A CURSE OF QUEENS

AMANDA BOUCHET

sourcebooks
casablanca

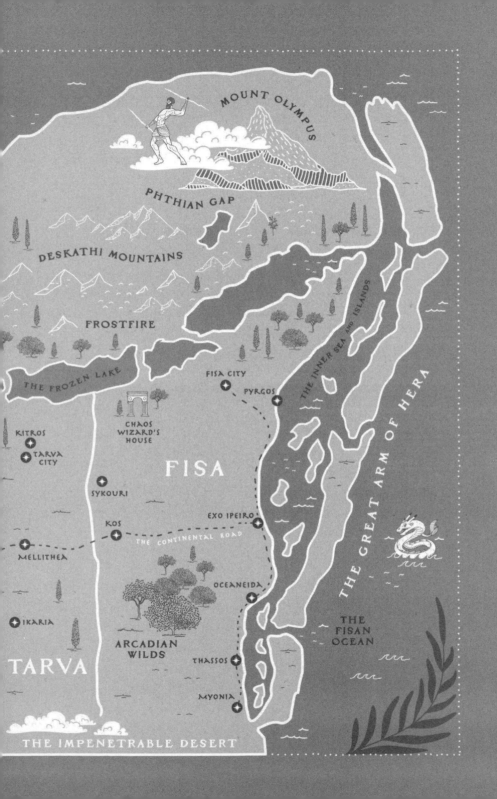

Published by Sourcebooks Casablanca, an imprint of Sourcebooks
P.O. Box 4410, Naperville, Illinois 60567-4410
(630) 961-3900
sourcebooks.com

Library of Congress Cataloging-in-Publication Data

Names: Bouchet, Amanda, author.
Title: A curse of queens / Amanda Bouchet.
Description: Naperville, Illinois : Sourcebooks Casablanca, [2022] |
  Series: The kingmaker chronicles ; book 4
Identifiers: LCCN 2022020743 (print) | LCCN 2022020744 (ebook) | (trade paperback) |
(epub)
Subjects: LCGFT: Novels.
Classification: LCC PS3602.O8878 C87 2022 (print) | LCC PS3602.O8878
  (ebook) | DDC 813/.6--dc23/eng/20220428
LC record available at https://lccn.loc.gov/2022020743
LC ebook record available at https://lccn.loc.gov/2022020744

Printed and bound in Canada.
MBP 10 9 8 7 6 5 4 3 2 1

For Lynn L.
Thank you for your unwavering friendship and support since the day
we met. I appreciate you so much!
And for Alexandra P.
Because I want the whole world to know how smart, kind, and
amazing you are. Polla filia.

PROLOGUE

It was **not** *a day like any other. It was Jocasta's eighteenth birth-*
day, and if the man she'd loved since she was six years old didn't
already know he had her heart, he would know it in the next
few minutes.

She took her brothers' makeshift bridge over the river
and cut through Flynn's olive grove rather than use the dirt
road between their two houses, avoiding gnarled old roots
that had twisted her ankles on more than one occasion. She'd
just washed from head to toe, and she had *plans*. Arriving at
Flynn's house with dusty toes poking out of her sandals wasn't
part of them.

Her stomach clenched, and Jocasta took a steadying breath.
This was it, then—everything finally coming together.

Really, she shouldn't be so nervous. Wasn't Flynn practically
a member of the family already? Her oldest brother's best friend?
Someone she'd known—quite literally—forever?

Besides, he was it for her—the one. She couldn't even remember a time when that wasn't her reality.

She stepped over a fallen branch and headed up the field,
Flynn's house a deceptively cheery whitewashed dot in the distance. He lived alone now. Old Hector was the last to go, leaving
Flynn parentless, brotherless, and sisterless after a decade-long
cycle of everything going wrong. Her heart had broken over
and over along with Flynn's, but now she could finally help him.

Wouldn't a family of his own be just the healing balm he needed after losing everyone?

Despite her positive—and logical—thoughts, panic still thrummed in Jocasta's veins, descending like a swarm of locusts on her fast-beating heart. Fear of rejection grew with every step toward Flynn's, but it wasn't as though she were about to spring herself on him from out of nowhere. She wasn't blind to signs or prone to inventing things out of sheer hopefulness. There was really only one way to interpret all the kind smiles and shared laughs, the near-daily inquiring after her health and projects, the long, private conversations down by the river between their two houses, and the frequent escorting her home, even when they both knew it wasn't necessary.

Flynn's attentiveness wasn't new exactly, just different somehow. He'd always looked out for her. And as independent as Jocasta liked to think herself, she *had* needed help at times.

Ice slid down her spine, and she slammed the door on the memory she mostly managed to avoid. It surged up anyway, and she walked more slowly through the sudden spike in her pulse, repeating thoughts like *done, over*, and *no!* until a colorful word mosaic of her own design patterned over the ugly images in her head.

Squaring her shoulders, she picked up her pace. There hadn't been a truly violent raid on their village in years, even if the last one still felt like yesterday at times. Sintan royal guards descending on their homes. Heartless soldiers demanding taxes far beyond what was due, thieving, destroying, and taking, especially from the women of the tribe. Seven babies were born roughly nine months after that last impromptu tax raid, and she'd had her first woman's cycle only a few months before.

She could've been one of those new mothers five years ago if Flynn hadn't pulled that rotten-toothed bastard off her in time.

He'd practically ripped the man limb from limb before spiriting her away to the hidden tunnels below the temple district. He'd raced off again to try to protect others, leaving her with his hunting knife and cloak. She'd been so cold down there, shivering in fear and shock beneath that big statue of Zeus. Sometimes, she still heard the eerie silence and felt the flood of dread deep under her skin like a sickness oozing its way out from within.

That distant day was a tangle of fear and gratitude in her memory, and Jocasta mentally stomped on it as she approached Flynn's house, each step driving the horror that could've been so much worse for her farther into the ground.

No one ever knew what happened that afternoon except for the two of them—how close her life came to being irrevocably changed. Not her parents. Not her brothers and sisters. No one. She should've been hiding in the secret room behind the kitchen pantry, but she'd been too far from home when the brutal, greed-driven soldiers arrived—and then not close enough when they truly closed in.

Flynn came for her when it was all over. Her family was intact but poorer, and he took her back to them. They never spoke of that day again.

Every now and then, when her mind hovered between asleep and awake, she saw Flynn's face as he killed that soldier above her. Most of it was a blur. Her groping wildly for a weapon. Rough, hard hands pawing at her new breasts and yanking up her dress. Suddenly knowing she'd lost—that she'd never stood a chance.

Another few seconds, and that would've been true. Flynn had snapped her attacker's neck so hard she sometimes still heard the crack. And then a huge auburn-haired beast had reached down for her, a roar in his chest and his features on fire with hate. All fear had vanished. As savage as he'd looked, he was *her* beast.

That day not only marked the moment her father became deadly serious about uniting the southern tribes into a coalition big and powerful enough to strike fear into the northern Sintan elite but also the day her love turned into passion. For as long as she could remember, she'd looked at Flynn with a child's adulation. After that raid, she'd understood what it felt like to look at a fierce, capable man and nearly combust with a woman's love.

Jocasta's steps slowed as she started down the flat, sun-warmed path of stones leading to Flynn's front doorway. Doubts rattled like swords, warning her away from the field of engagement. She knew how *she* felt, but what about Flynn? He'd never actually touched her or spoken to her in a way that indicated his feelings went deeper than friendship. It was just that lately, things hadn't felt the same.

The prospect of being alone with Flynn usually sent dragonflies swooping through her belly. Right now, their frantically beating wings churned up a wash of acid in her stomach, and Jocasta fought a nervous grimace. The closer she got to Flynn's door, the more her heart squeezed and burst and caught fire as though hit by a lightning bolt.

Finally on his doorstep, she shifted from foot to foot. Could this be a huge mistake? There was no *backward* from a confession of love.

But there was no forward without one—or at least not into a future she wanted.

Steeling herself, she lifted her hand and knocked. She'd always liked Flynn's whitewashed house with its sky-blue shutters—probably more than he did at this point. He kept the old farmhouse in perfect condition. The only things missing were his mother's big clay flowerpots with their bright-crimson hera's hearts and jaunty flushing dryads. He had the pots somewhere; she had no doubt. And Jocasta would replace the dead roots of bygone blooms with her kitchen herbs and medicinal plants as soon as it was her right.

Flynn was home now. He couldn't always be out honing his battle skills with her brothers and Kato. The five of them did little else these days, but homes and lands also needed tending. Even if Flynn hated every lonely second he spent in his empty house, a man like him would never let his family farm fall into ruin—or at least not the buildings. Harvests were a different story. Last season's fat black olives now stained the grove, shriveled and bird-pecked where they'd fallen while a new crop grew, waiting for a farmer to tend to it, when the only person who lived here now had a new occupation: war.

Jocasta waited for Flynn to answer her knock, which she'd made sure was loud enough to resonate. At this time of day, he was often in the back courtyard building something to furnish his house. If the telltale *thud, thud, thud* she'd heard was any indication, he was at it again. The steady fall of his hammer seemed to echo the beat of her heart these days, although if he built one more unnecessary chair or table, he'd have no place left to walk.

Maybe he could fashion them a cradle soon, one that rocked, and she'd try not to be too terrified when he rode off with the others to defend their border, which was slowly extending toward the north.

She knocked again, even more firmly this time. The hammering in the courtyard abruptly stopped, and Jocasta's heart tumbled, speeding up. She could make this empty house a home again. She *would*.

The door opened, jolting her pulse into a mad enough dash to make her hands shake. She hid them in the folds of her gown, all that floaty material draping down her hips and legs finally coming in handy. Flynn stood a head taller than her, his broad shoulders blocking out everything beyond. Limned in the golden glow of the sunset at Jocasta's back, his auburn hair looked almost blond. He hadn't cut a single lock since his father died, and the thick mass now brushed the strong curve of his jaw. She wished she could smooth it back with gentle, soothing strokes, the kind reserved for wounded animals. Or wounded souls.

Jocasta exhaled a slow, deceptively steady breath, her eyes fixed on Flynn's. Surprise flitted across his expression, quickly replaced by concern.

"Is everything all right, Jo?" He looked past her, around, and then at her again. He frowned. "It's getting late for you to be out alone."

His concern plucked at her heartstrings, sending a warm vibration through her chest. "Everything's fine," she answered. Except for her voice. It was already low and gravelly enough without creaking from nerves. She cleared her throat, wishing she didn't perpetually sound as if she just woke up. "As you know, the southern lands have never been safer."

Had wooden conversation ever led to seduction? Probably not. She fought a wince.

Flynn nodded, smiling despite how stiff and stilted she sounded. "Griffin's talking about going on the offensive soon. Next thing those murdering royals up in Sinta City know, *he'll* be king."

The idea made Jocasta shudder in fear for everyone she loved. It was entirely possible her brother would eventually make a bid for the throne. But a Hoi Polloi warlord ruling the realm? It had never happened. Magic always won.

"Happy birthday." Flynn stepped aside, leaving her room to enter. "I was going to stop by your house later, but since you're here, I have something for you."

Her heart leaped at his words. Jocasta followed him inside, her unruly pulse robbing her of breath and those dragonflies now carousing wildly in her stomach.

Inside, the house was dark except for the natural light slanting in through the deep-set windows. Flynn skirted an upturned stool with one leg still waiting to be attached and strode toward a side table. It was one of three lined up along the far wall.

"Is the upstairs this full?" Glancing around, she spotted several new pieces of furniture in varying stages of completion. There were far too many chairs for a one-man home. One was child-sized, and her heart gave a little thump. She could already see a red-haired imp in it. *Their* imp.

Flynn just shrugged, his silence seeming to invite her to ignore the fact that he was populating his house with inanimate objects because all the animate ones were gone.

Jocasta let it go, knowing she couldn't truly understand Flynn's suffering. Her family remained intact. Parents and siblings, all able-bodied and well.

Flynn picked up a small box tied with a thick hellipses-grass bow and held it out to her. His eyes gleamed the same warm brown as the olive-wood container he'd likely carved himself as he placed the gift in her hands, a smile tugging at his mouth.

Jocasta bit her lip. Flynn had given her many things over the last eighteen years, but never something *wrapped in a bow*.

She tried to hide how her fingers shook as she opened the box. Her breath caught. It was a bracelet. A beautiful bronze bracelet with fluted engravings on either side of a row of polished blue stones.

Her eyes jumped to his face, her heart pounding in her throat. Surely, giving her jewelry was a strong sign of his regard?

Flynn plucked the bracelet from the box and slipped it onto her wrist, squeezing to adjust the size. He set the box aside. "The stones match your eyes. They were the brightest and bluest I could find."

Elation made her dizzy. That was the most romantic thing

he'd ever said. To her—and probably ever. Jocasta moved without thinking. Happiness propelled her forward, and she threw her arms around Flynn's neck, stretched up, and crushed her lips to his. *Finally!* She closed her eyes, held on, and soared.

Flynn froze, his lips warm but unyielding, his arms at his sides, and his big, hard body not melding to hers. Jagged worry spiked her pulse. This might be her first kiss, but she still knew what was supposed to happen, and Flynn not kissing her back— *at all*—definitely wasn't it.

She stayed where she was, her lips pressed firmly to Flynn's and her breasts lightly brushing his clothes. She angled her head, the new, more intense pressure a silent plea for him to reciprocate. He was twenty-eight years old, a man who'd been on military campaigns, and she had no illusions about the women he must have kissed—and certainly more. Jocasta couldn't possibly be *that* bad at this.

Still, he didn't move. Just as hope started to crumble and die in her chest, Flynn kissed her back. His mouth suddenly surged against hers. He wrapped his arms around her and hauled her in close, a sound of pure hunger rising in his throat. Jocasta echoed it—a deep, primal moan of excitement and relief. Spearing her fingers into his hair, she arched into him with an instinctive roll of her hips.

Flynn's gasp punched her lips. He hesitated. Their mouths barely touched, their breathing ragged and loud. Then his grip tightened, and he brought her to her toes as he slanted his mouth over hers, softly at first, and then harder, parting her lips. Jocasta's legs grew heavy and weak. His tongue brushed her lower lip, feather soft and questioning. The thump of sensation low in her abdomen said *yes*, and she opened for him, catching fire from the heat of their kiss.

Flynn slid a hand to the nape of her neck. Tilting her head

back, he licked into her mouth. Jocasta sagged in his hold, the wildest jolt of pleasure hitting the space between her legs. A little whimper left her, swallowed up by the warmth of Flynn's mouth.

Learning quickly from him, she swept her tongue over his. He tasted of the mint sweets she'd made him. Chasing the flavor, she deepened the kiss. Triumph roared in her blood as Flynn fisted one hand in her hair. The other clenched the back of her dress, holding on to her as though she were *necessary.* Desire pulsed, hot and urgent. She devoured him, he ravaged her mouth, and it was glorious.

Until he reared back.

Jocasta staggered, nearly losing her balance. She opened her eyes, her mouth gaping. She glanced around, half expecting to see one of her overprotective brothers cocking back a fist. But no—they were alone. No one had yanked Flynn away from her.

The inferno inside her fizzled to wisps of smoke. Slowly, apprehensively, she looked back at Flynn. His expression turned her stomach to lead, and the knot forming in her middle dragged her hopes and dreams down with its cold, hard weight. She didn't want to let them die, but as she watched Flynn's hands curl into fists and his eyes go from stunned to horrified, the future she'd imagined for them started collapsing without waiting for the awful words she knew were on the tip of his tongue.

The man she'd loved for as long as she could remember stared at her, paling until his auburn hair glared a shocking red. "Forgive me," he finally said.

Jocasta expelled a trembling breath. "I kissed you. There's nothing to forgive."

"I took advantage." His measured tone cut like a knife. He took another step back. "I'm sorry. It won't happen again."

She swallowed. *It won't happen again.*

Those weren't idle words. He *meant* them.

Tears stung her eyes. Flynn didn't want her. He was supposed to claim her, she'd claim him back, they'd tell her parents, sign the temple registry, plan an official wedding if they felt like it, and likely start a family immediately. Maybe even right now. She'd been ready and willing. Apparently, she was the only one.

"I see." Her voice came from far away. Jocasta could barely feel her lips. Numbness rang in her head. A sickened daze smothered the thrill of their kiss, obliterating it from existence.

How stupid. She started to shake. *What a stupid, naïve fool I am.* It was all in her mind. Him. Her. Everything.

She shuffled back, even though he'd already put more than enough distance between them. She'd been waiting for this moment for years, for when Flynn couldn't use her age as an excuse, or his firm friendship with her brothers. She was a woman, fully grown and frankly well into marriageable age, according to their tribal traditions. Not that she *needed* to marry. She'd *wanted* Flynn.

Queasy, she turned to leave. "I... Goodbye."

Spiraling into a horrible, sinking pit of humiliation, she rushed for the door. Everything would be different now. She'd need to avoid Flynn for life. How in the name of the gods was she supposed to do that?

Flynn caught up in two steps, his nearness shocking compared to the sudden gulf between them. "I'll walk you home."

"No, please don't." Not looking at him, she yanked open the door and flew outside. The bracelet he'd given her glinted in the dull light, and the sight of it on her wrist broke her heart all over again.

He fell into step beside her anyway, flatly stating, "There's no way in the Underworld I'm letting you walk home alone in the dark."

Jocasta scoffed, the sharp sound somewhere between bitter and bruised. She finally stopped and looked at him, anger sparking even though her soul was one enormous festering wound. "I'm Anatole's daughter and Griffin's sister. No one within *days* of this place would dare lay a finger on me."

Flynn flinched, jerking his hands out of sight. *He'd* touched her. And gods, how he wished he hadn't. It was written all over his face.

They stood on his walkway, the ease that had always existed between them burned down to ash with one explosive kiss. A breeze swept over them, and Jocasta shivered, more devastated than cold. Flynn watched her, eyes wary, mouth flat. He didn't say a word.

Jocasta turned and started walking again, one foot in front of the other, already trying to shove lifelong feelings into a forgotten corner of herself where they wouldn't spring up like some horrible jack-in-the-box every time Flynn was around. Flynn followed her all the way home, now two steps behind and eerily quiet except for his tread. He'd started stomping like a Cyclops everywhere he went. She'd liked it. It had let her know when he was nearby.

A sob caught in her throat. She held her breath, keeping the shuddering howl inside.

Home finally loomed in sight. Jocasta didn't want to go in but had nowhere else to go. So home it was—with too many people inside. Flynn might've turned and left her at the gate, but her mother saw them through the window and waved them both toward the door. It would've been strange for him to refuse.

Stepping under the lintel and into the house, Flynn kissed her mother's rounded cheek, just as he had since he was a boy. "Hello, Nerissa."

Jocasta forced a quick smile for her mother but couldn't produce a word.

As they moved farther inside, her father strode over and dropped a kiss onto the top of her head. He clapped Flynn on the shoulder, his face splitting into the wide grin he reserved for his children. Anatole had always treated Flynn like one of his boys, especially after Flynn's real father, Old Hector, stopped caring about anything outside of his own grief.

Anatole beamed at them both, his focus shifting to Flynn as he spoke. "I see you found our wandering healer." Flynn simply nodded, and Jocasta's father turned to her. "Did you find those plants you were looking for?"

"No." In all honesty, she hadn't even looked. The sudden urge to search for althaea root had been an excuse to leave the house late in the afternoon—just when most of the people she knew would be finding their ways home and staying there, including Flynn. "Someone else must have gathered them up first." Having a naturally husky voice served her well for once. No one knew it was low and raw from holding back tears.

"There'll be more in a few days." Anatole's shrug accentuated the increasing stoop in his shoulders. Her father had recently begun looking his age and giving more responsibility to Griffin, who acted as co-head of the family now. It all meant change, when the only change Jocasta really wanted had just been denied to her. "And your competition doesn't stand a chance," Anatole added. "Whatever you concoct will be better."

"Thank you, Father," she murmured. His encouragement meant a great deal to her. Most tribal fathers didn't support their daughters in endeavors that had nothing to do with finding a husband and providing grandchildren. But Anatole had married a talented healer whose income supplying counsel, salves, and cures had been twice his own as a grain farmer, and he'd never batted an eye at Jocasta following in her mother's footsteps.

Out of sheer habit, Jocasta moved deeper into the house, but the moment she entered the great room, she knew she had to leave. Her entire family was there, and what if they could all see her chest ripped wide open and her heart falling out? It didn't matter that they barely looked up from their evening activities, her entrance with Flynn nothing unusual. *Everything* was different. Her shattered dreams cut like broken glass. She'd never stop bleeding.

At her back, Flynn blocked her path out, so she stood there, the wretched knot in her throat only growing. Jocasta's older sister, Egeria, sat by the fire with a scroll in her hands, reading. Her middle brother, Piers, did the same. Griffin and Carver played a strategy game, which their father rejoined. Kaia, at only nine, hopped like a flea as she talked to Kato. Kato, a de facto member of the family even more than Flynn, listened with his full attention, ignoring the game he'd probably started out playing with the others to hear about a typical Kaia adventure involving her beating the local boys her age at a footrace around the center of the village.

Jocasta had already heard the story twice. Kato probably had, too, but his effortless charm always came with a smile, and more importantly, his kindness ran deep. He'd listen ten times and always look just as interested.

Sometimes, Jocasta wondered why she hadn't fallen in love with him instead of Flynn. Kato was a few years closer to her in age and arguably the most handsome man in all the realms. His battle-sculpted body, blue-sky eyes, and sunshine hair were all most of her friends could talk about. They didn't know him like she did, though. They hadn't watched and learned as her mother cleaned and soothed Kato's cuts and bruises in the middle of the night, time and again. Jocasta was only waist-high at the time. She used to hold Kato's hand, thinking that might help—and he'd let her.

Some evils didn't come from the outside. Kato's parents were proof of that. Then one day, he just stopped going home. She'd lived under the same roof as Kato since before Kaia was born. Loving him the way she loved Flynn was impossible. He was her brother now.

Flynn got called into the game to replace Kato, clearing a path for her back out of the room. Jocasta joined her mother in the kitchen and began the monotonous task of kneading bread. It was mindless and numbing. It helped her stay blank instead of focusing on how her life had finally begun for an incendiary blink of an eye and then stopped. They didn't talk, and Nerissa threw her worried glances. Tears threatened every now and then, surging up with shocking heat and violence.

Flynn stayed just long enough to be polite and then returned home. After that, he started spending more time at his house than he did at hers. Then it stopped mattering where he chose to be, because Jocasta rarely saw any of the men in her life anymore. They were busy making her world a safer place and doing whatever it was that victorious warriors did. She tried not to use her imagination too much where Flynn was concerned.

Jocasta threw herself into honing her healing skills and becoming invaluable to her community. She improved on her mother's key recipes and invented new medicinal remedies in her dwindling spare time. Her ointments sold as quickly as she could make them, as did her herbal teas and tonics. She might not have a household of her own, but she was a household name, and that was almost enough for her.

But then one day, she was told to pack up and leave home. Griffin had won. The whole family was moving to Castle Sinta. She was a princess of the realm.

Jocasta packed her trunks, the life she'd begun building once again torn from her grasp. As her family rode out, a royal

army that included Griffin and his core team—that included
Flynn—surrounding them, she glimpsed a tightly shuttered-up
whitewashed farmhouse in the distance. Her heart too numb to
ache, she simply turned away from it.

No one ever knew what she'd done on her eighteenth birthday, how she'd thrown herself at Flynn. How he'd kissed her as if
his life depended on it and then leaped away from her as though
burned.

Had he been more horrified with himself or with her? In
the end, she never really knew.

That was another day they never spoke of. In fact, they
barely spoke at all.

PERSEPHONE

Persephone hadn't been the bearer of bad news to someone she cared about in eons. She'd almost forgotten how awful it was.

"You've been cursed." There. She'd said it. She looked at Cat. Queen Catalia Thalyria now—and the closest thing Persephone had to a human daughter. "There's powerful magic all over you. Not yours," she added.

Cat stared at her. Shock and fright widened her bright-green eyes to twin pools of panicked light. "Bad magic?"

"I believe you'll see it that way, yes." Persephone watched the new queen carefully. She'd known Cat since she was fifteen, a girl on the run from her abusive ·family and hiding from her destiny. As a powerful goddess and the queen of the Underworld, Persephone didn't usually preoccupy herself with concepts like fairness. Life was life. Death was death. But after everything Cat had been through, it seemed particularly unjust to bestow such a poisoned gift upon her.

"Cursed *how*?" the warlord-turned-king by Cat's side asked sharply. *Griffin*. Persephone was still getting used to him. His devotion to his wife made him tolerable, even if he had kidnapped Cat right out from under the goddess's nose. She'd grown quite fond of watching over Cat herself, but that hadn't been meant to last, had it?

"This particular state is usually a reward," she answered. "In Cat's case, though, it doesn't serve her purpose or give either of you what you want."

"What does that mean?" Cat gripped the arms of her chair, her knuckles sticking out like bone-white knobs. "Just tell us what we're dealing with."

Persephone hesitated. Everyone believed her cool and detached, but she wasn't. Not where Cat was concerned. "I'm starting to think someone powerful must not like the new rule in Thalyria. And they've found a rather wretched way to stir things up."

Griffin frowned. "Stir things up?"

Cat's hands curved protectively over the big swell of her middle. "What kind of curse?"

Persephone studied Cat again, wishing she were wrong but unable to find a fissure in her original analysis. "There's no doubt. You've been imbued with Olympian Evermagic."

Cat's brow drew down. Her arms coiled even more tightly around her unborn baby, fear and confusion draining the color from her face.

Persephone experienced a strong pang of worry. Now *that*, she was getting used to. The kingdom needed this baby as much as Cat and Griffin wanted her. The prophesied child, Eleni, was supposed to finish the work of bringing Thalyria full circle. The core Olympians, especially Zeus, had been working on it for generations. A perfect mix of Magoi from the northeast and Hoi Polloi from the southwest, Eleni was destined to be the embodiment of the peaceful and unified kingdom her parents had created out of three long-divided and warring realms.

"Evermagic?" Griffin asked. Cat shook her head. Neither appeared familiar with the term.

Unsurprising. The Elixir of Eternal Life was a closely guarded secret. And rarely used.

Persephone rose from her chair, leaving Cerberus to plop one head into her vacated seat. His other two heads watched Cat, as usual.

Ungrateful hound. She'd felt a twinge of hurt when he'd decided to leave the Underworld for good and become a permanent fixture at the castle. Hades had brooded for days.

Giving the pet who'd abandoned them for his human charge the cold shoulder, Persephone looked solemnly at Cat and then even at Griffin. "I believe someone put Cat into what's best described as active stasis—a balanced and unchanging state." She paused, waiting for the fierce twist in her chest to unwind. "I don't have the ability to reverse it."

Cat blanched. "You mean...I'll never change? Never age? Never..." She looked down at her hugely rounded belly. "Oh my gods."

"No," Griffin choked out.

Oddly, his broken whisper pierced Persephone's heart hardest. She'd never seen him falter.

"Someone really didn't want *that* to happen." Her eyes dipped to Cat's middle. "And now, it *can't.*"

Paling, Griffin dropped into a crouch next to Cat. He took her hand, but his shook just as much as hers did. "So what do we do? How do we undo it?"

Persephone pressed her lips together, reluctant to intensify bad news. "Evermagic is rare and precious, even on Mount Olympus. It's a well-protected elixir few have access to and is how we grant immortality to carefully selected demigod off-spring." She winced for what might be the first time in millennia. "As a direct descendant of Zeus, Cat has just enough ichor in her veins for it to work. The Elixir of Eternal Life bonded with her blood. She'll stay the same as she is right now—inside and out. Alive and well but unchanging."

Cat opened her mouth, but nothing came out. After several attempts at speaking, her quivering voice seeped across the room. "Eight and a half months pregnant—*forever*. I'll never be a mother. You'll never—" She looked at Griffin, her face crumpling.

Griffin's throat bobbed on a hard swallow. It was no secret how much they both wanted a family, how excited they'd been to fill this castle they'd claimed against all odds and turned into a home.

The warrior king looked at Persephone, eyes pleading, voice rough. "Please, there must be something…"

"Can you cut Eleni out? Open me up and take her out?" Cat asked in a sudden frenzy. "She'd be fine. She's almost ready."

"While that *is* possible," Persephone answered, "she's a part of you right now, so she absorbed the same magic. She'd never change. She'd be an infant forever."

"Never grow. Never *live*." Cat's heartbroken murmur shuddered at the end.

What was worse? Lifetimes of never holding your baby at all or having a newborn that never changed? Wasn't the joy of children interacting with them as they evolved? Seeing them *become*? "Cutting her out could be a last resort," Persephone said softly, "if only to relieve you of the physical strain."

"The physical strain…" New horror crossed Cat's face.

Griffin clutched her hand harder, his own knuckles turning white.

"This must be about Thalyria not getting its heir." Anger flared in Persephone's chest. "You're just caught in the cross fire."

"In the worst way possible!" Cat cried, showing a hint of her usual fire. It quickly disappeared, and Cat and Griffin gripped each other's hands like lifelines, his face a shipwreck, her eyes awash with tears.

Persephone's heart clenched in a new way. When was the last time she'd held on to Hades like that? It seemed an age.

Low and furious, Griffin demanded, "Who would do this?"

"Who's powerful enough?" Cat asked.

"An Olympian—likely one of the Dodekatheon." Instinctively, Persephone looked through the open window facing northeast toward Mount Olympus, even though the great snowcapped peak was too far away to see from the center of Thalyria. She narrowed her eyes, her gaze cutting across the kingdom. "I'd blame Ares, but he cares about you too much and is just waiting to insinuate his meaty, brutish self into your child's life."

"It's not Ares." Absolute certainty rang in Cat's voice. She knew the god of war as few humans ever could and trusted him with her life. Her eyes sliced across the same line as Persephone's. "But one of the twelve Olympians? Who? Why?"

Persephone shrugged. She didn't know, though she wasn't about to admit it aloud.

"There *must* be a way to undo it." A thousand emotions flitted behind Griffin's stark eyes, thoughts that read like ink on parchment. No children. He'd grow old and die while Cat lived on. They'd never reunite in the Underworld.

Watching their hard-won happiness shatter before her eyes, rage grew like a stain on Persephone's heart and mind. She hadn't felt this powerless since her pomegranate days. "Once in place, the gift of immortality is insulated from the magic of other Olympians. Otherwise, it would be too easy for rivals to undo each other's work."

"So there's...*nothing*?" Cat's voice broke. "How is that possible?" Tears leaked from her eyes. Her breath shuddered out.

Persephone impulsively reached for Cat's free hand, offering soothing magic to help calm the young queen's thundering pulse. It was the best she could do for now. "I'll consult with Hades. My husband might deal with the dead, but he knows more than most gods about how humans actually want to live. I'll do my best to come back with ideas."

And with that, she vanished. She couldn't bear the anguish on Cat's face.

CHAPTER 1

SIX YEARS AFTER THE KISS THAT SHOULD
NEVER HAVE HAPPENED

Jocasta shot a firm but sympathetic look across her worktable when the kitchen boy tried to jerk his arm away from her lightly probing touch. His injury was minor—a burn of the iron-pot-to-inner-wrist variety. She'd seen worse. How could she not have, when she'd been eyeballs-deep in chronic violence since birth?

Ironic, then, that her conquering family only ever allowed her to fight once. And the moment peace settled over Thalyria, they all conveniently forgot she knew how to hold a weapon.

To be fair, Cat was different. But now they rarely snuck away into little-used corners of the castle gardens to throw knives at targets and bang around with swords. Her new sister put on a brave face, but her growing despair hung like a storm cloud over the castle, making Jocasta think about little else other than trying to brighten her darkening spirits when they were together and find a cure for her when they weren't.

With a gentle tug, she guided the boy's arm over the folded-up cloth between them and carefully laid it down. His blistered wrist glared bright red against the pristine linen. She personally boiled all her healing supplies clean, even if it meant breaking her back over the laundry pot three times a week, the castle servants gaping at her as though she were insane. "Your name is Tycho, correct?"

The boy's eyes snapped up to meet hers, his jaw sagging in disbelief that a member of the royal family knew his name. At least his surprise distracted him, and he stopped twitching for the first time since he'd arrived. After trying—and mostly failing—to work out of one of the family rooms in the castle, Jocasta had commandeered an independent work space off the kitchen gardens, where she already grew most of her medicinal plants. Under the previous royal family, the bright, octagonal room had been used for potting flowers and drying herbs. And who knew? Maybe torture. She'd turned it into her clinic, although patients here were scarce.

Flynn had made her sturdy worktable. At least, she assumed it was Flynn. The big table was there the morning she opened her clinic to the castle residents, replacing the smaller table she'd taken from an unused room.

The brutal expand and contract of Jocasta's heart didn't take her by surprise. What she'd come to think of as the Flynn effect was a familiar ache now, and her chest knew it would survive.

"Yes, my lady," Tycho finally choked out, dropping his gaze and closing his mouth.

Jocasta pulled her oil lamp closer, peering at the raw skin and filtering through the most appropriate remedies in her mind. Kitchen boy or not, Tycho needn't be intimidated by her. She was painfully aware that she was a princess in name only. Duty had inexplicably passed her by, and the only place she had any real responsibility was here, in the little healing center she'd created when she finally realized no one expected or needed anything more from her than what she'd already been doing since she was a child.

"Would you like to know how to treat a burn?" she asked

Tycho. At least she still had this—someone to help from time to time.

He glanced up again and slowly nodded. The Hoi Polloi of Thalyria were still getting used to the idea that the new ruling family gave a fig about them. Were *like* them, at least on Griffin's side. Jocasta, her parents, and her four remaining siblings were as magicless as most Thalyrians across the known continent. Cat, on the other hand, was a Magoi of unparalleled power.

"There are, of course, Magoi healers who could fix this in mere seconds," Jocasta said, reaching for the jar of purified water mixed with lavender oil sitting on the shelf.

Wariness darkened the boy's eyes, his instant suspicion something she understood. Magoi healers had a history of self-absorbed elitism that wouldn't be easily forgotten—or forgiven—by a population they'd refused to help for so long. One of the new royal couple's first decrees made it punishable by six weeks of imprisonment for a Magoi healer to refuse to treat a Hoi Polloi patient. Now, prisons were bursting with angry magic-wielding healers who thought this egalitarian madness would surely pass. Patients in dire need—Hoi Polloi and Magoi alike—suffered because of deep-rooted prejudices that might still take generations to overcome. Cat and Griffin would make Thalyria better. But better took time.

"There's a Magoi healer just across the grounds," she continued, lifting the stopper from her jar and setting it aside, "and she treats anyone who comes to her." Because it was either that or get kicked out on her ear.

Tycho's mouth puckered into a frown. "Don't want no Magoi healer."

"I see…" Evidence that prejudice ran not only deep but in all directions. "I suppose I'd be out of a job if you did, but I'd like Magoi and Hoi Polloi healers to work together. There's no sense in taking a toll on a healer's magic for minor injuries, and there's no sense in letting someone die when magic can save them."

"Doesn't healing magic hurt?" he asked.

She nodded. "It's usually more painful than the wound itself."

Tycho grimaced. "This already hurts enough."

"Luckily, I know some tricks for soothing burns." Jocasta once again inspected the boy's wrist. "For example, lavender oil helps reduce pain and inflammation and chase away infection." The fragrance also calmed nervous patients. She swirled the contents of her jar, not only to mix the ingredients, which tended to separate, but to launch the scent into the air.

Tycho leaned forward and sniffed. "What else can you do?"

"All sorts of things. Make ointments and tonics. Herbal teas to help with different ailments. Deliver babies. Set bones. Clean and sew up wounds." She shrugged. "Amputate, if necessary."

Tycho looked at his wrist in horror.

"Not necessary in your case," Jocasta said.

"How did you learn all that?" His earnest curiosity made Jocasta wonder if she had a future healer on her hands.

"My mother taught me." She lowered her voice, as though adding a secret. "She's the greatest healer the southwest has ever known."

"Lady Nerissa? She looks too...soft for that."

Jocasta laughed, the sudden bubble of merriment the first true happiness she'd experienced all day. "I doubt many of the warriors she's treated over the years would call her soft. She's kind but *very* firm, especially with her patients."

"Like you." A shy smile spread across Tycho's face.

Jocasta smiled back. "Then I'm flattered. Kind but firm is an excellent thing to be." She tipped the mouth of her jar toward Tycho's wrist. Now that she seemed to have gained his trust and helped him relax, she poured some of her lavender water over the damaged skin. He winced, and she held his arm steady, not letting him move. "Burns hurt like Hades's own fire because of the lingering ache." She poured again, wanting to flush away any contaminants. "The pain goes deep, even when it's a surface wound."

Tycho's fiercely knit brow began to smooth out. "It feels better already."

"Lavender extract reduces pain. And the purified water it's mixed with will help wash away anything bad." She filtered and boiled—three times—any water that went into her concoctions. Tycho's arm hadn't been particularly clean to begin with, and Jocasta wasn't counting on the heat from the overturned cooking pot to have burned off all sources of infection. "When your arm is dry, we'll put my special honey on it. It'll speed up healing and prevent inflammation. Then we'll bandage it up. You'll see."

"What makes your honey special?" Tycho asked.

"It comes from very clean bees," a familiar voice rumbled from the open doorway.

Jocasta's pulse flash flooded her veins. What was Flynn doing here? Didn't he know they avoided each other at all costs?

"All bees are clean," she responded without looking over her shoulder.

"Maybe, but yours wouldn't dare drag a speck of dust into their honeycombs."

Was she really that exacting? Flynn made her sound like a shrew.

She finally turned. He leaned against the doorframe, his boots crossed at the ankles and his huge battle-ax peeking up over one shoulder. He might be the captain of the royal guard, but it wasn't as though they were under attack. He'd usually set aside that monstrosity by this time of day.

The light changed, and she saw him better. Flushed cheeks. Flared nostrils. Stiff posture, despite the casual pose.

She frowned. "Are you hurt?"

Flynn scowled. "Why would I be hurt?"

"Because you're here."

He stared at her, his face blank. Then he pushed off from the door. "Everyone's ready for dinner. Griffin asked me to find you."

Ah. Dinner was the last place Jocasta wanted to be. Not only because her brother and Cat expected Flynn to join them in the evenings—forcing him into her sphere *every day* since they took up residence—but because sometimes she just needed to breathe.

As much as she loved her family and the recent additions to it, sometimes she just couldn't stomach watching Griffin and Cat move around as if fused into one perfect—and perfectly destroyed—person, Carver and Bellanca peck at one another like angry crows, Kaia slowly guide Prometheus back to a semblance of normalcy after millennia of torture, and everyone tiptoe around the subject of Kato. Because he was gone.

Grief lanced her heart. Woodenly, she said, "I must've lost track of the hour."

"I'll escort you," Flynn offered.

"No need." She turned back to her patient. "I'm almost done. I'll meet you in the dining room."

Despite her clear dismissal, Flynn remained in the doorway. The feel of his eyes on her back made Jocasta's nape prickle with a storm-like heat. The charged, volatile pressure tingled against her skin, reminding her of the night air just before a lightning bolt cracked down and electrified her senses.

Suppressing a shiver, she inspected Tycho's arm to make sure it was dry. She always air-dried when possible. "My honey—which helps fight infection—is special because, like the water I used to clean your arm, it also contains drops of lavender oil. That means it smells good *and* continues to help with the pain." She gently spread a layer of the thick light-yellow substance over the burn. Her young patient didn't even flinch this time, possibly because a hero of Thalyria was watching.

"You'll thank the princess for her healing skills when you can sleep tonight, boy." Flynn's casual, low-pitched words seemed to resonate in Jocasta's chest cavity.

She kept silent. If only her healing skills extended to reversing magic elixirs. She researched documents and read scrolls until she was cross-eyed every day and found *nothing* to help Cat, Griffin, and baby Eleni.

She wrapped a clean bandage around Tycho's wrist and carefully tied it off. He immediately tried to look under the dressing.

"No peeking," she chided.

He pressed on the top.

"No touching."

He huffed. "But it doesn't even hurt."

"It'll hurt if you destroy all my hard work. No peeking, no touching, definitely no licking the honey, and come back tomorrow so that I can change your bandage." At least that guaranteed one patient for her little clinic.

A protest formed on the tip of Tycho's tongue.

"Or else," Jocasta said sternly.

Flynn cleared his throat, squashing what sounded suspiciously like a chuckle. She ignored him and held out a bowl of her homemade mints—another skill passed down from her mother. Tycho hesitated, his hand hovering over the sweets.

"Go on," she said as he stood. "You've been a good patient."

He smiled, took a mint, and bowed before turning to leave, probably late for his own dinner.

Flynn ruffled the boy's hair as he passed. "Come see me in about five years. We'll find out if you're more skilled with a kitchen knife or a sword."

Tycho looked ecstatic as he scampered out, her strict instructions probably forgotten as he basked in Flynn's attention. At least he wouldn't try to lick the lavender honey if he thought one of his idols' approval was on the line.

Jocasta sighed. Once Tycho was out of earshot, she turned to Flynn. "Don't encourage him." Kitchen boys rarely became warriors, and that probably wouldn't change, no matter how much her family was shaking up this new, united Thalyria. It was naïve to think otherwise.

Flynn's brows lifted in surprise. "Encourage everyone. You never know where life can take you—or have you forgotten that I used to be an olive farmer?"

No, she hadn't. Nor had she forgotten how much he'd liked it at the time.

She turned away without responding and dumped the damp, lavender-scented cloth into the wash pile, the imprint of Tycho's arm still denting the linen. He'd been her only patient today. She supposed she should be grateful that people were safe and healthy around her, and she certainly didn't need the income. She never charged for her healing services now.

Her little clinic off the courtyard was something, but wasn't she finally supposed to have more? Her older sister, Egeria, along with her partner, Lenore, were the royal family's arm in western Thalyria. They still called it Sinta—a province now instead of an independent realm. Jocasta had somehow assumed that Cat and Griffin would move east into what used to be Cat's home realm of Fisa, taking their Alpha Team—Carver, Bellanca, and Flynn—with them. That would've left her and Kaia here in Tarva, along with their parents and Prometheus. Essentially, because of her parents' age, Kaia's youth, and Prometheus's delicate emotional state, that would've made Jocasta responsible for the entire central region of the continent.

But none of that happened. Cat and Griffin established the royal seat here, in the newly named Castle Thalyria, and Ares, of all gods, was holding the east and its petulant Magoi in check with the help—or perhaps not—of Cat's two younger brothers. Laertes and Priam had come to visit recently and been odious to the entire family, although not enough for Cat to regret sparing their lives when she had the chance.

With Flynn still at her back like a heartbeat she couldn't stop hearing, Jocasta popped the stopper into the bottle of lavender water and put it away. Then she sealed off the jar of honey salve with a piece of oiled cloth, just as she had countless times over the course of her life. While she did, she thought about her older siblings now busy ruling and protecting a kingdom and her little sister responsible for a *god*. As she set the jar back into her cupboard, it was hard not to wonder... When would it be her turn?

CHAPTER 2

Flynn rolled his shoulders, trying to loosen the perpetual tension at the top of his spine.

Finally. On the road again. *Away*, if only for a few days.

Unfortunately, escaping the doom-heavy atmosphere of the royal seat didn't mean their problems had vanished.

And escaping Jo didn't mean she didn't barge into his every other thought, the same way she had for months now.

Neither issue would magically disappear. At least he still had hope for Cat and Griffin. His wayward thoughts about a certain blue-eyed healer were starting to feel like a lost cause to him.

Squinting, Flynn shaded his eyes from the morning sun, his thoughts inevitably straying to how Jo must be fretting over her garden. He could almost hear her husky voice grumbling about her plants not getting the long drink they needed before summer. Even when she was fussing or snapping, there was something perpetually erotic about her voice, as though all those silky little hitches were specifically designed to torture him. With this bizarre mission, he'd finally gotten out of that damn castle and was more than a day's ride from her constant, overwhelming presence. Distance used to help. Apparently, that was a thing of the past—along with his sanity.

Despite the early hour, sweat rolled down his temples. The dew glinting on the grass when Alpha Team set out at dawn had burned off within minutes, and the sunlight now baking his face just felt like one more thing battering his senses.

He turned away from the harsh rays. There hadn't been much of a rainy season, and they were already coming out on the other side of it. His farmer's senses tingled, fearing drought and maybe even fires this year. Time would tell. The ground-cracking heat wouldn't set in for several more weeks, and the grass was still lush and green up here on the northern Tarvan plateau.

Flynn reined in his mount when there was almost nowhere left to go. Griffin pulled Brown Horse to a halt on his left. Bellanca stopped on his right, her bright-red hair more blinding than the sun. Carver rode on a few more steps to where he could peer over the edge of the precipice. Flynn had already seen the carnage from below. He didn't need to see it again.

Carver let out a low whistle. "So this is where goats go to die."

Flynn's mouth twitched. It was good to hear Carver with a hint of humor in his voice, even if a bunch of dead goats wasn't exactly a joke.

Carver eyed the lifeless herd, one hand on his reins and the other curled around the hilt of his sword.

Bellanca urged her horse closer to Carver's, bumping into him as she advanced. Bellanca headed the Magoi soldiers of the Thalyrian army. Carver headed the Hoi Polloi troops. They'd somehow managed to get their warriors to work together even though they were constantly at each other's throats.

Carver's heavy focus shifted to Bellanca as she neared the edge of the cliff. "Stop there," he called in a sharp voice.

Bellanca tossed an annoyed look over her shoulder. "As if I've ever followed the herd."

Carver might've smiled. It was hard to tell these days.

Griffin echoed Carver's warning. "Careful, Bellanca. It's steep."

"Obviously. Otherwise, the fall would hardly have killed

three dozen goats." She stood in her stirrups and looked over the edge. A grimace twisted her face. "I thought goats were smarter than this."

"What does a Tarvan ex-princess know about goats?" Coming from anyone other than Carver, flinging Bellanca's former royal status at her would've been a caustic reminder of her family's reign of terror in these parts. From Carver, it was provocation as usual, but without malice.

A little flame of annoyance still sizzled down a curl on Bellanca's head, producing a wisp of smoke. "Enough to know that no four-legged animal willingly jumps to its death."

"Unless they're stampeding." Griffin glanced back at the shepherd who insisted his herd had been at the epicenter of what people in these parts were calling the Great Roar. The near-deafening shout had stretched for leagues and put the fear of the gods into anyone who heard it. Animals, though, had gone berserk. "Something strange happened here, and we need to find out what."

"Easier said than done." Flynn let his gaze slide over the undisturbed countryside. Everything was quiet now—except for the rumors, which were exploding into monsters with multiple heads. "We hear a different story from every person we talk to about what went on at…Dead Goats' Bluff?"

"Ooh. If we're naming it, I vote for Carcass Stench Hill." Bellanca wrinkled her nose, looking over the edge again. "Should I burn them, do you think?"

Griffin nodded toward the man puffing up the hill on his donkey. "Let the shepherd decide when he catches up."

Bellanca shrugged.

"This is the start of something more." Carver's mouth thinned, the hard, blade-flat line something they'd all grown used to. "First, the Elixir of Eternal Life. Now, the Great Roar…"

Flynn agreed. But what?

Worry sat in his throat like an olive stone he'd accidentally swallowed. This Great Roar was just one more problem on top of everything else. Persephone had disappeared and never come back. All of Thalyria had expected Cat to produce an heir days ago, and Alpha Team and the royal family were the only ones who knew she couldn't—and might never. Servants and guards had begun whispering about a miscalculated conception date— news that was spreading to nearby cities and would roll out across the kingdom on a wave of gossip. But even the most convincing chatter couldn't give them more than a month to restore Cat to her former, evolving state before Thalyrians went into a blind panic over their new queen and her highly anticipated baby. The first-ever royal child fusing Hoi Polloi and Magoi blood was one of the major forces keeping long-disparate people together. They *needed* her.

Squawks filled the air as a group of vultures lifted off from below and soared overhead.

"Oh look, Bel." Carver pointed to the birds. "Your coven's leaving without you."

Scowling, Bellanca flicked her hand, shooting red sparks at Carver. One bit into his cheek. He smacked it.

She smirked. "Thank you for slapping yourself. You saved me the trouble."

Carver didn't reply, but his expression promised more point-less bickering. It was all they'd done since the day they met, and Flynn was tired of it.

Jo's face flitted through his mind with a clarity that never failed to drive the air from his lungs. He'd welcome pointless bickering at this point if she would just *talk* to him. Now that they were living under the same roof, he didn't think he could face another day of exchanging a bare minimum of stilted, meaningless banalities with the one person whose thoughts and opinions mattered most to him.

And then every day, he did.

Flynn grimaced, assuming everyone would blame his pained expression on the stink of dead goats. *Talking, eh?* He'd muzzled himself a long time ago, and in doing so, he'd muzzled Jo. After that extravagant birthday gift and that haunting kiss, they'd lived in wary proximity of each other until he ran off to live with Griffin's expanding southern army. He'd abandoned his farm so he wouldn't have to face one small, curvy, raven-haired beauty with sapphire eyes, a healing touch, and lips he dreamed about day in and day out.

At least Jo had moved on a long time ago. She'd barely spared him a glance in years. She was a princess now anyway, and one day, a powerful, cultured noble would sweep her off her feet and give her everything he couldn't, including all those damn words that never seemed to come out of his mouth.

Flynn's nostrils flared, and he almost choked. "What a smell," he coughed out, even though it was really the thought of Jo with some rich Magoi that made him sick.

"Carcass Stench Hill," Bellanca affirmed with a nod.

The shepherd finally reined in next to them, red-faced and sweating. He eyed the edge of the bluff while swiping a crumpled handkerchief across his brow. "That's the place they all went over. Not even one lived."

"You said a loud noise sent your goats running." Griffin cut the shepherd a questioning glance. "Can you describe what happened? What you heard?"

Pivoting on his donkey, the shepherd waved a hand toward the grassy area behind them. "We were on that side of the plateau, away from the steep edge. The grass is good there right now, and with six nannies pregnant, I wanted them to have the best." His weathered features crinkled in distress. "The Great Roar came out of nowhere, from nothing. It scared me—I'm not ashamed to admit—but it terrified the goats."

"Could it have been thunder?" Griffin asked. "Or an earthquake?"

The shepherd shook his head. "Not unless the sky can howl and the ground can scream."

An all-encompassing screaming, howling yell was consistent with what people in the area had already told them. No one knew where it came from, though, and the speculation ranged from violently mating dragons to angry harpies to Hephaestus smashing his thumb in his forge.

"The closer and louder the Great Roar got, the more the herd panicked," the shepherd went on. "The noise seemed to come from that way"—he pointed behind them—"so they bolted away from it and ran straight over the cliff."

Flynn frowned in sympathy. That must've been awful to watch.

Griffin dug several coins out of the bag at his hip. He handed them to the shepherd. "I'm sorry for your loss. This should be enough to replace your herd."

The man stared at the gold in his hand. He'd probably never been so rich in his life. "My gods," he breathed out. "Th-thank you. I didn't expect…"

Griffin waved away his thanks. These coins were just more of the blood money from the royal coffers of Sinta, Tarva, and Fisa. The new royal family was enjoying using the previously hoarded wealth to finance free schools, new roads, healing centers, and tax cuts, especially in the long-deprived south.

"And you have no idea what might've caused the noise?" Flynn asked. It had only occurred in this region—that they knew of. Spread over leagues, but still contained.

The shepherd spread his hands. "No. It was just deafening. And everywhere at once."

Flynn nodded. At least the man hadn't offered up a new far-fetched theory. They'd ridden out here in the hopes of learning something useful, but he got the feeling they were going to leave with just as many questions as when they'd arrived.

"I can burn your dead goats if you want," Bellanca offered, glancing over the steep edge again. Sparks crackled between her fingertips, and then a larger flame wrapped around her hand. "It'll keep the vultures off them."

The shepherd looked at her, his expression hardening. "Aren't you Bellanca Tarva?"

Her back stiffened. "Yes."

"Offering an act of mercy?" He scoffed.

Bellanca's face turned blank, then red. She didn't respond, which Flynn knew couldn't be easy for a woman used to speaking her mind. Bellanca rarely censured her words and expected people to just deal with whatever she said.

Her restraint also proved she wasn't like her family. They'd have killed without thought or remorse for much less than a snide remark.

Flynn edged his mount closer to Bellanca's. They were a team and stood as one. Griffin did the same, and the shepherd would have to be dead to not feel the displeasure rolling off them both.

"Bellanca Tarva is a member of Alpha Team, a hero of the Battle of Sykouri, and a close friend of the new royal family, especially Queen Catalia." Carver's lethally soft voice whispered like the quiet hiss of a blade. "*Apologize.*"

Paling, the shepherd did his best to melt into his donkey while Bellanca stared at the back of Carver's head in utter shock. Carver's furious gaze stayed trained on the goat herder, hard as a rock.

Flynn watched in fascination. Other people showed their emotions so easily. Rage. Distress. Surprise. It baffled him.

"I apologize for my thoughtless words." The shepherd bowed his head at Bellanca.

Fear. Remorse.

It looked so easy for everyone else.

Jo jumped into his mind again. He couldn't get her out.

Bellanca finally snapped her jaw shut. "Do I burn the damn goats or not?" she asked.

The shepherd gathered his courage and glanced at her, nodding with little jerks of his head. "I would appreciate that."

Bellanca put whatever hurt and anger she felt at being tied to a murderous legacy into the inferno that sprang from her hands. In the end, she scorched the craggy hillside deep enough to leave a mark the gods would see from Mount Olympus—if they were still watching these parts.

CHAPTER 3

Jocasta flopped back in the grass, spreading her arms and looking up at the sky. The bright blue seared her eyes, but it felt good to be outdoors and as far from the castle as the walled-in grounds allowed. Each marble slab of the newly refurbished Castle Thalyria was starting to feel like an eye, watching her. Telling her to stay in her place. Stick to what she knew. Maybe find a man to love who actually loved her back.

Gods, wouldn't that be an improvement.

She sighed and then regretted it. She wasn't the one with things to sigh about.

Shading her eyes, she squinted up at Cat, who eyed the ground with a combination of longing and mistrust. Cat had come looking for her, needing to get away from the castle and pretend everything was normal for a little while, even if it wasn't, and even if it wouldn't last.

"If I sit down, I'll never get back up." Cat rubbed her lower back. She should already have been free of her aches and pains and holding her baby girl, except someone had slipped her a magic elixir and stopped them both in their tracks.

Someone with backing from Mount Olympus, which potentially put most of the powerful and disgruntled nobles in Thalyria on the list. Unfortunately, they'd been parading in and out of the castle for weeks, and trying to determine who'd cursed the queen was like looking for a stray obol on the bank of the Styx.

"I'll help you." Jocasta patted the ground beside her. She'd left the grassier patch for Cat, although the sparse spring covering was no velvet cushion.

Cat scoffed. "You can't lift me. You're barely taller than I am, and now I'm twice as wide."

Jocasta grinned. "If worst comes to worst, we'll shout for Prometheus."

Cat grunted at that. "Prometheus might remember his own strength at the wrong time and send me airborne if he tries to help."

Jocasta cupped her hands to her mouth and whisper-shouted, "There goes the queeeeen."

Cat giggled, a rare sound these days.

"Come on. The grass is lovely and cool and smells good." Jocasta got up and helped ease Cat to the ground before sitting again.

Cat curled up on her side, stuffing her brown hair under her head to use as a pillow. "Seriously, though, Prometheus wouldn't chuck me into the cosmos by accident. He's gentle enough with Kaia. She never comes back with a scratch on her. Nothing like when I was young and training with Ares."

Jocasta lay down again, breathing in the fresh scents of the shaded garden. "Ares was preparing you to conquer the realms and eliminate their rotten leaders. You needed to be able to withstand huge and terrible trials. It's not comparable."

"I hope Kaia never has to fight like we did."

Cat was generous to include Jocasta in that *we*. Her role had been minimal compared to what Cat, Griffin, and their Beta Team had accomplished. Alpha Team now. "I hope so, too, but you know Kaia—always looking for adventure."

Cat picked a blade of grass and started shredding it. "Anyway, Prometheus understands pain. He'll be careful."

Jocasta didn't think Prometheus even knew his own strength and magic anymore, and so far, he hadn't had to test them. Zeus locked him up for helping humanity by giving them fire from Olympus, and she could only imagine that the Titan was wary of overstepping again after eons of torture in Tartarus. Pretending to be a normal man had to be better than getting his liver pecked out by a giant eagle every day for millennia. But Cat sprang him from prison, and Zeus *let* them escape. Jocasta was suspicious enough to think there was a reason.

"I have a feeling Prometheus could do some damage if he wanted to." Especially if either Cat or Kaia were in danger.

"I just wish he'd *talk* more," Cat said.

"Kaia talks enough for both of them. *Three* of them. *Everyone.*" Jocasta chuckled, shaking her head. "But I wouldn't mind learning a few things from Prometheus. You know, about the old gods and Tartarus and magic…" She let her voice trail off. No one sought her out for those kinds of conversations. She got *What plant infusion should I use for my indigestion? How do I ease my sore throat?* Or *Good gods, my rheumatism!*

Not that those things weren't important, especially to the people affected by them. It just didn't seem on the same level as ruling a kingdom, protecting the population, or partnering with a god.

Cat tossed her ripped-up grass aside. "Kaia and Prometheus get to play all day. It's annoying."

Jocasta smiled. Cat might be the only person in Thalyria who understood her. Jocasta wasn't exactly envious of Kaia's freedom to do as she pleased, just wistful maybe. Kaia had Prometheus by her side, which meant she got to romp around the countryside—much as Jocasta used to back in their village. She missed that life.

"Apart from being terrified of the future if we can't break

this curse, my whole existence now is read-scrolls this and sign-scrolls that." Cat grimaced. "People needing something, people wanting something, people complaining about *everything*, Griffin putting out fires—half of which *I* start—and sometimes, *I just want out!*" Her voice rose to a frustrated shout.

Cat turned her face to the sky and yelled. Jocasta joined in, and they made enough noise to chase the birds from the nearby trees. A few of the feistier ones squawked along with them. They finished on a laugh, and Jocasta felt ten times lighter. Maybe she should start suggesting random screaming to her patients. It was therapeutic.

"Now *there's* a Great Roar for you," Cat said.

"Good thing there are no goats around." Jocasta reached over and squeezed Cat's hand. "And we *will* find a way to undo the elixir." Jocasta had been putting all her energy into finding a solution, especially since Cat's expected date had come and gone, and Persephone hadn't returned with any ideas, let alone answers. If Olympian allies and magic couldn't help, maybe, just maybe, there was a plant out there that could reverse this *active stasis*. Plants and their uses were Jocasta's domain. She didn't know every single one in Thalyria yet, but she was working on it.

"I'm starting to doubt," Cat admitted, fear edging into her voice. She seemed to sink into the ground. "Every day like this seems interminable."

"You're Elpis. *Hope.*" Jocasta looked at her friend. *Her sister.* "Unbreakable. Steadfast. You gave hope to everyone else. Now keep some for yourself, too."

Cat nodded, but it lacked conviction. She visibly tried to shake off her gloom. "I might not break, but I *will* break Nerissa if she tries to give me that tonic from yesterday again."

Jocasta's lips twitched. Her mother's tonics were effective but often disgusting. That was one of the reasons Jocasta experimented with old recipes. She'd managed to cut the bitterness and alleviate the metallic aftertaste in several. "Threatening to feed my mother to Cerberus was a little extreme, even for you," she said.

Cat shrugged. "That muck was repulsive, and Nerissa's *so insistent.*"

"Admit it." Jocasta turned her head, grinning at Cat. "You secretly love having her fuss all over you."

"She's overbearing."

Jocasta snorted. "You put up with Griffin."

"That's different!"

"Then say no to the wretched-tasting medicines." Cat gave her the stink eye, so Jocasta asked, "Did it help with the heartburn?"

"Yes." Cat spat the word at the sky.

"Good. That's my mother's tried-and-true recipe, but I'll see if I can come up with something that tastes better."

Cat shook her head. "No, it's fine. I know you're busy looking for more important things."

She deflated again, shivering despite the warm sun, and Jocasta worried that even their flesh-and-blood Elpis—hope in human form—really could lose faith about things eventually working out in the end.

"I got more scrolls from the knowledge temples," Jocasta said, trying to encourage Cat as best she could. "This time from the north of Fisa."

"They have the most precious ones," Cat muttered darkly, probably thinking about how her homicidal mother had hoarded magic, knowledge, riches, and power in just that region until only a few months ago. "Any luck?" she asked.

"I've seen some references to curse breaking using a

combination of incantations and plants," Jocasta admitted, "but the plants are all toxic. You might be able to handle the dosage and recover, but baby Eleni probably wouldn't."

"Oh." Cat deflated some more.

They all knew immortal didn't mean unkillable. It just meant the body wouldn't decay in the natural way.

"I'm still looking," Jocasta said. "I'll find something that's safe for you both." Or at least survivable. Safe was probably asking too much.

After a few minutes of staring at the sky in silence, Cat asked, "Have you seen much of Flynn lately?"

Jocasta's heart somersaulted in her chest. "Um, not really. Didn't Alpha Team just get back from that dead-goat thing up north?"

Cat nodded. "He just seems so distant these days."

"He's always distant." Or at least he had been to her ever since she ambushed him with a kiss.

"No, not like this. I don't think he's happy."

Were any of them? They were supposed to be basking in the peace and glory of a unified Thalyria and *oohing* and *aahing* over an infant right now. Instead, worry plagued them, and fear for the future stomped toward the castle gates with giant, unrelenting steps.

Jocasta just shrugged. She'd spent plenty of time wondering about and second-guessing all things Flynn-related. She couldn't do it anymore.

"He used to smile. And chat." Cat pursed her lips. "He didn't share *feelings* or anything, but he wasn't anywhere near this withdrawn."

Jocasta agreed—from what she'd seen, at least. "I think he misses Kato." They all did. But as Griffin had grown closer to Cat, Flynn and Kato had become inseparable. With Kato gone, Flynn probably felt more alone than ever. "Griffin and you have each other. Piers is in permanent exile. Carver is off with the army most of the time. He has his troops—and Bellanca." She winced.

Groaning, Cat shook her head. "Bellanca was the only person brave enough to call out Carver when he thought it was a great idea to pickle himself in wine for weeks. I wish he'd stop punishing her for it and be grateful."

"He is grateful." Jocasta was sure of it. Her brother was a surly beast these days but not stupid.

They lay there in silence again, eyes closed, lost in their own thoughts. After a while, Jocasta sighed. It just leaked out of her like steam from a punctured roast.

"Well, there's a dreary sound," Cat said.

Jocasta opened her eyes. "I thought you were asleep." Or she'd hoped. Cat was too uncomfortable to get a good night's rest anymore. And the idea of maybe living like that eternally... Along with everything else... Harrowing. She shuddered at the thought.

"I'm pretty sure only men have the ability to fall asleep that fast."

"I wouldn't know." Jocasta picked up a leaf from the ground beside her and scratched at the silvery underside until she tore a hole between the veins. She poked her finger through.

Cat's hand flew to her belly. "Little Bean's kicking." She reached for Jocasta's hand and placed it under hers over the baby. "Feel her?"

"I feel a foot." Jocasta gasped. "And toes!"

Cat grinned. "She's saying hello to her auntie." Her face fell. "But it shouldn't be like this."

"No," Jocasta said softly, drawing her hand back. "I'll do everything in my power to fix this," she vowed, more determined than ever. Emotion stabbed her eyes. She blinked.

Cat sniffed. Voice wobbling, she said, "I know you will." She closed her eyes again, but that didn't keep the tears from squeezing between her lashes.

Jocasta swallowed the lump in her throat. Doubts circled her potential solutions like hawks, ready to pick them apart and leave only the useless bones of her ideas. This supposedly unalterable magic—the Elixir of Eternal Life—was shielded from even Olympian power, so what did she, a Hoi Polloi herbalist, think she could do about it?

CHAPTER 4

Flynn trod a restless path around the family room. Everyone was here, but his eyes kept straying to one.

Jo slept in one of the smaller armchairs beside the hearth, her head drooping at a bad angle. He'd had the unyielding urge to tuck a cushion under her cheek for the last hour but didn't want to wake her. Or touch her. Touching her was like a burn to the senses, a quick, searing shock and then an ache that stayed with him.

Agitated, he glanced out the windows as he strode down the side of the room looking out over the inner garden with the fountain. Moonlight reflected off the running water, turning it to liquid silver as it crashed over the white marble statue of Apollo and Artemis. Flynn turned away from the twins. Someone should replace them with a statue of Poseidon. Poseidon had always protected Cat. And Cat protected everyone.

His hands curled into fists. Where was Poseidon now? Where were any of the Olympians that had brought Cat this far only to apparently wash their hands of her?

The evening calm started to wear on him, leaving him too much time to think. Carver and Bellanca were in Kitros with the army, Anatole and Nerissa had already gone to bed, and Cat played a card game with Kaia and Prometheus. She kept yawning, clearly exhausted. Dark circles shadowed her olive skin. Griffin tapped a finger against his leg as he read the scroll that had arrived earlier from Egeria with news about their projects in Sinta. He kept half an eye on Cat, his worry a dark cloud hanging over his head.

Flynn understood. They faced an intangible adversary they weren't at all sure they could vanquish. No one knew how to fix this unchanging state someone had inflicted on Cat and the baby—under *his* watch as captain of the royal guard.

Anger rose inside him, accompanying that gut-churning feeling of having failed people he cared about and who depended on him. There were endless questions and no answers. Jo was the only one with a plan.

Flynn glanced at her again, and his heart thumped hard. One gleaming curl had fallen forward since the last time he'd given in and looked. It dangled across her fire-warmed cheek like a midnight ribbon spun from black silk. The lock of hair led the eye straight toward the upper swells of her breasts, which rose and fell with each sleeping breath.

His abdomen tightened, tying his stomach into a knot. Flynn turned away and kept pacing. Jo was as exhausted as Cat. She'd sent out doves to all the knowledge temples around Thalyria, requesting parchments addressing anything even remotely related to medicinal plants, their uses, and breaking spells and curses. The influx of scrolls had been relentless for weeks, and she'd read every single one of them, all while staying available to castle patients in need of her healing skills.

No wonder she fell asleep every evening after dinner now. And everyone just…left her here.

Flynn frowned. She must drag herself up to bed during the night sometime.

A new scroll from Fisa sat in her lap, listing precariously from her limp fingers. Ancient knowledge shouldn't fall to the floor or, gods forbid, into the fire. Jo would be livid.

He stopped and gently tugged the scroll from her loose grip. He set it on the table and then practically leaped away from her. Only Cerberus seemed to notice, cracking open one eye and tracking Flynn across the room. The gigantic three-headed hound took up most of the space on Jo's right, his tail nearly roasting in the fire.

At least Cerberus still guarded Cat instead of the gates to the Underworld. Maybe he even guarded the rest of them.

Tension gripped Flynn's shoulders. He rolled his neck. All he wanted was to go upstairs and clear his head, but he never felt right about leaving before Griffin and Cat. They weren't obligated to include him in anything, and sometimes he wished they wouldn't. But since they always did, he refused to appear ungrateful.

Kaia finally won the game and said good night. Unsurprisingly, Prometheus disappeared shortly after.

Flynn's gaze flicked to Jo again. She still slept like the dead, her lips slightly parted and more hair falling over her shoulders. It struck him how much less tanned she was now, probably because she'd been thrust behind high walls and told to stay there. Jo used to love wandering. Now, she never went anywhere.

From her chair, Cat gave a huge yawn and looked pointedly at Griffin. He didn't need to be told twice—or at all. He scooped her up and carried her from the room with a good-night nod to Flynn. Cat waved to him.

Flynn nodded back. *Great.* Now he was alone with Jocasta. And Cerberus.

He stood halfway between the door and Jo for several minutes. He could leave like everyone else. She was in no danger—except of having a giant crick in her neck when she woke.

Flynn decided to go. But first, he moved around the room,

extinguishing the oil lamps. Servants could do it later, but he still wasn't used to having other people take care of things he could do himself. Finished with that, he walked out, leaving Jo in her chair with Cerberus watching over her.

He stopped three paces out. Her family loved her. He knew that. *She* knew that. But she'd been working herself into exhaustion—*for them*—and they'd all just left her without a second thought. Had it always been like that? Jo left behind to fend for herself?

Flynn pivoted, half turning around. He could bring her upstairs. She probably wouldn't even wake up, and it wasn't as though he didn't know which bedroom was hers. He walked by it all the time. Probably too much.

His pulse hammering, he pivoted again, facing the stairs. He should just go. It was late, and he had his own bedroom to get to. Flynn still didn't feel comfortable in the family wing. He wasn't family—not like Kato had been. He'd never lived in the same household as Griffin and his siblings. Kato had taken a step back when the new royals were first establishing themselves in Sinta, staying with Flynn in the barracks. Cat had stayed with them at first, too, and she'd been the first to switch over to castle living. Now, they all lived and ate and socialized together, and Flynn knew he was an imposter. He was a farmer and a soldier. He didn't belong here.

He was halfway up the marble staircase when he turned around with a growl.

Fine. He'd bring Jo upstairs.

Cerberus lifted all three heads when Flynn walked back into the family room, tracking him with eyes that gleamed as bright and shiny as new copper coins, even without much in the way of firelight. His upper lips curled, showing off curving fangs the size of Flynn's hands.

"Good dog." Flynn eased forward, both hands raised as a peace offering. Leave it to Hades to create a pet you couldn't play with or pat and then give it to Cat. She'd had to feed the hound six whole sheep today. "Jo's not comfortable," he quietly said. "I'm just going to help her upstairs with everyone else. They're already in bed. Then you can have this room all to yourself. Stretch out. Maybe get your tail out of the fire?"

Cerberus eyed him as if he might taste just like sheep—or better—before dropping his middle head back onto his paws. The other heads still watched him, but the snarling lips relaxed. Flynn took the final few steps to Jo, not sure what to do next.

Raking a hand through his hair, he looked down at her. Carrying her upstairs would involve touching her. He almost never did that. She seemed to be a heavy sleeper, though, so there was a good chance she'd never know who'd helped her. She wouldn't suspect *him*. They were barely even friends.

Since no one was around to witness him doing it, Flynn couldn't resist soaking in the sight of her unguarded. *Jo.* Gods, just her name in his head snapped everything tight inside him and sent an explosion of heat through his chest. He took a nervous step forward. This was going to be awkward.

Bending down, he got one arm under her knees and somehow wiggled the other behind her back, winding it around her shoulders. She lolled into him, making a husky little sound he'd hear into next year as her head fell back, exposing her neck and jawline.

Flynn froze, holding his breath. Jo settled back into slumber, only now her hair tickled his arm, and he had a view straight into the dark hollow between her breasts. Heat stirred in his groin, and he forced his eyes back up and cast about for something else to look at. Nothing was half as interesting. The gilt, the marble, the tapestries and vases… They all seemed dull and colorless compared to Jocasta's bosom.

He grimaced. For the gods' sakes, why didn't people make clothing that actually covered women's chests?

He inhaled deeply. *Be strong. You've fought monsters.* Should touching a woman really be this hard? Other men did it all the time and survived. Surely, he could.

But they weren't Jo. Or him. He wasn't so special, but she was. And they...

His heart cinched, and Flynn cut that thought short with a hard mental swing of his ax. There was no Jo and him.

Carefully juggling her higher into his arms, he lifted. Puzzled, he couldn't help looking down at her again. She didn't seem to weigh much. She wasn't particularly tall and felt less substantial in his arms than he'd imagined. Because of course he'd imagined. Her. In his arms. Sometimes naked.

Damn it. Often naked. Who wouldn't?

His skin burned from the sudden spike of heat in his blood, and he squeezed his eyes shut, trying to chase away the tantalizing images as fast as they assaulted him. A man would have to be dead to not admire Jo's hourglass figure. He saw others doing it, especially Magoi nobles with calculating gazes. When he saw them looking at her, a blistering rage always filled him. He wanted to carve out their eyeballs and serve them to Cerberus for dinner.

Quelling that thought, Flynn turned and tiptoed from the room. He'd do anything to not wake Jo, including send off a tentative prayer to Athena. He hadn't prayed in years. This seemed like the time to start.

It was almost comical how much one pocket-sized woman could unnerve a man who'd seen his fair share of battles and bloodshed. It didn't seem normal. And he wasn't laughing.

At least Jo mostly ignored him. He didn't ignore her back exactly. He just didn't engage with her when he could reasonably avoid it, all while being constantly aware of every place she went, every word she spoke, and every project she put her mind to.

He reached the wide, curving staircase and started climbing. Jo's forehead dropped into the crook of his neck. The warm, velvety caress of her breath sent a tremor through him and turned his heart into a battering ram against his ribs. *Good gods*, she cuddled in a little.

Flynn broke out in a sweat, his feverish body trying to cool down in any way it could. A long time ago, Jo had burrowed under his skin and started eating away at him. There didn't seem to be a cure for her—or this affliction. He just had to live with it, like a chronic illness.

Stepping onto the landing, he started down the corridor toward Jo's room. She muttered something unintelligible but didn't wake up, thank Olympus. The woman already made him awkward enough. The last thing he needed was to have to explain *this*.

Also, when did the bloody castle get so enormous? And why did she always have to smell so good? Like a summer garden. That honey-lavender scent made his head spin and his mouth water. It was a good thing it was socially unacceptable to lick people. Even when they were sleeping.

He neared her door—across the hall and three rooms down from his. He hated that. It just made everything harder.

Thank Zeus, her door was open. He didn't have to wiggle her around or risk squeaky hinges.

Flynn snuck like a thief across her bedroom, wary of getting caught, especially by Jo. If she woke up, there was a good chance he'd drop her and jump out the window.

Finally at the bed, he leaned over and gently deposited her. Her body went down lightly enough but one arm tangled with his, tugging a little. Jo groaned softly, and Flynn's heart nearly exploded. He didn't breathe again until his lungs demanded it.

She rolled onto her side, tucking her knees up. Slowly, he pulled the blanket at the foot of the bed up and over her.

There. Done.

But when he was finally free, he just stood there, unable to move.

What if she *did* wake up and see him? What if she looked at him with sleepy blue eyes and reached for him? What if she kissed him like she had more than six years ago and turned his world upside down again?

Flynn swallowed. He'd probably devour her like a lust-crazed animal, just as he'd done then. Obviously, that couldn't happen.

He backed away, every quiet step crushing down on something he desperately wanted. He'd barely been able to look Griffin in the eyes for weeks after he'd kissed Jo. Or kissed her *back*, more precisely. He'd kissed her, though—and thoroughly. Regret was all tied up with wishing he'd just kept going.

Turning, Flynn silently closed the door behind him. As he walked away, some idiot part of him wished Jo had woken up and forced him to explain. She would've looked at him with that sparks-on-flint expression until he said something, and then he really would've been in trouble.

What did a man say to the only woman he'd wanted for years? *I'm a thirty-four-year-old virgin with no title, no magic, some wages accumulated, and a farm that's probably been overrun by vermin?*

Not exactly a ringing endorsement. He could cleave heads with an ax. At least he had that going for him.

He'd missed his chance when they were on equal footing, but it didn't matter, since Jo didn't look at him the way she used to, and he'd vowed never to marry anyway. He'd watched his parents and siblings disappear one by one and had no intention of starting his own family just to go through endless rounds of death again.

He just wished he and Jo could talk again without the conversations feeling so forced and painful. Or that they could just sit together, like they used to. That would probably never happen, though, which made Flynn feel as if he were going through mourning all over again.

CHAPTER 5

"You're joking, right?" Jocasta set down her still-empty plate and forgot all about the lavish breakfast that had looked so appealing just seconds ago. She darted a wary look back and forth between Cat and Griffin.

Her brother shook his head. He looked utterly serious. Cat did, too, her expression holding a hint of her usual baiting smile, which Jocasta would've been thrilled to see again under circumstances that didn't involve baiting *her*.

Griffin offered an encouraging nod. "Alexander is a successful and powerful nobleman from central Tarva. He's been supportive of us from the start, and his entire household staff stayed with him *after* our takeover, which means he must've treated them fairly without being forced to by law. His magic is conducive to growing healthy plants, so that should interest you, and his orchards are the best in Thalyria—a fact that several sources have confirmed for us."

Jocasta narrowed her eyes. Griffin sounded like a scroll listing this man's qualifications to...

Do what, exactly? *Court her?*

"He's arriving later today," her brother added, "so try not to be late for dinner."

Jocasta arched her brows at him. Of course, the affairs of the kingdom hadn't stopped. The royal couple was just as busy as before the curse, which was a good thing, since distractions were the only remedy Jocasta could currently recommend.

That didn't mean their distractions needed to include meddling in Jocasta's life. She turned to Cat. "Really?" she asked through clenched teeth.

Cat shrugged. "He's young, handsome, and doesn't seem mean-spirited. We'd never throw him at you if he wasn't a good match."

"*Throw* him at me?" Jocasta could hardly believe her ears.

"Griffin and I have already met with him several times about the orchard deal. You'll like him. I'm sure of it." Cat nodded, as if to punctuate.

Jocasta pursed her lips. She'd rather scour the newly arrived scrolls for solutions than be forced to socialize, but at least this Alexander wasn't arriving until later, and she wasn't expected to attend negotiations. But Cat putting her on the spot with a Magoi nobleman she'd never met? Especially at a time like this? Cat's misguided efforts at matchmaking were both endearing and infuriating—an exact replica of Cat herself.

Making a tactical decision, Jocasta appealed to Griffin instead. "I'd rather work through dinner tonight. So many new scrolls to read. I could be up all night." Which was true. She'd barely made it through the last batch from the knowledge temples and more parchments were arriving today. She'd been setting aside the more promising scrolls in her healing room. She kept going back to one listing some of Circe's potions. Most of the scroll was gibberish about finding Circe's hidden island prison, but there were some interesting recipes using plants Jocasta wasn't familiar with. If she found and studied those plants, maybe she could devise new uses for them. *Elixir-reversing* uses.

"You haven't even met Alexander yet," Griffin pointed out. "Don't make any decisions until you do."

Jocasta sighed. "There's no decision to make. I'm busy with other things right now."

Griffin reached out and gently gripped her shoulder. "*Your* life doesn't have to stop. And honestly, ours can't, either. Alexander and his orchards—which we need if the southern tribes are going to get better fruit at reasonable prices—are a welcome distraction. We're going to have dinner tonight and pretend everything is fine. We have to."

Jocasta swallowed. Only the family and Alpha Team knew about the Elixir of Eternal Life, about Cat getting stopped in her tracks and baby Eleni along with her. They would keep it a secret as long as possible. Maybe long enough to find a remedy.

"I'm not interested in settling down," Jocasta said. At least, not with just anyone.

"Meeting him doesn't mean you have to marry him," Griffin said. "But inviting him here to talk about expanding his orchards seemed like a good way for you two to get to know each other." He smiled, releasing her shoulder. "Two birds. One stone."

"I'm a bird now, am I?" Jocasta turned to Cat. "I know who's the stone."

Her comment rolled off Cat quicker than water on oil. "You'll like him, even if you don't want anything else," she said.

"Fine." It wouldn't be *uninteresting* to meet someone, especially someone willing to help correct the imbalance of wealth and goods that had always existed in Thalyria. More magic and better soil gave the north an advantage over the predominately magicless, arid south. She wasn't surprised this Alexander's successful orchards sat squarely in the center of the continent, which had always fared well enough. "*One* dinner." Jocasta could agree to that, she supposed, although she was sick to death of her family deciding things for her without even *asking* first.

Carver arrived, windblown after riding in that morning from the army encampment outside nearby Kitros. He looped an arm around her shoulders. "Since when do family meetings start without me? And in the breakfast room, no less?"

"Since these two decided to play matchmaker." Jocasta gave her tall, wiry brother a quick hug back.

Carver's blade-sharp gaze swung to Griffin and Cat. "Ah, Alexander. Maybe he should prove his worth with a sword before meeting our sister."

Carver knew about this? Jocasta's mouth puckered with the sour taste of being the last to find out. "By all means, run him through and spare me the agony of small talk."

Carver chuckled, surprising her. It was good to see a spark of life from her brother that didn't involve annoying Bellanca into a blazing rage.

"I won't be here to meet him, actually." Carver moved toward the breakfast buffet and poked around the fruit and pastries. "Bellanca and I are heading back to Kitros later and staying until at least tomorrow. We're going to be running some nighttime exercises in and around the abandoned arena."

Jocasta shivered at the idea of anyone setting foot in the towering amphitheater that had seen so much bloodshed, including theirs, during the recent Agon Games. She still had nightmares about that place, heard the screams in her ears and felt the terror in her bones. A trial by fire, Cat had called it when Jocasta volunteered to complete their team. Alpha Team—Beta Team at the time—had accepted her offer out of sheer necessity, kept her alive, and won the games. Carver, though, almost died in that arena—protecting *her*. Magic literally pulled him back from the Underworld. Since then, he hadn't been the same.

"Let me guess…" Jocasta teased despite the way her stomach suddenly dove. "A competition?"

Carver nodded, his smile turning predatory. "Men versus women this time. I'll win."

Jocasta held back a snort. At least Magoi and Hoi Polloi soldiers were mixing better than anyone expected at first. "I'm happy you're confident, even if you're abandoning me tonight." She shot a prickly look at Cat as she grabbed a spice cake from the buffet and took a bite. There were advantages to being a princess, including excellent food she didn't have to help cook. "I'll be in the library," she said as hints of honey and cinnamon exploded on her tongue. "More scrolls came in from Fisa last night."

Cat reached for a spice cake, too. "If there are any in the old language, let me know. I can read them for you."

Jocasta nodded, taking another bite as she headed for the door. "Don't wait for me for lunch," she called over her shoulder. "I'll eat in the library when I'm hungry." Which meant she wouldn't have to see Flynn for hours. Always a relief—especially after that strange dream she'd had.

Heat billowed through her as she left the breakfast room. She'd dreamed about Flynn holding her tightly against his chest. She'd snuggled into his neck, inhaling a mix of leather, star anise, and cedar, the earthy scent of a man at work. She didn't know if he truly smelled of spice and raw wood anymore, but her dreaming nose still conjured up the intoxicating blend that had wrapped all around her the day they'd kissed.

Shaking her head, Jocasta exhaled with a gust, eliminating the phantom fragrance from her lungs. She pulled her shoulders back and focused her mind where it should be: on finding an antidote for the Elixir of Eternal Life.

———— ⑥ ————

Jocasta hurried toward the library, already feeling the press of time despite the early hour. Dozens of scrolls to read through, more on the way, and now a suitor she didn't want. And to think, not long ago, she'd been itching for something to keep her busy. This was one of those be-careful-what-you-wish-for situations. She'd happily have remained bored rather than have a curse hanging over her family.

Over the whole kingdom, really.

Thalyrians weren't aware of the problem yet. They'd been promised one prophesied child to truly unite the continent. Without that child, what would happen next? Griffin's and Cat's happiness wasn't the only thing at stake. The kingdom they'd fought so hard to create still stood on precarious legs.

Lost in her thoughts, Jocasta charged into the library just as Flynn stepped out. She ran smack into his large, hard chest. Startled, he reached out to steady her. She inhaled sharply, filling her lungs with traces of leather, cedar, and spice. Her dream came roaring back. Longing punched into her gut. Her eyes crashed into Flynn's, and they stared at each other in shock.

He finally spoke. "Are you all right?"

She swallowed. That voice. Deep and decadent. Who needed spice cakes? She knew exactly what she wanted to devour.

"Fine," Jocasta croaked, not sounding fine at all. He let her go, and they both stepped back, a thunderclap of awkwardness blowing them apart so fast that her heel caught on a crack. She tipped backward with a gasp.

Flynn's hands shot out. He pulled her upright, his grip eating up half her arms. His fingers tightened, drawing her closer, and Jocasta lifted her face to his, her lips parting and probably screaming for a kiss before her mind caught up and gave her— and her kiss-me-now mouth—a stern slap.

Flynn snatched his hands back, curling them into fists. "This floor is uneven."

She winced. "I noticed. Thank you. I probably would've cracked my head."

He nodded, and they slid away from each other. She shifted

uneasily. He shifted, too. In two shuffles, the usual gulf loomed between them.

"What are you doing down here?" Jocasta asked, glancing beyond Flynn's shoulder into the perpetually dim library. She should really request more lamps.

He angled his head toward the big table she'd colonized with her research. "A messenger just delivered more documents from the Fisan knowledge temples at the main gate. I was there for the changing of the guard, so I brought the scrolls here. For you," he added somewhat tensely.

Ah. Well, that explained his foray into the bowels of the castle. Only she came down here on purpose. "Thank you."

He nodded again, his mouth flattening.

The good news was that this exchange wasn't any more stilted than usual. Short. Awkward. Forced. *Fantastic.* So why did it feel so much worse?

Probably because she'd dreamed about Flynn so vividly last night. In her dream, he'd held her close, and now she wanted that in real life. Instead, she had this.

Jocasta involuntarily grimaced. She'd give anything to go back in time and take back that kiss. If she hadn't recklessly tempted fate, they'd still be friends. Friendship wasn't what she truly wanted, but it was better than nothing. She missed him.

"Are you busy, or do you have time to read through some of this information with me?" She regretted each stupid, impulsive word as they somehow flew from her mouth. "I've been doing this for weeks, and there's a lot..."

Flynn gaped at her as if she'd grown two heads. Or maybe horns. Whatever it was, it wasn't flattering.

"Ah..." His eyes darted down the hallway. "I..."

"Never mind." Jocasta waved a hand behind her, inviting him to leave. After all, he was very good at that.

He stiffened but stayed put. "No, I'll help. Where do we start?" He turned and strode back into the library, selecting a new scroll from the table piled high with parchments she'd yet to read.

Jocasta watched in astonishment as Flynn got to work. "Look for anything that mentions Circe," she murmured, joining him beside the table and picking up a document. Finding out more about the witch of Aeaea and her fabled garden might help her make sense of that scroll she'd put in her healing room.

After turning up an oil lamp, Jocasta read with only half her mind on the words. She blamed that on the Flynn effect. She made very little progress on the scrolls while her heart raced and her mind drifted all over the place. One would think total indifference got easier to fake, not harder. Wasn't practice supposed to make perfect? Frankly, whoever coined that phrase was a flaming idiot. Standing tensely next to Flynn in the chilly library, she started to almost miss the years she'd hardly seen him. He was more closed-off than ever, and it turned out that actually seeing him every day was relentlessly worse than just imagining him.

Why in the Underworld did she ask him to stay? Now, she was barely working, which wasn't helping anyone.

Flynn set aside the parchment he'd been reading and picked up another. "What happens when you find what you're looking for?"

"Then I'll go get whatever I need to help Griffin, Cat, and baby Eleni, assuming we don't have it already."

The look he turned on her was incredulous enough to raise her hackles. "You?"

Jocasta stared back, just as incredulous. "Yes, *me*. Why not?"

"By yourself?"

"I never said *by myself*, but why wouldn't I be part of a search party?"

His expression darkened. "It might be dangerous."

"Why? Thalyria is at peace."

"Being at peace doesn't mean everything is perfect and safe. If that were the case, I wouldn't have a job protecting the castle and the royal family. Carver and Bellanca wouldn't have positions maintaining an army. Griffin and Cat wouldn't constantly be dealing with issues, complaints, disputes, and everything else that lands on this doorstep. Prometheus might let Kaia out of his sight once in a while." Flynn let the scroll he was holding roll back up with a snap. "There are still bandits around... Bad people... Wolves."

Jocasta choked on a laugh. Flynn glared, and she cleared her throat.

"And this Great Roar now," he added stiffly. "Who knows what that's about."

"Yes, well, loud noises and wolves aside, I wouldn't just strike out on my own across the continent. Contrary to what you might think, I'm not stupid."

Flynn tossed the scroll onto the table and stepped forward. "When did I ever say you were stupid?"

Jocasta stepped back, her hip bumping into the table. "You didn't have to *say* it."

"I've never *thought* it," he growled.

"Then give me some credit. If I find something—*when* I find something—I'll gather a search party and travel safely."

"Being worried about the dangers doesn't mean..." He stopped midsentence, scrubbing a hand down his face. "You're always twisting my words. Turning them into something they're not."

She lifted her chin. "How can I twist your words when we never talk?"

Flynn's eyes narrowed. He leaned in, bracing one hand against the table beside her. His other arm twitched forward, nearly caging her, but then he let it drop. "We're talking right now."

His thunder-dark rumble sent a shiver through her. Her heart thumped behind her ribs. "You call this talking?" she challenged.

Slowly, he lifted his other hand and gripped the edge of the table. Her breathing sped up, flooding her senses with whispers of earthy spice and raw wood. *What did you make this time?* Just this morning, she'd listened to the rasp of sandpaper grating in his room.

Flynn didn't back off, and a swarm of honeybees buzzed in her blood. "I hear sounds, and they're coming from you and me." The gravel in his voice sank straight to the center of her body and smoldered there like a banked fire ready to blaze to life. "So yes. I call this talking."

"We're arguing," she corrected flatly.

His gaze held hers. "We argue too much."

"That's because you're argumentative."

Flynn's eyes flared. "*I'm* argumentative? You talk circles around me and leave me in the dust."

The volcanically charged heat rising inside her crumbled to ash. Dust reminded her of home, which reminded her of that kiss.

Which reminded Jocasta that she needed to protect herself.

Lifting her hands between them, she softly pushed. Flynn backed off easily—too easily. Her heart pinched. Couldn't he have resisted? Even a bit?

"Thank you for your help. I can take it from here." She turned to the table, giving Flynn her back. "And I'm sure you have other things to do."

"I said I'd help." He reached for a scroll, his arm nearly brushing hers as he picked it up. The heat from his body burned a line down her side, and suddenly, getting away from him was all she could think about.

"No, please don't," she blurted out. The misery-joy of having Flynn within kissing distance while knowing full well that he would *never* kiss her was too much.

Flynn froze, the parchment half-unrolled in his hands.

Jocasta awkwardly faced him. Was it too much to hope for that he didn't remember those *exact same words* flying from her mouth when he offered to walk her home after crushing her heart?

Unease shot across his expression. He put down the scroll and backed up.

No, he remembered.

Well, that made two of them—no matter how much she wanted to forget.

Jocasta turned back to the new scrolls and picked up one at random. Her hands shook. She didn't know what to think about Flynn anymore, except that she couldn't face six more years of unrelenting heartache.

"I'll...leave you, then." Flynn's boots scuffed over the stones, his voice already distant.

Jocasta didn't respond. He'd hear the tears in her throat.

She stood with her back to the door until she stopped shaking. Flynn's footsteps disappeared long before she sat down at the table, finding a brand-new cushioned footstool beneath it to shield her feet from the cold. Only she ever came down here, which meant that Flynn...

Her eyes stung, and her throat thickened all over again.

After several minutes of staring at nothing, Jocasta shook herself into action. She lit a second lamp, brought it closer, and started reading. She had a mission to accomplish, and time was running out. Without the promised heir, the kingdom might shatter. Magoi nobles who'd vied for power their entire lives would pounce the second they smelled blood. Unity didn't matter to them. Neither did peace. They'd carve the continent into countless warring city-states and rule from their thrones of blood.

Cat and Griffin were already falling apart, and Thalyria would be next—unless someone found a way to break the curse.

CHAPTER 6

What just happened?

Flynn could barely remember the exchange in the library, almost as if he'd taken a blow to the head. That was his usual reaction to Jo—hard to shake off. There'd been a bunch of words. He remembered being himself until he wasn't. And now, all he could recall was wanting to kiss her so much he nearly *did*.

The woman pulled him tight in every direction. Need stirred in his groin, and Flynn brutally suppressed it. Selfish desire meant nothing compared to the knot of tension sitting in his chest. Kissing Jo—if she even let him—meant starting down a path with a price, one he would never make either of them pay.

Flynn released a low growl as he clomped down the hallway, leaving one almost-impossible-to-resist blue-eyed beauty behind him. How did they always end up like this? Antagonistic sparks going up in a flaming mess? Did they really have to argue every time they spoke? He remembered a time when they could finish each other's sentences instead of misunderstanding them. Surely, they could do better than *this*?

He stopped and pivoted on one foot, half turning back to the library.

To say what?

Resolutely, he turned back around and kept walking in the direction he'd been heading—*away* from trouble. Words always failed him around Jo. For years, they'd been stuck in his head, but the thought of saying any of them aloud was a nightmare.

I can't forget our kiss. You seared my soul. I'm terrified you'll die—everyone else did. You're extraordinary. I want to fall on you like a ravening beast. Help me.

Flynn stopped and clamped his eyes shut, breathing hard through his nose.

Damn him. And damn that birthday gift. He never saw the bracelet again. Jo probably threw it in the river after he brought her home and couldn't figure out how to talk to her again. Apparently, *ever.*

He'd watched her for weeks, obsessed with everything she did and everywhere she went, sometimes trying to accompany her. She'd avoided him, turning a cold shoulder and going about her business. Then he'd run off, because leaving home to train with the growing southern army had been better than being constantly all twisted up inside over a woman he couldn't claim.

Never put a girl at risk unless you intend to marry her.

Old Hector's angry voice rang as clear as day in Flynn's head as he exited a little-used side door and stalked toward the barracks behind the castle. He didn't intend to marry anyone. For the first time in a long time, that certitude made him furious.

He didn't regret his father's vigorous slap and mortifying lecture. Humiliation aside, he was glad Old Hector stopped him from losing his virginity with a willing girl behind one of the fat old olive trees at the back end of their property. His father was right. Actions had consequences. Some could be permanent. He'd been seventeen and had no intention of marrying Dehla—then or ever. So he put his cock back in his pants where it belonged and didn't take it out again, even when he was tempted.

Then his mother got sick, sicker than usual. She faded so gradually they all had time for dread to eat them alive over and over. His siblings, all younger than him, died one by one, and the graveyard grew, also behind a fat old olive tree on their property. Eventually, it was just him and Old Hector. His father withered away, proving that dying of a broken heart really could happen. Flynn watched him go, too, both of them slowly suffering. And the day he shoveled a grave for the last of his kin, he vowed never to marry or have children. He knew exactly what happened to families. And since marriage wasn't in his future, sexual intercourse wasn't, either.

He understood well enough that there were methods for preventing pregnancy. Living with an army was an education in more than just weapons and tactics, and he'd heard more than he sometimes wanted about what went on between men and women or any combination of the sexes. But relying on those methods and offering nothing... It had never seemed right to him. Or foolproof.

And then there was the added complication of only wanting one specific person—which was why he needed to avoid her. Unfortunately, that was getting harder by the day. Hour. Minute.

Flynn grimaced. Was *he* the problem? Did he seek out Jo without realizing?

Being around him wouldn't end well for either of them, and he knew from experience that praying for anyone's health and safety didn't do a damn thing. He'd stopped trying years ago. Olympians didn't care about lives like his. Tragedy just happened. In the blink of an eye, like the strike of a lightning bolt, or slowly, so that everyone could live in constant, stomach-churning misery.

Losing Kato recently had been bad enough. But losing a wife? His children? Flynn had a good idea of how devastating that was, how it annihilated a strong man and turned him into dust. He also knew what it felt like to ramble around a big, empty house, the last one standing. That wouldn't be him again—not when he could avoid it.

Seventeen years after the night his father found him with Dehla, Flynn had never bedded a woman in his life and didn't intend to. The agony was finding himself in daily contact with the only one he wanted.

But claiming Jo—if by some miracle she even still wanted him—would have consequences. Maybe joyful ones at first, like love and children, but sickness and accidents would strike inevitably and when he least expected. They always did, and then he'd lose his family one by one and die of a broken heart, just like Old Hector.

And he'd decided a long time ago. That *would not* be him.

Flynn came across Griffin halfway to the training yard and fell in step beside him. It was unusual to see his friend headed toward the barracks at this time of day. Midmorning was when Thalyrian nobles crowded the throne room and buzzed around like insects, all wanting to drone in a royal ear.

He figured the courtiers were half the reason Jo escaped to that cold dungeon of a library every morning instead of taking her research somewhere more pleasant. From what he'd observed, conversation among the nobles was either vacuous or viperous, and Jo didn't tolerate either. It was a miracle Cat and Griffin could.

Nodding greetings to each other, the two men walked in silence until they reached the outdoor weapons rack and contemplated their options. It was a given they'd spar.

Various blades and bludgeons glinted in the sunlight. Flynn made sure the choice of arms came from all over Thalyria. He employed men and women from the four corners of the kingdom, and his soldiers needed weapons they felt comfortable with, whether they were Sintan, Tarvan, or Fisan. He had no issue with them maintaining their regional identities as long as they remembered they were all Thalyrians and here to protect the royals.

A frown settled over Griffin's face as he perused the options, eyeing a hefty sword that matched his height and size. He made no move to lift it.

Flynn lowered it from the rack. "Pointy end that way," he joked, offering the leather-wrapped hilt to a clearly preoccupied Griffin.

Griffin took it, the deep grooves around his mouth reflecting weeks of unrelenting worry.

"What happened now?" Flynn bypassed his usual double-bladed ax and selected a sword along with a dagger. Something for each hand. Doubling up might help. When they grappled, it was anyone's guess who'd come out on top, but with blades, Griffin almost always won.

Griffin's frown deepened. "Cat just insisted I come out here with you and get some exercise while she deals with the nobles and today's batch of issues. She told me to run away while I still could since she couldn't waddle fast enough to escape them."

Flynn cracked a smile. "She'll be fine."

"She hates court machinations."

And yet she'd been born into them. "Cat can handle the nobles." Flynn knew that. So did Griffin, or he wouldn't have left her.

"It's different now." Griffin shook his head, his face twisting with a combination of agitation and disgust. "The Thalyrian elite are always looking for a weakness to exploit, and it's exhausting pretending nothing's changed. It's even worse for Cat."

Flynn thought that was an understatement. Most of the

nobles would love to go back to the old ways, and only believing the new royals were at the top of their game would keep them from hatching takeover plots like the Hydra grew heads. "Cat gave you a gift. Take it. And next time, you deal with the nobles and find a way for Cat to escape."

Which would probably mean she'd bolt to the far reaches of the gardens with Jocasta. Close enough that Flynn couldn't follow them without looking overbearing and obsessively attentive—especially when it wasn't clear, even to him, which of the two women he watched more closely.

Ignoring the hot spark in his chest, Flynn started toward the small arena inside the castle grounds. The ex-Tarvan royals had used the ring beside the barracks for private entertainment, but his soldiers and he had cleaned out the bloodstained sand and begun using it for training and exercise. Bellanca refused to set foot in it. Her sister, Lystra, never even left the castle.

Griffin slowly followed. "Cat's not doing well. I'm worried."

"Tired?" Flynn asked in concern. "Uncomfortable?" Cat had to be sick of being pregnant too long already—and scared with no end in sight.

"Tired and uncomfortable are the least of it." Griffin flashed a somber look toward the castle. "We should already have a daughter. And an heir to the throne. We don't have either, and no one's any closer to reversing this curse. The days go by without a solution. No word from Persephone. No new ideas. Nothing changes, especially not Cat or the baby. She seems almost...defeated."

"Defeated?" Flynn rejected the idea with his whole being. Like a raindrop pinging off a hot slab of marble, it vaporized instantly, replaced by an image of Cat at the Battle of Sykouri. Winged punisher. Bringer of justice. Voice thunder-deep. Magic to topple tyrants. "'Cat' and 'defeated' don't belong in the same sentence. She's Elpis. She's hope—for everyone."

Griffin followed him into the empty arena, shutting the doors behind them. "Isn't that just another burden right now?" A shadow crossed his features. "Hope doesn't exclude fear. All we can think about is a future with no cure. A future with no baby—or with an infant that never grows. A future where Cat doesn't change but everyone else does—and leaves her alone. Masking her fear doesn't mean it's not there and getting stronger, or that it can't eventually break her."

Again, Flynn rejected the idea. *Unbreakable* was what made Cat the human embodiment of Elpis. She carried within her the original spark that gave hope to all mankind. She'd used it to champion a people who needed her. She overcame the worst, no matter what, no matter how. But Griffin needed a sympathetic ear more than a debate right now, and maybe Flynn was wrong. Maybe there were some trials even the strongest people couldn't emerge from more powerful. This curse came with immortality, and whoever had orchestrated it might just have found the one crack to split Elpis down the middle. *Forever* didn't have another side to it, no fire to burn through, no suffering to eventually overcome, no ashes to rise from. It just went on and on.

"She's not broken yet." Flynn squeezed his friend's shoulder. "I'm going to have hope a while longer."

His brow knitting, Griffin glanced at the sky as though expecting a sign from Olympus. Flynn had more faith in the people under this roof finding a solution. Gods moved on. Other amusements called. Even Persephone, who claimed to love Cat, delivered bad news and disappeared. The only Olympian still around was Ares, but he was in Fisa and didn't know how to counteract the elixir, either—or if counteracting it was even possible.

Fury Flynn knew would inhabit him until the annihilation of the worlds stirred deep inside. No one had breached their walls, but someone had still reached their queen, and no one knew how or when. Or why. This poisoned gift from Olympus felt like another sudden accident he had no control over. No say. No power. No turning back time to before tragedy struck and it was all over.

Flynn buried that thought—a shovel-full of dirt covering another grave—but the usual emotional distance didn't settle over him. Steadily blank hadn't helped him in months, and his commanding every soldier in this castle hadn't helped Cat. He could watch over the people he cared about with a vigilance that quietly bordered on compulsive, but it didn't keep them safe. Or alive. His entire family was testament to that.

Hiding his agitation, Flynn rallied for Griffin's sake. Griffin had no emotional distance from Cat. If something happened to her, he'd be Old Hector all over again. Probably worse.

But something had *already* happened. And they needed to fix it before everything they'd fought for unraveled along with his friends.

Flynn lifted his blades, knowing Griffin would do the same. "We still have time to figure this out." Not much, but maybe enough. "Jo's looking hard for a solution. The gods don't know everything, and she's awfully smart."

His own words sent a snap of heat through him. Distance and several minutes had done nothing to lessen Jo's impact. That was the way of it these days. She was a battering ram in a small and complicated package, relentlessly leveling him every time they met.

"She'll find a solution," he said hoarsely. "She's a gifted healer. If magic can't help Cat, then she will. She'll make it happen." Flynn was as certain of that as he was of the yearning prowling through his breath and blood.

Griffin nodded, some of the dread seeping from his features

as he raised his sword and looked around, his gaze darting over the freshly raked sand. "You ready?" He tightened his grip on his weapon.

Flynn was more than ready to get his mind off Jo's sapphire eyes, sharp chin, and gorgeous curves. "No holding back. I won't," he promised. And if his friend needed to pound on something to clear his head and keep panic at bay, it might as well be him.

Griffin used his blade to point to the center of the ring. "After you."

Flynn took his time walking to the middle of the arena, discreetly limbering up as he went. Sparring with Griffin could challenge muscles he didn't even know he had. Going in cold was a mistake he wouldn't make twice.

As if sensing Flynn's thoughts, Griffin let a slow smile spread across his face. "No holding back means I might not leave you in any shape for that mock invasion you have planned."

"I'll take my chances." Flynn rolled his shoulders and stretched his neck, noting that Griffin wasn't bothering with any of the same preparations. Living with a spitfire like Cat likely kept him in a constant state of readiness. "Training twice in one day will be the most action I'll have seen in months."

Griffin arched a brow. "Missing the good old days of running around and risking your life?"

"A little." At least quests and battles had kept him on the move and mostly away from… "And who says you'll beat me?" Flynn asked.

"Nearly thirty years of experience." Griffin flicked his wrist, sending his blade singing through the hot, dry air.

Flynn huffed. "You must have nearly thirty years of faulty memory."

Griffin's lips twitched, but then his expression flattened as he and Flynn began to circle. That flinty battle face made Griffin hard to beat. His eyes never gave anything away but saw his opponent's next move before they made it. The ease with which Griffin predicted an upcoming strike was almost oracular. He and Cat were made for each other—god-touched beyond the rest.

Griffin struck first, a lightning-fast lunge that came out of nowhere. Flynn barely sidestepped, then shifted his balance to go on the offensive with a blow that would've knocked the blade from nine hands out of ten. Griffin parried, shoved Flynn away, and took back the offensive.

The first ten seconds of sparring finished warming Flynn up better than ten laps around the arena. He countered Griffin's next strike. Attack and defense went back and forth, the scrape of metal filling his ears as training kicked in and instinct took over. This was exactly what he needed: reaction, not thought.

To be ruled by reflexive self-preservation.

To hammer out some frustrations.

The next time they circled, they both breathed harder. Flynn's feet churned in the sand, stirring up patterns around the arena. His senses sharpened. Sweat and dust. Hot steel. Dry leather. Sounds and smells filled him with the echoes of past battles—of aching arms, ringing teeth, and deafening noises. Not that either of them would ever mistake this for a real battle, one born of intent and underlined with danger. Fighting for your life was something different. Fighting for others was something beyond even that.

But sparring didn't mean easy, especially with Griffin. Flynn's muscles burned. His lungs strained like bellows. Perspiration rolled down his face, making him almost miss all that hair that used to absorb it. *Almost*—because the day he'd chopped it all off, Jo had said she liked it.

"How can I twist your words when we never talk?"

Her earlier question distracted him, and Flynn sidestepped a second too late. Griffin took advantage with a punishing blow that sent him to one knee. Flynn whipped up his dagger and pushed with both hands, shoving Griffin back with a snarl. He sprang up, and strike for strike, they fought again, neither finding an opening.

He never found an opening to talk to Jo, either.

"No, please don't."

Griffin delivered a whip-fast hit with the flat of his sword. The heavy steel struck Flynn's wrist with a thud that echoed into every nerve and bone of his body. He exhaled sharply and dropped the dagger.

"Son of a Cyclops." Flynn flexed his fingers. He could barely feel his hand. The ache went to his shoulder.

A smirk pulled at Griffin's mouth. "That's one blade down."

Scowling, Flynn launched an unrelenting offensive, trying to knock Griffin's sword from his hand. He could win, but probably not with blades. Grappling was how to even the odds between them.

Strain started showing on Griffin's face. The two men exchanged heavy blows. Flynn blocked out everything else and let the frustration he felt every waking hour push him to the brink of his strength. Griffin's sword arm finally wavered. *Got you!*

"No rest and royal obligations make Griffin a sloppy warrior," Flynn taunted. He had him this time.

"All duty and no intimacy make Flynn bored and lonely."

Shock punched into Flynn. All it took was one hard downward strike, and Griffin knocked the sword from his hand. A sharp metallic vibration rang between them, ending abruptly in the sand.

"Gods damn it," Flynn muttered, dropping his hands to his hips. He bowed his head, breathing hard. His two practice blades stared up at him in accusation. He should've won this time.

Bored and lonely.

Griffin picked up the blades. "What happened?"

Flynn barked a laugh. As if Griffin didn't know. He shook his head, not angry or even disappointed at losing. Just…restless. Restless and tense. Sparring hadn't gotten rid of it. Nothing did.

He eyed his friend. "You can wipe that smug look off your face. I got your message."

Griffin frowned. "What message?"

Flynn just shook his head again. He wasn't bored. As for lonely…

Maybe. Griffin had Cat. Carver had family. Kato was gone. And Flynn just put one foot in front of the other and lived each day as it came. What else was he supposed to do?

Flynn kept his mouth shut, so Griffin started toward the exit. "I'd better get cleaned up and go rescue Cat."

Nodding, Flynn followed, some of the tightness easing from around his ribs. "I doubt Cat needs rescuing." Even haunted by this curse, she was a force to be reckoned with. Not to mention that his guards would've alerted them to a problem anywhere in the castle, especially the throne room.

Griffin's quick, almost pitying smile made Flynn think he'd missed something important. "Never underestimate the value of moral support."

Jo instantly filled his mind. It was more the idea of her than an actual image, but the sinking feeling that pitched straight through him had Jo written all over it.

The only time she'd needed his support in recent years, he'd withheld it. He'd even threatened to walk away from his duty and his team to keep her from risking her life in the Agon Games. In the end, she'd fought, and survived, but the thought of Jo in that blood-soaked arena still jolted a convulsive beat from his heart. Even now, he tasted an ashy layer of fear on his tongue.

"I saw Lukos organizing the guards in the throne room this morning," Griffin said, loading the blades back onto the rack outside the training venue. Flynn would need them later for the mock-invasion drill with his soldiers. "He's come a long way."

Flynn confirmed with a nod. "From Fisan shepherd to my right-hand man. He's loyal to the core and a natural with a blade." Lukos could've led his own contingent of Hoi Polloi soldiers under Carver's command but had chosen to join Flynn and remain at the castle. His duty was to Cat, his queen, and he'd made that clear from the moment he kneeled before her. He was now second-in-command of the royal guard and quickly becoming indispensable.

"I could've sworn I saw him ogling Kaia when she wasn't looking." Griffin's expression darkened.

Flynn shrugged, unsurprised, especially since he'd seen the same thing himself. "That's what young men and women do. They ogle each other."

Griffin gaped at him. "Kaia's only sixteen."

"Just because you're practically old enough to be her father instead of her brother doesn't make her a child," Flynn pointed out.

Griffin stared at him in shock. If his friend expected indignant and protective posturing over younger sisters and the men who noticed them, Flynn was about to disappoint. First, didn't Griffin know by now that Flynn would rather try to pat Cerberus than discuss women, especially the ones close to him? Second, Flynn didn't have a leg to stand on.

How long had he been ogling Jo? He knew exactly when it started. It was that day she fell into the river while they were fishing. She'd come up laughing, her black hair dripping down her arms, her eyelashes spiked with water, and her pale dress clinging to her body, revealing more than she realized. Flynn had barely been able to breathe for an hour.

He wiped sweat and dust from his brow. "Just leave them be. I doubt anything will come of it."

Griffin's mouth thinned. "He's always popping up when Kaia's around."

Flynn grunted. He wasn't about to judge. He didn't realize it at the time, but he was lucid enough now to look back and see how he'd always managed to put himself in Jo's path for one reason or another. He'd asked question after question about medicinal herbs he didn't give a Cyclops's eye about just so he could hear her talk.

And gods, that voice... Low. Melodious. Smoky rich. It was the kind of voice that sank deep inside a man and stirred his blood.

Flynn cleared his throat, uncomfortably aware of standing two feet from Jo's older brother. Whom he'd known since birth.

He was also aware of the stonelike guilt dragging at his innards. Jo kissed him for a reason that day. He'd spent years seeking her out and making himself a part of her everyday existence. He'd sent her signals without knowing what he was doing—or why. She'd understood. And acted on it.

Jo was the brave one, the clever one. No wonder he'd nearly come unhinged when her lips touched his. He hadn't even realized he'd been dying for that explosive kiss.

Flynn scrubbed a hand down his face, weary somewhere deep in his bones. He hadn't meant to hurt her. Or lose her altogether. But with one kiss and a few hasty words, he'd done both.

Glancing toward the castle, he said, "So what if Lukos pops up? He might just be doing his job, and Kaia doesn't seem uncomfortable." Flynn trusted his second-in-command. He also wasn't convinced that Kaia had noticed Lukos to begin with. To see the soldier, she'd have to look past Prometheus.

And *that* wasn't a talk Flynn was going to have with Griffin. Cat could handle that hornet's nest.

"I guess you're right," Griffin said. "Just...keep an eye on them, all right?"

Flynn nodded. He kept an eye on everyone.

Griffin glanced down at himself and then over at the entrance to the royal bathhouse. "One quick stop and then I'll help Cat close out the morning session with the nobles. I'm sure she's handling things admirably—and possibly even diplomatically," he added with a laugh.

Flynn chuckled. "I haven't heard any screams, so she probably hasn't fed anyone to Cerberus."

"*Yet*," Griffin said archly.

Flynn knew she wouldn't—not unless the person really deserved it. "Cat's learning to be more diplomatic. Anyone with a sense of humor can see that. And don't worry about Kaia," he added. "She's more interested in strategy and weapons than she is in men at the moment."

Griffin pursed his lips, seeming unconvinced. Maybe Flynn just didn't understand because he hadn't had younger sisters to fret over in years and didn't know what it felt like to see them grow up and turn into women.

Two little flame-top heads bent over a weaving project flashed in his mind. Flynn shoved the mental image aside as fast as it assaulted him. The memory of his sisters still left him wondering if the twins' fiery locks would've eventually faded to auburn. His had.

Griffin thumped him on the back with a wry smile Flynn wasn't sure how to interpret. "See you at dinner." He strode toward the bathhouse, already tugging his sweat-dampened shirt from his trousers.

Flynn watched his friend disappear into the bathhouse. As

for himself, he'd clean up later. He'd be encrusted with sweat, sand, and possibly blood soon, so why bother?

He also wouldn't use the royal bathhouse and risk running into Jo. Right now, he couldn't think of anything more torturous than seeing her slip into a private bathing chamber where he knew she'd be naked, wet, and unguarded.

Heat swirled through his middle. Suddenly, Flynn's feet wanted to carry him back to the library. He turned to the barracks, but it was harder than usual to put one foot in front of the other and walk in what felt like the wrong direction.

CHAPTER 7

As usual, Jocasta did her best to look more comfortable than she felt. Unsurprisingly, Cat seated her next to Alexander at dinner. Despite a lingering prickle of irritation, Jocasta sat where she was told and couldn't even try to claim her customary place at the table with three of their numbers missing. Carver and Bellanca were in Kitros with the army, and Lystra never appeared at dinner if her older sister was absent. Flynn ended up opposite her, and it was infuriating to be more aware of the withdrawn, scowling man across the table than of the handsome, relaxed, *talkative* man beside her.

Jocasta resisted the urge to pluck at her dress and get some air moving across her skin. Fidgeting was for those who couldn't calm their nerves from the inside out, and overheating…

Well, ideally, sweating could also be controlled with focused breathing.

Flynn's fork clanged against his plate. His cheeks darkened. He looked readier than usual to bolt from the formal dining room and would probably find an excuse to escape the after-dinner socializing. What would it be this time? Anything that didn't involve feeling unwell, because gods forbid someone suggest he speak to the castle healer. She could've helped him lessen the monstrous black eye glaring out at her like a taunt it was too late to respond to, but of course, he hadn't come to her, and now there was no limiting the vicious bruising. Did he consciously fight the idea of blending in with the royal family? He'd washed and dressed for dinner but still managed to look as if he were facing a battlefield instead of a banquet.

Was it some kind of statement, as though turning up for dinner with raw knuckles and a black eye would prove he didn't have a place at the table?

If that were the case, they should all pack up their trunks and abandon the castle—especially Cat, who could be positively feral.

Jocasta reached for her wine and sipped the cool, fruity liquid as she dragged her attention back to Alexander, thinking that Thalyrian wine tasted exactly the same in a clay cup as in a golden goblet. She doubted a Magoi nobleman was interested in that bit of wisdom from a former village healer and farmer's daughter, so she simply took another sip. Alexander didn't put on airs as she'd feared he would, but the luminous green brightening his eyes to a striking turquoise against his brown skin spoke of a hefty supply of gods-given magic and reminded her that they came from very different backgrounds.

"Your orchards aren't far from here, I think. A few days' journey to the south?" It had taken mere minutes for them both to understand that their common interest in plants could cure any lull in their conversation. Alexander had capitalized on that discovery earlier, and now Jocasta returned the favor. Both times, she was guilty of letting her mind wander.

"The spring flowers on apricot trees are stunning. Have you ever seen them stretch as far as the eye can see?" He fully snared her attention when he produced a bloom from seemingly out of nowhere and offered it to her.

"I can't say that I have," Jocasta murmured, taking the delicate pinkish-white blossom from his hand. It was lovely. Far too crushable for a person used to kicking at stumps and swinging from branches. She worked with herbs. They were hardy, growing up just as she had, wild and free to roam the hillsides.

Her fingers tightened on the flower, crumpling an almost-translucent petal. She set it down and picked up her goblet. A sip of wine slid down her throat. Then another. She'd be inebriated soon if she wasn't careful.

Apparently, she considered lifting her drink to her lips the only acceptable form of fidgeting. She should try eating instead. After all, this was dinner. Unfortunately, her appetite was missing.

"Apricot blossoms are white with pink on the inside. The petals flutter to the ground like dancers." Alexander's jewel-bright eyes smiled as he moved his slightly work-worn fingers to demonstrate. "When they fall, they carpet the whole orchard, and we say it snows in Mellithea, even though we barely see frost there."

His enthusiasm for apricots and their blossoms turned out to be infectious instead of ridiculous, and Jocasta found herself smiling back at him. "It snows spring flowers?" She could almost see it, a soft blanket of petals hugging the land and holding in moisture for as long as it could before the dry season.

He nodded. "Sometimes deep enough to cover your feet to the ankles."

"It sounds delightful. Do you sell to presses or only to markets? I'm always on the lookout for high-quality apricot kernel oil. It's good for treating skin and hair conditions." She purchased her supplies since she'd never been in a position to produce her own stock of anything.

A surprising thought wriggled into her mind. If she married this man, she could build an oil press.

She mostly ignored the idea. That was a big *if*—but maybe one worth considering?

At this point, decisions about her not-so-distant future came down to one thing: she wanted children, or to at least try for them. She wasn't in a family or a position to go about that in an...unconventional way. Oh, it happened. Of course it did. But not to a royal princess. Not to Anatole's daughter. Not to Griffin's sister. Jocasta knew her older brother had nearly twitched himself to death at the idea of having children out of wedlock or any official claiming that equaled marriage to him—Cat had told her that.

"I've heard you're a gifted healer." Genuine interest lit Alexander's face, and Jocasta felt a stirring of warmth. "I sell a small amount of fruit to presses. My plant magic mostly prevents damage, but weather or insects occasionally get the best of a swath of trees and render the fruit inedible—or at least unattractive. Oil presses only seem interested in my apricots and figs. They're ravenous for nuts, though, which I don't grow. Nuts make for a change from the ubiquitous olive oil."

At *olive oil*, Jocasta instinctively looked at Flynn. Flynn looked away from her.

Her chest pinched. She turned back to Alexander. "Not all seeds produce useful oils, even if you repeatedly squeeze them to a pulpy death."

He chuckled, saying dryly, "So I've been told. If I'd been smarter, I would've started a vineyard. Grapes, wine, and grape-seed oil. A commercial trifecta, according to my mother." He popped a mini tiropita into his mouth with a self-deprecating smile.

Jocasta glanced at Nerissa. Across from her at the other end of the table, her mother fussed over Kaia while Prometheus looked on with what appeared to be a certain amount of confusion. Shrunk down to a Flynn-sized man—in other words, still quite large—the Titan kept trying to interrupt with zero success, his mouth opening and closing like a fish out of water. Leave it to her mother to plow right over a god—who'd been the recipient of his own fair share of maternal clucking since his unexpected arrival.

"Mothers often have strong opinions." Jocasta layered enough humor into her tone to convey fondness rather than bite. "My own advises me daily on how to eat, live, and breathe—with love, of course." Although Nerissa had been suspiciously silent on the subject of a potential marriage alliance with a powerful Magoi landowner in the center of Thalyria.

Alexander's smile widened. His voice dropped, lightly teasing and leaving them firmly cocooned in their private conversation. "If the henpecking wasn't done with love, you probably wouldn't listen."

Soft laughter bubbled out of Jocasta. "I see you know me already."

"I can hardly claim that." His eyes suddenly sparked with something different, hotter. Alexander looked at her intently. "But I wouldn't mind the opportunity."

A weight shifted in her belly. It wasn't a flutter. More like nerves—and a possible sinking sensation.

Jocasta reached for her wine again only to find the goblet empty. Well, that was two full servings down. It was a good thing no one expected her to stand anytime soon. She switched to water.

"Tell me more about your orchards," she prompted, side-stepping his attempt at flirtation and cutting a bite-sized piece of honey-glazed lamb from the larger portion on her plate. She paired it with a baby root vegetable and brought it to her mouth, despite her lack of appetite.

Alexander easily went back to his favorite subject. "The orchards surround the city of Mellithea. Some sections have been established for generations, but I've been expanding to cover several new slopes and working on irrigation."

"It must take a tremendous amount of work to maintain all that. How many people do you employ?" Jocasta asked, truly interested.

"Hundreds," he answered. "But different growing schedules help keep the workload reasonable. If everything needed care and harvesting all at once, the operation would become unmanageable."

"Even with the help of magic?"

"Plant magic helps grow healthy crops, and luckily runs in my family, but it doesn't do everything."

Jocasta liked the idea of a man who worked. Actual labor. There was something vigorous about it, and judging by the width of Alexander's shoulders and the way he filled out his tunic, he had vigor aplenty. "My brother told me the land we're offering has water."

He nodded. "More land and more water mean more fruit. I can increase supply to the southern markets at prices everyone can agree on."

Jocasta couldn't argue with that logic. "I've never been to Mellithea, but I've heard impressive things about its temple district."

Alexander huffed. "Zeus's temple is almost so grand as to be offensive."

"Shouldn't it be grand? He's the king of Olympus."

"It can be grand without being plated in gold. Those riches could be better used to serve the people."

Jocasta gazed at him in astonishment. Alexander certainly wasn't cut from the same cloth as your typical Thalyrian noble. No wonder Griffin and Cat liked him. *She* liked him.

But did that mean she wanted to *marry* him?

Across the table, the server offered a second portion of lamb to Flynn. Jocasta knew from a lifetime of experience that he burned through food like the sun through Icarus's wings, but he refused the extra helping with a shake of his head and a murmured "No, thank you" that barely reached her ears.

Her heart gave a sudden twist. Was he in pain? He certainly looked a mess. He should've come to her. She'd been in her healing room for at least an hour before dinner and seen several of his guards, who'd clearly had a hard day's training. Obviously, Flynn had gotten personally involved in the tests.

Personally involved. She nearly snorted aloud. Flynn didn't get personal—not with her, at least.

She turned back to her dinner companion. "I'm not sure Zeus would agree, but then again, I don't know him myself."

Alexander laughed. "The gods are known for having quick tempers and volatile moods." His eyebrows rose. "This conversation might be bordering on dangerous."

"Only if the intent were malicious," she said, a playful smile tugging at her lips. "Otherwise, I doubt they'll care."

Warmth filled his magic-rich eyes again, and Jocasta found herself easily smiling back. Magoi nobles, men and women alike, generally left her feeling either snakebitten or unsure of herself. This man did neither and had a subtle sense of humor and slight irreverence that made conversation easy and time fly.

"Mellithea is large and lively and has some of the best shopping and entertainment you can find. It's right in the middle of the kingdom and on the Continental Road. Everything goes by us. Some call it the Jewel of Thalyria." Alexander obviously loved what he did and where he lived, and Jocasta could relate to that—although not any longer. She also had the sense that he was selling his home—to her—and was uncertain if she should encourage him.

"I've been told the climate's especially lovely. Perfect for orchards," she teased before she could stop herself.

He chuckled, perhaps realizing his pitch had been too transparent. "Apricots—my biggest and most successful crop, in case I haven't already made that painfully obvious—do especially well there."

"Do they? I hadn't heard," she deadpanned.

He laughed outright, his turquoise eyes sparkling with amusement.

Flynn cleared his throat, pulling her attention away from Alexander. Her smile faded. Why did she feel sudden guilt when she and Flynn had no relationship? Their friendship was barely even standing. Showing he cared about her safety wasn't anything to go by. Flynn tried to protect everyone. Gods forbid someone else die on him.

Her meal turned over in her stomach. Her appetite truly gone, she focused again on Alexander—or tried to. Damn Flynn for distracting her without even moving. Or talking. Or eating. At dinner.

Alexander, though, had been snagged by her father, who was giving farming advice to a farmer. The Magoi listened with interest—as he should. Anatole's irrigation setup had been the envy of their community. He'd even piped water directly into the house and found ways to filter and heat it. She'd been spoiled by hot, clean baths long before Griffin conquered a kingdom.

Jocasta sighed in spite of herself. The others chattered boisterously, Cat and Griffin the center of attention, while an awkward silence settled over her end of the table. One that was her fault. And Flynn's. She refused to take the blame entirely, not when he was glowering at his plate as though it had personally offended him.

Alexander eventually escaped her father's somewhat one-sided conversation and turned back to her. "I have a very big house." The information catapulted from his mouth. Even he looked startled. "You could visit. And bring your mother. I'm sure mine would be delighted." A flush stole across his face, deepening his brown skin to a dusky mauve.

"Oh. Thank you…" Not sure what to answer, Jocasta tried to imagine life in a city she'd never set foot in and the scope of Alexander's orchards. His operation was clearly grander than anything from their old village, including Flynn's olive groves, which had always seemed grand enough to her.

Alexander's smile looked painful, and empathy rose within her. What had her family told this man? He obviously had high hopes for their meeting, and while she'd discovered she liked him enough to entertain vague thoughts about a future, she'd been thrust into this encounter without much of an option and with very little warning.

Her discomfort grew, along with her awareness of Flynn's flat, steady stare. *Now* he decided to look at her? Heat prickled her entire body.

"That's a kind offer, but I'm right in the middle of an important project. I…couldn't possibly go anywhere." As soon as she said it, the rejection churned in her mouth like chalk and left a bitter taste behind. Her brain told her she was being shortsighted and possibly idiotic, but her heart spoke for her the second she realized how carefully Flynn was watching her from across the table.

Hope leaped inside her, and she nearly grimaced. What a disaster. Meeting a potential suitor she liked should help purge her of her pointless obsession with Flynn, not make it *worse* again.

Alexander glanced quickly at Flynn and then back at her. "Maybe another time? When you've finished your project?"

Jocasta didn't know what to say, and awkwardness grew between them like a weed strangling a plant they'd been successfully nurturing. Not that she was nurturing anything beyond an acquaintance. In fact, she suddenly found Alexander's interest in her a little suspicious. Did he think he wouldn't get the property he wanted without her hand in marriage?

"I'm sure your land negotiations will go well regardless," she said a little more frostily than she'd intended.

His brow furrowed. "My invitation has nothing to do with that. We've already come to an agreement."

Oh. Her pulse sped up. Sweat pricked at her nape. Did anyone else find it uncomfortably hot in the dining room?

As if on cue, Cat flung her hand toward the hearth. "*Why* are we heating this place? It's not even the rainy season anymore, so don't talk to me about dampness. I already have a little inferno inside me. I don't need one behind me." Pointedly, she looked at Griffin.

Griffin rose, skirted a sprawled-out Cerberus, and thoroughly soaked the fireplace with the large bucket of water that had been keeping the wine chilled earlier. "It was for your pet monster. He likes the heat."

Cat turned her scowl on Cerberus. "Only two of his heads like the heat. The other one is sensible."

Not even trying to swallow his snort, Griffin gave the hound a wide berth as he strode back to the table. No one got too close to Cerberus, not even Cat. The creature was entirely unpattable. From snouts to tail, no part of him invited touching.

"Majority rules," Griffin said as he took his seat again.

Cat huffed. "I'll find you some reading on monarchies. The scrolls are pretty clear, but I'll give you a hint: that's not how it works."

"Is Cerberus his own monarchy now?" Griffin asked, glancing over his shoulder at the three-headed beast.

Cat followed his gaze. Her lips pursed. "He certainly rules

the hearths in this place. But I say no more heat until the next rainy season."

"And I say you'll change your mind the next time Cerberus uses puppy eyes on you."

Cat's jaw dropped. "Puppy eyes? Take that back or Cerberus might eat you."

"He could try," Griffin said smoothly, picking up his utensils.

Cat sputtered a laugh. Almost immediately, what looked like a sudden twinge of pain sliced through her smile. She hid it well, but Jocasta saw it, and sympathy rolled into a tight ball behind her breastbone. Late pregnancy came with practice contractions, and Cat's unwanted immortality—and stasis—had set in *after* that preparation began. Now, she was stuck with aches and pains and fatigue—indefinitely. And no baby.

Unless Jocasta found a solution.

As Cat and Griffin one-upped each other in an argument about Cerberus and his heads, entertaining everyone and doing a convincing job of showing their guest that all was well at Castle Thalyria, doubt crept over Jocasta's shoulder like a poisonous spider. What if she couldn't find a solution? This child, a combination of Cat and Griffin to truly unify Thalyria, was *foretold*, and only unimaginable power could alter a prophetic thread. Ares didn't know what to do. Persephone hadn't even come back. Prometheus had been out of the loop for millennia and had his own torture to deal with. How was she, a Hoi Polloi healer, supposed to find knowledge not even the gods possessed?

Somehow, she'd thought she could make a difference.

A flash of village life hit her along with an intense feeling of belonging and understanding where she fit in. The phantom of her old life haunted her with things she missed. Her medicinal herb garden must be a mess, just a tangle of pungent weeds now.

And what about the people who'd counted on her? Who did they go to for tonics and advice?

Alexander glanced nervously in her direction when Cerberus's low growl thundered through the discussion. Taking pity on the Magoi, Jocasta adjusted her expression. She'd been conjuring up convincing smiles long enough to do it with ease. All she had to do was imagine turning up the wick of an oil lamp until the desired brightness beamed across the room.

She angled her head toward her table neighbor. "He's definitely a menace, but don't worry, Cerberus won't eat you. Not without good reason." While she spoke the truth, it was clear she was teasing.

Alexander jumped on the life raft she offered and added paddles in the form of conversation. "Are you sure? I've heard at least one of his heads is highly unpredictable."

Her smile turned genuine. She leaned closer, lowering her tone to a conspiratorial whisper. "But no one can tell you which one. The rogue head changes according to region."

Alexander let out a low chuckle.

"It's the one on the right," Flynn said flatly, looking straight at her. "Don't trust it."

Jocasta scowled at him while Alexander stiffened. Cerberus didn't have a rogue head, Alexander was on her right, and Flynn wasn't helping.

Annoyance grated inside her—and not only with Flynn. He was a lot of things, but impolite wasn't usually one of them. Why in the Underworld had Cat seated them in this odd—and frankly uncomfortable—grouping? And how dare Flynn make such a pointed comment after not uttering a word for the entire dinner? What right did he have? None. None whatsoever.

Jocasta glared at the hulking boulder across from her. Flynn might be expressionless, but she had no doubt the look on her face was blistering enough for both of them.

"Why is there meat in front of me?" Cat said loudly. Her narrowed gaze jumped from Jocasta to her own dinner plate. She wrinkled her nose. "I hate meat."

"Yesterday, you were craving meat," Griffin said. "You wanted it."

Revulsion flashed across Cat's face, making it clear that was the wildest tale she'd heard in a decade. Stabbing her lamb steak, she lifted it from her plate and tossed it at Cerberus, fork and all. His middle head was quickest. The fork disappeared, too. "I never crave meat. I want fruit. Lots of fruit." She pointed at Alexander. "You. Apricot man. Do you have apricots?"

All eyes landed on Alexander.

To his credit in Jocasta's opinion, he proved he wasn't a fidgeter, either. "I...do, actually." He brightened, endearingly so. "I brought three dozen crates of the earliest blooming variety as a gift to your household."

"Excellent. Thank you." Cat sat back and waited.

Jocasta bit her lip to cover an unstoppable smile. She'd heard more about stone fruits, orchard pests, and pollinating partners in the last two hours than she had in her entire lifetime. *Of course* the man had apricots.

"I'll send for them." Alexander waved for his personal servant and quietly instructed the man to bring the queen her apricots.

"Well done. You saved the day," Jocasta whispered. "Or at least the dinner."

Alexander angled her way, murmuring, "As long as I saved myself from being the next morsel thrown to Cerberus."

They laughed, genuine and spontaneous, but true merriment eluded Jocasta. Alexander kept rising in her esteem, and she liked him immensely, which made it even more unfortunate to know that she was still, and always would be, more aware of Flynn than of anyone else at the table.

But what of the life she wanted? Her own household? The chance for children?

She studied Alexander out of the corner of her eye. The children she'd imagined for herself always had thick red hair, soulful brown eyes, and possible chin dimples. And the man she'd imagined sharing a bed with had a jaw that could cut slabs of marble, strong arms that held her tight, and shoulders she could barely see around. Alexander was certainly handsome, but he wasn't...

Her eyes flicked up, meeting Flynn's across the table. She swallowed.

"*Try* it," Kaia insisted, waving something in Cat's face and capturing everyone's attention. "It tastes different than usual. Not at all goaty."

Griffin snatched the offending blob and ate it before Kaia could shove goat cheese under his wife's nose again.

"My hero," Cat breathed out with utter sincerity. Then she turned to Kaia. "Do that again and Cerberus gets to lick you."

Kaia burst out laughing. Prometheus took his social signals from her and relaxed as soon as he realized Kaia wasn't truly in danger of death by poison slobber. Cat's apricots arrived, and the rest of the family buzzed with perhaps almost genuinely happy chatter for once while Jocasta struggled for something to say to her neighbor.

"Does having plant magic mean you can grow something specific?" she asked Alexander.

His was a rare gift, from what she understood. Very unusual. Not even Cat seemed to know much about it.

An idea sparked, sending a shock through her. "Something brand-new? A plant that doesn't already exist?" Something that could nullify a magic elixir.

Her heart pounded. Could Alexander be the answer they'd been waiting for?

His wistful smile told her she'd just hit on a fantasy he'd love to believe in. "My magic nurtures and protects what's already there. Seeds, vines, trees, buds… But no, I can't invent a new plant or fruit or nut variety. Those would have to come from a place like Circe's garden."

Circe again. Jocasta kept circling back to the witch's potions, but half the plants in them seemed utterly absent from Thalyria. "If only Circe's garden were real." The fabled garden would certainly solve their problem. A plant didn't already have to exist when a powerful sorceress could *create* it for you. But no one had ever found Circe's prison island or the magical garden there. It was either on another world they couldn't access—Atlantis or Attica maybe—or a myth, and myths didn't grow the antidote she needed.

Flynn's chair scraped back. "Excuse me." He stood. "Some of my soldiers took a beating during training today, and I need to check on them before it gets too late." He swept a quick glance around the table out of ingrained politeness, his eyes not meeting Jocasta's. He focused on Cat and Griffin. "I hope you don't mind."

"Of course not. Go." Cat waved a hand dripping with apricot juice. Griffin nodded in agreement.

Flynn gave a curt nod of thanks, turned, and left as though his heels were on fire.

Jocasta frowned. Leaving before the end of dinner was unusual, even if he wanted to check on his soldiers.

"What makes you think Circe's garden isn't real?" Alexander asked.

She dragged her eyes away from the now-empty doorway and back to him. "No one's ever found Aeaea. Rulers have tried and failed over millennia. If the island is out there, it must not be in Thalyria." Which was as good as not real to Jocasta. And definitely not useful.

"Just because no one's found it doesn't mean it's not there."

"Do you think Circe's island is out there? In Thalyria?" Because if so, that scroll in her healing room could become infinitely more useful. She'd mostly set it aside for the plants and potions, but there was also some kind of map in there— vague directions through dangers to reach the ultimate reward of Circe's garden. She'd gone back to it time and again over the last weeks, drawn to both sections, even though she'd considered the orientation parts to be nothing more than the poetic ramblings of thwarted adventures.

Five trials by sea and land.

But what if she *could* access Circe's garden? The sudden itch to go find that scroll nearly lifted Jocasta from her chair. She resisted. Another hasty departure from the table would look very odd to their dinner guest. And someone might think she was running after Flynn.

"Alexander?" she prompted.

Wariness tightened his expression. "I rarely say this aloud because being scoffed at isn't much fun, but I'm convinced my plant magic comes from Aeaea."

"But...magic comes from Mount Olympus."

"Not mine." He flushed a little. "I don't think so."

Her pulse leaping with new hope, Jocasta asked, "How can you know?"

"When I use my magic, I feel it in my bones. They tell me the island's out there." Flushing deeper, he flicked his eyes away from her. "I know. It sounds ridiculous."

"Why ridiculous? Bones tell stories all the time. They reveal height and approximate age. Sex. Diseases. Injuries. Why wouldn't they reveal magic?" she asked.

He turned back to her, watching her intently. "Do you really believe that?"

She nodded. "How does it work? What does it feel like?" *How can it help me find Aeaea?*

"It's hard to explain." Alexander shook his head. "When that deepest part of me springs to life, I don't feel any link to Olympus. The mountain means nothing to me. I look toward the Fisan Ocean instead."

Jocasta's heart pounded harder with each word he said. She suddenly understood why Alexander might be so different from other Magoi. Their magic might not have the same source. And if his magic *did* come from Aeaea, then Circe's island existed in Thalyria. It was out there—somewhere. Circe, who predated Olympus. Circe, granddaughter of Titans and daughter of the sun god, Helios. Witch. Spell caster. Potion master. *Maker* of plants.

She tried to keep her voice from trembling—and her hopes from soaring too high. "Wouldn't explorers have found Aeaea by now? I know people have looked."

"Maybe they have." He leveled a cautioning look on her. "And maybe they never came back."

Jocasta bit her lip. Circe wasn't known for a friendly welcome. Or a friendly anything. But this was exactly what they needed. Aeaea. A garden where anything could grow. And a witch to grow it for them.

Alexander's brow drew down. "You have a look. You're worrying me."

Warmth spread through her chest. Alexander was lovely. If only she wanted to marry him. Then at least one of her problems would be solved. "That project I was telling you about... I need a plant that doesn't exist." *Yet.* "I need Circe to create it."

He stared at her in shock. "That's a fool's errand. And people have died on it."

She was sure they had. But Jocasta was willing to risk her life for her family, and after weeks of dead ends, she was actually starting to form a plan. This could work. If she found Circe and her magical garden, there was a chance she could come home with a potion brewed from a plant that currently only grew in her mind. *Olympus* couldn't reverse its own magic in this case. She needed magic that came from *somewhere else.*

Spontaneously, she reached out and squeezed Alexander's hand. She let go just as quickly, not wanting to give him the wrong idea.

Ironically, she *could* envision a life with this man. He potentially offered exactly what she wanted. Companionship and her own household. Someone who listened to her. A family, if all went well. But even when she tried to peer into that possible future, a hulking redhead got in the way and took up all the space as though he alone belonged there.

"Fool's errand or no, can you tell me more? Anything you know?" She knew her eyes pleaded with him.

"I've heard rumors..." He paused. "They're rather far-fetched."

"Humor me?"

His mouth flattened, and uncertainty darkened the magic in his eyes.

"What harm can it do," she coaxed, "if you think Aeaea can't even be found?"

"I don't think it can't be found. I think no one comes *back* from it." He treated her to a hard look that made him fit right in with the rest of the men in her life. No wonder Griffin liked him.

"I promise not to do anything dangerous. I'm a *princess.* I wouldn't just go off on an impossible quest." She smiled to reassure him, half-certain that *liar* was writing itself across her teeth as she spoke.

Alexander scoffed. "Somehow, I don't believe you."

"By myself," she amended. Dishonesty had never come naturally to her.

He laughed. There wasn't much humor in it. "This better not get you killed."

Jocasta simply waited, her insides twisting, her outside utterly still.

He gave in with a grimace. "I don't know how to find the island. All I can tell you is that I've never felt closer to my magic than in Thassos, on the south coast of Fisa. My power just... sang there. All through me, everywhere, and the source of it was coming from the ocean."

"You felt it in your bones," she murmured.

He nodded. "But it lessened as I traveled north on the Fisan coastal road, toward the Ice Plains and Mount Olympus."

"So the exact opposite of other Magoi."

Again, he nodded. "The strong feeling got me interested in what's out there, beyond the Inner Sea and the Great Arm of Hera. Information is sparse," he said with a wry twist of his mouth, "but I've been at it for about ten years now and have pieced together a few things."

Jocasta knew exactly nothing about what lay beyond the enormous peninsula protecting the east coast of Thalyria from the great Fisan Ocean. Like all the unexplored areas surrounding the known continent, the ocean was god touched. Humans didn't go there. And if they tried to... Well, there was a reason no one knew anything about it.

"Supposedly"—Alexander drew out the word, underlining the pure conjecture in it—"if you somehow manage to reach the marble statue of Circe at the center of her island, you can describe what you want, and—as long as she can grow it in her garden—she'll be obligated to give it to you."

Obligated to give it to you. That was even better. The idea
of earning a gift was threaded throughout the parchment she'd
been studying, so Jocasta had a feeling Alexander's speculation
was spot-on. Not only that, she *felt* it. Maybe in her bones. This
was it. The solution—and possibly the only one. If she reached
Circe using the frankly terrifying directions in her scroll, she
could *force* the witch of Aeaea to make her a nontoxic plant-
based potion with the right magical properties to reverse the
Elixir of Eternal Life.

She had no doubt that finding the exiled goddess would be
the hardest thing she'd ever do in her life. But the reward…

It was finally her turn to go on a quest. What were her
chances of success? Of *survival*? Her heart hammered in her chest.

"Thank you for this. I can't tell you what it means to me."
Sincerity rang in her low, trembling voice.

The troubled crease between Alexander's brows told her he
wanted to dissuade her from whatever she had planned. She
liked him even more when he didn't try. "Maybe you'll come
visit me in Mellithea after you finish your project."

She smiled. "I'd enjoy seeing your orchards. And would
value your friendship very much."

He nodded, taking that for what it was—her best offer.

Jocasta escaped as soon as she could, excitement knotting
with dread in her stomach. The Fates had dumped her into
the middle of an exceptional family and then passed her over,
forgetting to weave in *her* thread. Alexander had just handed
her a loom, and if she was right about that scroll in her healing
room, she had a pattern to follow, a map of sorts.

She'd spin her own destiny, starting tonight. And if she got
Alpha Team on her side, she might just have a fighting chance of
reaching Circe's not-so-mythical garden alive. And maybe even
making it back.

CHAPTER 8

Someone was in Jo's healing room. Flynn narrowed his eyes, tracking the shadowy figure shuffling around in the dark. On his way back from the barracks, he'd noticed the door ajar and stopped to investigate. Someone was snooping around, or maybe stealing something. Now *that* wasn't about to happen—not on his watch.

The person moved toward the back, where Jo kept all the bits and pieces she didn't need within easy reach from her worktable. He liked catching glimpses of her at the big, sturdy table he'd made for her.

Actually, he didn't. It did strange things to him.

Scowling, Flynn moved on silent feet toward the partially open door. He could be quiet when he put his mind to it, and he put his mind to it now. He slipped inside as the figure—a woman, judging by the size of her—took something from the back cupboard.

Anger flared. Someone had come in here to take something from Jo while she was busy at dinner with that glossy-haired, fruit-this, fruit-godsdamned-that suitor of hers who smiled so much his face should break.

Flynn lunged forward and grabbed the offender's wrist.

The woman swung around with a shriek. His eyes widened a split second before Jo grabbed his shoulder with her free hand and brought her knee up. Her aim was off, but Flynn still leaped back with a hiss. Forgetting to let go of her, he yanked her with him, and Jo thumped against his chest. They both gasped. She stumbled, and he wrapped an arm around her waist.

"Flynn?" Jo quickly regained her balance, but his world tilted, his muscles locking tight. He knew he should release her, but he just stood there, holding on, his breath coming in short bursts. This was his dream and his nightmare. All at once.

"What are you doing?" Her words whispered over his collarbone. "Here?" she added in that husky voice.

He opened his mouth to answer, but his mind was too filled with the feel of her in his arms to find words. Warm. Soft. Small but strong. Just as he remembered. A hint of honeyed lavender teased his nose, and he almost groaned.

"I thought you were an intruder," he finally choked out.

After a long beat of silence, she said, "I'm not."

Flynn swallowed. Could she feel his heart thundering like a herd of centaurs behind his ribs? For the second time in his life, he had Jo pressed up hard against him, chest to chest.

A long curl slid across his wrist. When had his other arm come around her back? And why wasn't she trying to break free? If anything, she was holding on just as tightly and looking at him in a way she never did—in a way that screamed *kiss*.

Heat licked down his spine. His groin stirred. He needed to let go of her before he grew thick and hard against her. He needed to let go of her, period. Why was he doing this?

She stared up at him, her tip-tilted eyes bright, even in the darkness.

Now. Let go now.

Flynn dropped his gaze to her mouth, ignoring the warning bells clamoring in his head.

Jo's lips parted. She gripped his shoulders, the sensual press of each small, smooth nail sinking deep. Flynn shuddered. He wanted to kiss her so badly he shook. He relived her kisses in his sleep and then almost couldn't bear the daytimes without them. He'd nearly given in to temptation twice now. Once, months ago, in the castle kitchens, and the other time... Was it only this morning?

Would she even welcome a kiss?

Probably not. He couldn't follow it up with anything meaningful, and Jo didn't dally. *He* didn't dally. *So stop.*

"Flynn." His name whispered across her lips. She angled her head back, her thumb skating up his neck and brushing his earlobe.

He sucked in a breath and dropped her. Jo landed hard on her heels. Surprise shot across her expression. Goose bumps washed down his arms, and he stepped back, putting some much-needed distance between them.

Flynn braced for Jo's reaction. For her shoulders to go back, her spine to stiffen, and her whole face to tell him what a colossal back end of a donkey he was. None of that happened. She stood there, looking adorably owlish in the moonlight.

Flynn swiped a hand down his face. "I'm sorry."

She gripped the edge of her worktable. "For what?"

"For..." Where to start? Scaring her? Grabbing her? Wanting to toss her onto that damn table, lift her dress, and drive into her until all his pent-up desire exploded in a long, hot rush?

His cock pulsed. It would take two thrusts.

"Startling me?" Jo asked.

He nodded. *Right. That.*

She waved a hand through the air, brushing aside the fact that they'd just been locked together like lovers. "I'm fine. You surprised me. That's all."

He took a calming breath without it being obvious. He'd learned that from Jo years ago, just from watching her. Slow in. Slow out. He needed to get control of himself.

Flynn searched for something to say that wasn't *Thank Olympus it's dark, since I have a raging erection pointed your way.* "We surprised each other." He cleared his throat. "Why aren't you at dinner?"

"Dinner's over."

"Already?" He must've spent longer in the barracks with his soldiers than he'd thought.

"You left ages ago." She picked up the scroll she'd dropped, smoothing out the wrinkled end before setting it on the table. "Dinner seemed to bore you tonight."

"You looked properly entertained." The thought of Jo's Magoi farmer helped calm his lust. Anger replaced it, jealousy he had no right to raging through his veins.

Her eyes snapped to his. "I have a working knowledge of fruit trees now."

"Enough to be the Lady of the Orchard?" he bit out. This was degenerating fast.

Her chin notched up. "I've no intention of marrying him."

"Why not?"

"Do you *want* me to?"

Gods no! "I didn't say that."

"What's going on with you, Flynn?" Her hands landed on her hips. She shook her head. "You've been odd all night."

His gaze dropped. Those hips. Just round enough to fit his hands. His fingers twitched.

"Flynn?"

He looked back up, and his throat worked, trying to produce an answer. None came. So much the better. He'd rather be mute than say something he'd regret, which was all he seemed able to do with Jocasta.

He rubbed his forehead. *Think of something. Change the subject.*

"Is it a headache?" She stepped forward. "That black eye

must throb. How did it happen? Did you lose consciousness?" Frowning, she reached out to touch his head.

Flynn caught her fingers and lowered them. He didn't have a headache, and he didn't even feel the black eye. His aches were elsewhere. Deep. Internal. He let go of her hand, keeping only the heat it left on his fingers.

"No one knocked me out," he said gruffly. It would take a lot more than a *training exercise* for that.

Jo pulled out a stool and pushed him toward it. He let her have her way and sat.

"No wonder you were so quiet at dinner. Have you felt any confusion? Dizziness? Did you get bashed anywhere else up here?" She ran her fingers over his scalp, lightly threading them through his short hair. Flynn's body went bowstring tight again even though she did it with a healer's efficiency. He still felt every stroke down to his toes.

"I don't feel any lumps." She did a second pass to make sure she hadn't missed anything, prolonging the torture of having her hands on him and her body so close that if he just tipped forward, he could...

What? Nuzzle her chest? Take comfort? Rip off her clothes?

Flynn grimaced. He never had sane thoughts when it came to Jo.

"Oh, sorry. Did that hurt?" She leaned even closer and swept her fingers along the base of his skull, her forehead crinkling into an adorable little frown. "I don't feel anything," she said.

That made one of them.

Flynn closed his eyes. Jo's summer-garden scent surrounded him. He curled his hands into fists on his thighs and sat as still as she always seemed to. Sometimes, he wished she'd stop weighing every movement she allowed herself and regulating every breath she took. But Jo… She needed to control something in her life, so she controlled herself.

"Hmm." He felt her move away from him, the air cooling at his front. "Everything seems normal, but I should still watch you tonight. You can sleep, but only in small intervals. I'll have to wake you every few hours to make sure you're all right."

Flynn's eyes flew open. He popped off the stool. "I'm fine."

"But you—"

"Have a black eye," he growled. "That's all."

Jo pursed her lips. Then she lifted her hands, backing up. "Fine. I surrender."

It was all Flynn could do to not reach out and pull her back to him.

He didn't. He *wouldn't*. Not only was it grossly egotistical to assume she'd still welcome his touch after all these years, but there was no way he was contaminating her with his bad luck.

Lifting his gaze over Jo's head, he glanced around the dark healing room, barely making out the cabinet where he'd found her. He couldn't bring himself to leave her yet, even though he knew he should. If they talked too long, they'd fight.

"Should I light you a lamp?" Maybe she still needed something in the cupboard. She could get it. He could walk her back. That would be that.

Her brows crept ominously up her forehead. It wasn't too dark to see *that*. "Princess doesn't equal useless. I can still light a lamp."

"I didn't say you were useless." Flynn stared at her in disbelief. "You twist everything I say. Why do you do that?"

"Don't loom over me in the dark."

He backed up. Jo stepped forward. As far as he could tell, he was still looming if she stuck herself right in front of him. Flynn clasped his hands behind his back. He didn't trust himself not to grab her and kiss her senseless—if he even still remembered how to kiss.

Slowly, Jo lifted her hand to his chest. Her touch nearly undid him. His heart hammered beneath her palm, and he let out a quiet sound of distress.

Her eyes met his. "I'm sorry. I snapped at you for no reason. I don't know why I do that."

"No, I'm sorry." His hand covered hers. He couldn't stop himself. "I never seem to say the right thing. Now, or..." He couldn't finish. He couldn't bring up that kiss that had changed his life. He squeezed her fingers instead.

"I wish I'd taken the olive branch."

Flynn froze, dumbstruck. Several days after that kiss—and Jo resolutely ignoring him—he'd snapped a branch off one of his trees and tried to give it to her. She'd turned her back on the peace offering without a word.

"Did you just offer one back to me? An olive branch?" His question rasped with the emotion of too many years.

Jo nodded. "If you want it."

"Yes." He squeezed her hand again.

They stood together like statues, scarcely breathing. It had been years since she'd kissed him, and they'd hardly seen each other for most of them, but Flynn couldn't help wondering if maybe Jo still felt something for him.

Should that be so hard to believe? He still wanted her so much she scrambled his brain like eggs and turned his body to molten lava. But he didn't have anything to offer, except himself, and that would probably be her downfall. Too many women died in childbirth. And even if she survived that and so did the babies, there were still lung infections, flash floods, wasting diseases, a cart in a ditch, a snakebite, a fall from a tree—red hair mixing with blood, glassy, sightless eyes, and a little hand still clutching a dolly.

His stomach tilted. That was one family. It wouldn't be another.

Flynn opened his hand, releasing her.

Biting her lip, Jo moved to the edge of the table. She hopped up, her legs swinging and reminding him of when she was younger. "Do you remember that time we went fishing?" she asked.

His voice as thick as wet sand, he said, "We went fishing all the time." The day that stuck out in his memory was the afternoon he'd fished *her* out of the water. Gods, that sodden dress... He swallowed.

"True, but I'm thinking of the time you made sure I caught *all* the fish."

He shrugged, not sure where she was going with this. "You had a good net."

"My net was mediocre at best. But you stomped and splashed so much on your side of the river that all the fish fled my way, and I snapped them up."

Flynn still didn't understand her point. It had been a good way to help her catch fish. If they didn't practically jump into her net, Jo got distracted by water plants and river rocks—those smooth red ones she always liked to pick up—and went home without enough dinner for a big family with huge appetites. He couldn't have that.

"I don't always say the right thing, either. Maybe neither of us is good with words." Shaking her head, she glanced down at her swinging toes. "But you've always been there for me when it counted—for as long as I can remember. Saving me during that last raid. Keeping me company on long, dusty walks home. Making sure I caught so many fish I could barely carry my bucket. Protecting me during those horrible Agon Games." She took a deep breath. It shuddered out again. "Those were the most terrifying days of my life."

Fear twisted his chest. They'd all suffered, but Jo... She hadn't been trained for that.

Her eyes captured his, and his heart nearly stopped.

"Maybe we could try to be friends again?" she asked softly. "To stop misunderstanding each other at every turn?"

Flynn stood stock-still. Living under the same roof as Jo for the last several months had been torture, even with as little interaction as possible between them. If they spent more time together, he might volcanically erupt.

He stared at her, even though he already knew her by heart. Stubborn chin. Up-tilted blue eyes. Delicate brows. Black hair he yearned to sink his hands into. The most kissable mouth under the sun.

A dull buzzing droned in his ears. Maybe it was time to look for a new home. New employment. New companions. He could start over. It couldn't be *that* hard.

Jo's brow furrowed. "Flynn?"

"Of course we can be friends," he heard himself answer. "We *are* friends."

"Good." Smiling, she picked up her scroll, hopped off the table, and moved toward the exit. She left the healing room, waiting just beyond the doorframe for him to follow.

Flynn trailed her out, shutting the door behind them.

For the first time in years, Jo threaded her arm through his as they began walking. He matched his stride to hers, the warmth of her body against his side making awareness vibrate inside him.

"I've actually never really liked apricots all that much." She tilted a little closer. "I've always preferred olives."

Flynn nearly stumbled. Her words ricocheted through him. Unless he was criminally obtuse—which was always possible— *he* was the olive.

With a few words, Jo nearly brought him to his knees, his chest hot and tight and aching.

That was more than an olive branch. That was the whole damn tree.

He could picture them together so easily, their bodies interlocked, their destinies entwined. That had never been the problem. The problem was dooming Jo to the fate of anyone who'd ever been *his*. The problem was ending up like his father, fading from this world so that he could try to find his love again, regardless of who he left behind. Being a grown man hadn't made Flynn ready to lose Old Hector. Who was ever ready to be orphaned and alone?

Flynn's heart pounded. He'd battled men, monsters, terrifying sorcerers, grief, and his own nightmares where he couldn't save anyone from anything. He'd survived it all, but right then, he wasn't sure if he could survive this woman. Jo might be the end of him.

Worse, he could be the end of her. And he would *never* let that happen.

CHAPTER 9

Jocasta called a meeting the following afternoon, waiting until Carver and Bellanca were set to return from the army encampment and Alexander had already departed for home. Standing in front of the unlit hearth in the castle's family room, she clutched the scroll she'd read over and over the night before and then again this morning. Jittery excitement buzzed in her veins like a swarm of honeybees headed for summer flowers.

People started arriving at the designated hour, her parents first, Kaia and Prometheus next, and then Cat and Griffin. A few steps behind a slow-moving Cat, Cerberus plodded in on huge paws, his razor-sharp nails *tick-tacking* on the stone floor in a way that scraped straight through her and tried to shred her confidence.

Suppressing a grimace, she shifted from foot to foot, and all three of the hound's monstrous heads turned in her direction. He growled.

Jocasta's lip curled in spontaneous retaliation. She was already going to have to prove herself to everyone here. She didn't need the *dog* against her.

The thunder in Cerberus's throats gradually faded. He circled twice and then sat in front of the cold fireplace, one set of eyes on her, one on Cat, and one on Jocasta's mother. Nerissa kept coming up with gigantic bones to give him, and now Cerberus stalked her, always looking for another.

If Hades tried to call his hound back to the Underworld, Jocasta wondered if he'd obey. Cerberus didn't lack for anything at Castle Thalyria, including affection from a cautious distance. He had quite the life here. For that matter, so did she—one she was about to abandon.

If her family let her.

And maybe even if they didn't.

She was perfectly capable of walking out of here on her own. Or riding. Or sneaking. She had at least one devious bone in her body. She'd find it if she had to.

A nervous bubble popped inside her. She'd never liked sneaking. And she wanted help—muscle and magic and people she trusted. She knew what teamwork could accomplish, and going rogue felt like a terrible idea.

She squared her shoulders, her heart thumping. She'd just have to be convincing.

A mud-encrusted Carver arrived next, stalking in on a swirl of dark energy. He mumbled greetings to those already present and collapsed into one of the large armchairs, stretching his long legs out in front of him. His head fell back against the plush, ruby-toned cushion, and he closed his eyes, some of the tension leaving his face and softening the hard lines around his mouth until they faded into the shadow of late-day stubble.

Watching her brother summarily shut out the world, including his own family, Jocasta had to consciously repress a scowl. Carver had quickly gotten into the habit of not being around to witness Griffin's and Cat's glowing contentment, and he still wasn't around much to witness their increasing fatigue and anxiety. Did he even realize how dire the situation had become? How Cat's unchanging state frayed their happiness and the future security of Thalyria day by day? Hour by hour now?

Carver *cared*. She had no doubt about that. He ran himself

ragged trying to keep the people he cared about safe with an obsessive protectiveness that extended to everyone except for Bellanca, who got his ire instead. Jocasta feared Carver's increasing spiral into extremes would work against her today, but she was prepared to fight him—and hope for his help.

A swallow scraped down her throat. She'd no doubt have a fight on her hands with Flynn, too. Neither Flynn nor Carver had supported her offer to take their murdered team member's place in the Agon Games. Jocasta had been the only available option to fight alongside Beta Team, and she hadn't died, which was saying something considering the competition's brutal reputation.

Brutal was putting it mildly. Stack a nightmare on top of a nightmare, and that was just the beginning of what the Agon Games were about. How did people find entertainment in that?

Carver died protecting her. Only Persephone's magic brought him back. Carver told her she would get them killed out there in the arena with her inexperience, and he was right. No wonder he didn't trust her anymore. They'd hardly talked in months.

Jocasta tensed as Carver opened his eyes, his dark-gray gaze landing on her like a slab of granite. At least his stone-flat stare was clear of any wine haze now. It was sharp and wary, and if she hadn't already known he would fight her on this, she would be able to guess just by the way he watched her now, focused and preparing for battle.

Jocasta looked back at her brother, confrontation-ready but also wishing she could somehow stitch up his broken heart. Carver's short-lived death sent him to a place that shattered the shell he'd built around himself, and no one had suspected how much pain he was still in until his misery started oozing out from the cracks.

She supposed it was better that he hadn't fallen back on his old disguise of flirting wildly and making light of everything, even though he growled now more than Cerberus.

Jocasta's gaze shifted back and forth between her older siblings. Just as Griffin got less overbearing under Cat's influence, Carver became more so. Even though they were the safest they'd ever been in their lives, Carver had somehow decided that his sisters—she and Kaia to be exact—might die of a splinter or a stubbed toe or a bite from a gnat.

Oh yes, her brother would fight her on this.

Carver remained in his chair, his cheeks too hollow and his long fingers drumming against the armrest. He studied her holding her scroll and obviously ready to make an announcement, and Jocasta could practically see him building a glass tower around her in his mind and throwing the key into a harpy's nest.

Piers might have supported her. He might have discovered a less dangerous potential solution than she had. He'd always been more of a scholar than a warrior. But he was gone, banished to Attica.

The ache of loss throbbed inside her, dulled by the days that passed. Her middle brother wasn't dead, but he was in a place they could never reach him. The family rarely spoke of Piers, and Griffin never did.

Jocasta caught Cat's curious but encouraging nod and forced a fragile smile to her lips. What if she was just giving her family false hope? What if she got someone *killed*?

Slightly queasy now, she glanced out the open double doors. They were still waiting for Flynn and Bellanca. Jocasta hadn't bothered inviting Lystra. Bellanca's younger sister did her best not to be a part of anything, so she wouldn't be a part of this.

Anatole and Nerissa whispered together, throwing increasingly uneasy looks her way. Carver was the eye of the storm, quiet yet charged and ready to turn into a gale force against her. Jocasta still feared her biggest obstacle would be Flynn, and she hated the idea of fighting with him again.

Her stomach dipped. She swallowed hard.

Feet scuffed on marble, and Jocasta's heart jerked. She held her breath, but it wasn't Flynn. Bellanca burst through the doors to the family room, frustration crackling beneath her skin. Smudged with dirt, her flaming-red hair a mess, she stomped in and scowled at Carver, barely glancing at the rest of them and not offering a greeting of any sort.

"You had a head start," she seethed. "And the faster horse."

Carver smirked. "Is 'No fair' coming next?"

"No, it's 'Rematch.' And next time, on equal mounts." Bellanca crossed her arms and stared down at him with a glare that could scorch worlds.

Carver shrugged. "If you want to chase me again for an hour, be my guest."

"You'll be chasing *me*." Bellanca leaned forward, her eyes narrowing to slits. "And you might cause an 'incendiary incident' if you don't stop giving me that obnoxious look."

Carver at least half wiped the gloating smirk off his face. Bellanca straightened and backed away, each precise movement hinting at barely stifled fury. She'd started calling it an *incendiary incident* when she erupted in a flaming rage. Since only Griffin was immune to harmful magic, and the furnishings certainly weren't, the Tarvan ex-princess was making an effort to keep the light-ups to a minimum—inside, anyway.

Bellanca kept backing away and sat in a chair that gave her a direct view of Carver, probably to keep glowering at him with that burning ice stare. He stared back, just as frosty hot, and Jocasta could only be grateful that the other woman had taken his focus off *her* for now.

Everyone else was still looking at her. Waiting. She cleared her throat. Apparently, Flynn wasn't coming. He was usually punctual to a fault, never giving her enough time to prepare herself for the sight of him. He must've had other things to attend to, things more important than—

She cut off that thought. Maybe Flynn was right, and she attributed words to him that he didn't say and intentions that weren't true. The rawness inside her when it came to him made her twist meanings and spew dry, brittle accusations like volcanic ash. When the ash fell, maybe it covered the terrain in a way that hid the real shape of the land.

Just as that unhappy realization settled heavily inside her, Flynn's unmistakable tread thudded in the hallway. The stone in her gut abruptly zagged sideways. His steps drew close, his pace hurried. He could be quiet, stealthy even, but when there was no need, his clomping footfalls could fill a house. Jocasta didn't remember that from her childhood. It started later. Empty houses needed sound, and Flynn's steps got loud when Old Hector passed.

He breached the doorway, his brown eyes going straight to her and locking on to her face. A heated shiver coursed through her. Jocasta looked away first. Her insides had been holding a riot since their encounter in her healing room last night. It had taken her hours to fall asleep, her skin vibrating and her body on edge. She couldn't tell how much was Flynn and his mountain-deep voice and how much was realizing that Circe's garden might actually be accessible to them. It was a whole stomach-clenching mix of both.

Without a word, Flynn took up position beside her parents. He didn't sit even though everyone else had. Like her, he remained standing. He was probably bracing for an argument, and she doubted she'd disappoint. They'd conversed almost normally last night for the first time in ages, but Jocasta had a feeling their new peace was fragile. She'd lashed out at him more times than she cared to remember since they'd been living under the same roof. Lately, he'd been pushing back.

Jocasta slowly exhaled, focusing on the whole room again. With everyone there and waiting for her to speak, she carefully worked the ribbon free from her scroll but kept the aged parchment rolled up in her hand. Expectant silence filled the room, making her whumping heartbeat that much louder. Destiny didn't entirely write itself. Choices filled the spaces between patterns, giving the predrawn lines color and texture and life. She had a choice now, and whether anyone else supported her, she chose *this*.

Chin up. Back straight. Deep breath.

"I know how to break the curse," Jocasta announced. "If we succeed, we can make Cat mortal again. We can end all this."

CHAPTER 10

Everyone stared at Jocasta in shock. No excited murmurs. No gasps. Nothing. Then Cat breathed, and the whole room vibrated again just as suddenly as it had stopped. Cat's bright-green eyes turned huge, hope spilling from them like magic. She leaned forward, Griffin tilting with her as though linked by an invisible thread.

"Are you serious? How?" Cat asked.

"It won't harm Cat? Or the baby?" Griffin's eyes pleaded for a *no*, fear mixing with cautious hope.

Jocasta shook her head. "Not if I do this right." Wording would be crucial, but she had time to plan it out.

"You mean brew it right? What do you need?" Her brother half stood, evidently ready to gather the ingredients right now and dump them in her lap.

If only it were that simple. Jocasta held up a stalling hand. At the shake of her head, Griffin sat back down, a grimace erasing the eagerness on his face.

"I've had the knowledge of the kingdom delivered to our doorstep and found nothing that can counteract the Elixir of Eternal Life. Our plants can't. Our magic can't. Even Olympian magic can't help."

Griffin's brows snapped together. "Then what is it? What did you find?"

She hesitated, fear of giving false hope springing up again.

Griffin was her brother. She loved Cat like a sister. And beyond their family, the entire kingdom looked to the two of them, and especially to Cat. She was their new hope, their steadfast, indomitable, unbreakable, gods-chosen queen of Thalyria. They'd seen her burn in magical fire and come out stronger on the other side of the flames, climb a Cyclops and stab it in the eye, sprout wings and fly, call Cerberus to heel, and rain down thunderbolts. She was victory. She was judgment. She was *law*. Nothing could break her…except maybe this.

"Jo?" Flynn prompted softly.

Her eyes jumped to his. He gave her a reassuring nod, and the cramping in her chest tripled. Quadrupled. Nearly did her in.

She cleared her throat. "It's a… It requires a journey."

"What kind of a journey?" Flynn asked.

His tone wasn't suspicious or sharp, simply curious and almost encouraging. Some of the tension locking her in place melted into confusion that felt much warmer and more dangerous. Flynn was taking her seriously. She was so grateful for that—especially considering the wary looks from everyone else.

"A long and dangerous one," she said. "Involving boats."

"I can already tell this is going to be madness," Bellanca muttered.

Annoyance stirred, and Jocasta arched her brows. "Madness or not, I have an idea. Do you have one?"

Her mouth pursing, Bellanca waved her hand as if to say *Carry on*. Jocasta swallowed any further comment. She had more important things to argue over—or in favor of.

"There's a goddess with vast knowledge of potions and plants. She also has an infinite garden. She can grow anything, even something that doesn't exist—until she creates it." Jocasta glanced at Cat, then Griffin. "We need to get her to grow a plant specific to Cat's needs and then brew a potion with it."

Cat stared at her, unblinking. "You're talking about Circe. You want to look for Circe's garden."

It wasn't a question. It was a statement—of disbelief.

Jocasta nodded anyway.

Cat's tentative optimism wilted, fear and fatigue visibly sprouting up again in its place. Shaking her head, she wrapped a protective hand around her belly. "Circe's garden doesn't exist... at least not in Thalyria." Her voice dulled to a monotone. "And looking for it is a death sentence."

"Just because no one's found it doesn't mean someone can't." Despite her confident words, Jocasta took a step back, everyone's sudden disappointment pressing on her. She unrolled the scroll she'd been clutching and held it open. "Something Alexander said last night helped me put the pieces together. I know where to start. In Fisa."

"What? Two days off Thassos?" Cat sighed. "Don't you think my mother tried to find it? Any herb? Any plant? Any poison? Any *cure*? It's not there. She lost at least sixteen ships and hundreds of soldiers looking for Circe's garden—and those are only the ones I know about. They left. They tried to sail beyond the Inner Sea and never came back."

"But she didn't have this." Jocasta showed them the scroll. "I found it in *our* library—the Tarvan ex-royals' library that your mother didn't have access to—and put it in my healing room. At first, I thought it was the plant and potion listings that might be useful. I didn't put much store in the part about Circe and sea creatures and trials and rewards until last night, when I realized what this scroll really is."

"Which is?" Griffin asked.

"A map. A guide to reaching her garden."

Keen attention and maybe even hope sharpened his features. Cat just looked queasy now.

Jocasta pressed on, trying not to let doubt sneak in and un-settle her resolve. "Have you ever wondered why Fisa has such strong magic compared to the other realms? Provinces, now?"

"Because Mount Olympus sits directly above it," Carver said. "We all know that. The magic trickles down through the land and water. Fisa's in the best position to soak it up."

"Even so, Fisan magic is nearly as strong in the south as it is in the north," she pointed out. "It's not like that anywhere else. Southern Sinta and southern Tarva are almost completely without magic. Even Magoi can have trouble using their abilities there."

"Bu—"

"That's true," Flynn said, cutting off Carver's budding argu-ment. "Why do you think that is, Jo?"

Jocasta could only stare at Flynn, too surprised by what felt like his support to move or talk or breathe at first. Flynn looked at her expectantly. They all did.

"Maybe magic is traveling to southern Fisa from another power source. One off the coast," she said.

Cat sat up straighter. "I never thought of that."

"The north–south magic discrepancy is still there but hugely diminished." Jocasta wasn't an expert on magic or gods, but Fisan magical superiority was well known, and the reason why seemed infinitely clear to her after thinking about it all night. "Olympus in the north. Aeaea in the south. They're both places of power, almost worlds unto themselves. They generate magic. They *are* magic. Fisan Magoi aren't so powerful just because of Mount Olympus. They have Circe's garden off their coast. Persephone told us that magic tied to Mount Olympus can't undo the curse. Circe is the granddaughter of Titans and the sorceress daughter of the sun god, Helios. She's not an Olympian. Her *Titan* plant magic is what we need for this."

Her family and de facto family looked at her with expressions ranging from *You're insane* to *Hmm* to *You might be a strategic asset I never considered before.* The old parchment crinkled in her fingers. She'd take *strategic asset*, please.

Cat rolled her lower lip between her teeth. "Say Circe's garden is out there—and I'm not saying it is—you can't just walk up to an ancient goddess—the *witch* of Aeaea—and ask for what you want. In my experience, gods only show up when they want to and not a second before, and they don't just hand over powerful weapons—or potions—out of the goodness of their hearts. There's always an ulterior motive, a trial to endure, a life-or-death situation to overcome." She spread her hands to encompass the people in the room, her expression saying *Been there, done that.*

Jocasta felt her lungs tighten. They had. And Jocasta had barely been a part of it. Maybe that was why she was ready to start again.

"Even if you find her, Circe's not easy to deal with," Prometheus warned from his perch on the arm of Kaia's chair. He somehow dwarfed the solid piece of furniture without diminishing Kaia at all.

"Are any of them?" Cat huffed.

"What do you mean?" Kaia asked, glancing up at the Titan.

"She's bitter, violent, predatory." Prometheus shrugged. "She has a wicked temper, and there's almost always a trick up her sleeve. There's a reason her own brethren exiled her. No one wanted Circe around."

"Aeaea is her prison," Bellanca said. "From the history I've read, Zeus and Helios locked her up and made her island as inaccessible as possible because she was smarter than everyone else. Males can't stand a female threat." She looked pointedly at Carver.

He arched dark brows that seemed to mock her without effort. If Bellanca was insinuating that she threatened Carver with her intelligence, she was wrong. Jocasta knew her brother. He loved a challenge and didn't tolerate fools.

"Count her lucky, then," Cat murmured. "It has to be better than ending up in Tartarus with most of the Titans and their ancestors." She shuddered, exchanging a troubled look with Prometheus. When their eyes met, millennia of torture flashed across his wide, square features before he tucked all that suffering away again beneath a seemingly placid expression that immediately started to crack.

A chill skittered down Jocasta's spine. No god was placid. She was certain they all boiled with heat and wants and rage. Prometheus was no different, except he'd been in Tartarus for eons before Cat broke him out, and life with them must seem wonderful and safe compared to reliving the same torment every day. He'd remember what he was capable of soon enough, what it meant to be a god. Would he leave them then and go on his way?

"Do you know where Circe's island is?" Kaia asked Prometheus, not blinking an eye at how the Titan hovered over her like a storm cloud ready to burst. "Have you been there?"

"No." Prometheus shook his head, actual calm settling over him when he focused on Kaia again. "I've been...otherwise occupied."

Right. Busy stealing fire from Zeus, giving it to humans, and being eternally punished for it. Poor Prometheus.

"This scroll tells us how to find Aeaea and approach Circe," Jocasta said, pulling everyone's focus back to her parchment. "It's a map—a heavily riddled map—but I think I've deciphered most of it."

Cat shifted her weight before settling into her chair at a

different angle. She radiated discomfort, as any woman already weeks past utterly ready to give birth would. "I'm still skeptical, but let's hear it. What does the scroll say?"

Jocasta would take skeptical. It was better than the looks she was getting from Carver and Bellanca. Her parents hadn't said a thing—which wasn't usually a blessing. It meant her mother was worried and her father was thinking too hard. Flynn was less expressionless than usual. He still looked curious, almost encouraging.

Something shifted inside her, maybe a block of courage added to the ones she'd already gathered and carefully stacked along her backbone to call this meeting in the first place. Her tower of mettle had wobbled a few times in the past quarter hour, but it felt shored up now, stronger.

Jocasta flexed the fingers of her free hand, her only concession to the nerves still riding her. So what if her family almost never supported her ideas outside of the healing arts? That didn't mean they'd reject this one.

She didn't need to look at the scroll to tell them what it said. She'd read it enough times to recite it in her sleep, so she paraphrased instead. "A lot of what's written here is purely poetic, but the vital information is that Circe, sorceress and plant master, will reward anyone who makes it to the marble statue of her in the center of her garden."

"And here comes the hard part." Griffin scrubbed a hand down his face. He didn't look as tired and miserable as his wife, but desperation was creeping up on him like a fast-falling twilight, dimming the brightness in his eyes, even when he looked at Cat.

What they needed was dawn. Light on the horizon. Elpis was a miracle they knew all about. Hope gave people strength beyond their limits. The strength to take one step, then another, and another, until the job was done.

"Five trials by sea and land." Jocasta met her brother's somber gaze with a determined nod. This time, she glanced at the scroll, reading directly from the parchment. "Evade Charybdis's swirling fall, heed not the deadly sirens' call, navigate the maze where Asterion rules all, fall not into the lotus eaters' indifferent thrall, and"—she looked up to deliver the last of the bad news—"pass Circe's final test or lose what makes man proud and tall."

"Well, that doesn't sound dire *at all*," Cat muttered, shifting back to her previous position with a grimace.

"Or impossib-*all*." Carver shook his head at no one in particular.

Jocasta set the scroll aside and crossed her arms. "'Impossible' shouldn't even be in your vocabulary." She launched a spear-tipped look at Carver before sweeping the same lancing glare around the room. "You're the heroes of Thalyria. You're *Elpis*." She tossed that at Cat, who shrugged indifferently. "You killed a dragon, you fought the Hydra, you bested a Cyclops and won the Agon Games. You dethroned not one, not two, but *three* powerful and brutal Magoi rulers. Nothing's impossible—not for Beta Team."

"Alpha Team," Bellanca corrected, shooting a finger into the air in a way that made Jocasta want to grab it and snap it off. And she was a *healer*.

"Is now really the time for this argument?" Flynn asked Bellanca with a tight-lipped smile.

"It's just that no one gets it right." Bellanca thrust a hand toward Cat and Griffin. "Alpha. Alpha." Her usual knack for conveying how colossally stupid everyone was burst through in her huff of annoyance. "*Alpha* Team."

"Bellanca's right," Griffin said. "But more to the point, Jocasta's find is something to consider. Five labors for an immense prize that will affect all our lives and futures?" He turned to Cat and gripped her hand. "This is what we've been looking for. A solution to the impossible—or a chance for one, which is more than we had yesterday."

Warmth flushed Jocasta. Griffin believed her. He took her side in front of everyone. That hard nugget in her chest that protected her against her family's usual quick dismissal dislodged and bounced with happiness until Carver's hands hit his thighs with a strong and disgusted *thwack*.

Her closest brother glared at Griffin. "You can't be serious. Just *send* our sister to her death?"

"No one said Jocasta would go," Griffin answered sharply.

"Excuse me?" Startled, Jocasta looked back and forth between her brothers. "*You* can't be serious. I found this!"

"And we should send the best team for it," Griffin said.

"I *am* the best team for it," she shot back, her voice rising in pitch.

"How do you figure that?" Carver drawled.

Her nostrils flared. She wanted to kick him for his chafing tone but settled for narrowing her eyes instead. "Circe's final test? In her *garden*? There's a good chance the test will involve potions and plants, and I'm by far the most well versed."

Anatole cleared his throat. "Be that as it may," her father began in a harder tone than she'd heard from him in months, "you'd have to make it through the other four trials first. Your brothers are right. Without magic or battle training, this quest sounds like a death sentence."

"I wasn't planning on doing it alone." Jocasta threw up her hands in disgust.

The men in her family still looked unconvinced. Instead of appealing to her mother or Cat for support, as usual, or even to Kaia and Prometheus, Jocasta turned to Flynn. Her heart gave a massive thud and jumped into her throat when she realized what she'd done. Flynn hadn't championed her before the Agon Games. He'd made himself an obstacle to her participation and nearly kept them *all* out of the arena just to keep *her* out. Why would she look to him now, when this undertaking was potentially even more dangerous than the deadly tournament? Why would her body just *do* that?

Every frantic beat of her pulse told her why, rushing the truth through her blood. *Oh no.* After spending the better part of a decade trying to move on from this man, she was right back to where she started—utterly in love with him.

CHAPTER 11

Flynn stared back at Jo, both of them frozen solid like two hapless souls who'd stumbled across Medusa. Distress flashed like a lightning bolt across her face, and Flynn's mouth opened without his permission.

"I'll go with her." The words just tumbled out. More kept coming. "And she does have battle experience. The Agon Games packed years of warfare, terror, and bloodshed into a few days. I'm sure no one's forgotten that, including Jocasta." Flynn nodded toward Jo as she looked at him, her mouth ajar. He was almost as shocked as she was. But underneath the shock, oddly committed. No going back now, come flood, fire, or epic disaster. "If she's offering to go, it means she's an asset. Jo wouldn't jeopardize her family just to get out of the castle."

Jo released a long, slow breath, and Flynn could've sworn he felt it breeze over him along with a hint of lavender. Impossible, since she was several feet away from him. His skin still shivered when she smiled. That surprised blush. The happy spark he'd put in her eyes for once—eyes that danced away from him and then darted back again. Her smile widened, and he felt ten mountains tall. His chest expanded by the second.

Good gods, he was doomed. Death by Jocasta—but not before he brought her home safely.

"Excellent." On board from the beginning, Griffin agreed with him. "Flynn will go, and Lukos can take over as captain of the guard here at the castle." He looked around. "Who else will go? We're the only ones who know about the curse, and no one else can get wind of it for as long as possible. Who here is best suited to the tasks?" he asked the room in general, although he turned to Cat for her answer.

Cat barely hesitated. "Prometheus." Everyone winced, except for Kaia, who immediately perked up.

"Oh good, then I can go, too." The sixteen-year-old looked ready to take on Olympus.

"No!" everyone shouted at once. Except for Flynn. He kept his mouth shut.

Kaia frowned up at Prometheus. "What do you mean, *no?*" She focused on the Titan, even though his weren't the only vocal cords still ringing.

"It means there's not a chance in the Underworld I'm letting you near any of those trials," he growled.

"*Letting me?*" Her brows rose along with her voice.

Prometheus snapped his mouth shut, but Anatole filled the void. "That's my call, and it's a definite no," the old man said with a sharpness that reminded Flynn of the fierce and intimidating warlord Anatole had been not so many years ago.

"But I fight better than Jocasta!" Kaia turned to her sister for help. "I'm much more skilled."

"That may be true," Jo admitted, clearly trying not to take offense, "but—"

"But nothing. I want to help my family just as much as you do," Kaia insisted.

"And you *can,*" Jo said. "By staying here to help protect the castle. There are still rumbles of unrest across Thalyria. Not everyone wants one kingdom under one rule. Not everyone wants a Fisan queen. Or a Sintan king. Not everyone wants equal rights for Hoi Polloi. A dozen powerful Magoi families from across northern Thalyria are probably plotting right now to try to take the throne before a new royal dynasty forms—one that represents them *all*. That's why baby Eleni is so important. She needs to unite us before existing divisions can fissure the kingdom again or we're forced into the war we somehow mostly managed to avoid."

"East, west. North, south. Magoi, Hoi Polloi." Kaia blew out a frustrated breath. "I *know* how important the baby is to the future of Thalyria. That's why I want to help."

"You can help here, where the baby is, even if she isn't born yet. Besides, do you really think Lukos is ready for all that responsibility on his own?" Jo asked.

Frowning, Kaia said, "Don't you?"

"I think that with at least Flynn and maybe Prometheus gone, Griffin and Cat need someone they can trust helping to keep threats away from the castle. I also think you have good ideas to offer and that Lukos would like to hear them."

Kaia's eyes narrowed to suspicious gray-blue slits. "You're just trying to placate me."

"I'd actually feel better if you're here," Cat said. "You're a more-than-capable warrior, and we might have threats to face we'll need help handling, especially with the Great Roar making new appearances."

More reports had come in from across Thalyria. Panic. Stampeding. Flynn didn't know how wise it was to leave the royals right now, but the most pressing matter was curing Cat—and baby Eleni—of this maliciously imposed stasis.

"Okay." Kaia sat back, capitulating. "I'll stay and help Lukos."

"Good." Grimacing, Cat rubbed the side of her belly where a little elbow, knee, or foot was making a knobbly lump. Flynn had to stifle a wince on Cat's behalf. She needed that baby out for more reasons than he could count.

He caught Cat's eye. She nodded to him what seemed to be a slow, strained thank-you, and Flynn nodded back. He knew why he'd volunteered so quickly, and Cat probably did, too. His path was set. Any internal debate had gone silent, and his main concern right now was surviving a possibly weeks-long journey with the woman who turned him inside out.

Cat shoved herself up to standing and shuffled toward the hearth. She leaned against the mantelpiece, Cerberus at her feet. The beast lifted one head, stretched his neck, and sniffed in her direction. Cat knew better than to touch the hound but let Cerberus come as close as he wanted. His choice.

"I can't go this time. I can't help you." She glanced around the room, her heart and soul in her eyes—along with the growing cracks in them. If they didn't succeed, Flynn feared Griffin could be right. Cat might break from the inside out, and then so would Thalyria. She lifted her chin, her features hardening. "Neither can Griffin. I can't put Eleni at risk, and we both need to be here, strengthening the transition to a central power and keeping twitchy nobles from getting too ambitious. The Fisan ones are especially obnoxious."

From what Flynn had seen, that was an understatement. Cat was going to need to show them—and her two younger brothers—a firm hand, or she could lose control of Fisa only months after winning it, even with Ares watching over the province for her. Flynn knew she was testing her brothers' loyalty and integrity by giving them responsibilities in eastern Thalyria, like Griffin's sister Egeria had in the west, but Ares had already reported Priam's unexplained disappearance on two occasions and Laertes's total lack of interest in anything honest or work-related. When the two young men had visited Castle Thalyria, they'd barely said a word to anyone without magic, which excluded most of the royal family. Flynn had seen the resignation in Cat's eyes at the end of their stay and watched her pen the scroll to Ares asking him to keep an even closer eye on her brothers. Showing them mercy didn't mean she'd get any from them in return—a reality that was increasingly clear to everyone.

Griffin stood and joined Cat in front of the unlit fireplace. "So it's settled, then? Flynn and Jocasta will go. Maybe Prometheus?" He glanced at the Titan and received a shallow nod in response. Prometheus would go, even if it meant leaving behind Cat and Kaia—his anchors.

Griffin nodded back in thanks. His brow creased as his gaze left the reclusive Titan and skimmed over both him and Jo. It wouldn't sit well with Griffin to send his younger sister off with one unattached male, let alone two. Flynn doubted Griffin was worried about Prometheus and his sister, but frankly, Griffin was right not to trust *him*. It was a constant battle to not fall to his knees in front of Jocasta, beg her to kiss him, and entreat her to erase the years.

I prefer olives to apricots.

Flynn swallowed. And he preferred Jo to just about anything. Brave. Smart. Beautiful. A challenge.

His gut clenched. He should be *leaving* instead of leaving *with her*.

But that option left an ashy taste in his mouth. He couldn't leave the only people who actually needed him for something, people he cared about as deeply as he'd let himself care about anyone since shoveling dirt over that final grave in the shade of his olive grove.

His—because the large property belonged to him now. The farm. The house. The memories…

His eyes strayed to the raven-haired healer who haunted his dreams, waking and asleep.

As for Jocasta, he'd make the best of it. Try to keep the peace.

"Any other volunteers?" Griffin asked. "Us here... We're it. No one else can know about this until we've exhausted every option. Secrecy is the only way to protect Cat and Thalyria."

"Won't it be too late at some point?" Bellanca looked pointedly at Cat's belly. "I'm already hearing rumors about a fake pregnancy, and that's from our own soldiers."

Cat winced. Griffin sucked in a harsh breath.

"That's why we need to move fast," Flynn said with a hint of impatience. "Who's with us? Anyone?"

Jo's eyes flashed to his. The bright blue crashed into him, making his heart kick at the base of his throat.

"I'll go." Carver slouched in his chair again, his expression turned inward in a way that reminded Flynn of Old Hector. Carver got that Old Hector look about him sometimes, but while Carver was too vigorous to simply fade away, there was a chance he might go looking for a fight he couldn't win.

"Me too," Bellanca declared. "Obviously."

Carver shot upright, all nonchalance shattered as he turned to the redhead in disbelief. "Who'll run the army?"

Bellanca glanced at her fingernails. She flicked a piece of half-dried mud off one, looking up just in time to see it hit Carver in the chin. "Cat and Griffin, for example."

Carver swatted the mud off his jaw. "They're busy."

Bellanca huffed. "They can still oversee things. And we have underlings."

"Underlings?" Carver's brows rose.

"You call them captains. I call them underlings." Bellanca shrugged.

"We have the entire spring mapped out, *princess*. Someone needs to stay and direct the *underlings*."

"I can do it," Kaia said. "Kitros isn't far. I can go back and forth."

"You're sixteen!" Carver shot back at her.

"Yes. And I can read, follow directions, *and* talk. You have it all mapped out? I'll have everyone do what you already planned. Besides, being busy will help keep me from constantly worrying about you lot."

"You're supposed to be here, helping Lukos," Nerissa pointed out.

Kaia rolled her eyes. "Griffin and Cat will be here, and Lukos will look to them for advice, not to me. But if I spend my days at the army encampment, I'll be the royal representative there. Top dog." She winked at Cerberus.

Cerberus lifted all three heads and thumped his tail, giving Kaia's plan his clear approval. She grinned.

"Fine. Kaia can hone her leadership and battle skills with the army." Griffin leveled a hard look on his youngest sister. "Just have a healer with you at all times. Practicing with weapons can be dangerous. And be home in time for dinner every evening. You are *not* sleeping there in a tent surrounded by soldiers."

Kaia nodded.

"And Cerberus will go with you," Cat added. "Right, pooch? You'll be her shadow?"

The hound thumped his tail again, settling the matter.

Kaia sat up straighter, but her flush of pleasure disappeared as Carver shook his head, scowling at her. She even shrank a little, his dark stare a poison dart to her confidence.

Flynn's blood boiled, and he barely controlled the urge to smack Carver upside the head. It was times like this when he missed the old Carver, the one who buried all his pain under a joke. Did Carver really need to doubt and hurt everyone around him just because he was doubting and hurting himself? Flynn was a firm believer in keeping it on the inside. What was the point of opening your chest and bleeding out your wounds for everyone to see? All that did was drag everybody else down and rot the atmosphere. Wasn't the atmosphere already rotten enough here?

Carver let out the most humorless grunt of a laugh Flynn had ever heard. "You've all gone insane. Even the dog. Flynn's needed here. Kaia running the army?" He snorted. "And Jocasta? Her skills are in the healing room." He glared at everyone, his jaw so stiff a muscle twitched. "This is madness. I'll go—*alone*. The scroll tells us what to expect. There's no need to risk anyone."

"Because you're no one?" Bellanca gave him a lofty once-over. "Last time I looked, you had two legs, two arms, and half a brain. That makes someone. You, to be exact."

Carver opened his mouth. Nothing came out, and he snapped it shut with an audible clack.

"Oh!" Jo lit up like a lantern, drawing everyone's eyes, most of all his. Flynn recognized that fire-flash look. She was on to something. She opened the scroll again, reading aloud. "'Lose what makes man proud and tall.'"

"That was part of the fifth trial, right?" A crease slashed down between Cat's brows. "For failing?"

"For failing Circe's test." Jo nodded, her eyes racing over the parchment. Her lips moved on certain words, forming little dips and O's that utterly captured Flynn's attention. "Bellanca just helped me figure out this last part." Excited, she pivoted toward her parents. "Do you remember that bard who used to come through the village? He always had stories from Attica and claimed he heard them from a wise old centaur—Chiron—who came to Thalyria after both Attica and Atlantis lost their magic."

"I remember him," Anatole said, his rheumy eyes brightening. "I always paid him well to entertain the tribe during the harvest festival."

"Yes, that one!" Triumph sparked from Jo like little banked

embers flaming to life. Her radiance burned through Flynn's defenses like nothing else, and he wished only for her to look that jubilant every day for the rest of her life. "Circe's not well known in Thalyria because Aeaea is—so far—inaccessible. But he had tales from Attica. So many. Do you remember?" She glanced around at Griffin, Carver, and him. They hadn't seen that bard in years, so Kaia might be too young to recall the man's stories. "There were a few about Circe. One theme kept coming back. If she feels threatened by someone or they don't do as she wants, she turns them into an animal. Swine, wasn't it?"

Flynn nodded. He remembered some of those tales—and thinking Circe was a witch he never wanted to run into.

"Birds, too. Some monsters. But mostly pigs," Cat said. "Ares told me he spurned Circe's advances once upon a time and spent the next century or two oinking and grunting instead of laughing, although her full-blown spell didn't work on him."

Jo turned to Prometheus. "Wasn't that part of why the gods exiled her to begin with—practicing witchcraft on anyone who vexed her?"

The Titan paused, his expression distant and vague as he appeared to sort through memories from centuries ago. "That's right. Mostly swine. One horrible sea creature. A bird or two, like Cat said."

Jo spread her arms in a don't-you-see gesture wide enough to encompass even Cerberus. "I'm betting that if we don't pass her test, that's what she'll do to us. We have to succeed, and not anger her in the process, or she'll take from us what makes man proud and tall: two legs."

"This is getting more appealing by the second," Carver muttered, scraping a hand down his face.

"It's perfect for you. Wild"—Bellanca looked Carver up and

down from the chair across from his—"boar. And make that *b-o-r-e,*" she added with a smirk.

"She'd turn you into a woodpecker," Carver snapped. "Since all you do is peck, peck, peck."

"At least I'd still have two legs. And wings. And pecking is better than fight, mope, fight, mope. We all have our specialties," Bellanca said with a shrug.

"I don't *mope,*" Carver huffed in affront.

The red brows Bellanca arched nearly to her hairline said everything she didn't. For once, she kept her mouth shut.

"Let's call it brooding. It's more masculine," Cat cut in before the argument could degenerate. "There's still one problem. Well, a lot more than one, but I'm focusing on the most obvious. No living soul that we know of has been to Aeaea and back. Are you certain it's out there?" She directed the question at Jocasta.

Jo's chin lifted, that stubborn angle probably more attractive to Flynn than it should be. "As certain as I can be. As for no one finding the island yet... I think I discovered a clue to that in this parchment." She wet her lips, a nervous tick she rarely indulged in, and worry tightened Flynn's gut. "If I'm correct, this would indicate that no living soul has been to Circe's garden from Thalyria because, to reach Aeaea from here, you have to be dead."

Flynn flinched. Everyone else exploded, sending Cerberus into high alert. He lifted all three heads and growled deep in his throats, his six eyes blazing like copper coins at sunset.

"How in the name of Zeus does this help us?" Griffin finally boomed above the chaos. He gripped the back of his neck, letting out a growl to match Cerberus's.

Distress flashed across Cat's face. She looked up at Griffin, her eyes wide and shining with tears. "It *doesn't.*" She blinked hard and fast.

Tucking Cat close to him, Griffin swung a rock-hard look on Jocasta. For the first time, Flynn saw Griffin look at his sister in real disappointment, almost fury, and he took an automatic step in Jo's direction. Best friend or not, he wouldn't stand by and let Griffin intimidate her.

"What are you playing at, Jocasta?" Griffin ground out. "You know we can't communicate with the dead."

"Playing?" Jo's jaw dropped, hurt and outrage a silent scream in her open mouth that maybe only Flynn heard. It nearly deafened him, echoing inside his head.

He took another step in her direction, but she only had eyes for Griffin and Cat, the people she'd worked day in and day out to help. She simply stared at them in shock, and he wanted to bellow on her behalf. Jo deserved better than this. Better than Carver's and Bellanca's constant bickering. Better than her parents' fearful looks. Better than Griffin's quick doubt. Flynn couldn't remember one important idea of hers that had failed. Not one.

He opened his mouth to say so, but Jo didn't need his help.

"I have a plan." With four words, Jo yanked all eyes back to her and killed the noise in the room.

Pride flared in his chest, and Flynn went back to his previous position, arms crossed, ears open. Waiting.

"A plan? What plan?" Skepticism exploded from Griffin's bark of a laugh. "The dead can't perform the labors. They can't bring us what we need."

"Death can be faked, you idiot," Jo snapped. "All we have to do is trick Aeaea into thinking we're a ghost ship."

Cat's head cocked in interest. "How?"

"Nyx's Shallow Grave." Jo's chin hit that stubborn angle again. "I've already started brewing it."

Cat's lips parted in surprise. Looking at Jo, she hissed out a slow, impressed, "Yes."

"Can someone please explain?" Kaia asked. "For those of us who *aren't* trained with magic or potions?"

Flynn grunted his agreement, as confused as Kaia in this case.

Cat nodded to Jo, leaving the explanation—and credit—to her. No wonder Cat was a champion. *Elpis*. Flynn's heart swelled with gratitude.

Despite the momentary setback, Jo squared her shoulders, projecting that competence that had half his soldiers in love with her and always looking for an excuse to end up in her healing room. Flynn couldn't blame them. He'd contemplated letting himself get stabbed only yesterday just to have an excuse to talk to her.

"Nyx is the goddess of the night. With this potion, you fall into such a deep, dark slumber that even your own body thinks it's dead. Your heart slows and your breathing practically stops, but it's a shallow grave, as the name indicates." Jo's long, chest-expanding inhalation demonstrated a rejuvenation of sorts. "It wears off, your body goes back to normal, and you *live* again."

"So it's a sleeping draught?" Kaia said.

"Yes, but a very strong one," Jo answered. "Too much, and it could be fatal. Nyx is the mother of both sleep and death, but she also birthed brightness and day. Just like in nature, it's an unbroken cycle. As long as the dosage isn't botched, the shallow grave will last through one night and then give way to a new dawn."

Leaning forward, Prometheus frowned. "One *actual* night or the span of hours a person usually sleeps?"

"Either," Jo said. "It's not literally tied to night and day. The principal plant ingredient is simply named after Nyx because of its potent soporific qualities—enough to send a person into a death-like sleep for about twelve hours."

"But who'll steer the boat?" Cat asked. "You can't just all fall asleep and hope you stay afloat, don't hit anything, and don't go wildly off course."

Jo bit her bottom lip. "Carver." She glanced at her brother. A swallow moved her throat. "He died. He came back, but he died. We all know that."

"And you think that's enough for me to be able to see Aeaea?" Carver asked. "One quick trip to the Underworld and back?"

Jo flinched, the little jerk of her body so small that Flynn might've imagined it but somehow knew he didn't. "This entire endeavor is dependent upon it, so I hope so." Guilt over her part in Carver's temporary death warred with what Flynn thought was cautious but real optimism in her low, husky voice. Her fingers fluttered over the pleats of her gown. The almost imperceptible movement told him how nervous she was. For such a strong, independent person, Jo still craved her family's approval in a way that was almost pathological. Some days, he thought it might be the only thing keeping her here.

"My other hope," Jo added, "is that the rest of us will be *dead enough* with Nyx's Shallow Grave to trick whatever magic is blocking the living from the island into letting us—the dead—pass."

"That's a lot of *hopes*," Carver muttered.

"We'll wake up where we need to be," Flynn said at the same time, covering Carver's cynical words. Jo's cleverness never ceased to amaze him. "Ingenious."

The corners of Jo's mouth jumped up in happy surprise, and her pleasure pierced him like an arrow to the sternum. An increasingly familiar heart-aching, blood-pumping elation overtook everything else. He'd made her smile. In other circumstances, Flynn could've *lived* to make her smile.

What's stopping you? a quietly mutinous voice whispered inside his head.

Old Hector instantly popped into his mind, larger than life—and then wholly diminished.

Flynn turned away from Jocasta, his nape prickling as the ghost of his father skittered across his skin. He might not have believed a hearty, healthy man could die of a broken heart if he hadn't seen it for himself, *lived it* day by day until he had another grave to dig.

"Won't Circe be angry if we trick her?" Bellanca asked as she played with sparks between her fingertips. A rebellious little flame jumped toward her wrist, and she flattened it like an insect, crushing with a twist. "She might turn us into animals just for that, and then we fail before we even get started." She abruptly closed her fist, absorbing the fire and looking up. "And then we're *animals*. How do you propose we come back from that?" she asked Jo. "You can't *baaaa* yourself back into a body."

Jo's mouth flattened. Her nostrils pinched. "It might not be Circe's magic hiding the island," she answered evenly, despite signs of annoyance at Bellanca's snide remark. "That could be part of her exile, connecting her to the dead rather than to the living. Who'd want that for all of eternity? She might welcome visitors."

Bellanca scoffed. "There's a lot of *hope* and *maybe* and *might* in all this and not much actual knowledge." She gusted out a loud breath. "Your plan stinks like donkey."

Jo's eyes flared. "We're trying to counteract magic even the greatest gods on Olympus can't undo. Did you really think it would be *easy?*"

Bellanca opened her mouth to respond but then caught the flash of angry-hot power in Cat's warning glare. In the face of that eerie green luminescence, she shrugged and went back to playing with fire.

Carver glanced at the redhead, his eyes reflecting Bellanca's flames until he turned his skeptical gaze on Jo again. "Bellanca has a point. There are a lot of unknowns here. What about Nyx's Shallow Grave? Are you sure you know how to dose the potion? It sounds as if a drop too little might not be enough and a drop too much could be fatal."

"I've done it before." Jo paused. "On rabbits."

"Rabbits?" Bellanca snorted loud enough to annoy Cerberus into lifting his middle head. "Why don't you test it on a full-grown person, and then we'll see about the rest?"

Flynn felt a growl rise in his chest. Carver might be a broody pain in the backside lately, but he was right about Bellanca—peck, peck, peck.

"Do you volunteer?" Jo asked tartly.

Bellanca shrugged, unaffected by Jo's icicle tone and glacial look. "Sure. Why not?"

Carver's dark brows slashed across his forehead. "Out of the question. Test it on me," he said.

"Or me," Flynn volunteered. He had utter faith in Jo's brewing skills. Utter faith in *her*.

Prometheus stood, his large, booted feet scuffing next to Kaia's delicate, sandaled toes. "Or me. I could use a good night's sleep." That haunted look crept across his features again, the shadows of Tartarus deepening the hollows beneath his cheekbones.

Sympathy panged inside Flynn. Their experiences weren't comparable, but he knew all about sleepless nights, his whirring, anguished mind screaming *Why?* and *How?* and *No!* No answers ever came, just waves of sorrow, helplessness, and guilt. Those feelings still surged up, rattling him sometimes, especially since Kato's death. He'd almost made his peace with life—or the one he had anyway—until his friend's eyes went dark. Now, the old questions haunted him again. Why did he remain strong and hale while the people he loved fell one by one?

Lately, though, most of his sleepless nights had been tied to something else. Wishes...desires...

He glanced at Jo, and a searing heat burned his soul. He'd seen her deflate like one of her dried-up mushrooms too many times, the spores of her ideas and efforts dispersing in a cloud of resignation and disappointed hopes. He'd been the cause of her disillusionment at least twice, but he'd make damn sure that didn't happen to her this time. Not because of him—or anyone else.

"Will Nyx's Shallow Grave work on a god? Or work differently?" Flynn asked, trying to move the discussion along—and away from doubting Jo's plan, which was the most solid strategy any of them had come up with. "Testing the brew on a human might make more sense."

"Flynn's right." Anatole rubbed his grizzled chin. "Use me instead."

Nerissa gasped. "Absolutely not." She eyed her aging husband in a way that said a shallow grave might still be *his* grave. She was right. The old man had been fragile of late. "There comes a time in life when these strong potions don't mesh well with the body anymore, no matter how skilled the healer is. Me, then," she declared primly, turning to her daughter. "I'll do it."

"Good gods. 'Test it on me.' 'No, me.'" Groaning in utter annoyance, Bellanca shook her head. "I withdraw my offer. Poison Carver instead."

"I'm not...poisoning...anyone!" Jo ground out from between clenched teeth. "If I didn't think I could do it"—she spread her hands in emphasis—"I wouldn't!"

"That makes no sense!" Bellanca tossed both hands out wide, mimicking Jo—as if that would help. "You can't *know* until you try it. And then someone might be dead."

"No one will be dead." Jo stared the redhead down until Bellanca lowered her mocking hands and folded her arms across her chest. "I pick Carver to test it out. You withdrew your offer, and he offered next."

Approval banged inside Flynn. He'd tell Jo he was proud of her later. Or maybe he wouldn't. It didn't matter what *he* thought, only what *she* did.

Bellanca pursed her lips, but the argument died there. Maybe she knew Carver needed a full night's sleep just as much as Prometheus.

"When will the mixture be ready?" Griffin asked.

"I should have a first dose ready to test tonight." Jo glanced at Carver, confirming that she was allotting the test sample to him even though he wouldn't be taking the sleeping draught again. He nodded, accepting. "Then, I'll need another two days to make enough for everyone on the boat."

"I've used Nyx's Shallow Grave to induce deep sleep during amputations," Nerissa said. "I can oversee your preparations, if you'd like."

"Two herbalists are always better than one." Jocasta accepted her mother's offer with a grateful nod of her head.

"So that's Jocasta, Flynn, Prometheus, Carver, and Bellanca," Cat said. "Alpha Team."

"Team Elpis," Flynn blurted out on instinct, catching Cat's troubled gaze and holding it with his. "Team *Hope*."

Cat sucked in a breath. Tears sprang to her eyes, but as if by magic, some of the fear she'd been carrying visibly dissolved. "Team Elpis," she echoed in a firm voice.

Emotion swelled in Flynn's chest. They'd bring Cat an antidote to the Elixir of Eternal Life, that cursed gift she hadn't asked for, or die trying. He silently vowed it.

"Team Elpis. That's perfect, Flynn," Jo murmured, her eyes

shining with unshed tears. She blinked them back, just as Cat had. "Thank you."

His throat suddenly thick and burning, he nodded, incapable of speech. Team Elpis would die soon, at least for the equivalent of one long sleep. And then maybe Cat, Griffin, and baby Eleni could *live.*

CHAPTER 12

Dressed for travel and equipped with what weapons she knew how to use—including herb powders, ointments, and healing tonics—Jocasta arrived early and waited in the outer courtyard for everyone to assemble with their mounts and gear. Early morning sunlight slanted over the castle walls, hitting dawn-crisp air with a golden glow that worked hard to chase away shadows and shivers. A few guards patrolled the area. Noise swelled along with the sunshine and warmth, each dewdrop evaporating into someone waking up to begin their day as usual.

For Jocasta, today was anything but usual.

Bellanca and Carver showed up first, leading their horses behind them and waving their greetings toward her. Jocasta waved back as they gravitated off to one side, a heated conversation kicking up about the two new Great Roars that had been reported over the last few days on opposite sides of the kingdom. After a moment, Carver muscled his way in to check Bellanca's girth strap. Bellanca mounted, kneeing Carver in the process.

Once she had the high ground, she shoved something at him that looked like a charm to ward off the evil eye. Whatever Carver said as he took the necklace made her visibly bristle, and she tried to snatch it back again. Carver hopped away and dropped the charm around his neck. Bellanca's red-hot glare hit the back of Carver's head as he turned to his horse, tucking the coin-sized medallion under his leather armor.

Kaia arrived next along with Prometheus. She jogged over and hugged Carver before he mounted and then turned back to the Titan, chattering in that way of hers that meant he only had to listen and nod, which they all knew Prometheus found soothing. She fussed over him, handing him something covered in blue cloth before wrapping her arms around his waist and squeezing. Prometheus mounted, looking rather sick, truth be told. Atop his very large horse, he tried to open his present, but Kaia shook her head and made him tuck it into his saddlebag for later.

Anatole and Nerissa came to see them off, their arms linked as they moved toward Carver, Bellanca, and Prometheus on their horses. Jocasta hung back with Kaia. She'd get a final hug from them both, but she'd said goodbye to her parents inside already, barely containing the tears trying to drown her courage. She knew what she was facing, what they were up against. Not coming back whole—or at all—were very real and terrifying possibilities.

She swallowed the lump of fear in her throat and hugged her sister. "Don't do anything deranged, like follow us."

A laugh erupted from Kaia, rough with those tears she wasn't shedding, either. "I have an army to run and a temporary captain of the guard to oversee. I'll be too busy for mischief."

"That sounds like nothing *but* mischief to me." Jocasta gave Kaia a final squeeze, marveling at how grown-up the baby of the family suddenly felt to her, and not only physically. Both Kaia and Egeria were more like their brothers, tall and lean, whereas Jocasta had inherited their mother's smaller, curvier stature. "Speaking of temporary captains…" Her voice trailed off as she watched Lukos descend from his quarters in the gatehouse to open the portcullis for them. Trim and well muscled, the ex-shepherd looked more suited to war than to guarding flocks after his months of vigorous training under Carver and then rising to be Flynn's second-in-command. Lukos bounded down the steep stairs two at a time, nimble and energetic even at just past sunrise. "He's quite handsome," Jocasta remarked.

Kaia beamed at her. "Oh! Are you interested? I couldn't tell how you felt about Alexander."

Jocasta gaped at her sister. "N–no," she spluttered. "Are you?"

Kaia shrugged, a little smile tugging at her lips. "I notice a lot of things about a lot of people."

Jocasta snorted. "How enigmatic—and egalitarian—of you."

Kaia's laugh lost the edge of tears and pealed across the courtyard, drawing all eyes to them. Poor Lukos tripped on the last step and nearly fell face-first onto the cobbles. His fierce blush lit up the morning, and he lunged for the wheel to raise the portcullis, turning his back to them.

Jocasta noticed things, too. Lukos's straining shoulder muscles beneath his fitted tunic were one. How he lost all sense of balance when Kaia caught his attention was another. Kaia was looking, too, and for the first time, Jocasta thought maybe her sister wasn't as oblivious to men's attention as she seemed. Kaia's main focuses were weapons, puppies, and Prometheus, though, and she doubted that was about to change.

The portcullis started to groan. Jocasta shivered at the grinding noise and slow opening. She'd hated that gate from her first day here, with its sharp teeth and bolts of iron. It made her feel more trapped than protected, like this beast of a castle had swallowed her whole and she couldn't breathe from the pit of its belly.

Luckily, she rarely saw it. If the royal family wanted to enjoy the outdoors, they had the inner courtyard with its glittering marble walkways, fountains, and flowers. Undeniably beautiful as the private yard was, Jocasta preferred the sprawling gardens and wooded grounds beyond the barracks and bathhouses. There were dusty, root-strewn paths there, rocks that weren't polished to a shimmer and carved into statues, and big old trees with gnarled branches, reminding her of the places she'd roamed in what felt like another lifetime.

She even found the occasional useful wild plant for her healing room and some edible mushrooms. The kitchen staff here turned their noses up at anything that wasn't bought at the principal city agora, though, as if paying coppers for fungus made it any tastier once the sauce was poured on. She'd stopped picking anything for them once she realized her findings went straight into the fire—and not for cooking.

"Where's your horse?" Kaia perched on her toes and looked around as though Jocasta's gray mare had mysteriously vanished but might suddenly appear again. "And Flynn?"

"I don't know where Flynn is. I imagine he's coming." How could just saying his name make her chest clench? What would traveling with him do to her? She might implode-explode-liquefy-evaporate. Now wouldn't that be an accomplishment. "As for Elektra, Griffin and Cat said they'd saddle her for me and bring her out while I said goodbye to Mother and Father."

Kaia murmured a response while smiling and waving at Prometheus, who nodded back, his dark eyes serious.

Jocasta shifted from foot to foot, impatient now to start their journey. It had been a busy few days, complicated by the fact that every time she saw Flynn, she wanted to grip his golden-red stubbled jaw, rock up on her toes, and whisper against his lips that he was her champion, that he'd *always* been her champion, and that she was mad for him.

A hot, tight whip of feeling spiraled through her. Her over-active imagination kept picturing things that were never going to happen. Namely, Flynn and her.

She knew very well that wanting something didn't make it happen. She'd wanted Flynn and a family of her own. She'd wanted to stay in their village and maintain her thriving healing practice when Griffin brought the family to Castle Sinta and put Egeria on the throne. She'd wanted to travel the kingdom and help establish the new schools her eldest sister was building in Hoi Polloi communities that had lacked any positive attention from their previous royals. She'd wanted to teach the mixing and uses of herbal remedies at the new healing centers Griffin, Cat, and Egeria had worked so hard to establish in Sinta, then in Tarva, and soon in Fisa as well.

But no. She was safer with her family. Safer behind high walls. Safer—and miserable—near Flynn. She could *leave*; she knew that. She wasn't a prisoner here, and yet she was. No force in Thalyria, the Underworld, or on Mount Olympus could make her abandon her family to simply strike out on her own. No force could make her disobey her parents if they truly put their foot down. No force could make her disappoint and worry her siblings, who only wanted what was best for her. No force could make Flynn fall in love with her, no matter how much she wanted him to.

She was stuck, a bird in a cage with an open door she couldn't fly through—until now.

She glanced in the direction of the path that led from the stables to the front entrance, wondering where the others were. Was it odd to feel fully prepared and yet not ready at all? Excited yet terrified? Slightly unwell?

After a last embrace and a kiss on the cheek, Kaia wandered back toward Prometheus. Jocasta stayed where she was, taking mental inventory of her preparations. The stiff little pouch at her belt contained the most essential of them. Carver had slept for only nine hours and still twitched when she poked him, so she'd added another drop of nyx-shadow essence to her potion and tried again on Bellanca, who'd slept like the dead for a little longer than Jocasta expected. After adjustments, she had vials marked for each of them with personalized doses of Nyx's Shallow Grave. The most potent concoction was for Prometheus, the largest of them all, and the least potent was for herself, the smallest of the company.

Ducking into the shadows along the east wall, Jocasta gave her right boot a tug, attempting to get comfortable in her unfamiliar clothing and equipment. The day before, Cat had surprised Jocasta with her own leather armor, short sword, and daggers. They'd barely needed to adjust the buckles and ignored the scrapes and gouges in the tough leather. Evidence of battles fought—and hard-won sometimes.

Jocasta looked up at the sound of hoofbeats on cobbles, and her heart zoomed sideways at the speed of Hermes. Cat wasn't leading Jocasta's mare, Elektra, who despite her name being rather kinetic could be quite plodding sometimes. She was leading her own horse, Panotii, into the courtyard, and Jocasta nearly burst into tears when she saw Cat's parting gift to her.

They walked toward each other, Jocasta moving slowly until she mastered her emotions. She waved in greeting, sure her voice would be unsteady.

"He's smart, strong, and has a heart of gold." Cat put Panotii's reins into Jocasta's hand, not commenting on the tremble she must've felt in Jocasta's fingers.

Jocasta stroked Panotii's nose, rough with whiskers, smooth as silk. The chestnut gelding was neither the biggest nor the fastest horse in their stable, but Jocasta agreed that he was the strongest. Like Cat, Panotii didn't break. He'd come through, again and again, resolute to the end, relentless until success.

"But…" Cat glanced over her shoulder at Griffin and Flynn,

who emerged leading Brown Horse behind them. The big stallion's hooves thudded rhythmically, drowning out the sudden buzzing in Jocasta's eardrums. "These two refuse to be separated, so Flynn's going to take Brown Horse and leave his usual mount here for Griffin."

A teary laugh burst from Jocasta. She blinked rapidly. Brown Horse and Panotii were just as inseparable as Cat and Griffin. "Thank you."

Smiling, Cat patted Panotii's neck, and his oversized ears twitched in her direction. "Panotii will take care of you—and the rest of Team Elpis. He's very dependable."

Panotii nodded. Honest to gods, nodded. The horse was made of heart and courage, and Jocasta just hoped she had as much of both as he did.

Reaching out, she ran her hand down the chestnut's well-groomed neck, thinking his coloring was close to Flynn's—reddish with hints of gold and brown. They might even have big ears in common. Flynn's were more evident now that he'd cut his hair. And they were both dependable. Kind. There when you needed them. Good looking. Strong.

She smiled a little wistfully. "We'll take care of each other. Right, boy?" Panotii's donkey ears pricked forward. Her smile widened. Inside and out, the chestnut gelding was truly a magnificent beast. "My, you are a handsome fellow," Jocasta crooned in admiration.

"Thank you." Griffin winked, stopping beside her. Brown Horse nickered.

"Yes, you too, Brown Horse." Jocasta gave her teasing brother an indulgent smile while Flynn, head down, busied himself with strapping on his saddlebag.

She gently scratched under Brown Horse's jaw when the stallion extended his head to sniff her shoulder. He'd answered to Horse until Cat insisted Griffin name him. Griffin's sad attempt at humor stuck, and now the stallion was Brown Horse to everyone—and Panotii's faithful friend.

"What's making you grin, little sister?" Griffin asked.

Jocasta shrugged, the jumble of emotions inside her difficult to separate and name. "I'm not sure. Maybe I'm...hopeful."

Flynn finally turned at her words, his gaze locking on her and flaring with something Jocasta didn't dare name in case she'd imagined it. It was gone in an instant, but her body still flamed up from the lick of heat she thought she glimpsed in his eyes.

She brushed a hand against the side of her formfitting leather armor, her pulse battering her veins. Swallowing, she turned back to Griffin. "*Cautiously* hopeful," she amended in a low rasp.

But suddenly, she wasn't sure. Did she mean Flynn or the mission? Or both?

She bit her lip. It was too soon to be hopeful about anything, and the mission came first.

In fact, the mission was growing. "I heard Carver and Bellanca saying we need to investigate another Great Roar on the way to Thassos," Jocasta said. "How many is that now? Half a dozen?"

Griffin nodded as he handed Brown Horse's reins to Flynn. "There've been two new incidents. We sent word to Egeria asking her to look into the Great Roar near Velos. Something happened in the nearby forest that sent the animals into a panic. Now, hunters are complaining that the game has vanished and the agora in Velos is suffering from the loss of it."

"Angry hunters. Worried merchants." Cat pursed her lips. "Annoyed customers who want meat."

Jocasta grimaced. "In other words, an unsettled and nervous city right in the middle of Sinta."

Griffin's expression darkened. "In Fisa, it's even more

worrisome. The people who've crossed through the Arcadian Wilds are talking about dry rivers and wilted trees. It isn't just the animals that fled. It's as if a whole section of woodland just...*died.*"

"Isn't that forest said to be populated by nymphs?" Jocasta asked. "Blessed by the gods and eternally thriving?"

"Thriving until a few days ago," Cat muttered. "The reports say *panikos* set in, and the nymphs took off, probably for the Ice Plains." She resorted to the old language to describe the sudden fear that sent the nature sprites scattering.

"And the abrupt loss of them killed the trees?" Jocasta asked.

"I guess so." Cat smoothed her hand down Panotii's neck. "Losing the dryads so quickly must've weakened the whole forest. It sounds as if they crushed the moisture and life from it somehow."

"A stampede," Flynn said. "The tree nymphs could've stampeded like the animals we've been hearing about and trampled the woods in their frenzy to escape the noise."

A vague memory scratched at Jocasta's thoughts. Flynn's rich, cavern-deep voice never failed to resonate inside her. His idea did, too, reminding her of something she couldn't quite put her finger on. Isolated places... Angry shouts... Had she come across a scroll somewhere?

"Nymphs running amok. Vanishing game. Entire herds— dead." Cat sighed, rubbing her forehead. "Just what we need when everything's already a mess."

"We'll figure it out, *agapi mou*. All of it," Griffin said.

Cat nodded, but the faraway look in her eyes as she curved a hand around her belly seemed to veer more toward fear than hope again.

Cat's worried frown faded as she pulled a pendant from her pocket. A small, egg-shaped gemstone dangled from a delicate gold chain. "This heliotrope is spelled to cure one mortal wound. Persephone made it and gave it to me months ago in case of...a difficult childbirth." She handed the necklace to Jocasta, a shadow flitting through her eyes. "You're a capable healer, so I know you'll only use the magic if there's damage beyond your skill."

Jocasta took the pendant with a murmured thank-you, emotion clogging her throat again. Persephone was an unparalleled healer, and she could see signs of the goddess all over the necklace. Thin spirals of gold wire cradled the polished green stone in branching patterns of small leaves and spring flowers. Bright-red flecks smattered the gem's dark surface like drops of blood. Magic throbbed from the stone, thumping against Jocasta's hand like a pulse. She swallowed. "It'll be a little like having a Magoi healer with us."

Cat nodded. "Just hold the gemstone against the injury until the magic ignites. But it'll only work once—unless Persephone renews the spell."

"I understand." Jocasta looped the chain around her neck and tucked the smooth, almost flat pendant inside her leather breastplate. Even through her tunic, the bloodstone felt like an open artery against her chest—hot and pumping. It was a heartbeat, she realized. *A heartbeat to give life back to a heart about to stop.* She shivered.

"Now go, before I figure out a way to escape court and come with you." Cat made a shooing motion, slapping humor across her face like armor. "If someone had told me that being *Queen Elpis* meant I couldn't run around killing miscreants and slaying monsters, I'd have turned down the job faster than Dionysus can fill an empty wine goblet." She shot a sour look at Griffin. "You did this."

Griffin dropped a kiss onto the top of her dark head. "*We* did this."

"Well, you still owe me about eighteen adventures," she grumbled.

Griffin's brows rose. "You're counting, are you?"

"Yes. I started yesterday. By tomorrow, you'll be up to thirty-six. After that, I'm just picking fights with Cerberus."

Griffin chuckled. They all did, and it felt good. Laughter was another parting gift from Cat—maybe the most needed one.

Smiling, Jocasta met Flynn's eyes without even thinking. He smiled back, his lips curling into a delicious grin, and the Flynn effect exploded inside her. Heat and butterflies. The jolt of awareness threw her off-balance. Her breath came short, her heart pounding.

Just then, the rest of the departing group converged on them along with her parents and Kaia. They urged Jocasta and Flynn to mount up before the sun got higher and the travel day shorter. Her mother clucked and hovered. Flynn, Carver, and she were used to the smothering affection—Nerissa had been fussing over all of them since they were infants—but Bellanca managed to look both annoyed and greedy for more attention. If Prometheus thought anything about Nerissa trying to baby the lot of them, including the ancient Titan, he didn't show it.

Her father was more reserved, which either meant he wasn't feeling well or worry plagued him, making him subdued and thoughtful. It could be both. He'd been quieter and quieter lately.

Jocasta took a moment to soak in the sight of everyone together, her chest tightening. Carver and Flynn were with her, but that wasn't even half the people she loved the most. Saying goodbye and preparing to ride out the gate without knowing if she'd come back was harder than she ever imagined. She'd stumbled into her last-minute participation in the Agon Games. This departure into danger was a deliberate, planned decision.

And so, when the final goodbyes had been said, her back straight and her eyes burning, Jocasta deliberately turned Panotii toward the gate and pressed her heels to his sides, sending him forward. Her course was set. First, the Arcadian Wilds on their way to the Fisan coast and Thassos. Then, hopefully, Aeaea.

Her throat thick with tears she somehow managed to hold back, Jocasta took the lead, riding straight into the rising sun. As Team Elpis set a steady pace to the east, she had to wonder if the real reason she hadn't ever left her family before was fear of never seeing them again.

CHAPTER 13

Flynn wasn't sure what was worse: riding next to Jocasta and being aware of every breath she took or having her ahead of him and watching her body sway in that graceful, enticing way it did. *Hips. Waist. Hips. Waist. A little turn of her head.*

He never let her ride behind him. He'd keep an eye on her, even if it killed him.

Prometheus rode point. Flynn took up the rear. And for two people who wouldn't stop needling each other, it was surprisingly hard to separate Carver and Bellanca.

Right now, the team rode in single file. As usual, Prometheus scouted ahead, avoiding all conversation. The woodland road they'd veered onto the previous day took them off the beaten path. It was their most direct route toward the border city of Kos and then to the Arcadian Wilds, but it kept funneling them into a strung-out formation Flynn wouldn't have liked had he sensed there was anything to worry about. As it was, the only thing he needed to fret over was internal brawling, which probably should've concerned him more as he suddenly seemed to be in charge of this group. How did that happen?

"I don't need a watchdog," Carver snarled.

"Mangy, ill-tempered, in need of a bath?" Bellanca glanced over her shoulder at Carver, one red brow arching high enough to remind Flynn that no one did imperious like a Magoi princess, even a deposed one. "One of us is the animal here. Guess who?"

"Probably the one watching my every move like she's about to pounce," Carver snapped in annoyance.

Flynn urged Brown Horse to pick up the pace, closing the small gap he'd let form between Jo and him. Behind Carver but now directly ahead of him, Jo tilted her head skyward in what Flynn had decided was a silent supplication to the gods to spare them all another argument. He smiled, his mouth curving and stretching in a way his facial muscles seemed to have forgotten after Kato died and Beta Team ran out of missions. It was the tenth time this morning Jo had sent a silent prayer toward Mount Olympus. Yesterday, he'd counted thirty-two in all. Oddly enough, he didn't mind the incessant bickering. It filled the silences that came with long journeys and reminded him of the early days with Cat, when she'd been all vinegar and violence.

Just like back then, the claws-out squabbling provided a distraction, especially since he'd started cataloging Jo's reactions to the volatile pair that usually rode right in front of her, forcing her to be audience, buffer, and oft-times mediator. She went from aggravated to amused to fed up to deeply interested—along with a dozen other subtle responses he kept trying to identify now just from the set of her shoulders, the angle of her back, or the tilt of her chin as she listened.

Flynn batted an insect away, its hard carapace pinging against the back of his hand like a blunt little hammer. Maybe he shouldn't watch Jo so carefully? Wasn't it strange, even unsavory? Men weren't supposed to know when a woman sighed. Or yawned. Or stretched. Or silently giggled. Were they? Granted, there wasn't much else to do as they rode—and definitely nothing more captivating to look at. So what if his gaze was drawn to her like a stargazer's to the brightest light in the cosmos? Somewhere in the past days, he'd accepted that Jocasta was his Polaris, his only compass, no matter which direction she faced or where she led him. As long as *she* didn't know that, he figured he was safe from temptation.

Up ahead, Bellanca slowed enough to wedge her mount next to Carver's, despite the tightness of the path and the branches that scraped at them. As a pair, they formed a horse-behind blockade in front of Jocasta. Turning in her saddle, Jo shot him an impish look over her shoulder, her sparkling blue eyes saying, *Brace yourself.* Flynn's heart gave a great wallop against his ribs. He nodded, although he didn't think they were bracing for the same reasons.

"There are limits to my patience." Carver's flat tone gained bite when their new position nearly forced his horse off the path and into a prickly bramble. His mount twitched sideways, bumping into Bellanca's.

"Ooh, did someone learn a new word today?" Angling toward him, she let a syrupy smile bend her mouth and didn't give even a fingernail's worth of space back to Carver. "Let's try spelling it. P...A...T..."

"I..." Carver swiveled to face her, his countenance darkening.

"Don't know what comes next?" Bellanca patted his shoulder. "Poor darling."

A laugh cracked out of Jocasta. Her hand flew to her mouth, trying to contain the sound as Carver turned in his saddle, his entire body reminding Flynn of a cloudburst just waiting to happen.

"She boils the wine if I even look at it. I'm not that weak." His scowl turned thunderous as he glared at his sister. "Do *you* think I'm that weak?"

"Don't get me involved!" Jo cried, slowing Panotii.

"Does that mean yes?" Carver demanded.

"Who said you're weak?" Bellanca reclaimed Carver's

attention with a hearty scowl of her own. "No one else dared get involved when you turned into a sloppy, growling drunk. That means *they're* weak."

"Thank you. That's lovely," Jo said.

Unfortunately, Flynn had to agree with Bellanca on that one, and from the way Jo's shoulders slumped, he thought she did, too.

"Sloppy?" Carver stared at the redhead. "*Growling?*"

Bellanca shrugged. "What's weak is tiptoeing across each other's feelings like a little truth might shatter someone's spun-sugar filigree coating. People are tougher than they look. Mean what you say, and say what you mean. It makes life easier."

"Because your life has been so easy?" Carver challenged.

"No, but at least it's been honest in its brutality and horridness." Bellanca turned to him with a grin. "It's better now."

Carver gave her the evil eye—halfhearted, in Flynn's opinion. "That's because you have me to torment," he muttered.

Bellanca waved that off with a flick of her hand. "Torment. Watch out for. Potato. Potahto."

Carver snort-laughed, genuine amusement shaving ten years off him in seconds. Flynn couldn't remember the last time he'd laughed like that and figured he must look halfway to the grave if mirth erased years and wear like magic.

Bellanca looked at Carver, startled at first and then suspicious. Her eyes narrowed. "Stop that!"

"Stop what?" Carver asked, his shoulders still shaking.

"Whatever *that* is." She waved her hand up and down, encompassing his head and torso.

"Don't drink. Don't laugh. Don't pick fights. Don't cheat at races." Shaking his head, Carver tossed his next words back to Jocasta. "She's a killjoy of epic proportions."

"And that's my cue to leave the arena." Jo reined in and

ended up next to Flynn, their knees brushing. His blood pumped harder, his body heating. There was barely enough room on the path for both their horses, but for the life of him, he couldn't steer Brown Horse away from her.

"Fine. *She* will stop boiling the wine," Bellanca hissed, sounding a lot like that damp log they'd accidentally put on the campfire last night. A stray spark leaped out from the flame-red wisps at her hairline. "*She* doesn't care if you end up in a ditch. *She* has better things to do with her time."

Jo leaned toward him, whispering, "Who's oppressively overprotective now?"

Flynn chuckled. "What goes around comes around."

"False." Jo shook her head. "Bellanca's the only person in this family other than Cat that Carver actually trusts to take care of herself."

This family. Was he included in that? He wasn't any more a blood relation than Bellanca.

His next words rasped in his throat even though they were meant to be lighthearted. "When you can turn into a vicious little fireball and aren't inherently opposed to killing, your chances of survival improve somewhat."

Jo giggled. It was a sound from a long time ago, from a time of olive groves, farmhouses, lazy afternoons down by the river, and Jo in dusty sandals with twin braids down her back instead of the sophisticated way she swept her hair up nowadays.

Their eyes met, and her smile made it hard to breathe until she faced forward again, breaking the spell her every look cast over him. Considering they'd been traveling, eating, and sleeping all within a few steps of each other for the last four days, Flynn wasn't sure how he was still functioning. He found himself constantly holding his breath, as though life were on the cusp of revealing a tremendous surprise—one that could either be incredible or devastating. No wonder he was always light-headed around Jocasta.

He guided Brown Horse around a fallen log, giving more room to Jo and Panotii. She ended up ahead of him again, riding single file. Flynn told himself it was better that way and to ignore the part of him that missed her company and smile already. Smiling didn't come easily to him anymore, although he liked it when Jo did. Her laughter made him feel lighter.

CHAPTER 14

Jocasta had never considered herself a slave to comforts but being accustomed to daily hot baths made full-body immersion in cold streams genuinely miserable. Since smelling like horse and sweat was even more miserable, she did the necessary each time the opportunity presented itself. Bellanca insisted on accompanying her, and arguing for a moment of privacy proved fruitless. The ex-princess's overprotectiveness extended to Jocasta, who it seemed was in danger of drowning in three feet of water. They'd taken to washing first and then leaving the creek to the men, who never left them for more than a few minutes.

Kos was still two days away, so real beds and baths weren't for tonight or even for tomorrow. And Flynn had started talking about bypassing the border city altogether, since their evening hunts had provided enough food for them to avoid dipping into their dried, smoked, or otherwise-preserved provisions.

Routines were quickly established on road trips, Jocasta discovered, and they'd fallen into a pattern of sorts from the very first evening. Prometheus hunted, only coming back with what they could cook and eat on the spot, which Jocasta appreciated. Carver and Bellanca patrolled the perimeter, gathering edible greens and berries if they found any, and Flynn did the cooking. As usual, she had no role. When she offered to help, Jocasta was told to rest and relax. If she heard *rest and relax* one more time, it was entirely possible her internal scream would burst out and scare the lot of them.

The only advantage to having nothing to do besides pat horses and sit beside the campfire was spending time with Flynn. He automatically took on the role of team cook, which placed him next to the fire, too. He took pride in his cooking, not letting anyone meddle with his pans or spices. Jocasta always offered to help, but they both knew she wasn't gifted in the kitchen unless it was to mix medicines, which no one ever expected to taste good.

From what she'd heard, Flynn had always cooked for Beta Team, too. No one seemed to have questioned the habit, but Jocasta had to wonder if the time and effort Flynn put into their on-the-road meals wasn't his way of taking care of a family.

Watching him, she discreetly smiled, recognizing it as that chest-tightening secret smile only Flynn brought out in her. His brow furrowed as he looked at his spice pouches, clearly hesitating between two choices. He had several dried herbs with him, which he kept in little drawstring bags in a rolled-up oilcloth in his saddlebag to protect them from bad weather. It was rather adorable.

He glanced her way. "Marjoram or fennel?"

Flynn wanted her opinion? On cooking? The warmth that billowed inside her could in no way be attributed to the fire. "They're quite different." She braided her still-damp hair into one thick plait as she thought about it. "For the rabbit?"

He nodded.

"I prefer the more delicate spice on the meat." She finished her braid and gripped the end to keep it from unraveling. "Is it too late to add fennel to the flatbread? That way you can get both flavors."

Flynn's eyes brightened, sending a little ripple of pleasure through her. "I like the way you think." The flattened dough hadn't gone into the hot pan yet, and he added a pinch of fennel to it, pressing gently. Then he lightly spiced the already-cooking meat with the marjoram and brushed his hands off, looking satisfied. "There. Some of everything."

"The exact opposite of my life," Jocasta murmured without thinking.

Flynn glanced at her, frowning. "What do you mean?"

She pressed her lips together. She hadn't meant to say that aloud. The answer was complicated and not for Flynn's ears—not if she wanted to maintain this new ease between them.

"I…" She searched for something vague that wouldn't make either of them uncomfortable. "I just feel as if something's missing. I have so much, but oddly, none of it's really what I want. Or wanted." Belatedly, she realized he might still think she was talking about him. She hadn't been. Not really. But it applied to him, too, in the end.

Flynn gazed at her, the forest shadows and the flicker of flames making it hard to tell if he was sympathetic, neutral, or frozen in place. Probably the latter. Flynn didn't talk about feelings. Each death in his family had bit into that ability a little more until Old Hector's passing swallowed it whole, leaving him silent.

"I'm sorry." Grimacing, she gripped her braid like a lifeline. How could she complain about anything? She'd made it through twenty-four years and a kingdom-altering war without even a fraction of the pain and loss Flynn had known by her age.

He cocked his head, and instead of backing away, he stepped closer. Firelight danced over his features, highlighting golden-red stubble, stern yet generous lips, and a jawline that would make Apollo jealous. She shivered, even though his proximity warmed her in a way the fire couldn't seem to—from the inside out, permeating every layer.

"Why are you sorry?" Genuine interest creased Flynn's brow, maybe even concern. He looked at her with an intensity Jocasta felt like an actual touch, and her mouth went dry in an instant.

Why indeed? Her thoughts scattered and vanished like sparks from the blaze as her senses instinctively focused on Flynn's voice, all woodsmoke and resonance. It was unfair that voice, hypnotic. And the way he looked at her made everything else fade away.

Jocasta forced her surroundings back into focus. "That was insensitive of me. I'm lucky and should recognize it and be grateful instead of wanting more. Or different," she added.

Flynn seemed to hesitate but then sat beside her on the log they'd rolled over to the fire, ending up close enough for the heat of his body to seep into hers, although no part of him touched her. He stayed quiet for a good minute—which felt like an hour—before finally asking, "Why do you think you can't want something? Who put that idea in your head?"

His question startled her. It was profoundly simple, and yet she'd never really thought to ask herself that, let alone expected the question from someone else. "No one, I suppose. I just have a hard time reconciling wanting more when I know what I have."

Nodding, Flynn leaned toward the fire. "I understand." He gave both spits a quarter turn to brown another section of the two rabbits Prometheus had caught for them and then rested his forearms on his thighs, watching the meat drip.

Jocasta wanted him to look at her again and scooted closer, not ready to lose the cautious intimacy forming between them. "You understand?" she asked, her heart beating like a hummingbird's wings inside the cage of her chest.

"I think so." He winced, conveying just how comfortable he was with this conversation. He stayed put, though, and seemed to search for the right words before saying, "There's a sense of wrongness at wanting anything when you know you're the lucky one." He half turned to her before glancing away again. "Does that make sense?"

It did. For her—and for him. She'd fallen into a life of luxury, ease, and total irrelevance without ever pursuing it, and Flynn… The domino-like deaths of his entire family had left him riddled with guilt. Over and over, he'd asked, *Why him?* and *Why her?* but what he'd really been saying was *Why them and not me?* Kato's death must have brought all that back to the surface.

"It makes perfect sense," she said gently. It couldn't be easy to embrace life when you felt guilty for living it. "And I think it's normal to give in to those feelings from time to time. The gods know they can be overwhelming. Stronger than us, sometimes."

"But should they rule you? Dominate your life?" Flynn followed his questions with a soft sound of derision. Did he regret his words? Supposedly, they were talking about her, but that didn't feel true anymore.

Jocasta's thoughts tiptoed across eggshells, trying to find the answer Flynn needed. Her aching heart wanted to cry for his losses—and it definitely didn't want to make a mistake that would hurt him.

"No. Not forever, anyway." The cocoon of near dark made the wide-open clearing seem smaller and just for them. Angling to fully face him, her knees brushing Flynn's now, Jocasta all but forgot about the rest of Team Elpis hovering on the periphery. "Some things dominate your life for a time, and maybe there's no helping that, or stopping it. Maybe those are things to recognize and try to understand—and eventually overcome, if possible."

"Overcome." His mouth puckered, as though the things he held inside tasted terrible. "So what's holding you back, then? From the more *you* want?" Flynn softly nudged her with his elbow, neatly putting the olive back on her branch and making her smile.

Jocasta glanced down, a flash of heat and a whole new kind of tension snapping through her. She folded her hands on her lap, squeezing her thumbnail for balance. It was a little trick she'd developed to make it look as if she wasn't fidgeting, when really, she was mashing the Olympian stuffing out of her finger. Since a big part of the *more* she wanted was Flynn, she chose her words carefully.

"It's simple, really. I always feel enormous guilt at not being satisfied. On the outside, what more could I want? On the inside, I'm…unfulfilled." She looked back up, releasing her thumb and letting the blood flow again. "I didn't used to feel that way."

Sympathy softened Flynn's features. She didn't seem to have surprised him. "Back home, you were always the satisfied one, not looking for more like the others did."

Her huff rang bitter, even to her ears. "That was when I had purpose and people who counted on me. Daily. Hourly, sometimes. New lives in my hands. Old lives. Everything in between. A plan…"

She glanced away again, her heart cinching. She'd had everything all mapped out. Unfortunately, life hadn't cooperated.

"People still count on you. My soldiers, the servants—"

"Could all get instant treatment from a Magoi healer," she interrupted. "Magoi healers might look down their noses at Hoi Polloi, but Griffin and Cat would have their hides if they didn't cooperate. I'm superfluous."

"Not true," Flynn argued. "Unless an injury or illness is immediately life-threatening, every Hoi Polloi I know would rather go to you than to a Magoi healer."

She made a noncommittal sound, shrugging one shoulder because the other seemed too heavy to move. Maybe disappointed hopes sat there. They weighed a lot sometimes.

"And this quest? We're here because of *you*. You gave us a way to help Cat and baby Eleni. It'll save Griffin, too."

"It might not work. We might not even…" She didn't add *survive*. She wrinkled her nose instead.

"Stop selling yourself short, Jo. You're vital."

She was? To whom? It was a nice thought, even though she didn't believe it.

"Well, now I've officially joined the merry band of ambitious siblings." She spread her hands, encompassing the life-threatening quest she'd sent them on based on an old scroll and some hearsay. Yes, she had doubts. "Cerberus is our stay-at-home mascot. Watch out for fangs, your livestock, and poison drool."

Flynn chuckled. "Good. Ambition makes things happen. Look where it took Anatole, and then Griffin. And isn't it human nature to want more? As a people, we wouldn't accomplish much if everyone was satisfied with the minimum."

Grease hissed, a flame licked higher, and Jocasta's stomach gave a little rumble. The meal already smelled delicious. "I can't say I have the minimum. That would be an affront to anyone who doesn't live in a castle."

Flynn grinned at her. "Point taken."

Her heart flipped over. He grinned so rarely these days. She grinned back. It was inevitable.

"And wanting more?" he added. "Or something else? There's no harm in that. Or shame. It's not a question of ingratitude. It's a question of personal..." He searched for a word, not finding it. Or perhaps not wanting to utter it. His mouth flattened.

"Desires?" she asked huskily.

He nodded. A swallow moved his throat. Dark pools in the dim light, his brown eyes were as guarded as usual but far from expressionless. The raw emotion she saw in them for once made Jocasta want to ask what *he* desired, but she feared that would be the end of their conversation—now and likely for days. Maybe forever. It had taken them more than six years to talk again almost normally. She wasn't about to risk it.

She also wasn't going to risk suggesting he apply that advice to himself, although if the shoe fit, he might think about slipping it on and walking a few miles.

Not knowing what else to say, Jocasta looked away first. Flynn busied himself adding more wood to the fire and turning the meat again, so she fished in her pocket for a rawhide lace to tie off the end of her braid, which still dangled across her shoulder. She fumbled the knot twice before muttering, "This is impossible one-handed."

"Easier with a maid?" Flynn plucked the tie from her fingers.

"Yes." Her lips twitched, a little jolt of sensation lashing up her arm from where he'd touched her. "You know...the minimum."

He smiled, wide and genuine. "If you'd said that back in the village, I would've laughed in your face."

"How kind of you," she drawled, her heart swooping in her chest. "You, with your grand speeches about humanity and ambition."

"Ah, but your ambition was never to be served, was it?" He tied off the end of her braid, double knotting the lace with deft fingers. His hand lingered on her hair just a second longer than necessary, and Jocasta shivered. "It was to serve others."

Their eyes met, and her lips parted in surprise. Flynn still knew her better than anyone.

"I miss my patients back home," she admitted. "The people who needed me in and around the village. I knew them all by heart." Her voice quavered, and she dipped her head, hiding how she squeezed her eyes shut. *This* was why she rarely spoke aloud what was in her heart. If she did, all the holes in her life overwhelmed her, and all the questions blazing through her mind threatened to burn her down.

Was someone helping Old Man Timeo with his gout? Could the elderly midwife still handle the difficult births? Did little

Yannis keep getting splinters in his foot? Had Phoebe gotten rid of that chronic cough? What did her herb garden look like now? Was Flynn's farmhouse still standing strong or had it crumbled like her heart?

She gulped down a breath.

"I've no doubt they wish you'd never left." Flynn tilted her chin back up, his touch coaxing and featherlight.

Heat spiked inside her, but the gentle pressure wasn't enough. She wanted to *feel* him—his warmth, his calluses, his strength—but then… "Wishes never seem to matter much."

Her fatalistic statement drew a sad smile from Flynn. He dropped his hand from her chin. "Your wishes matter." *To me,* he left unsaid. She heard the words anyway, echoing in his eyes.

Jocasta wet her lips, and his gaze dropped to her mouth. Something shifted in the air, a charge heating between them. Everything went still—her, him—and then hunger flashed across his expression. Her body reacted like a thunderclap. Suddenly, she was eighteen again and ready to offer him her heart, soul, and virginity, right there on the spot.

Flynn cleared his throat. "Funny," he murmured, meeting her gaze again, "how no one seems to know you in your own house."

Except you. Heat billowed through her. Low down, her stomach clenched. "I don't think it's funny at all," she countered, barely hearing the words over the hot rush of her pulse.

"No, I suppose you don't." Inching closer, he tucked a wisp of hair behind her ear. There was nothing awkward about it. It felt natural, right—and like they should've been talking and touching like this for years.

"Flynn… I…" She swallowed hard. Was she brave enough? Rejection was awful. She knew that for a fact.

"Ugh. Rabbit again? It's a good thing I'm famished." Bellanca surged from out of nowhere and plopped down on the ground beside them. Startled, they scooted apart as Bellanca sniffed the air, her nose wrinkling. "I think the meat's burning. And is that a charred foot?" Oblivious to interrupting what might've become one of the most important moments of Jocasta's recent life, Bellanca looked back and forth between them, a scowl on her face. "Aren't you two paying attention to this?"

Jocasta couldn't answer. She was too twisted up inside to utter a single word. She might've managed a kick, however, if the redhead had been within striking distance.

As quiet as she was, Flynn bent forward and turned the spits. Jocasta didn't see any too-crispy meat. Flynn made sure the flames didn't touch the flesh, and the feet had already been cut off.

"Carver and Pro are off peeing in the woods. Or something." Bellanca made a face at the *or something* and started picking up the rot-speckled leaves the last rainy season had brought to the ground and left moldering in the clearing. "We've established that there's no one around for *days*"—she rolled her eyes—"and that this is the most boring stretch of woods in Thalyria."

"Pro?" Jocasta coughed out.

"Metheus?" Bellanca shot Jocasta her signature are-you-stupid look. "You know? Big? God? Slightly unhinged?"

"Yes, I know who he is." Jocasta chose not to be annoyed. She let humor take the upper hand and felt her lips curl in a reluctant smile. Bellanca might've disrupted her private moment with Flynn, but the other woman might also have saved her from making a huge mistake—again. "I didn't know he had a nickname."

"I'm trying it out." Bellanca shrugged. "He hates it."

"And so you persist." Jocasta shook her head, letting another wry smile sneak out.

Bellanca grinned at her. "Of course."

"Maybe *don't* irritate the jumpy Titan?" Flynn started to fry the savory dough now that the rabbits were nearly cooked. His lips twitched, too, setting off a giddy little tumble in Jocasta's chest.

"See? That's where you lot always get it wrong. I need to irritate the jumpy Titan, so that when something really worth jumping at jumps out at him, he'll be toughened up and ready."

"Bellanca's logic makes sense," Jocasta admitted, catching Flynn's eye as he set the pan on top of the hot embers he'd gathered from the now low-burning fire. "Prometheus spends most of his time with Kaia, and she's not exactly dangerous. Even he said he wasn't sure he was ready for this, and he does startle easily."

"Maybe, but words aren't the same as weapons," Flynn said. "Or magic."

"Oh, I can do weapons and magic, too." Bellanca smiled evilly. "Can I?"

"No." Flynn looked at her hard—and kept looking. "Leave the man alone."

"Absolutely not." Bellanca threw one of her leaves into the fire. "It starts with Pro, and it'll end with flames and pointy objects. Then he might be ready for Circe's garden."

"*If* we find it," Jocasta murmured.

Bellanca scowled at her. "Your scroll. Your quest. At least *you* should believe it."

"I do. Fully." Jocasta plastered a sweet smile on her face that took a last-second dive into bared-teeth territory. "Lovely pep talk. Can you go back to annoying Carver now?"

"I'll pretend I didn't hear that," Carver grumbled from the shadows. He carried an armload of wood to fuel the fire once Flynn didn't need the lower cooking flames any longer.

Sighing, Jocasta looked up at the night sky in hopeless sup-plication. *Really?* Such terrible timing had to be predetermined by some ill-natured deity.

Carver set the wood down on the far side of the campfire and brushed off his hands and tunic. He leaned over to smell the dinner. "Mmm, Flynn's famous rabbit. My favorite."

"It's edible," Bellanca conceded. "But growing up on dust and shoe leather doesn't exactly fine-tune the palate."

Frowning, Carver wandered closer. "Do you picture me as a starving urchin begging for scraps in the street?"

Jocasta snorted. They'd lived comfortably and with a healthy and varied diet, thank you very much.

"I don't picture you at all," Bellanca retorted.

"I…" Shaking his head, Carver scowled and sat on the log beside Jocasta. Flynn was up and cooking again, standing by the fire. Carver might've been at a loss for words, but his choice of seats probably had little to do with sitting next to her and a lot to do with being higher than Bellanca.

Carver gently nudged her. "What's this about callously throwing me to the wolves?" He gave Bellanca the stink eye.

Jocasta leaned her head on her brother's shoulder in silent apology. "Sacrificial lamb?" she said hopefully.

"Now I'm a lamb?" Carver protested with humor.

"I'm not some evil witch you need to throw the innocent to in order to appease my villainous hunger." Bellanca tossed her whole handful of damp, dead leaves into the campfire.

Flynn grimaced. "It's not supposed to be smoked rabbit," he muttered, scraping what smoldering leaves he could back out and stomping on them.

"We should set you up in a cave." Slipping away from Jocasta, Carver bent down to goad Bellanca. "I can see it now… Dark and dank. Harpies guarding the entrance. Bats in the corners.

Broken cauldrons. Children's bones littering the floor. You'd obviously be missing some teeth—and maybe an eyebrow."

Bellanca arched her brows at him—both perfectly intact for the moment. "Save some insults for Circe. She's the real witch."

Carver's eyes narrowed. "What? No fury and fire?"

"Would you rather?" Bellanca asked innocently.

"Maybe." Practically nose to nose with her, Carver drew out the word, seeming wary. "Can't have you going soft before we get to Circe's garden." His arm brushed Jocasta's as he sat upright again and stretched out his legs, crossing them at the ankles and crowding Bellanca. The Magoi gave his boots a hard shove with flaming fingers, at least momentarily curing him of trying to annoy her again.

"I'd stop saying her name." Prometheus emerged from the shadows and joined them by the fire. "Each time a god's name is said several times in close succession, his or her focus is drawn to the general location. That's why humans began erecting temples."

"In that case, you'd think prayer would be worth something," Flynn said so low that Jocasta might've been the only one to hear him.

"Pro, Pro, Pro." Bellanca circled her arms around her updrawn knees and looked at the Titan expectantly. "Did it work?"

Carver stifled a chuckle. Prometheus ignored her, conjured what looked like a solid-gold throne with red velvet cushions, and sat on the other side of Jocasta.

"I'll take one of those." Bellanca eyed the opulent chair as though she were perusing luxury items at the agora. "In black."

Prometheus snapped his fingers—which they all knew was just for show—and conjured a much smaller chair with petal-pink cushions that clashed with Bellanca's fiery hair. She sat in the almost child-sized seat anyway. "Luckily, I'm incapable of looking ridiculous," she said with enough conviction to make it true.

Carver grinned outright. "Your knees are practically hitting your face."

"Of course they are." Bellanca looked down her nose at him. "It's the latest fashion."

His smile lit his eyes. So often, it didn't these days. "Setting a new trend?"

"I imagine so. I'm sure it'll catch on better than your mud-scruff scowl. Thalyrians have some taste, you know."

"I just bathed. And shaved." Carver turned his head from side to side, showing off his clean jaw.

"Ah, missed a spot." Bellanca pointed toward his neck. "Don't worry. I'll get it later when I slit your throat."

"We'll take watch together," Carver announced.

"Scared of me?" Bellanca smirked. "Finally, a sign of intelligence."

Carver paused, something almost tangible hovering on the tip of his tongue before he simply turned to the fire, leaving Bellanca with a confused look on her face.

Jocasta wiggled uncomfortably—and not only because of the awkward silence. "Well, don't stop there," she encouraged with a pointed look at Prometheus's velvet-cushioned chair. "This log is making my bottom numb."

Two seconds later, she had a massive throne of her own. She sat, although she would've preferred a cozy pink chair like Bellanca's. She liked when her feet touched the ground.

Likely out of sheer masculine stubbornness, neither Flynn nor Carver requested a chair to help them sit more comfortably around the campfire. Carver stayed on the bumpy log, and Flynn finished cooking and served them all in metal camp bowls before sitting cross-legged on the ground. No one asked for a table or fancier dishes. They never really knew what magic Prometheus was comfortable testing out after millennia of having his immense power as chained up as he was in Tartarus. It was clear from his daily choices that Prometheus didn't know, either. He mostly conjured inconsequential objects and changed his own size and power-bright aura to fit in better. He tended to err on the side of next to nothing rather than lose control. All in all, that seemed like a wise choice to Jocasta.

The last thing they needed was Prometheus getting showy and bringing down the wrath of Olympus. The charred scars across the continent proved that the twelve ruling Olympians never really turned a blind eye to Thalyria, especially Zeus with his destructive thunderbolts.

Prometheus was of Titan descent. His brethren were locked up, exiled, or—at best—continuing their existence in the Underworld. He shouldn't be free, let alone in Thalyria. She'd rather he act almost Hoi Polloi than accidentally draw the wrong type of attention. A god bolt could destroy them all—or worse, send them straight to Tartarus.

CHAPTER 15

Flynn still thought bypassing the border city of Kos was a good idea, despite the grumblings from Team Elpis. Who didn't want a hot bath, fresh fruit, and a real bed? He liked a few comforts just as much as anyone else. He also knew they could all live without. They were on a quest, not a touring jaunt. He had priorities, and the amenities of one of Fisa's principal cities weren't among them.

He scratched his jaw, his fingers rasping over what was quickly turning into a beard. Brown Horse's ears twitched. The animal might not be a born leader—Panotii too easily snatched that role from him—but his senses were nothing to scoff at. The smallest noise caught his attention, making his rider aware that something was afoot, even if it was just a deer picking its way through the forest. If a twig cracked within half a league of them, Brown Horse let him know. Best of all, the stallion's overactive senses didn't make him skittish. He moved along without fault, his shifting ears relaying information.

The team had spread out sometimes in the quiet countryside of eastern Tarva, but they'd hit the Continental Road on the far side of Kos and now traveled as a tight-knit group. The wide, busy roadway traversed the continent from east to west. Like any major metropolis, Kos drew in as many people as it spit out, and the constant flow of humanity and goods circulated like blood not only into the nearby townships and villages but into all of Thalyria.

Merchants and other travelers passed them by, some selling their products right from their wagons. Assorted fruits, fresh, crusty loaves of bread, and honey-glazed rolls fell into their laps in exchange for a few coins without them needing to go into the city after all. The morning's bounty helped eliminate lingering complaints about skipping Kos and made Flynn feel better about momentarily using the main road until they could veer southeast into the Arcadian Wilds.

"How long until we reach the road into the hinterlands?" he called to Prometheus. Since leaving Castle Thalyria, the Titan had discovered that the lay of the land unfolded before him in his mind's eye as he moved toward it. His ability to see the terrain before they got there had started out small but was gaining in power. Now that Prometheus was aware of it and honing the skill, he seemed able to project up to two days ahead and indicate routes that would also lead them to water. Flynn hadn't taken the map out of his saddlebag in three days and was letting Prometheus guide them.

"Not today," the Titan replied. "Midday tomorrow—unless we push the horses to their limit."

Flynn shook his head. He didn't plan on dawdling, but they'd avoid combining hard riding and heat when they could. They were heading into the afternoon, and the dry season hadn't been joking around when it decided to roll up its sleeves and punch the moisture from Thalyria earlier than ever.

No royal baby as promised. Rumors and questions snaking across the land. Great Roars popping up out of nowhere to scare people and animals. A drought in the making.

At least they had a plan now, if only for the baby part. They just had to survive it.

"Excellent. That means a bed and a bath after all." Bellanca tossed back a handful of grapes and spoke with her mouth full.

"This road is littered with inns. I get to choose later—something nice. Fit for a princess." She winked at Jocasta.

"Or two." Jo grinned at her.

"I'm deposed," Bellanca said gleefully. "The job's all yours, darling."

"And yet you still get to live in a castle," Carver remarked archly.

"But I don't have to deal with backstabbing nobles, slimy suitors, or even attend dinner if I don't want to." Bellanca spit a seed out and wiped grape juice from her chin. "I don't even have to act like I have manners. I knew burning my evil brother to a crisp was a good idea."

"It was pretty epic," Carver admitted.

"*Pretty epic?*" Bellanca cocked a brow at him. "I won the realm for you."

Carver shrugged, a smile lurking on the fringes of the surly expression that always seemed plastered to his face these days. "We had it under control."

Bellanca rolled her eyes. "Maybe Cerberus did."

"Did you ever act like you had manners?" Prometheus asked.

"Well, now who's being rude?" Bellanca said with a scowl.

"I…" Prometheus opened and closed his mouth like a fish out of water. He frowned.

"Oh, Pro…" Bellanca shook her head. "You're a god. Get it together."

"Would you rather he smite you?" Jo asked.

Bellanca gave Prometheus an assessing once-over. "Can you do that? That would be useful."

"I might have some smiting in me. Somewhere." Prometheus shifted in his saddle, looking uncomfortable at the idea.

"Perfect!" Bellanca beamed at Flynn, as though he had something to do with this ridiculous conversation. "Possible smiting this afternoon and a proper dinner and bed this evening. What could be better?"

From the look on Jo's face, she agreed wholeheartedly with Bellanca—at least about the dinner and bed part. Flynn hated to disappoint her, but the "something nice" the ex-princess was envisioning might need to land closer to mediocre.

"I didn't bring the royal coffers, you know, and we still have to buy a boat in Thassos." Providing his team with a night of luxury and comfort might make him feel like he'd accomplished something on this journey so far other than traveling in the right direction, but he'd never even seen the Fisan Ocean and had no idea how much a boat might cost. Flynn needed to keep as much gold as possible in his pocket.

"Oh, don't worry about that." Bellanca patted one of the pouches dangling from her belt. "I brought some of my mother's jewelry to help pay for the boat. She had a ring with three big fat rubies on it that she'd always turn around on her finger before she slapped me. I think I'll barter that away first. And then maybe the ruby-and-pearl-tipped hairpins she used to stab my sister with if poor Appoline produced a vision Mother didn't like. A set of six—solid gold. Should fetch a good price."

Flynn tried to hold in his shock at her words. It wasn't what she'd said—they all knew what the royal families they'd deposed had been like—but that she'd said them. Bellanca almost never mentioned the family she'd turned against when the hour of choice was upon her. He thought she just wanted to forget them, apart from shy, skittish, magic-deprived Lystra and the now-dead seer, Appoline. But forgetting them might not be as easy as Bellanca let on. She touched her cheekbone, as if the strike of her mother's rubies still pained more than her flesh, her eyes turning distant as she gazed down the long, straight road ahead of them.

"Then an inn it is! Your choice." Flynn's too-chipper voice earned him an odd look from Bellanca, but she dropped her hand and focused on a smattering of signposts, as though already searching for her fine lodgings for the night.

Brown Horse nickered and tossed his head. Panotii moved closer, bringing Jocasta's leg nearly against his. Flynn's abdomen tightened, and for several heartbeats, he held his breath. Would their calves touch? Would he get that warm, heady rush? Parts of him tingled at the mere thought of an innocent brush against her, and he had to resist the urge to close the gap between their boots. Their *boots*, for the gods' sakes. There must be something wrong with him. He was so constantly aware of the woman beside him that he didn't know how his senses had time for anything else.

A little shudder rippled over Brown Horse. Tossing his head again, the stallion jigged a few steps. Flynn softened his back and settled more firmly into the saddle, riding out the hiccup. Out of the corner of his eye, he saw Jo glance over curiously. His leg wasn't right next to hers anymore. Should he edge back toward her? He could make it look accidental. He was getting good at that.

His mount sniffed the air with chuffing breaths, finally drawing Flynn's full attention. The back of his neck prickled. If Brown Horse was antsy, he wanted to know why.

"Do you hear something?" he asked Jo.

She listened, then shook her head. "No. Do you?"

"No, but I think Brown Horse does." Shading his eyes from the sun, Flynn scanned the area, finding nothing but large villas and thriving farms and orchards on both sides of the busy thoroughfare. He didn't see any disturbances. Even the weather was pleasant, offering a bit of a breeze to offset the mounting heat. He pursed his lips. Maybe it was nothing, Brown Horse just reacting to the bustle and scents.

He subtly eased Brown Horse closer to Panotii. "I can't say I'm looking forward to the Arcadian Wilds. I'd rather stay on this road all the way to Exo Ipeiro and then take the coast road south." The huge port city at the edge of the continent might be a better place to buy a boat than in Thassos. More importantly, it was the safer route. "Cat said the Arcadian Wilds are the only known region south of the Ice Plains where magical creatures live. She said to watch out."

Jo touched her bloodstone necklace, swiping her thumb back and forth across the pendant. She'd told him she barely felt Persephone's magic anymore and had gotten used to the pulsing heat. "Maybe the magical creatures all fled along with the nymphs," she said.

"Maybe, but I wouldn't count on it." Flynn wasn't a pessimist about most things, but he'd also learned that blind optimism rarely did a man any good.

"What's the fun in the easy, well-traveled path?" Jo's chin notched up, and a hint of playful challenge made her blue eyes spark. Her smile said she was teasing—though not entirely. The woman had a wild streak that kept peeking out.

Everything in Flynn's chest tightened and expanded all at once. "Not having to fight for your life?"

Her laughter chimed between them, making his breath catch and Panotii's ears swivel back. "Let's not assume the worst. And we know next to nothing about these Great Roars happening all over the place. Maybe we'll find some clues to help us."

Flynn nodded, conceding the point, even though taking the potentially dangerous path through the hinterlands of Fisa didn't sit well with him. The nymphs might've taken off during the Great Roar, but what about bandits and other dangers? And if parts of the forest really were dead, what game and water would they find? It would take them at least three days to cross the Wilds, a secluded pocket of land they knew little about.

Flynn began paying attention to the merchants crossing their path again. He'd stock up on food supplies before they left the main road in case the Arcadian Wilds were as inhospitable as he imagined.

He was about to flag down a woman leading a vegetable-laden donkey—a hearty soup would make for a nice change of pace—when Brown Horse let out a nervous snort. Frowning, he reached down and stroked the stallion's neck. "What is it, boy?"

Brown Horse pranced sideways. Panotii followed, trying to herd him around to face west. Flynn did a full circle to face east again, his heart starting to hammer in his chest.

"Flynn?" Jo tightened her grip on her reins as Panotii gathered himself beneath her, bumping into them again. Her horse called out a warning whinny, stopping Team Elpis in its tracks.

Both Carver's and Bellanca's heads whipped around, identical frowns pulling at their mouths.

"What is it?" called Carver.

Prometheus peered down the road, his magic-charged eyes narrowing to slits. "Something's wrong. There's a…force. I'm not familiar with it."

Flynn's eyes met Jo's. She swallowed and turned to the Titan. "A malevolent force?" she asked.

Prometheus didn't answer. He didn't need to. The air abruptly changed, biting with menace. The sky darkened without there being a cloud in sight, and the breeze that was warm just moments before suddenly carried a sharp, icy scent.

A warning chill burst up Flynn's spine. Something was coming all right, and they were in the most open, vulnerable spot since setting out on this journey. With *dozens* of people around.

"Get off the road! Get behind us! Go!" He waved the woman, her donkey, and other nearby travelers off the road. A peddler was among them. "Use the wagon for cover. Stay behind it. Stay low!"

People shouted out to their companions and tugged on their animals, pulling on children and livestock that instinctively dug in their heels. From in front and behind, frightened travelers converged on them, scrambling over the wide drainage ditch and onto the grass beyond. More raced their way, jostling whoever was in their path. Panicked families struggled to stay together. An elderly man lost his walking stick and tottered, alone.

Flynn galloped out, scooped him up with one arm, and raced him to the wagon, dropping him off behind one high, red-painted wheel. The man gripped the spokes with gnarled, arthritic fingers, his rheumy eyes peeking through.

"There's magic coming this way." Bellanca circled, unable to keep her restless mount still. Just as antsy, she craned her neck, her searching gaze whipping back and forth across the darkening landscape. "Something old. Something powerful."

Something angry, Flynn wanted to add, his blood turning cold.

He took in his team with a glance, people he cared about. No, more than that. Bellanca and Prometheus had carved out places in his heart, when he'd sworn to himself that no one new would get in. Carver was a brother in all the ways that counted. And then there was Jocasta. *Care* was a weak, insipid word.

Poison fear hit his bloodstream, a toxic and paralyzing mix that had already dictated some of the biggest decisions of his life. A team was a family, and he was responsible for this one. He wasn't any good at keeping a family alive, even when he wasn't in charge. Why would this be any different?

Bellanca's horse chopped at the cobbles, ratcheting up

Flynn's anxiety with every ringing step. An enemy he couldn't see? Unknown magic? Those were a Hoi Polloi soldier's worst nightmares. No wonder the cold fist of panic gripped his chest.

Jo shivered beside him, clutching her reins in white-knuckled fists. Panotii was the steadiest of them all, and even his big liquid-brown eyes started to roll wildly in his head. "It's like someone moved aside a giant boulder and opened a cavern that hasn't seen light or heat in years." Visible breath whispered from Jo's lips, quickly vanishing as if any human warmth sought to flee the coming beast.

Flynn nodded, wholeheartedly agreeing. Stale air slapped his eyes and lungs, tasting like the deepest depths of a dungeon holding a thousand years' worth of must and bones. The cold seeped into him, penetrating straight to the marrow while the open road mocked him, as did the flat farmland around. He had no idea what was coming. He only knew that a fight was inevitable. There was no doubt in his mind.

"Jocasta!" Carver's sharp call rose above the general cacophony. "Get behind the wagon!"

She glanced over her shoulder. Carver frantically waved at her from his position beside the peddler's home. She ignored him and turned back around.

"With me." Flynn signaled to Jo, even though his gut twisted at the idea of her out in the open. It seemed important to keep her close. Better than pushing her away.

She nudged Panotii and joined him as he cajoled Brown Horse forward to form a first line of defense with Jocasta beside him. Bellanca got her horse under control and took up position in front of the cowering travelers while Carver and Prometheus continued to frantically round up more people, herding them into a defensible group. Those who remained in sight but out of reach, some in front and some behind, all ran west. Whatever was coming bore down from the east, and man or animal, they felt it and fled.

Flynn reconsidered telling Jo to take shelter with the others but then bit his tongue. She wouldn't. She would fight. Against what, he didn't know. Every quick, hard beat of his heart told him it was something dreadful. This was Jo, though—a woman who'd never run from anything. She'd grown up holding her own in one of the most determined and ambitious families in Thalyria. Who was he kidding if he thought she would hide?

Behind them, another wagon joined the barricade. A goat bleated, tied tight to its stocky owner and straining to break loose. The vegetable woman's donkey kicked out and ran, the baskets on its back flopping like wicker wings about to break off. She popped out from behind the refuge and chased after it, shouting as the terrified ass flat-out galloped in the direction of Kos.

Just then, a ghastly wind barreled down the road, ripping past him and Jo first. It slammed into the others with enough force to snatch the gasps right from their mouths. The woman's hat tumbled after her donkey, a splash of color zigzagging away so fast it disappeared in a blink. She stopped dead in her tracks and turned back to them, her skirts snapping around her legs and her face frozen in dread.

With a growled curse, Carver galloped out and grabbed her, dropping her behind the wagons again just as the ground shook. A rumble filled the air. Dust kicked up ahead of them as animals stampeded down the road—horses, pack beasts, dogs, livestock. People, too, desperately fleeing an unknown and unseen force. Some dove into the ditch to avoid the unstoppable onslaught. Others lost their footing and went down, trampled under the wild rush.

"Good gods," Flynn murmured. "Off the road! Now!"

Jocasta obeyed instantly, digging her heels into Panotii's sides. They leaped right just as he and Brown Horse shied left, leaving them on opposite sides of the road.

"Jo!" Flynn caught her frightened stare, his heart in his throat.

"Flynn!" She looked ready to bolt back across the cobbles, and Flynn nearly had a heart attack right there.

"Stay where you are!" he yelled just as the stampede arrived, led by a crazed, riderless horse. Animals pounded past them, making Brown Horse shudder and twitch. The last of the human stragglers dove behind the barricade, except for one unlucky man who wasn't fast enough. A huge bull veered into him and gored him in the stomach, tossing him backward into the chaotic herd to be crushed.

"It's the Great Roar," Jo shouted across the road to him. "It's coming. Can you hear it?"

Flynn nodded. The terrible sound built and built, rolling over the land and crashing into them, a huge, screaming, icy wave. His lungs froze tight, and he instantly understood all those flocks, herds, nymphs, and whatever else that had bolted in abject fear. He wanted to gather his team and do the same, and only years of fighting villains and monsters kept him resolutely in place.

Across from him, Jo's face distilled into a mask of terror, and he flinched from the inside out.

"Jo!" Her head snapped around, her panic-filled eyes landing on him with the force of a house that came crashing down on a man because he hadn't shored up the foundation. Terrified shouts rang out, calling out to Team Elpis for answers, for reassurance, for help. He focused on Jo instead. "It's just a noise. It can't touch you." Gods, he hoped that was true. The fury and menace felt real enough.

She blinked at him, then slowly nodded, her expression regaining that ever-intrepid look. Worry still gripped Flynn's chest. This stampede wasn't in a remote area like the others. It was coming straight down the busiest road in Thalyria. Why? What changed?

He turned, and his eyes found Prometheus's. The Titan shrugged. Flynn swung his gaze to Bellanca. The Magoi shook her head.

A nervous swallow scraped down Flynn's throat. Then he choked when a little girl with orange-red hair shot out from behind the barricade to chase her dog, the two of them dashing into the road.

"No!" The raw scream tore from his throat. For a petrifying second, he thought it was one of the twins—Stella, with her chipped front tooth and freckled nose.

But that was madness. His sisters were dead. Bright hair, pretty little smock dresses, and favorite dollies six feet under the olive trees, along with the rest of them.

His body didn't remember the truth as fast as his brain, and bile slammed up his throat. Darkness crowded the edges of his vision as he wheeled Brown Horse around. He had to reach her, save her. His entire dead family seemed to count on it.

From across the road, Jo and Panotii raced out onto the cobbles first, dodging a Great-Roar-fevered horse. Pure panic erupted inside him, volcanic heat when everything else went cold.

"Jo!" Flynn pulled up short. He didn't want to drive the herd *into* her. The crazed stampede was already dangerous enough.

"Go! Go!" she cried to Panotii, grabbing a handful of mane and stretching her other hand toward the child. Flynn's heart stopped dead. His stomach in knots, he watched as horse and rider darted between frenzied bulls and runaway livestock. Jo snatched the girl out of the road by her shirt collar, hauling the screaming child across her lap just as a goat ran into Panotii and nearly sent him tumbling. The chestnut recovered his footing, jumped a zigzagging sheep, and skidded to a halt behind the peddler's wagon.

Flynn wheezed in a breath. "Gods help me," he murmured. It was the first time he'd truly meant a prayer since Old Hector's death.

The girl's petrified parents flapped their arms and called out. Jo handed the child to them before circling around the back of the wagons and joining him again. She drew her bow and nocked an arrow.

Flynn did his best to swallow his pounding heart. "That was brave." *Great Zeus.* His voice almost shook.

"I was terrified," she said. "The dog's gone. Run away with the rest."

Their eyes met, and it was all he could do to not reach out and haul her across his lap. He drew his sword instead.

The tail end of the stampede approached. Dust clouded the air. The horrible roar continued, one long, loud, hair-raising shout. Whoever—or whatever—was making the awful noise couldn't need to breathe like a regular human. They'd have keeled over from lack of air by now.

Flynn's pulse drummed to the heavy rhythm of panic around him. Hooves beat the ground. It was mayhem. Total, utter, deafening chaos. His spine tingled as the Great Roar built, and pandemonium reached a terrible crescendo. Fainting people. Bucking horses. A sky the color of dread.

Ears aching from the pressure, he moved closer to Jo. She was pain, but she was also the remedy sometimes, and right now, he needed her by his side. Maybe she needed him, too. Once upon a time, she'd counted on him for a lot of things. And she'd been the center of his life when he'd been too stupid to realize it.

But now she was again, wasn't she? And he hadn't even seen it happen.

Reaching her unscrewed one of the bolts locking down Flynn's lungs. Brown Horse gained confidence next to Panotii, more manageable once he brushed up against his friend.

The roar suddenly blew past them, the enraged noise ending as abruptly as it began. The stampede clattered off, losing momentum, the wind died, and the chill melted away, leaving a silence that thumped between Flynn's ears. He shifted uneasily.

Jo glanced at him in question, her mouth pulling down as she rode out an edgy little hop from Panotii.

He shook his head. He didn't think it was over.

Her frown deepened. He wanted to comfort her, but an empty, silent farmhouse flashed in his mind with stinging-nettle heat, its loneliness clinging like burrs to his heart.

Suddenly, an earsplitting shriek rent the air. Flynn's pulse took off at a gallop. He grimaced against the piercing sound.

Fear drained all the color from Jo's face. "Flynn?" They both searched for the source of the sound. "Good gods, what *is* that?" The cry seemed to come from above.

"I don't know." The new noise was dreadful. Grim. Apocalyptic.

A second ghastly shriek joined the first, then a third, all of them layering one on top of the other in an infernal chorus.

Flynn's skin puckered into goose bumps as Brown Horse shuddered beneath him. He didn't know what this was, but *here* was the fight. The Great Roar was just the prelude.

The gray sky in front of them split open with a flash of lightning and a crack of thunder. The bright-hot noise rolled out, driving away the unnatural storm color and bringing back blue sky and sunshine. The sudden brightness hit Flynn like a spike in the eye. He squinted up through lowered lashes. *What in the Underworld?*

Dots in the sky—moving fast and growing bigger. As if loosed from the hand of a god, three winged females dropped from the heavens. Boar tusks. Claws. Hair made of living snakes. Golden masks covering their terrible visages.

"No…" Flynn's gut sank like a stone. There were monsters you could fight. And then there were the Gorgons.

CHAPTER 16

Jocasta stared in horror at the creatures above them. She sucked in a breath that stuck in her throat. "Oh my gods, Flynn. That's Medusa."

"And her sisters." Beside her, Flynn was the only thing keeping her backbone from crumbling and the scream shoved down her throat. His perpetually even tone reassured her for once instead of annoying her. If he'd screamed, "And her sisters!" she might've fled in terror—which was exactly what every sensible bone in her body railed at her to do.

She blinked hard to make sure this wasn't a nightmare. She had those now, ever since the Agon Games. Before, she never did.

Stheno. Euryale. Medusa. Ancient. Deadly. Vicious. A second blink didn't help. The black-winged Gorgons still loomed above them, crows in the sky, omens of death.

Jocasta gulped down a mouthful of fear and steadied her bow and arrow. She wasn't prone to hallucinations, and there was no reason for them to start now—sadly—which meant they had to deal with this.

"Did any of the other Great Roars make the Gorgons appear?" She hadn't heard about any stone statues left in the wakes of those horrific shouts.

Flynn shook his head.

"Just us then?" Did that terror-laced wobble come from *her* mouth?

"As far as I know. Put me in charge and look what happens. Lucky us." The cynicism in that tacked-on sentiment made Jocasta cut the man next to her a sharp look. Did Flynn believe *he* brought bad luck?

"Why is this time different?" she asked. "Aren't panic, stampedes, fear, and death already enough?"

Flynn didn't answer, his mouth pressing into a tight, tense seam as he peered up. The creatures sank lower, their huge wings beating the air with a percussive thump that jolted against Jocasta's heart. Her hands rattled, and her arrow slid out of place. She righted it, swallowing hard. Heroes didn't flee. They fought. And protected the innocent.

She tore her gaze from the dreadful sisters and looked behind her at the dozens of people cowering behind the two wagons, their makeshift barricade shifting as the harnessed donkeys threw their weight around and tried to escape. Her heart banged in her chest. Animal instinct lashed at her to run. The new menace terrified everyone—those who knew what approached and those who didn't. All except for one. The old man who nearly got trampled earlier stared at her as though he could see straight through her, his expression blank.

Jocasta lifted her eyes to look past him. "Blindfold yourselves! And each other!" Her clipped tone got everyone's attention. "Hurry now! And stay behind the wagons. Whatever you do, don't come out and *don't* look!"

Children started to cry. So did some adults. The old man just stood there as if he didn't have a pulse.

"What she said. Do it! Now!" Flynn's firm support made her chest clench so tight it hurt.

Jocasta pivoted back around without waiting to see if anyone obeyed. No one expected merchants, travelers, and families to fight, but they'd damn well better hide their eyes if they didn't want to turn into stone statues lining the ditch on the road to Kos.

The question now was how to protect *themselves* from this.

The Gorgons swooped lower and hovered, pure, dark menace in the sky. Jocasta glanced over her shoulder at Carver. He gave her a look that rolled *I love you* and *Don't make me kill you* into one hard glower. Oddly, Bellanca gave her much the same look.

Swallowing, Jocasta turned back around. In her peripheral vision, Prometheus shifted nervously, muttering a curse.

"What are they waiting for? What do they want?" she murmured to Flynn. Not knowing what the Gorgons were after triple knotted her intestines.

Urging Brown Horse even closer to her, Flynn asked, "What do we know about the Gorgons?" He spoke fast and low, for her ears only. Their legs brushed, his solid thigh a hot, hard jolt of muscle against her fear-locked body.

What do we know about the Gorgons? "Sisters," she said. Shock had rattled her, but knowledge was power, and Jocasta never forgot a thing. Tell her a story, and it stuck in her mind like a fly in honey. "Perpetually furious. Their likenesses are put on protective talismans to strike fear into enemy hearts."

Was Team Elpis the enemy for some reason? Because the hideous winged creatures were doing an excellent job of scaring her to death.

Flynn's grunt acknowledged her words as he tracked the Gorgons with narrowed eyes. They shrieked again, yanking a flinch from him and catapulting her hammering heart straight into her esophagus.

"So not inherently bad?" he asked.

Jocasta's eyes flicked to his, the split-second connection shoring her up before they both turned back to the creatures. "Maybe not. But they've been pushed in that direction."

He nodded. Flynn had never been particularly interested in history, Thalyrian, Olympian, or otherwise, but the way his marble-cut jaw sharpened with tension suggested he knew how and why the sisters became monsters.

The dark-winged females dropped closer, tattered skirts flapping, voices raised in fury, masks glinting in the sun. There were no eyeholes in the solid-gold half masks. Lifeless metal instead of deadly hypnotic gazes stared down at them.

Hope flickered inside her. "If they were inherently bad, they wouldn't care who they turned to stone." Unfortunately, good logic didn't lessen her terror.

Flynn frowned. "Do you think they can be reasoned with?"

"Maybe. They haven't attacked yet. It depends on why they're here." What she knew about the Gorgons came from listening to that bard who always told Chiron's thrilling—and chilling—stories at harvest festivals. In Attica, they thought Medusa was dead, beheaded. She wasn't, and the "hero" Perseus was a liar. Unlike her sisters, Medusa was a two-headed beast, and he only took one snake-topped appendage. Stheno and Euryale brought their injured sister to Thalyria to recover and escape Perseus's continued assaults at the secret behest of his sister, Athena. "There must be a reason they dropped from the sky right here, right now, in front of us."

"I've never heard of them leaving the Ice Plains before." Flynn seemed unable to shift his focus from the blunt stump rising from the torso of the middle Gorgon. It was easy to tell which was Medusa. She'd been cursed worse than her sisters— and turned into the bigger prize for the monster slayer who'd persecuted them.

"Me either." As far as Jocasta knew, the sisters had never crossed below the natural border of the northern lakes, staying deep inside the domain of gods, monsters, and magical creatures.

Few humans ventured into the frozen north, and tales from survivors of direct encounters with the Gorgons were so rare she could count the ones she'd heard on two fingers.

Two.

She kept that information to herself.

Behind them, Carver, Bellanca, and Prometheus murmured in hushed tones with hard edges. *Hair of venomous snakes. Wings. Fast. Strong. Angry. Spiteful. Don't make eye contact, or you'll turn to stone.* Their litany of traits snuck forward and gripped the back of Jocasta's neck, icing her to the bone.

She shivered. As terrifying as those things were, Gorgon basics didn't help them. Team Elpis needed more. They needed a way to potentially fight what they couldn't look at directly. And they needed a *why*. Why here? Why them? Why now?

Medusa reached up and yanked a snake from her head. Jocasta's mind blanked in fear when the writhing reptile turned into a long, hard spear in the Gorgon's hand. Medusa hurled the weapon, fangs first, venom dripping. Jocasta's heart barely had time to strike a savage beat against her ribs before the deadly green spike stuck in the ground in front of them. It split a large paving cobble straight down the middle and rose like a flag, marking the battlefield.

Jocasta stared at the clear-cut warning, her pulse pounding. The air still sang with the metallic ring of impact. The team cursed and murmured. Panotii—not a dumb animal—backed up a few steps. Brown Horse inevitably followed. She met Flynn's eyes. His were ink splats in a pale face. She doubted she looked different.

"She who rules will crumble." Medusa boomed the darkly prophetic words like thunder. Their echo reverberated inside Jocasta's chest with tight, thorny resonance.

"The new reign falls like sand through an hourglass."

Stheno—Jocasta was certain. The oldest and most brutal of the Gorgon sisters had red snakes for hair instead of green ones, blood-red tusks, gold-tipped claws filed into needle-sharp points, and viciously curved talons slicing through her sandals. A belt made of circling crimson-and-black serpents spun around her narrow waist, cinching, sliding, pulsing.

Stheno loosed one of the belt serpents, and it fell to the ground with a dull flop before slithering across the roadway just behind the snake spear. It left a thin, smoldering crater in the cobbles—a line of demarcation.

Jocasta shuddered. A bitter-sharp odor stung her nostrils. Cooked scales. Melted stone. One step past that serpentine line, and they'd be at war with the Gorgons.

"They're talking about Cat," she whispered out of the corner of her mouth. "About Elpis—failing."

Flynn nodded, the furrow between his brows so deep it rivaled the gnarled old bark of his olive trees back home in the village.

"Cat doesn't fail," Carver said. He had faith, flat and resolute. Prometheus concurred.

Bellanca made a cynical sound, and for once, Jocasta had to agree with her. No one was infallible. They'd all seen Cat face down monsters and conquer, but what happened when she became her own monster? Eternity without the people she loved or the family she'd dreamed of? Robbed of the future she fought so hard for? There were some bottomless abysses even the strongest people didn't climb their way out of.

"Her time is almost finished. Their work will be undone. The fall of undying Elpis heralds the Olympianomachy to come!" As if sealing a prophesy, the final sister, Euryale, let out a giant shout that crumbled the cobbles beneath her to sand.

Jocasta gasped. The horses stamped and whined. Brown

Horse reared, and for a few fractured heartbeats, chaos exploded on the road again. In a feat of horsemanship, Carver leaped up next to her on her open side, leaving Bellanca and Prometheus as their second line. Her brother flashed her a look rife with conflict. He didn't want her here.

She squared her shoulders. Too late. Too bad. She focused ahead again.

Gorgons overhead. Destruction in front. More snakes on the ground, slithering out of shattered stone and cobbles as if called into existence by their mistresses above. Panotii snorted, his nostrils flaring. He still settled down faster than the other horses, helping to calm Jocasta's nerves. Her gaze flicked over the broken road. Upright spear. Burned line. Crushed stone. The boundary couldn't be clearer. It screamed *Stop here!* in a silent voice as deafening as the Great Roar.

"They're here to thwart Team Elpis." Wide-eyed, she looked at Flynn. "They've come to stop our quest."

Flynn cursed. "Olympianomachy?"

"War," Prometheus intoned darkly from behind.

"Like the Titanomachy?" Bellanca asked. "When the Olympians overthrew the Titans?"

Jocasta glanced over her shoulder in time to see the Titan nod. Prometheus should know. He'd lived through it.

Prometheus looked northeast toward Mount Olympus, his brow heavy with a scowl. "This time, they battle each other. It looks like civil war."

Carver hissed in a breath. Fury lit his eyes. "So they've finally decided to backstab each other into an all-out power grab but the daggers go through Griffin and Cat first?"

"Who wants to steal the rule of Olympus from Zeus?" Jocasta asked.

Bellanca huffed. "Everyone. And their goat."

Jocasta threw the other woman a sour look.

The Gorgons suddenly shrieked in unison. More stone crumbled. Snakes slithered from the cracks. Her ears aching, Jocasta's stomach turned over in disgust. Panotii stamped down hard, crushing a serpent under his hoof. She shuddered. One down, about a hundred to go. They needed Cerberus. Cerberus loved snakes.

Voices layered and deep, the sisters spoke as one, "Retreat now and return to your home. Cross the line and be turned to stone!"

Goose bumps shivered down Jocasta's arms.

"I *hate* threats," Bellanca growled. She sliced her head to the side, probably trying to dislodge the resonance lingering in the air like the jarring music of an untuned harp. "And the Gorgons hate the Olympians. Why are they even taking sides?"

"Vengeance." A sudden burst of clarity snapped Jocasta's thoughts into place. "They want revenge on the gods who wronged them. They're out to get Poseidon and Athena." Poseidon, who'd staunchly supported Cat.

Flynn scraped a hand down his auburn scruff. He swiveled his head, and their gazes collided, a new spike of worry darkening his brown eyes to almost black. "And if the enemy of my enemy is my friend, then..."

"The friend of my enemy is my enemy." A sinking feeling dropped straight through her. "Poseidon gifted Cat with magic. He stood by her, saved her, protected her. Pushed her toward the throne, pushed her toward Griffin."

A muscle ticked near Flynn's jaw. "And Athena?"

Jocasta thought back to what she knew. "She hasn't been *inactive* in bringing Thalyria its new Alpha couple. And she's always been Griffin's favorite."

"The Gorgons want Poseidon and Athena to suffer." Bellanca appeared convinced already. "Now, what do we do about it?"

Everyone looked at Jocasta. Fine, it was her quest, but that didn't mean she had all the answers.

Her anxious gaze skipped back and forth between Team Elpis and the Gorgons. She wouldn't say it aloud—she wasn't that stupid—but frankly, Poseidon and Athena *did* deserve to suffer for what they'd done to the sisters. But not at the expense of Cat, Griffin, and their baby. None of them had anything to do with what happened in Attica epochs ago. Why should her family suffer for it? Why should all of Thalyria?

Besides, abandoning their mission wasn't an option. Jocasta would rather not return to the castle at all than return empty-handed.

"We're not your enemy," she called out. Helping her family at all costs might be her primary reason for living, but she was a long way from having a death wish. Death by Gorgon seemed especially fiendish. "Destabilizing Thalyria only punishes people—humans—who never wronged you."

The Gorgons stared down with blank metal eyes, flat disks in golden masks, snakes curling up the sides.

In the face of their stony silence, Jocasta mentally dove back into the harvest-festival bard's detailed stories from ancient Attica, looking for a way to reason with the equally ancient females. The tragic tale of Medusa and her sisters started before the chapter most people knew about. They hadn't always been winged Gorgons with death eyes, snake hair, and shrieks that crumbled stone. Humans feared the monsters the sisters became rather than the gods who made them that way. Poseidon. Athena. The first grievously mistreated Medusa in Athena's own house. The second transformed the beautiful daughters of primordial sea deities into hideous monsters for daring to protest.

Rape. Indifference. Those were the legacy of beings who were accountable to no one. Jocasta's nostrils flared on a fury-tight breath. She had words to describe the Olympians, and most of them weren't flattering, especially for the males. They rarely took no for an answer.

In a show of good faith, Jocasta slung her bow over her shoulder and dropped her arrow back into its quiver. With a little effort on both sides, they could resolve this terrifying standoff without aggression.

Flynn gave her a sidelong glance. His hand tightened on his sword. "Stopping us hurts Cat. Hurting Cat thwarts what several gods worked toward for years, including Poseidon."

Beside her, Carver muttered a curse. "As if this quest wasn't already enough of a long shot."

Ignoring what her brother probably hadn't meant as a barb, Jocasta said, "The Olympians aren't our friends, and these creatures aren't our enemies. Several prominent gods and goddesses might've helped Cat gain the throne in Thalyria, but that doesn't make them our permanent allies." Or make them any less violent, cruel, selfish, and scheming. They shook things up when they got bored. "Cat was a pawn in their games, just like Medusa. We have no quarrel with the Gorgons."

"How do you figure?" Prometheus's question rumbled forward, quiet with skepticism.

"Cat and Griffin need those prominent gods more than ever right now, but they've moved on to their next amusement. They didn't even care that Cat stole you from Tartarus." She scoffed, caustic. "Only Ares hasn't disappeared, but he's always been on the outs with the other Olympians. They've hated him since the beginning."

"Exactly. And where's Persephone?" Bellanca edged her mount closer. "She claims to love Cat, but we haven't heard a peep from her or Hades since she identified the curse."

Jocasta was so used to fighting for every idea she set forth that receiving instant backing made emotion tighten her throat. She glanced at the redhead, grateful for the support.

"Decide!" The Gorgons suddenly flew straight at them. Her pulse surging, Jocasta flattened herself against Panotii's neck. He reared up, kicking out. She clamped her legs around him, grabbed a handful of mane, and held on. Whip fast, the Gorgons veered off at the last second and zigzagged in crazed patterns above their heads. They cawed and shrieked. The road beneath them cracked. People screamed behind the barricade. Children wailed, their frightened sobs piercing Jocasta's heart.

"Get away from them!" she yelled, popping up and flapping her arms.

The Gorgons turned in unison, their focus slamming into her with the force of a physical blow. How did they see? Their masks looked solid. Maybe tiny pinprick holes in the gold. Maybe magic she couldn't conceive of. Maybe senses honed by eons of being hunted and abhorred.

"Jo…" Warning vibrated in Flynn's tone. She snapped her mouth shut, fear freezing over the second shout on her tongue.

The Gorgons dove. They arrowed straight at her with sharp cries, claws bared. She ducked just as Flynn yanked her onto his lap. The Gorgons slammed into Panotii, knocking him flat. He skidded across the broken cobbles, squealing in anguish.

"No!" Jocasta tried to fly off Flynn, but he snatched her back. Her head collided with his jaw, making them both gasp. Snakes converged on Panotii. Bigger serpents slithered over smaller ones, racing toward easy prey. "Panotii!" The horse lifted his head, his sides heaving. He tried to clamber to his feet, but his hooves scrabbled over the sharp and shattered stones. "Get up! You can do it!" A monstrous pair of snakes poised to strike Panotii's exposed belly. Jocasta's eyes flared. Panic beat in her chest.

Fire suddenly shot past her shoulder. Bellanca bombarded the road with exploding fireballs, driving back the snakes. They advanced. She volleyed. Panotii finally scrambled upright, his dazed eyes reflecting the red-hot blaze. Sizzling serpents filled the roadway in front of him. He turned unsteadily, revealing deep gashes and bloody claw marks all over his frame.

"Oh gods." Jocasta's heart ached. "Come!" she called. Panotii's ears twitched.

"He'll be fine," Flynn murmured, his chin sliding over her hair as he watched the Gorgons circle overhead. "If they'd wanted to kill him, they would have."

She gripped the rock-solid arm around her waist. "So what are they doing?"

"My guess? A final warning."

Panotii shook himself out and took a steadier step. He stomped on a snake and kicked it across the line of demarcation. He threatened another with a cutting hoof, making it abruptly veer off.

Pride burst inside Jocasta. That was some horse.

She twisted in Flynn's lap, frantically telling him, "I know the problem, but I don't have a solution."

"Then we fight." Grim determination hardened the lines of his face. Those three words meant he wouldn't back down, that he believed in their quest—believed in *her* somehow.

"We fight." She nodded, fear twisting her gut. "Don't look in their eyes. Promise you won't."

His grip tightened around her waist. "I'll protect you with my life."

That wasn't an answer. Her stomach dropped.

The creatures suddenly shrieked again and landed with an explosion of stone dust on Team Elpis's side of the road. As one, they strode forward, cold with purpose.

The way they advanced made Jocasta's hair stand on end. Or maybe it was the hissing snakes writhing all around their heads, hundreds of sharp, tiny fangs dripping venom. She swallowed hard. "I think our time is up."

"I think we never had our time," Flynn murmured.

His soft words seared a hole in her chest as she slipped from his lap. She landed on a snake head with a satisfying crunch that made her want to shatter bones instead of healing them. Grinding the ball of her foot down with a decisive twist, she quickly scanned the ruined roadway for her fallen bow and picked it up, telling herself this was no different than hunting rabbits. Draw. Shoot. Kill.

Except the sisters were immortal.

She slung her bow across her shoulder. Immortal didn't mean unkillable. It just meant that severing their heads from their bodies was the only thing that worked.

She drew her sword instead, even though the double-edged blade wasn't her preferred weapon. Hands not quite steady, she pulled out a dagger as well and backed toward the barricade to stand between Bellanca and Prometheus.

Jocasta's short, sharp sword glinted in front of her. Leaf-shaped blade. Straight cross guard. Hack. Slash. Stab. She could do that.

"Panotii!" Her quiet shout made the chestnut swing his head around. She didn't want him out in the open like that. He was too vulnerable there. "Come! Behind us!"

Panotii trotted toward the wagons and stopped in front of the old man, snorting a breath at him. Unlike the other travelers, he hadn't protected his eyes from the threat of the Gorgons.

"Blindfold yourself!" Jocasta hissed in his direction. Had no one helped him? "Use this." She handed him a handkerchief from her pocket, hoping it was long enough.

He ignored her and lifted a hand to Panotii's neck, stroking him with knobbly fingers. Eyes wide open, he peered over Panotii's back.

Fine. Suit yourself. Jocasta pocketed her handkerchief and turned back around.

"You cannot fight us." A shriek rent the air—Medusa's shrill cry. "Your choice. Your doom." She reached for her mask. Her sisters followed her lead without question.

"Don't look!" Flynn shouted.

Jocasta dropped her eyes, keeping her sword up. She shook with fear. "Prometheus! Can you conjure masks to distort our vision?"

The Titan grunted. A second later, a clear helmet covered her entire head, and her hot, trembling breath bounced back at her. Jocasta blinked, trying to focus. Everything looked bent, puffed up, and distorted. The helmet sloshed when she turned her head.

A smile curved her lips—wholly premature, but she didn't care. Raising a flinty gaze to the unmasked Gorgons, her vision altered by rounded glass and a sheet of water, she whispered, "I see you." And they were a dreadful sight.

Anger sparked in three sets of deadly, swirling eyes.

Beside her, Prometheus dismounted. Fishbowl-helmeted like the rest of them, he grew three feet in height and two in width, ripping his pants and tunic. "*You* cannot fight us," he ground out, a long, sharp blade appearing in one massive hand with a bright pop. "Your choice. Your doom."

Jocasta's heart thundered. The rest of Team Elpis dismounted, urging their horses toward Panotii and the protection of the barricade. The five of them formed a line, all shielded by Prometheus's helmets, the curved bowls and layer of water altering their vision enough to thwart the Gorgons' deadly stares.

The sisters shrieked in unison. Birds dropped from the sky. Insects too. Cicadas. Bees. Larks and sparrows. The horrifying noise killed anything smaller than Jocasta's fist, and death fell like hailstones, battering them.

The Gorgons attacked in a burst of violence. Swords clashed against claws, knives on fangs. Everything blurred, and Jocasta reacted without thinking. *Guard up. Keep moving. Block. Strike!* She punctured Euryale's wing, and the Gorgon swung on her, hissing in pain and punching out with a metal-encased fist. Jocasta deflected at the last second, the hit reverberating up her arm and sending her reeling. Flynn jumped in front of her, blocking Euryale's killing blow with the battle-ax he heaved between them. He bellowed. The monster bellowed back, and savagery charged the battlefield.

Snakes slithered at them in relentless droves. Bellanca scorched the roadway. Prometheus protected her as she drove back the serpents, his face gray, sweat sheening his forehead. Stheno attacked from the sky, hurling down vipers. She aimed for Prometheus. A snake bounced off his helmet. He grabbed another serpent out of midair by the tail and whipped it back at Stheno. Another struck Bellanca from above, its jaws opening on her shoulder. She shrieked and went up in flames from feet to hairline. The scorched serpent disintegrated, and she batted snake ash from her shoulder.

Carver jumped in front of Bellanca and went berserk on the nearest Gorgon. Jocasta barely saw his sword move, the blade so fast her eyes couldn't track it. He drove Medusa back until she took flight and spiraled skyward to join Stheno with a rage-thick howl.

Euryale hammered at Flynn. Her screams crumbled the ground between them, the uneven footing throwing him off-balance. He dropped and rolled under a swiping talon, popping up on the other side of her, blades ready. She swung around to face him, her hypnotic eyes spitting deadly magic and her wings a terrible shadow. Flynn lunged, low and fast, plunging the dagger in his left hand into her side before she knew what hit her. He tore the blade upward through her middle, opening her from waist to sternum.

The Gorgon bayed a crazed animal sound like nothing Jocasta had ever heard in her life. Primal. Shattering. Gut-shriveling and wrathful. The female-turned-monster focused on Flynn like she wanted to pluck his bones from his body one by one and suck them clean while he was still living.

Jocasta yelled and flung her dagger. It glanced off Euryale's shoulder, but the Gorgon whipped around, snarling. Flynn swung his ax the second he saw the opening. Blood splattered Jocasta's feet, and Euryale's head hit the ground, snakes still writhing and hissing.

She stared in shock. They'd killed her. They'd killed Euryale.

With the tip of her boot, she flipped the head over so that the still-lethal eyes stared downward.

Flynn suddenly spun her around, his arm around her middle as he scooted sideways. A hard snake spear stuck in the ground where she'd just stood. She glanced up, her heart in her throat. Medusa glared down at them.

The youngest sister threw another spear. Then another. Jocasta and Flynn dodged, hopping over choppy ground and blackened snake carcasses. Carver raced over to help them. He grabbed a spear and heaved it at Medusa. She swooped sideways, wings beating the air. Carver plucked the spears from the ground one by one and hurled them back at the Gorgon.

Stheno saw her dead sister on the ground and let out a scream of heartbroken fury. She unleashed two long serpents from her belt and wielded them like whips against Flynn and Jocasta.

The snakes unfurled like striking cobras. Fangs cracked against Jocasta's helmet. She flinched. A fissure formed in the glass shell, and water splashed her shoulders. She stumbled back, bumping into the barricade. Flynn severed the head from one snake whip. The other chased him toward Prometheus. Bellanca shot flames into the sky. Stheno's robes caught fire and the barrage stopped. Medusa screeched and raced to help her sister.

The old man Jocasta stood in front of again tapped her leaking helmet from behind. She turned, her eyes enormous and her chest heaving.

He tipped his head toward the Gorgons. "They can't look directly at each other, either."

Jocasta took half a second to understand him. Then she raced off at full speed and scooped up Euryale's head. The snakes were limp and dead now, but that didn't mean the magic eyes were. She brandished the gory trophy skyward, screaming at the top of her lungs. At least one of the Gorgons was bound to look at her.

The helmet water fell below her vision, and Jocasta slammed her eyes shut. A heartbeat later, a huge thud shook the ground. Looking down and through her lashes, she opened her eyes. A stone Stheno stuck out of the crumbled roadway ahead of them, her body frozen in rock, her deadly eyes gone statue-silent.

Jocasta dropped Euryale's head facedown and scrambled back. Two down. One to go. "Prometheus! My helmet!" she cried.

"Take it off!" he yelled back.

She ripped off the clear covering. Another popped onto her head. "Thank the gods," she breathed out, water blurring and bending her vision again.

"*You* thank the gods." Medusa crashed down in front of her and grabbed her arms. Jocasta gasped. Fear knifed through her along with sharp stabs from Medusa's metal-tipped nails. "*I* curse them!"

The Gorgon's spiked fingers sank into Jocasta's flesh. Pain burst from every puncture, cauterization hot. Jocasta thrashed but couldn't shake free of Medusa's steely grip. Agony lanced down her arms. Blood dripped from her elbows. Gritting her teeth, she kicked out. The Gorgon snarled and yanked her clear off her feet. Team Elpis converged on them and attacked from all sides, but Medusa ignored both flames and blades, her terrifying eyes boring into Jocasta's as if sheer force of will could turn her enemy to stone.

"I curse *you.*" Medusa gave her a brutal shake. Jocasta flopped like a rag doll, trying to keep her neck from snapping. "Death to Poseidon, his brothers, and their offspring. Death to their precious Elpis. Death to the woman who killed my sisters. Death to—"

Flynn slammed into Medusa from the side, breaking the Gorgon's hold. Jocasta fell into the broken roadway as Flynn and Medusa rolled across the ground. They snarled, kicked, and struck, both viciously battling for the upper hand. Medusa twisted like a snake and used her inhuman strength to pin Flynn beneath her. She brought her forehead down, cracking his helmet. She did it again. The glass shattered, and he squeezed his eyes shut, water drenching him.

Team Elpis raced in to help. Jocasta was closest and moved like a lightning bolt. She picked up Flynn's ax and severed Medusa's remaining head with a low-to-high sweep of the blade that came dangerously close to hitting Flynn. The Gorgon dropped, lifeless, her blood gushing all over Flynn. He clamped his mouth shut, keeping his eyes closed and turning away his head.

"Flynn. She's dead." Her fingers numb, Jocasta let the ax slip from her hand. It thudded to the ground. Carver sprang to her side and kicked Medusa's head away from them. Bellanca charred it until there was nothing left, and the echo of hissing snakes finally faded from the air. The stink of burning skin remained, but that didn't stop Prometheus from ripping off his helmet and gulping down a breath.

Jocasta met the Titan's eyes before he turned away to smash a snake with his helmet, destroying both with one hit. Gratitude nearly wrenched a sob from her. They were alive because of his fishbowl helmets. Prometheus had come through under pressure. She knew he would.

Light-headed, shaking, and ready to thoroughly break down if she let herself, Jocasta dropped to her knees next to Flynn. He was the only man she would ever want in her whole life, so there was absolutely no way he was dying on her before at least the ripe old age of eighty-seven, preferably after.

Flynn opened his eyes, revealing the dearest color in the world to her, the brown of olive bark and deep Sintan soil. "Eighty-seven?"

"What?" She'd said that aloud? She frowned.

"You told me I'd better live until I'm eighty-seven."

"Make that ninety-seven." She thumped his blood-soaked chest as Team Elpis spread out again, scorching and beheading the remaining snakes and reassuring the people behind the barricade. Jocasta curled her fingers into Flynn's tunic, the material hot with Medusa's blood. "You saved me," she whispered.

"You saved *me*." He reached up and covered her hand above his heart. "I'm in awe of your bravery." He squeezed her fingers, and the pressure traveled all the way through her, clamping down on every part.

Her eyes burned, and her vision turned watery without any help from her helmet. She ripped it off and tossed it aside. Flynn reached up and brushed sweat-dampened hair back from her forehead with the gentlest touch, never looking away from her face.

Jocasta's heart galloped back in time to the one kiss they'd shared. The gory battlefield fell away. Everything blurred except for them, and resolve hardened like molten metal inside her, casting a new mold.

Her future wasn't shaping up to be what she wanted? Then she'd change the framework. She'd already begun.

As they looked at each other, her pulse beating hard, Jocasta decided that the life she'd dreamed of wouldn't dance just out of reach anymore. She wouldn't let it.

Standing on unsteady legs, she held out a hand to the man she loved. She would seduce Flynn or die trying. This quest would see to that.

CHAPTER 17

"Jo." Flynn gently shook Jo's shoulder, trying not to startle her. He didn't know about the first night after the Gorgon attack— they'd slept at an inn—but these last two nights on the desolate road through the Arcadian Wilds, Jo's sleep had been a long way from peaceful. "Wake up, *kar*—" He cut off the endearment. *Kardoula mou.* She might be his sweetheart, but there was no reason to *tell* her that. It would just complicate things.

She sat up slowly, looking confused and rubbing her eyes. Emotion expanded in his chest like a bubble stretched to bursting. Gods, if only he could take her in his arms.

"Flynn? Is something wrong?" Her gaze sharpened on their surroundings. She shivered, and he understood why. He'd had a constant itch on the back of his neck since they'd entered the hinterlands of Fisa, the kind of primal chill that kept his nerves on edge and his ax hand ready. The Great Roar really had killed the forest. Evidence of the nymph stampede was everywhere, as though the woodland creatures had ripped the essence from the trees and the liquid from the streams.

"No." He awkwardly patted her bent knee. "It's just… You were having another nightmare."

Her mouth scrunched up. She nodded. Her eyes dropped to the ground.

"The Agon Games?" he asked softly.

She shook her head.

"This place?" The dead forest was more of a waking nightmare, but it had even crept into his dreams. Skeleton trees.
Cracked streambeds. Everywhere they went, decaying moss
hung, strung like cobwebs across the path. There wasn't even
enough grass for the horses to eat. They'd had to dig into their
supply of oats.

"It's not this place. Or the Agon Games." She huffed a quiet
laugh. "Although I'm sure those nightmares will be back soon."

Jo's voice was even huskier in the middle of the night, that
rich, smoky hitch amplified by sleep. She cleared her throat, and
Flynn wished she hadn't. He could rub his senses up against that
voice forever. It was as addictive as smoothing a hand back and
forth over the rough-soft nap of a velvet cushion. Hypnotic.
Soothing.

He scooted a little closer, shielding her from the chilly night
breeze. "Then what was it?" His voice gruff, he cleared *his*
throat. "I mean, if you want to talk about it."

She breathed out slowly, using one of those controlled ex-
halations to keep herself entirely still. Same for the slow inhalation, filling her lungs again. Nothing moved except for her
chest, rising and falling over the space of several heartbeats that
pounded against his ribs. Finally, she said, "It was Medusa."

Flynn nodded, wondering if someone had once told Jo that
fidgeting would make her less of a person and she'd taken it to
heart. He didn't care if she fidgeted. She could hop around like
a flea if she wanted. Sometimes, letting go of strict self-control
helped—or so he'd been told. He wasn't good at it himself.
"The Gorgons were terrifying. Deadly. It's normal to be afraid,
even after they're gone."

She rubbed her arms, careful of the deep puncture wounds
and heavy bruises circling her biceps. Unlike Panotii, who'd
recovered from his cuts and abrasions with miraculous speed, Jo

still bore purple-blue skin and ten scabbed-over claw marks that had to be a lot more painful than she'd been letting on. He'd barely seen her wince since the battle.

"Were you? Afraid?" she asked.

"Of course." He puffed up his chest, posturing as though proud of his fear. In a way, maybe he was. He'd be a lot more ashamed of blind arrogance than caution, especially with lives on the line. *Jocasta's* life. His insides still churned at the thought of her in Medusa's murderous grasp.

She chuckled, the low sound bridging a little more of the gap that always seemed to loom between them. "Fearless and brave are the same thing for some people." Her eyes flicked up, twin pools of silvered darkness framed by thick, curving lashes. Jo's impishly up-tilted eyes had rendered him breathless for as long as he could remember. He wanted to dive straight into her midnight-blue gaze and take up permanent residence.

"Then they're idiots," he murmured. "You can be scared and still act with courage."

She tilted her head in thought. Nightmare pallor gave way to interest as her expression turned pensive. "Without fear, is any act truly courageous?"

"No."

Her eyebrows flew up. "Well, I guess that's settled."

Had he been too abrupt? Her wry tone told him he could add something—and probably should. "If you go into a situation without fear, then courage isn't required. True bravery is unnecessary to success and doesn't play a role in actions or outcome."

She made a soft humming sound in the back of her throat—one he heard in his dreams sometimes. "You might've missed your calling as a philosopher."

"Flynn the Wise?" he joked.

"Exactly." Her wide smile looped around his chest and squeezed so hard his heart skipped a beat.

His expression sternly serious, he said, "You can add this to the pearls of knowledge I've dropped in my life. There must be another one somewhere."

She rolled her lips in, holding back a giggle. Laughter shimmered in her eyes, making him feel as if he'd succeeded somehow.

But *gods!* What was going on in his chest? It felt like a whole school of fish had started zipping around in there.

He wasn't any good at teasing or dealing with feelings— or *great Zeus*, was this flirting?—and silence quickly stretched between them again.

Jo regulated her breathing like before and pulled her blanket higher, tucking it against her chest. "The nightmare wasn't about fighting the Gorgons." Her gaze dropped to the ground. "Medusa, she…" Jo paused, swallowing. "She was accusing me."

"Of killing her?"

"I guess, but it was more than that. She called me a traitor." Her gaze still lowered, she actually started to pluck at her blanket, pulling on a golden tassel decorating the edge.

"A traitor?" Flynn's hand crept toward hers. He stopped before their fingers touched. "I don't understand."

"Traitor to abused women." Jo looked up, biting her lip. "Betrayer of women wronged."

He peered into her face, frowning. "That's what she said to you in your nightmare?"

Jo nodded, her fingers methodically rolling that tassel into a tight little spike of thread. "Maybe she's shouting at me from the Underworld. Maybe she should."

Flynn didn't believe for a second that Jo deserved nightmares of any kind, especially for defending herself, her team, and innocent people on the road. Knee-jerk denial wasn't what she needed, though. He knew her, and that would only make her dig into her ideas harder. She had no idea how stubborn she was.

He tried to take apart what she was saying and put his own thoughts together in a way that might help. "Kill or be killed. Isn't that what Cat always says? How she had to live?"

Looking at him, Jo nodded again. He had her attention, and it was almost too much. What if he couldn't help? What if he made things worse? He was the man on the sidelines, swinging an ax and trying to help others achieve great things. He didn't know how to achieve them himself.

But what if he somehow managed to take that distressed look out of Jo's eyes tonight? He'd like to accomplish that.

He reached for her hand. To the Underworld with it. He could touch her without the cosmos crashing down.

"*You* didn't pick a fight." He put gentle pressure on her fingers. He couldn't help himself. Her eyes went round, locking on their joined hands before jumping to his face again. "*You* didn't hunt down the Gorgon sisters like the monster slayers that have tracked them across two worlds. You tried to understand them and think of a way to avoid conflict. They're the ones who had no interest in compromise. They didn't even wait for us to decide. They attacked before we crossed their line."

She gripped his hand back, the tassel forgotten. "So it's not our fault? They're still dead because of us."

"They're dead because of *them*. What choice did we have? Tilt our heads up, point to our necks, and say, 'Insert knife here'?"

She laughed. There was more surprise than humor in the sudden sound, but it still warmed him. A laugh was a laugh. Maybe he was doing something right.

"You defended yourself." He squeezed her hand again. "Us. Me."

"You defended me, too," she whispered.

"Always."

She shivered. He felt the tremor in her fingertips. "It's been three days, and I still can't think of a solution. I don't know what we could've done differently, other than giving up."

"None of us even considered giving up. I promise you that."

She arched a brow. "Because you're all so excited about this possible wild-goose chase?"

Flynn shook his head. "Because when you have an idea, it works."

Her lips pursed, forming a perfect pink heart. Well, not quite a heart, but close enough. And not quite pink, either. More of a dusky rose, one of those sunset colors that slashed across the horizon and made a person stop and look. Jo moved her plumped-up mouth back and forth in thought, torturing him—although probably not on purpose. Her eyes slowly narrowed. "You didn't seem to think that when my idea was to join Beta Team in the Agon Games."

"I was wrong." It didn't even pain him to admit it. "It was a gamble—and a damn terrifying one—but winning those games put Cat and Griffin exactly where they needed to be. We couldn't have done that without you. We would've had to forfeit."

As if reeled in by his words, Jo tipped closer. Her back softened, some of the tension she always carried slipping down her spine and away from them. With her armor set aside for once, the air between them swelled with something Flynn knew was coming from him: desire. Her thumb swept across his knuckles, a tiny movement for her, an electrifying jolt of sensation for him. His speeding pulse carried the terrifying thrill of her touch to his entire body. Heat billowed through him. His heart pounded. His groin tightened. He stopped breathing. He couldn't imagine what would happen if he kissed her. Cardiac arrest? Aneurysm? Ejaculation?

He slipped his hand from hers. If Jo could turn his world inside out with one fleeting little caress, there was no way he could pay attention to this conversation while she was touching him.

Were they even talking anymore? All he could remember was the silky warmth of her skin. The soft sound of her breath in the night. The hints of honeyed lavender clinging to her hair. He wanted to bury his face in her raven curls and inhale so deeply he took a part of her into his lungs and kept it there.

That would be a weird thing to do. Why was he even thinking that? Dear gods, he'd better stay away from her.

Flynn tucked the tasseled edge of her blanket between her fingers and sat back on his heels, putting some distance between them. Jo frowned at the lump of fabric. She smoothed it out, leaving her hands loosely folded in her lap and totally motionless again.

Damn it. He'd ruined her fidgeting.

Unsure what to do next, Flynn kept quiet. With Jo, saying nothing was better than saying the wrong thing. The wrong thing led to a fight.

"Would you listen to strangers? Or compromise?" she eventually asked. "If you'd been through what the Gorgons had?"

"I don't blame innocent people for the crimes of gods."

"Are we innocent, though?" she asked.

"Yes."

"Another simple answer. I'm not sure it's so black and white." Doubt clouded her expression. "What would we do if faced with the allies of our enemies?"

"Probably end up in a battle for our lives," Flynn said. "But that doesn't mean we'd have sought out the fight."

Jo looked unconvinced. "So the distinction is who attacks first?"

"The distinction is between needlessly killing and defending yourself."

"To the death?" Her cynical snort was so unlike her that Flynn almost took offense.

"Yes, to the death. Do you really think they'd have left you alive? Or me? Or anyone else?"

"I guess we'll never know, will we? You and I made sure of that. But their anger... It was justified, Flynn. What a terrible existence they had." She shuddered, then her gaze flicked sideways when Carver snored loudly enough to wake himself up. Carver lifted his head, looked around, and then settled down to sleep again when he saw that Flynn was on watch—if one could call it that. He was so fixated on Jo that a Cyclops could probably stomp into the camp and club them all to death before he even noticed.

"Listen to me." He leveled the same hard look on her that he'd seen Griffin use on Cat. It seemed to work—or at least get Cat's attention. "We had nothing to do with what happened to Medusa and her sisters lifetimes ago in a place we can't even get to. My sympathy was with them until they attacked. No one puts you in danger. I draw the line at that."

A blush stole across Jo's cheeks, and Flynn cursed himself for not watching his words more carefully. Jo blushed, and he got *ideas*. It was always like that.

"But we killed them." Her knuckles turned white, although he didn't see her fingers move. "All three."

He nodded, itching to reach for her hands and help them relax somehow. Instead, he thought back to the battle on the road. Jo had been magnificent—smart, courageous, and decisive when she'd needed to be. But she'd killed two living beings and helped kill a third. For a healer, bringing death couldn't be easy.

"And we lived. All of us." He leaned over and dropped another log onto the fading fire, pushing it into place with a thin branch he'd snapped off a half-dead tree earlier. When he was done, he left his poking stick within Jo's reach, pointing right at her. It might help her fidget again. "Maybe try not to focus on the lives lost," he suggested. "Focus on the ones saved instead."

Jo reached for the stick. She only touched it at first, brushing her fingertip against the bark in a light circular pattern and then gouging at a knot with her thumbnail. The moment she decided to really grip the branch, she picked it up and poked at that damn campfire like anything she set her mind to—with vigor and intent.

Flynn felt a stirring of pride. He'd done that.

"It's all a blur now." She jabbed harder, and a charred log split in half. Another tumbled into the center of the pit, sending sparks flying. They put amber flecks in her eyes and shadows into the hollows of her cheeks. "Turning Stheno to stone was really just dumb luck, and I think I almost chopped off your head along with Medusa's." She grimaced.

More than ever, Flynn wished he could take Jo in his arms and comfort her, especially when she sat there looking so dubious about her own skill and worth. Against his better judgment, he took her hands again. Her skin was cool to the touch, soft. "There was no dumb luck or sloppy chopping about it. You fought well."

Her breath caught. He heard the hitch, loud in the dead forest. She leaned forward. Slowly. So slowly. She closed three-quarters of the distance between them and stopped. Her eyes flicked up, locking with his.

Flynn froze, caught in her glittering, jewel-dark gaze. Heat buffeted him from the inside out, flooding him with that feeling he simultaneously craved and feared: urgent desire wrapped tightly around enduring, gut-wrenching love. Gods, he hated this feeling. It ripped down his walls.

He swallowed. He could draw back. He should. He had willpower. Didn't he? Where was it?

Jo's mouth hovered in front of his. Flynn waited, torn in half. He'd lost the ability to move. His stomach tumbled and clenched. Jo wouldn't walk away, would she? Unless he got up right now, he was making a choice.

Her gaze dipped to his mouth. "Flynn?"

He nearly groaned at the warm whisper of her breath across his lips. Jo's smoke-and-velvet voice sank into him, resolve-melting and rich. He could taste her on his tongue, feel her in his arms. So vivid. Like yesterday. That was what one searing kiss and years of erotic dreams did—tore a man's peace of mind to shreds.

Before he knew it, he blurted out his worst nightmare. "If I kiss you, I'll be lost." One crack was all it would take. One opening led to everything else.

Jo's small hand slipped from his. She touched his cheek, her fingers featherlight. "Maybe you'll be found."

Or maybe he'd give her what they both seemed to want and all his deepest fears would come to pass.

Flynn shook his head. Her hand stayed with him, cupping his jaw. He lifted his hand to lower hers, but all he ended up doing was pressing her fingers harder against his cheek. Walking away seemed impossible, but a kiss was a promise of more. Jo wasn't some plaything. He didn't have playthings, especially female ones.

He kissed her; he married her. Unless she rejected him.

"Empty farmhouse." He squeezed his eyes shut and saw grave markers lined up under a row of ancient trees. He saw his father aimlessly wandering the house, little by little leaving his will to live in empty bedrooms and never looking for it again.

He could be Old Hector. It could be Jo and their children under the silvery-green leaves, silent and waiting for him to pass.

Her other hand touched his cheek, framing his face. "I want you to kiss me. What's holding you back?"

"I'll lose you." He opened his eyes, his heart pounding so hard it hurt.

"Why?" She moved closer. The tip of her nose brushed his. Once. Twice. He shuddered. His hands twitched. "I'm not so easily gotten rid of, you know. Rather like a parasite. It's one of my many qualities."

He smiled, even though it was convulsive and rough. "You're nothing like a parasite."

"See how good at compliments you are?" She tipped forward, and her lips touched his. A wild jolt of heat raced straight to his middle. Jo barely pulled back, staying all-too-reachable with just the slightest dip of his head. "And I know you're good at kissing."

Was he? He only remembered one kiss.

"I'm out of practice." The gravel-thick croak that scraped out of his throat was an embarrassment to men. Flynn hoped she didn't notice.

Jo's fingers swept over his jaw and grazed his earlobes. His neck tingled. The skin all the way down to his thighs tightened. Who knew earlobes were so sensitive? He wondered if she'd touch them again.

"How much out of practice?" she asked.

Flynn could barely think. He was feeling too much. "Going on several years now. Between six and seven, I guess."

She drew back in shock. "*I'm* the last person you kissed?"

He met her incredulous stare, fear and want thumping inside him so hard he felt sick. The shut-up-and-don't-say-anything method would have to do once more, because he was incapable of speaking right then.

Her sudden grin split him open like a thunderbolt cracking the night sky. "Well, you're the *only* person I've kissed." Slowly, as though not to startle him, she rose onto her knees, leaned forward, and brushed her lips against his. This time, she *pressed*.

"Jo." Her name was half moan, half plea. Half stop and half don't stop. Flynn didn't know what he wanted anymore. He only knew he couldn't decide, couldn't move, couldn't turn his back on her to save his life.

"You won't lose me." Another light kiss shook him like an earthquake. "If you want me, I'm yours."

Flynn slid his hands into her hair, his heart thundering in his chest. Jo was right there—eyes open, lips parted, breath suspended. Waiting. For him.

"Want isn't the problem." Gods, no. He throbbed for her, body and soul. But she didn't understand the fear he lived with. The fear of watching her blue eyes go sightless and blank. The fear of threads they might weave together unraveling one by one until the whole tapestry of his life fell apart and left just one solitary string, dangling and alone.

Abruptly, he let Jo go. Better to empty his hands himself than have the Fates yank everything he loved most in life from his fingers. *Again.*

"Flynn, what happened to your family was bad luck. Sickness and accidents." She brushed his earlobes again, sending a heated shiver through his veins. "That doesn't mean it'll happen to us."

"That doesn't mean it won't." Stubbornly, those grave markers filled his mind again. Six in all. He'd dug the last three himself.

Her brow furrowed. "That's surrender before a fight even starts."

"That's self-preservation. I can't..."

"Live through that again?" she asked when he paused.

He nodded, not surprised Jo understood the root of his fears when he'd barely said two words. She'd been through those dark years with him. Her whole family had, but she'd been the one who could walk into a room and make him forget the ache in his chest until she left again.

He knew exactly why she'd kissed him on her eighteenth birthday. He finally understood just what she'd believed and expected and why. Not *meaning* to fall in love with her didn't mean it hadn't happened. And not *knowing* he was in love with her at the time just meant she was smarter than he was, which was no surprise.

"Jo…" Flynn knew if he touched her, he might never want to stop. He kept his hands balled into fists. "It could all be the same. Only *worse*." *His* wife. *His* daughters and sons.

"I'm stronger than any of them." She met what must've been his haunted gaze with a firm stare of her own. "And you're not Old Hector. I know you idolized him and took everything he ever said to heart like it was written in Zeus's blood, but he was selfish. You're better than him."

Flynn's eyes pricked with heat. He shook his head.

She slipped her fingers around the back of his neck and touched her forehead to his. "Life is unpredictable and full of tragedy. I won't pretend otherwise or try to convince you of something that isn't true. But you're not to blame for *surviving*. Carrying on is what makes you strong. Old Hector abandoned life. And you. He forgot that hearts heal—and that he wasn't alone."

Flynn's breath shuddered. "Sometimes, hearts don't heal." His wouldn't. The closer he got to Jo, the more certain he was that she'd own his heart in mere minutes if he let it happen. She was already most of the way there.

No, she was *all* the way there. But without a physical connection, he could preserve himself somehow.

Her fingernails lightly scored the back of his head. Goose bumps cascaded down his spine. Flynn's lips parted, and he let out a low, desperate sound.

Jo angled her head and pressed her lips to the corner of his mouth. "If fear rules your life, you'll miss out on the rest."

His hands uncurled between them. The ache to reach for her was almost too much. "Are you calling me a coward?" he murmured, barely able to form words, let alone tease her, which was what he'd somehow done.

He felt a hint of her soft smile against his lips. "Didn't we just say that fearless and brave aren't the same thing?"

He huffed in reluctant amusement, his hands somehow moving to her waist. The flare of her hips was so enticing that he slid his hands down, gripping the softer flesh. "You could have a noble. A Magoi. Anyone you want."

This time, she huffed—incredulous. "Is it not clear by now what I want? Shall I make it clearer?" She gripped his shoulders, inched forward, and straddled his lap.

Flynn's eyes flared. His hands clamped down, locking her in place. But *gods*, he wanted her to move. He almost rocked her up against his hardening cock. Jo's knees hugged his thighs. Her breasts brushed his chest. She still managed to wiggle and tense her legs around him, holding him tight. Heat flooded his groin. His fingers shook.

"Kiss me, Flynn. I won't break."

Jo's smoke-and-silk voice broke *him*. The soft weight of her on his lap broke him. The siren call of her mouth *broke him*, and he dipped his head, a low groan resonating in his chest.

The second their lips touched, another tremor shook him from the ground up. He angled his head, fitting their mouths together and deepening the kiss. Jo moaned and wrapped her arms around his neck. She pressed her body flush against his, all tentativeness gone in a flash.

Flynn's pulse surged. Desire exploded inside him. Jo's hidden boldness had haunted him for nearly a decade, taunting him in his dreams and filling him with forbidden fantasies that brought him to his knees.

Echoing her moan, he gripped her bottom and rocked her in his lap. He shuddered, sensation blocking everything but Jo from his mind. She melted against him, her back softening and her hips rolling in. Her breath sped up. Flynn ached for more. His blood thundered in his veins, pounding her name through his body until he couldn't hear anything else.

The kiss, the feel of her in his arms, it was everything he knew it would be and more—a double-edged sword splitting his life in half. Pain was inevitable, especially since she'd already crawled inside him and claimed his soul.

And now that she had, he wanted more.

Flynn flicked his tongue against the seam of her lips. Jo opened for him without hesitation. He quaked again.

Worry intruded on his haze of lust, keeping him from thrusting his tongue into her mouth. Was that an earthquake? He'd thought it was just him falling apart.

The ground shook again, a longer rumble growling up from beneath. Flynn leaped to his feet, hauling Jo up with him, one arm around her waist and her lips still clinging to his.

Her eyes popped open, her startled gasp hitting his mouth. "Flynn?"

Wrapping his hand around the back of her head, he tucked her close and shouted a warning to the others. Something was coming for them.

CHAPTER 18

Jocasta's heart went from pounding with desire to racing in fear.

"Carver! Bel!" Flynn roared above her head.

"What's happening?" Jocasta turned with him, gripping his tunic. On the far side of the campfire, Carver sprang into action, fast on his feet and reaching for Bellanca. Prometheus rolled to his knees. He pressed one hand against the ground and looked sideways into the forest.

"Earthquake." Flynn widened his stance for balance.

Behind them, the horses stamped and whined. Brown Horse nickered uneasily. The trees surrounding the clearing groaned and trembled. Adrenaline-spiked fear made Jocasta rattle like the branches. Flynn's arm tightened around her. Dead leaves fluttered to the ground, and the two of them swayed together, trying to stay upright as another tremor shook them.

Prometheus looked over sharply, his eyes flashing bronze in the firelight. "Go!" he yelled, pointing them back from the center of the clearing.

Flynn gripped her hand, and they ran toward the horses. Prometheus, Carver, and Bellanca raced in the other direction, reaching the far edge of the clearing just as the ground split down the middle, engulfing the campfire and their blankets.

Jocasta's jaw dropped. "Oh my gods." She and Flynn backed into the trees, herding the horses with them. The fissure grew, crowding them farther into the forest and utterly crumbling the space where they'd just been sleeping. The clearing disappeared, a wide fracture in its place that stretched in both directions, separating them.

"Carver!" Jocasta shouted. He didn't look over. The noise was terrible.

Bellanca shrieked as the ground gave way beneath her. Jocasta's heart volleyed against her ribs, and she cried out a warning. Prometheus lunged, grabbing Bellanca's hand as she fell. Her feet dangled into the rift. Carver leaned over the edge, gripped her belt, and hauled her up, rolling away with her. Prometheus snatched them both up like toys and sped away from the deepening chasm. It reached the edges of the clearing, claiming the first dead trees around it and gulping them down like a hungry, saw-toothed animal.

Jocasta clapped her hand over her mouth, her pulse bucking in horror. What if someone had fallen in? How could they ever cross that? They were separated now, on two sides of a massive division.

The ground finally stopped shaking and growling. Only now, a wide crevasse with no bottom she could see stretched between them. Team Elpis—divided.

"Someone did this on purpose," she seethed.

Flynn glanced at her. "The same person who sent the Gorgons to stop us?"

"Person?" She scoffed. "What *person* has this power?"

"Olympianomachy," Flynn murmured.

She nodded. "If this is the start of a Power Bid on Mount Olympus, we seem to be caught in the middle of it."

"Everyone all right over there?" Carver shouted across the gap.

She and Flynn shouted back their assurances and got the same in return. No one was hurt, but they weren't *together*.

And they *could* have been hurt. In fact, Jocasta was starting to think that the ground swallowing them whole had been the idea. If she and Flynn hadn't already been awake, it might very well have happened.

"Prometheus! Can you do something?" Flynn called, letting go of her hand and moving cautiously toward the edge of the chasm. The ground started to crumble. Rocks tumbled down the sharp incline, and Flynn hastily backpedaled.

"I can't jump that far." The Titan flapped his arms. "And do you see wings? Or special floating powers?"

Flynn grunted. "It was just a question."

"He's still touchy about magic," Jocasta said. But Prometheus was good at one thing. "Can you conjure a bridge?" she shouted.

"Too big," Prometheus called back. "And the ground on either side isn't stable. I think the sides will just keep collapsing."

Next to her, Flynn gripped the back of his neck, his brow creasing. "Can you use that mapping ability you discovered to see how far the chasm stretches? Maybe we can get around it in just a few hours."

"Good idea," Jocasta said.

The Titan got down on one knee and touched the ground again, bending low and looking along the path of the crevasse into the dark forest. "It stretches the entire length of the Arcadian Wilds. It's *only* in the wilds. It splits the woods right down the middle."

Well, that confirmed Jocasta's suspicion about the earthquake being sent to take them out—or at least separate them. As far as she could tell, there wasn't another living being in the woods. There wasn't even a living tree here. The only things an earthquake in the Arcadian Wilds impacted were them and their mission.

So what god was against them? Or worse, which *gods*.

Flynn groaned in frustration. "We're still a lot closer to Kos than to the coast. Jo and I are on the right side to continue southeast. We'll take the horses, ride to Thassos, buy a boat, and start figuring out how to sail it. You three will head back to Kos on foot, acquire new horses, take the Continental Road to Exo Ipeiro, and then head straight down the coast. We'll meet you in Thassos."

"On *foot?*" Bellanca squealed with all the ingrained privilege of a Magoi princess.

Carver snorted. Jocasta didn't actually hear his snort from across the distance, but she knew it just from the way Bellanca turned on him.

Shivering, she leaned into Flynn, the aftermath of fear and adrenaline leaving her cold and shaky. She didn't like the idea of a delay or of Team Elpis being separated, but several days without listening to constant bickering and alone with Flynn didn't seem like such a terrible thing. In fact, it was just what she needed to seduce him.

———— (6) ————

"Your mind is working so hard I can hear the wheels grinding from here," Flynn teased. He rode beside her on the grim path through the nightmarish forest, leading Bellanca's and Prometheus's mounts behind him. Carver's horse followed her and Panotii.

Jocasta glanced over, finding it almost impossible to keep the grin off her face. She couldn't remember the last time she'd felt this energetic and hopeful. Flynn *kissed* her! Sure, she'd asked him to—practically begged—but he'd participated. *More than* participated. That light, exploring touch of his tongue kept surging back to her senses and shocking a giddy little leap from her heart.

Heat flooded her. She took a low, trembling breath and

forced her mind back to where it had been just moments ago, turning over the usual questions—or at least the ones *not* about Flynn. Something about the Great Roar kept cycling into her thoughts, hinting at the source of the strange and destructive noise. Maybe optimism and excitement had somehow unlocked the idea in her head. In any case, the more present the notion became, the quicker she was to discard the rest.

"There's something I can't stop thinking about." She ducked to avoid a brittle branch. "It's about the cause of the Great Roar. I keep coming back to an idea, and now it seems impossible to give credit to anything else."

Flynn looked at her with interest before side-eyeing the animals trailing behind him. One of them balked at a gnarled root, and Flynn gave the lead line a tug, clicking his tongue to keep the horses moving while Jocasta slowed, waiting for him to catch up. Once the horses fell back into line, he said, "Now I'm doubly curious. I doubt you'd say a word if you weren't convinced."

"Because I don't like being wrong?" she asked with a laugh.

"Who likes being wrong?" The corners of his mouth tipped up. "But that's not what I meant."

"You mean I'm prudent."

He chuckled. "Not always. But you're cautious when it counts." He didn't explain further, and it almost felt as if he were teasing her again. She wouldn't go so far as to say flirting, but maybe that would come next.

In an unexpected twist, Flynn seemed more at ease with her since their kiss. He hadn't kissed her again, but he also hadn't avoided her or seemed uncomfortable in her presence. It was reassuring—and made her belly clench.

"So?" His brows rose in question. "Don't keep me in suspense."

"Pan," she said. "We don't know much about him here, do we? Cat never mentions him. Bellanca doesn't, either. I've never heard Persephone say his name, although she and I don't typically chat or anything." The idea was laughable. The goddess of spring exuded more frostiness than sunshine, except toward Cat and possibly Cerberus. "But I remembered something. In Attica, at least, he's apparently known for frolicking with…um…vigor… and then taking really long, deep naps in secluded places where he won't be disturbed to recover his energy."

Flynn's brows lifted another notch. "Is he, then?"

She almost giggled at his expression. "According to stories passed down from one wise old centaur, yes. It didn't occur to me at first, but then another one of that bard's stories—one he learned from Chiron at some point—came back to me after we talked about the Titanomachy and this Olympianomachy that seems to have begun—possibly a new War of Gods. Pan supposedly inadvertently helped Zeus overthrow the Titans in the original conflict by letting out a huge screech that terrified the enemy and sent them running. They scattered in fright at his unexpected shout."

"His Great Roar?" Flynn's eyes narrowed in thought. "This sounds familiar, but…" He shook his head. "I remember jugs of wine and dancing around the bonfire better than the stories."

Jocasta wasn't surprised. Wine had certainly flowed at harvest festivals, and she'd been too young to imbibe, as opposed to her older brothers and their friends. There was a good chance she remembered the bard's tales better than they did because she'd had a clear head.

"Well, according to what I remember, ever since the Titanomachy—and Pan's fortuitous help—all the other gods and magical creatures are careful not to startle Pan awake. He hunkers down for long sleeps in vast grazing meadows, secret grottos, isolated woodlands like the Arcadian Wilds..." Jocasta swept a hand toward the now dead and dying trees. "If he wakes up on his own, no problem. All is peaceful and quiet, and Pan goes about his business until he settles down somewhere for his next long nap. If he's unexpectedly jolted out of slumber, he lets out a *pan*icked shout, like the one that scattered the Titans and gave Zeus the upper hand."

"*Panikos.*" Admiration lit Flynn's face. How had she ever thought him expressionless? It seemed impossible now. "Cat even said it before we left."

Jocasta nodded, irked that she hadn't put the pieces together before when it seemed so obvious to her now. "I think Pan is in Thalyria, and that someone—or something—keeps waking him up on purpose and making him cry out in fright. *Panikos.*" She also remembered Cat using the old language to describe the nymph stampede that killed the ancient and magical forest. "It's not something you think about every day, but both the old and the new word for pure fright come from the god himself. A startled Pan *panics* and sows *panic* around him by shouting his head off."

"It makes perfect sense." Flynn's now arrow-sharp gaze shot to hers across the path. "Someone who wants to undermine confidence in the new royal family is creating Thalyria-wide panic by shocking Pan into huge shouts."

"Pan might not even be doing it on purpose. He could just be someone's pawn in this Olympian power play, like the rest of us."

"The Great Roar is Pan." Flynn gave her the proudest look. "You solved it."

A thrill gripped her ribs, tightening her lungs. He believed her. "Whoever is responsible for jolting Pan awake and causing panic in Thalyria is probably responsible for slipping Cat the elixir and blocking any hope of the promised line of succession. That not only damages Cat and Griffin in all the ways we already know, but it prevents Thalyria from being truly united again under a direct descendant of Zeus. Cat is Thalyria's hero for now, but Eleni would've been everyone's darling. Cat and Griffin united the realms on parchment. It takes more than that for hearts to really follow."

"Do you think Zeus is the real target?"

"Zeus and his allies," Jocasta said. "Their big win in Thalyria is already crumbling—along with the royal family."

A shadow crossed Flynn's features. "And when you found a possible solution to Cat's immortality, which also puts baby Eleni in stasis, whoever is behind this rebellion on Mount Olympus sent the Gorgons to scare us back to Castle Thalyria empty-handed."

Jocasta nodded. "Up until the earthquake, I don't think it was about us or even about Cat. Instead of trying to kill Cat, whoever it is made her immortal. A god could justify that as a gift. They wouldn't see stasis the way Cat does—as a fate worse than death. And the Gorgons were sent to scare us off. The encounter degenerated fast, but I don't think killing us was their mission to begin with."

"Then which god is behind all this?" A frown pulled at Flynn's mouth. "Who wants war on Olympus?"

Shrugging, Jocasta looked around at the shriveled forest whose soul had been ripped away when its stewards fled. "Someone who's tired of Zeus?"

"Does Zeus really care that much about Thalyria?" Flynn asked. "He and his brothers got what they wanted—new rulers, one kingdom. My guess is they'll move on to something else."

"I know we're playthings to them as they live out their immortal lives. Even Cat is just a heartbeat. A blink. But she's the *latest* blink." Jocasta shook her head, helpless to explain the feeling that made her think Cat and their family were just another line of demarcation, as the Gorgons had drawn. Any human, god, or creature even remotely involved in Thalyria would have to stand on one side or the other. They'd have to choose. "Those who actively helped Cat win the crown are Zeus's closest allies. It's easy to identify them and set them aside. Poseidon, Hades, Persephone, Ares, Athena, Artemis. They've all intervened on Cat's behalf. Those who didn't… Well, they're up for grabs now, targets for seduction."

"Seduction in the can-be-swayed-to-new-leadership sense?" Flynn asked.

Jocasta nodded, her cheeks heating at her choice of words. "And any god, demigod, or lesser deity coming to Cat's defense now—trying to help her or simply showing sympathy—can be discarded, too. Cat's their line in the sand, their sneaky way of filtering out anyone unsympathetic to their rebellion."

"So Cat—and anyone close to her—is being used as a filter by someone trying to gain support on Olympus?" Fury hardened Flynn's voice. A muscle ticked in his jaw. "Are you saying some god or goddess ruined her chance at happiness to see who might *care*?"

Their eyes met, and her nostrils flared. "That's exactly what I'm saying." And it enraged her, too.

CHAPTER 19

Flynn set up camp on their fourth night alone while Jo refreshed herself by the stream. He kept his back carefully turned while he built up a campfire, took out his cooking supplies, and plucked their dinner, giving her privacy since there was little more than half a bush and a few squat boulders to hide behind. He could hear her splashing around, pretty much see her in his mind, but—*ow!*

Flynn frowned at his hand. That was the first time he'd nicked his thumb like that in years.

He sucked the drop of blood off and got back to work. There wasn't much game in the scrubby hills southeast of the Arcadian Wilds, but with her sharp eyes and good aim, Jo managed to shoot and kill some kind of Fisan fowl neither of them had ever seen before. It was plump, which was all that mattered. Since they had no idea what to call the bird, they decided on Perses, after the Titan god of destruction. No one liked him anyway. Tonight, they'd have baths and eat and drink their fill for the first time in days.

Despite now-refilled supplies and relatively good progress, unease remained a low droning inside Flynn that refused to go silent. His gaze flicked up, taking in their modest camp. The Arcadian Wilds might've been eerie, but even dead trees provided cover. They were out in the open now in a way he didn't like. As one of five travelers including a powerful fire-wielding Magoi, an expert swordsman, and a god, he wouldn't have worried about it. As a man and a woman with no magic between them, traipsing around the Fisan countryside felt like an invitation for trouble.

He yanked at a particularly tough patch of dull-brown feathers to finish cleaning the bird, hoping Perses was more tender on the inside than out. As he prepared Perses for cooking, Flynn calculated distances from what he'd seen on his map. In another two days—three, at most—they'd reach Thassos. He'd never seen the ocean. He'd never looked across a lake he couldn't see the other side of. Endless sameness was one of the more terrifying things he could think of. A horizon that never got closer, nothing in every direction, nowhere to aim.

They were aiming for something, though—Circe's island. According to Jo's scroll, they just had to point themselves toward dangerous sea monsters and fake their own deaths to be on the right track. Excellent.

He grimaced. Even in his head, he didn't do sarcasm well.

Brushing his hands off, Flynn surveyed his work. He'd plucked, gutted, seasoned, and impaled Perses, who'd soon start dripping grease onto the fire and making it pop. All Jo had to do was turn the spit from time to time while he took his bath. Which he needed—two days ago.

"It's a good thing nothing of yours fell into the earthquake crevasse, or eating would be a challenge." Jo smiled at him as she approached, dressed in a fresh white tunic and finger combing her hair. "If you'd lost your pots and spices and we had to rely on my cooking abilities, we'd likely starve to death within a week."

A primal thrill thumped in Flynn's chest. Who'd have guessed the satisfaction of *providing* could make a man want to growl like a beast, scoop up his woman, and—

Gods almighty. He blinked. "We're eating fresh meat tonight because of your skill with a bow and arrow," he said in a voice that sounded drugged.

She waved a hand, dismissing that. "This time. Not always." She eyed the cooking fire. "Perses looks good."

Perses needed to cook so they could eat and Jo could go to sleep before he did something irreversible, like undress her.

She propped her leather satchel by the fire and laid the tunic she'd been wearing earlier over it. She'd washed it, along with what looked like some underthings that she draped over a stick she propped against the bag diagonally. He averted his gaze again.

Flynn had never believed he was a man with much imagination, but traveling alone with Jo was proving him wrong—hourly.

He grabbed his soap and drying cloth as blood rushed to his groin. He'd get in that stream not a second too early and kill his lust with a sharp slap of cold. "How icy is the stream?" he called out as he fled.

"Not cold at all," Jo called back. "Really pleasant."

"Excellent," he muttered under his breath. His sarcasm was better this time.

Flynn settled down by the low-burning campfire and pulled his cloak around him. He used a bunched-up tunic for a pillow. Jo had his bedroll and blanket. He'd insisted, just as he had since the earthquake. He couldn't fathom why she argued every time. Her sleeping things had fallen into the chasm. He'd been on watch and hadn't spread out his gear before the disaster happened. Did she really think he'd sleep on a pad and let her feel every lump in the cold, hard ground?

And it was cold. As soon as night fell, a strong, chilly wind started blowing down from the north, reminding him that the hot, dry season hadn't quite settled in for good.

"Flynn?" Jo's voice barely reached him even though they were mere feet apart.

"Jo." Was she afraid of waking him? He was so on edge with awareness of her, he thought he might never sleep again.

"I'm cold." She paused. "My hair's still damp, and that wind seems to be coming right through the blanket."

Flynn went utterly still, two imperatives colliding inside him. *Must warm woman.*

Run!

He swallowed. He'd been a little cold himself a second ago. The sudden bonfire in his veins fixed that and then some. He was a bloody volcano now.

"Flynn?"

He grunted.

"I can't sleep when my feet are cold."

"Do you...want me..." He couldn't believe he was about to say this. All logic told him it was the beginning of the end. "To help warm you?"

"That would be nice." She shifted, lifting a corner of the blanket in invitation.

Oh gods.

Flynn got up, moving as though his limbs weren't attached to his brain. Maybe they weren't. Maybe another part of his body was controlling him, because all his blood seemed to be flooding south and leaving him light-headed.

He unfastened his cloak and spread it over Jo before sliding under the now-double blanket next to her. She immediately snuggled into him, sliding one leg between his and laying a hand across his chest. With Jo tucked into the crook of his arm, her head on his shoulder, Flynn stared up at the cloudless sky, as still and silent as the stars above. Fear kept his cock in check. He wasn't sure which god to thank for that, since none of them seemed able to keep their own cocks in check. Still, he was thankful. He needed all the help he could get.

"Hmm. That's better." Her words whispered across his collarbone, her low smoke-and-velvet voice as erotic as the silky-hot caress of her breath.

"Warmer?" he managed to ask.

"Much." Her fingers started to move back and forth on his chest. Heat coiled in his abdomen. His damn cock twitched. "Flynn?"

He pushed out a sound in response. Jo had reduced him to a monosyllabic idiot, burning up while frozen in place.

"I wouldn't mind if you kissed me again."

White-hot desire and bone-chilling anxiety crashed like a storm inside him, tying his wildly thumping heart into a solid knot.

Marriage. Family.

Loss. Empty house.

They were so tangled up in his mind, he knew one couldn't come without the other, no matter what Jo said. Other people might want to tempt fate, but not him. He couldn't do that to Jo. He wouldn't do that to himself.

His arm tightened around her. "I'm afraid," he said before he realized the words were even in his mouth.

"I know. I'm afraid, too, Flynn. I'm afraid you won't even give us a chance."

He didn't answer. He couldn't form a sentence out of the chaotic jumble in his head. Pressure sat like a stone in his upper abdomen, heavy with dread, aching with want.

Jo seemed to hold her breath for a long time before finally relaxing against him and giving in to slumber. He didn't sleep at all—which was why he was wide awake when the Fisan brigands entered their camp.

CHAPTER 20

Jocasta lifted heavy lids when Flynn whispered her name. She sighed, still half-asleep. It was the first time she'd been warm and comfortable in days, and judging from the darkness, even Helios wasn't on his way yet. Did they really have to be?

"Tired," she mumbled. "Sleep some more."

"Shhh." Flynn's nose brushed her forehead as he lightly pressed a finger against her lips. It was so unlike him that she instantly snapped awake.

"What is it?" she whispered.

"Someone's trying to steal our horses and gear."

Steal Panotii and Brown Horse? She huffed. "That'll never happen." The three others might let themselves be led away, but not them.

Flynn's stubble rasped her cheek. "Lie still. Maybe they won't even know you're here." He rose silently, leaving her to look like a lump of blankets while he crept around the back side of the still-smoldering fire. He already had a dagger in one hand. He picked up his ax with the other, staying low to the ground.

Jocasta's heart thudded. She watched him creep toward the thieves, torn between doing what Flynn told her and making some move to help.

"Get those horses moving!" one of the thieves hissed as he slung Flynn's saddlebag over his shoulder. Two pans clanked together, and he hugged the bag close to his body, silencing the metal.

"I'm trying," another grumbled back.

"Just pull on the reins." The third was a woman's voice—sharp and in command.

Jocasta lifted her head a little more and saw three blobs moving around in the dark. What looked like a fourth, smaller blob huddled on a flat-topped rock farther off.

"I did. It's not working. Stupid things won't move," the thief closest to the horses muttered under his breath.

"Maybe this'll work." The woman clambered onto Panotii's back as if scaling a cliff before righting herself and giving him a solid kick.

Panotii ignored her. Brown Horse nipped her leg.

The woman thief growled in frustration. "We have to *move*." She pointed forward, as though that might help.

"I'm cold, Momma," the little blob whispered from her perch.

Jocasta's heart lurched. A child? Dragged into this?

"Steady, Zephyra. We'll get you to a healer faster this way," the woman whispered back.

Jocasta sat up. "What's happening here?"

Everyone stopped. Two short swords pointed her way while Flynn grabbed the woman and dragged her off Panotii, the handle of his ax around her middle and his knife at her throat.

"Momma!" the child cried, jumping up. The little blob toppled off the rock. Jocasta gasped along with the child's mother and the man—probably the girl's father—who stood by Panotii's head.

"Zephyra!" the woman cried. The child moaned and staggered back up, leaning heavily against the rock.

Jocasta stood. "What's wrong with her? I'm a healer." She moved toward the shocked thieves, who didn't look much like thieves at all. Their blades barely glinted in the moonlight, the steel old and dull. Their faces held far more fear than malice, and none of them made any move to actually use the weapons they brandished with more bravado than skill. "And *don't* touch my horse," she added to the man still holding the reins.

He let go immediately. Panotii snorted and shook his head.

"We saw the smoke from your fire before sunset," the woman said, keeping statue still behind Flynn's blade. Only her eyes shifted, jumping between her daughter and Jocasta. "We—my husband, daughter, and father—have a farm just beyond that hill." Her focus flicked to the rise south of them, outlined in the dull gray of approaching dawn. "The nearest healer is in Thassos, and my daughter… Something's wrong. She can barely move her right side, and she has this…lump." The woman touched her neck, presumably to show where her daughter's lump was.

Jocasta immediately started filtering the symptoms through the knowledge in her head. Partial paralysis. Swelling. Likely a fever—she'd have to check.

Snakebite was her first thought. Spider bite came next. Toxic plant after that, although she hoped it wasn't vegetal because with the sheer number of poisonous plants in Thalyria, it was hard to know them all—or their antidotes.

She needed more information. And to examine the child.

Flynn released the woman but kept his weapons at the ready. "And you decided to steal from us instead of asking for help?" Suspicion lined his every word as he cocked his head in doubt.

"Magoi don't help us," she said.

Jocasta gaped, taken aback. "What makes you think we're Magoi?"

"Fine horses. Rich clothing." The woman cautiously waved a hand in her direction. "Lighting a fire with no fear even though you're in brigand territory."

"You live in brigand territory," Jocasta pointed out.

"We struck a deal. We give them food and wine without question when they come knocking, and they take their thieving and violence elsewhere. My family has been here for generations. We're not giving up our farm." Something soured in the woman's voice. "We have nothing left to steal anyway, especially now that we're feeding dozens whenever they want."

The older man spat on the ground, maybe trying to rid himself of the taste of poverty and fear. "Whatever happened in the Arcadian Wilds flushed even more bandits out. You're either brave or stupid to be flaunting your wealth in these hills. Or Magoi—which gives you half a chance."

"Half?" Flynn asked, taking a few sidesteps that brought him closer to Jocasta.

"Who do you think leads the rovers? Magoi." The husband dredged up a bitter laugh. "All they've ever done is take."

"I told you this plan wouldn't work," the old man grumbled just as Jocasta was about to propose taking a closer look at the little girl. "Zephyra will probably be fine in a few days. Children get sick."

"Children. Get. Sick?" Flynn ground out. "And you wait around to see if they *die*?" The fury in his voice drove the old man back a step. Zephyra's parents gasped while the grandfather spread his hands in a mix of entreaty and defiance.

"What choice do we have? Wars for that witch of a Fisan queen emptied the villages in these parts. She's gone, but that doesn't give us our people back—the healthy ones who died because of her greed and violence. Every passerby for months cried *Elpis, Elpis* after Andromeda fell, but what has Queen Catalia given us? Hope?" His caustic laugh cut like a knife, especially them. "We haven't seen her *once*. All the new royals' grand projects haven't made it here. Healing centers? Schools? We still barely subsist. The nearest healer is still days away on foot. A sick child either gets better or not."

As if to prove his point, the girl moaned. "Momma, I just want to go home." Her teeth chattered with audible clacks.

The woman, so sharp and in control a moment ago, suddenly burst into tears. "Zephyra's the last of five. She's all I have left."

Jocasta's heart lurched. Flynn didn't move, but everything about him changed, saturating the air around him with a thundering energy full of darkness and pain. She didn't need full daylight to know how much his face had paled. She didn't need to be inside him to know how his stomach had dropped and how nausea had roiled up in its place.

She pulled up her sleeves. "I'm coming over to you, Zephyra. Don't move. Just rest." Jocasta bent down and pushed her still-damp tunic aside to open her satchel with her ointments and herbs and very clean, very sharp knives. She took out her healing equipment and left the rest. "I'm not a Magoi healer, but I'm still a healer. And a very good one, if I do say so myself."

The child watched her approach, her whole right side sagging against the rock. "Are ladies supposed to boast?" she asked in a shaky voice.

"I'm not a lady." Technically, that was true. She was a princess. "And it's not boasting if it's the truth."

Closer up and with the increasing light of dawn, Jocasta understood why Zephyra's parents were desperate enough to try to steal horses to reach a healer as fast as they could. The child was visibly flushed and feverish, but that wasn't what would terrify most parents into robbery. It was the huge and horrifying bulge on the side of her neck and the completely limp arm and mostly limp leg that would do the trick.

"My mother was a great healer," Jocasta said, still visually examining the girl without trying to touch her yet. Swollen red skin. What had to be fist-sized balls of pus underneath what she actually thought were at least two conjoining lumps. Fever. Chills. "I learned from the best."

"Is that boasting again?" Zephyra asked, curious and shy all at once—and bravely using questions to try to distract herself from fear and pain. Children were best at this. Adults usually just sat there, grimacing and focusing on how much something hurt.

"Again, not if it's the truth." Jocasta reached out without actually touching the girl. "May I?" she asked.

Zephyra nodded, and Jocasta gently felt the girl's neck. The lump was hot and hard to the touch. Zephyra winced.

"Have you lost your appetite?" she asked.

The child nodded.

"Have you upchucked?"

Embarrassment flashed across Zephyra's pain-gray face. "Twice," she said. "It was awful."

Her mother approached from the side and stood close without crowding Jocasta. "All that happened yesterday. The lump started the day before that. It just keeps getting bigger. Seems to double in size every time I look. And now she has trouble walking and can't use her right arm."

"Hmm. You're about ten years old?" Jocasta asked, carefully tugging the neck of Zephyra's tunic down. The skin over the bulge was so distended it was hard to tell anything from it. She *thought* she was seeing white-ringed bull's-eyes with red dots in the centers. She wasn't sure yet, but with this amount of swelling, she was almost certain she was looking for multiple spider bites.

She carefully righted the girl's tunic, keeping it away from the sore lump on her neck.

"Twelve," Zephyra answered. "I'm small for my age."

"I was always small for my age, too." Jocasta lifted Zephyra's loose blonde hair back and examined her hairline and then the little nook behind her ear. And there it was: a definite ringed target around two distinctive jab marks, one next to the other. The swelling was less here, which also helped narrow the remaining suspects down to one vicious little spider. By the third or fourth bite in a row, two-headed spotted hydrachnes were almost always out of venom.

Jocasta smoothed the girl's hair back behind her bony shoulder. Even if this family had managed to steal the horses and ride toward Thassos, Zephyra would've been dead before they ever reached a healer.

Fortunately, she was here, and she would save this girl's life. "Being small makes it harder to climb trees," she said with a teasing smile.

"And to get out of them," Flynn rumbled behind her.

"Yes," Jocasta agreed, remembering him lifting her down from the big ash tree between their houses more than once.

"We hardly have any trees," Zephyra said.

"Maybe not, but you still have tree spiders, like the sneaky little spotted hydrachne that gave you this large lump on your neck."

Zephyra's eyes widened. "Is it poisonous?"

"Unfortunately, yes. That's why your neck is swollen and hot and you have a fever."

"And my arm won't move?" Zephyra tried to bend her right leg, showing that it wasn't working well, either. She winced, clearly in pain all over.

"That, too," Jocasta said. "But I can help you. You'll need to be very brave, because it's not easy. Right now, that big lump is still holding most of the spider's poison, but it's slowly leaking out and reaching other places in your body. We have to drain the venom before it does any more damage." Such as shut down all the muscles and organs of her body. "You see, that big ball of fluids on your neck is actually your body's natural defense against the spotted hydrachne. Think of it as a barricade, trying to keep the poison from attacking the rest of you. It gives you time to find a healer—like me." She smiled reassuringly. "But let's get you home first. You'll be happier in your own bed, and then you can stay there and rest for a few days while your family treats you like a princess." She gave a pointed look at the mother, who nodded without hesitation, and then at the father, who did the same.

She didn't bother looking at the grandfather. She'd written him off the moment he turned Flynn inside out with a few careless words that had probably cut his own family just as deeply.

She turned to Flynn. "What do you need?" he asked before she even opened her mouth.

"Let's get them to their farm as fast as possible. Zephyra can ride with one of her parents. We even have horses for everyone."

———————— 🌀 ————————

Jocasta rolled her stiff shoulders and took several deep breaths, enjoying the warm, sage-scented air that breezed over the hills and the low drone of insects that reminded her of home. They'd saved a life, and despite the fatigue of leaning over a bedside for hours, she floated on that indefinable feeling she got as a healer, that gladness that she'd been in the right place at the right time.

Flynn joined her outside and leaned against the fence next to her, resting his forearms on the rough-hewn wood and staring out across the Fisan countryside. It was well past noon, the sun high in the sky and that nasty north wind a distant memory.

Honestly, it had been since the moment Flynn held her in his arms.

"That was extraordinary." He turned to her. "You're extraordinary. You saved that girl."

A warm flush of pleasure swept through her. Simple, heartfelt words were all she'd ever wanted from Flynn, and they seemed to come more easily now.

"I'm happy I knew what to do. The spotted hydrachne's not common." Or it wasn't in Sinta, where they were from. "They say it's a leftover from a fight between Hera and Zeus. He cheated, as usual, and she retaliated by creating a horde of two-headed spiders that bit her rival to death—a human, here in Fisa." That would explain there being more spotted hydrachnes in the Thalyrian east. "The human woman supposedly attracted Zeus's attention because she was such a graceful, athletic dancer, and so Hera's spider poison took away her ability to move. Then breathe. Then live."

Flynn grunted in distaste. "It seems unfair that the rival paid for Zeus's disloyalty, especially when he probably didn't give her much choice."

Pursing her lips, Jocasta glanced north toward Mount Olympus, almost afraid to voice her true thoughts. The gods likely weren't listening, but she wasn't *sure* of that. "That's the Olympians. Look at Medusa and her sisters. There was nothing fair about that." And now they were dead.

Traitor to abused women. Betrayer of women wronged.

A shiver peppered her arms with goose bumps.

Kill or be killed.

Jocasta had every intention of staying alive.

"Life isn't fair." Flynn's face darkened. But then he drew his shoulders back and made a visible effort to shake off whatever somber thought or memory plagued him this time. "But sometimes... Lately, really"—he lifted a hand and smoothed her hair back, tucking a lock behind the shell of her ear—"some of the things I think about don't seem so scary anymore. Maybe, like today for these people, it doesn't have to all go wrong."

Jocasta looked up at him in shock, replaying his words in her head. *It doesn't have to all go wrong.* Her heart suddenly beat with a hard, battering rhythm that stole her breath. She wet her lips, and Flynn's gaze dropped to her mouth. His work-roughened fingertips glided down her neck. Then, deliberately, he slid his big palm around her nape and gripped.

Heat washed through her. A little sound lodged in her throat.

His searing gaze flicked back up. "Jo?"

"Yes." Her answer shot from her so quickly it might've been comical if she hadn't been waiting for this her whole life.

His eyes flared. "Yes to what?"

"Anything," she murmured. "Everything. You."

Flynn trapped a low groan behind closed lips. His expression set her skin on fire. His hand pulsed on the back of her neck, and Jocasta's legs grew heavy while her breathing sped up.

He swallowed hard. "You could keep them alive. *You.* Just like you did today."

She wasn't sure who *they* were, but a lightning bolt of hope told her this was about their future together, the family they might have. "I could try. I *would* try. I would move the cosmos."

"But you?" He tugged her closer, his shadow over her a comfort, as though he offered the tower of his strength. "Who would help you?"

I'm a tower, too, just a smaller one. "I'll have to train a son or daughter to be a healer, won't I?" she said in a low and breathless rush.

A familiar expression crossed his face. What she'd taken for unresponsiveness for years was actually a brittle mask of pain. "That would take too long. Too much could happen..."

Jocasta felt him about to back off and slid her hands over his shoulders, stepping near enough for their chests to touch. "I'm not going anywhere, Flynn." They were so close that the temptation to crush herself against his big warm body almost won out, but it was more important for Jocasta to look at him, to show him the truth on her face. "I'm strong. I'm healthy. And we're in the lucky position now of having powerful allies, wealth, and Magoi healers if we need them."

His breath shuddered out. He squeezed his eyes shut and leaned down, his deliciously rasping golden-red stubble teasing her cheekbone. He stayed there for a long time, perfectly still, cheek to cheek, breathing hard. "I want you so badly."

Jocasta's insides took flight on wings of fire. "Then claim me," she whispered back, sliding her hands into his short hair and gripping. She could hardly believe the words that left her mouth. She hadn't been this bold even when she'd been so sure of everything on her eighteenth birthday. She'd kissed him, but she hadn't said *this*. "Claim me, Flynn," she said again, throwing all caution to the wind.

He breathed jaggedly against her jaw, one hand still wrapped around her nape. Jocasta waited, tension gathering in her middle, fear sneaking into her thoughts, and her whole body trembling with ice and heat. *Say the words,* she silently begged.

Her stomach twisted into knots as she waited. Claiming was an old-fashioned southern Sintan ritual that sounded barbaric to outsiders who didn't understand. It was a promise of protection and devotion. In many cases, it replaced marriage, because it meant the same thing. If Flynn claimed her, he wasn't telling her, *You're mine*; he was telling her, *I'm yours*. And then she could do the same.

CHAPTER 21

"I…" *Flynn gently tugged Jo against his chest and held her there,* torn straight down the middle.

Gods, he wanted her. And not just physically, although that was a constant weight in his groin. He loved her intelligence, her determination, her kindness, her prickliness, her courage, her everything. He loved her.

But he could love from a distance. The gods knew, he had practice enough. Claiming, though… Claiming led to every-thing he'd sworn to forgo.

He squeezed his eyes shut, wet heat pricking his lids. Did she really say those words aloud? *Claim me, Flynn.* She wanted him enough to bind herself to him for life? Wanted him anyway, knowing he wasn't half as smart, wealthy, or ambitious as she was?

In a rough rasp, he finally said, "I don't know how to do anything but fight and farm."

Jo hummed, low and soft. "Fight and farm." She nodded against his chest, despite his firm hold on the back of her head. "Protect. Provide."

Flynn couldn't help the incredulous smile that lifted his mouth. "You hear what I didn't say and change my words around."

Her arms came around his middle and linked behind his back. "I'm exceedingly good at that."

He choked back a laugh. "How can you make me smile when I feel like I've been struck by a meteor?"

"Am I a meteor now?" She tilted her head back, her sapphire eyes narrowing. "How flattering."

"Not flattering?" A meteor was the most spectacular thing he could think of, rare and beautiful. Fire in the sky. "You're straight from the heavens, and I don't know what to do with you."

Her look turned impish, a hint of pleasure flushing her cheeks. "Kiss me, Flynn. That could be a start."

His pulse leaped. So did other parts of him. "If I do, will you try to stop twisting my words from now on?"

"If you do, I'll be too breathless to talk."

Emotion burst inside him so hard he reeled. What a gift, to be able to make him feel ten feet tall and utterly desirable when he knew neither was true. "A kiss could never be just a kiss with you."

Her eyes searched his, and he found himself falling hopelessly into their jewel-bright depths. "What if..." She hesitated. "What if we made it just you and me? If that's what you truly want, I know how to avoid pregnancy. Would that ease your mind?"

Jo's proposition stunned him. He couldn't lose what he didn't have. That had been his objective all along, the reason he'd run from her years ago. Jo herself would still be a constant worry, but he knew how capable she was. Something would have to be worse than the Agon Games, the Gorgon sisters, three obsessively overprotective brothers, and a variety of even the most severe injuries and illnesses to get the better of her. Her offer was the most selfless, compassionate compromise he'd ever heard. So why did it feel like a knife in the gut? Twisting, turning. Not right.

He shook his head before he knew he was doing it. "I can't do that to you." To himself, maybe. To *them*, because he doubted a decision like that wouldn't come back to haunt them.

Jo's hard little laugh didn't sound like her at all. "Flynn, I don't want to be intimate with anyone but you, so without you, I won't have children anyway. Not my own."

He let her go and took a step back, everything starting to feel heavy and constricted inside. His chest grew tight. Unease flooded him, and his heartbeat took off, hammering an agitated rhythm that chopped up his breath.

This was why he didn't *talk* about anything—especially feelings. It made him sweat.

His voice reedy, he said, "You could change your mind."

"About being with someone else? Or about needing children?"

"Either." His ribs seemed to close in and squeeze his heart. "Both."

She frowned. "Do you think you know me better than I know myself?"

"I know you pretty well." Gods, his lungs felt tight. He tugged at the collar of his tunic, perspiration heating the back of his neck. "I've known you since birth."

"Is that the problem?" She glared, crossing her arms. "I'm still your best friend's little sister? My gods, Flynn. Let it go. I'm an adult."

"That's not the problem." His heart pounded so hard he heard it in his mouth.

"Then what is? Tell me?"

"I…" *Duh-dun. Duh-dun. Duh-dun.* He blinked and tried to swallow down the thuds.

Jo stepped back, half turning from him. "I've offered every solution I can think of. I've thrown myself at you—twice. Three times, really." A bitter laugh burst from her throat. "Well, don't worry. I won't do it again." Her brilliant blue eyes flashed with anger and hurt. "I'll be a daughter, a sister, eventually an aunt, and a healer, and that will have to be enough. And you can have a grand old time being *alone*." She whirled and stomped off.

Flynn lunged after her without thought. He wrapped his hand around her elbow and coaxed her to a stop. "No."

She pivoted to face him, belligerence a thunderclap across her face. "No *what*?"

"Don't walk away."

She pressed her mouth flat. Then her delicate nostrils flared on a deep breath. "Why not? I'm not walking away from anything."

He growled at that. "You're walking away from *me*."

"So? What does it matter? You don't want me. Not enough."

"I want you more than life itself!" Sheer disbelief overcame his anxiety, and for the first time, Flynn was as brave with her as he was in battle, where it was simply do or die, and his thoughts didn't get all jumbled up and impossible to bear. "You, everything you represent, everything you offer, it's my dream *and* my nightmare. You don't know what it's like to lose *everyone*. To know it can happen again."

"You never lost everyone! You had Griffin, Carver, me, Kato." Jo's voice broke on Kato's name, and Flynn's chest lurched with familiar pain. "You were happy when you were fighting and making a difference, being a part of Griffin's team."

He nodded slowly, wary of ever claiming happiness. He hadn't been *unhappy*. There'd been kinship, some laughter, common goals, and victories. "As happy as I can be. But that's all different now." The Power Bid was over. Griffin married Cat. Carver changed. Kato was dead, just like Flynn's entire birth family. "Why am I still here when so many others aren't? I haven't done anything worthy of being spared."

Her jaw dropped. He'd never seen her look so aghast. "You're only one of the half-dozen people who *changed the world*. Cat and Griffin didn't take Thalyria by themselves. But beyond that, maybe you're still here for *me*. And maybe you're wasting your chance."

Jo's words hit him like a Cyclops's club to the head. Could she be right?

Old Hector flashed in his mind, slapping him hard across the face for almost bedding a girl without intending to claim her. Years later, the only person Flynn had ever wanted to claim was still Jocasta. Would she laugh at him for being a virgin? No one knew that about him besides Kato, who wasn't talking from the Underworld. Flynn had told her he hadn't kissed anyone since her, but Jo probably hadn't taken that to mean he'd never had sex. Fear of fumbling like an idiot and disappointing her in bed was just one more thing holding him back.

He gripped the back of his sweaty neck. What a joke. He was a renowned warrior who'd come out on the winning side of inconceivably deadly situations time and again, and yet it was fear of intimacy, domesticity, and *other* people's deaths that ruled his life.

Flynn was silent for too long and saw the moment Jo lost her spark.

"I'm finished here." She glanced at the farmhouse where a recovering little girl slept, but she really meant she was done with this conversation, with him. "Let's get back to our quest."

"Stop." He reached out and gripped her arms. Not hard, just enough to make her halt midstep and look at him again. "You're torturing me."

Her eyebrows flew up. "*I'm* torturing you?"

For a second, Flynn thought she was going to knee him in the balls. She didn't, and he blurted out, "You're the first thing I think about when I wake up. Yours is the face in my mind when I fall asleep. You haunt my dreams, daytime and night." Great Zeus, he couldn't stop talking. Jo stared at him, wide-eyed. For once, she didn't interrupt. "But you terrify me. If we go down this path together, and I lose you, *I will break.* I already knew it six years ago. If anything, now it's *worse.*"

Her brow creased. "Why worse?"

Because I love you so damn much it turns me inside out. Admitting that seemed too much. "Because I know myself better," was all he said.

"You're not Old Hector."

"I *am.*"

Her frown deepened. "Well, I'm not your mother."

He grimaced. "I know that."

"I don't mean in an Oedipal way," she snapped, frustration sharpening her voice. "I mean she was weak—physically. I only remember her that way. *My* mother only remembers her that way. She always had a cough, an ache, a sore something. Every time she got sick, it lasted for weeks, not days." Jo shook off his grip but didn't step away. "Old Hector might've let himself wither away from a broken heart when he still had a son to take care of, but your mother died because she was ill. She'd *always* been ill. I. Am. Not."

Flynn stared at her, his pulse racing and his palms a sweaty mess. Some of what she said penetrated his fears, even though he tried to make her logic bounce off. "The rest were all accidents. My brothers and sisters weren't weak and ill."

"Maybe not," Jo agreed. "I don't understand the workings of the Fates. The Moirai choose how long to make our threads of life and when to cut them and how. There are things we can't control, Flynn. You need to accept that."

But he could control things in his own way. No wife. No children. No family to lose.

No turning into Old Hector.

"What you *can* control is what you do with your life. How you live the time you're given." She lifted a hand and lightly placed it over his rapidly beating heart. "Do you know what I dream of?"

He shook his head, snared in the bright-blue depths of her earnest gaze and trapped by the small, capable hand that barely touched his chest.

"I dream of a big farmhouse with blue shutters and little red hera's hearts blooming by the doorstep. I dream of vast, rolling olive groves and year after year of bountiful harvests. I dream of a huge medicinal herb garden behind my kitchen—where I do almost none of the cooking—and of villagers I've known their whole lives coming and going so frequently for my help, tonics, and advice that the stone walkway leading to the house is smoothed by countless feet until it's slippery when it rains, and you have to replace it."

"Me?"

"Of course *you*, Flynn." She dropped her hand. He caught it and brought it back to his chest. She swallowed, looking at their hands together. "I want you. And I want to go home. If you at all want what I want, please let me know before I leave for the village."

Panic rocked him. "Leave?"

"I'll leave sometime after Cat and Griffin have their baby." She tugged her hand away. "Assuming we survive this and find a solution for them."

His panic doubled. They still had to face the five trials. Face Circe. What if he lost Jo anyway, without ever kissing her again? Without claiming her? Without telling her she was everything to him?

With a groan, Flynn pulled her against him and buried his

face in her hair. He was a heartbeat away from bellowing his love for her, but his throat closed up so tightly he could barely draw air.

Jo's arms came around him. She gently stroked his back, soothing and unhurried. He realized then how patient she was, how patient she'd always been with him, even when she'd been snapping and twisting his words and…waiting. Always waiting. For him.

"I have so much to say," he whispered. "But it never comes out."

"I usually talk enough for both of us."

The surge of air that left his mouth might've been a laugh. "I love to hear you talk."

He felt her smile against his jaw. "That's a relief."

"You're the most interesting person I know." He slowly slid his nose across her cheek. "And the most desirable."

Her breath turned rough and unsteady against the corner of his mouth. "Flynn?"

His abdomen clenched, heating, tightening. "I'll never be the same again."

"Isn't that the idea?" she murmured. "When one chooses a new path?"

Agreement vibrated in his throat. He slid his mouth to hers and softly pressed. Jo doubled the pressure, her lips warm and full, and he groaned from that place he kept locked up tight inside his chest. He wrapped his arms around her and angled his head. Jo did the same, inviting him deeper with a coaxing little sound Flynn would crave for the rest of his life. She was everything a man could want. Everything *he* wanted. Fire raced through his blood. Every sensation grew brighter, hotter. His hands fell to the flare of her waist. He squeezed. She flicked her tongue out, and he nearly collapsed.

Flynn turned and pressed her up against the fence. Jo wrapped one leg around his hip and angled into him. Their bodies rubbed together. She gasped.

"*This*," she breathed out. "*Yes*." Her fingers swept into his hair and massaged his head. With a little whimper, she drew his lower lip into her mouth and sucked.

Flynn shuddered, the tug of her mouth pulling straight down to his cock. He was so hard, he hurt. Wild centaurs couldn't drag him away the next time he had this beautiful, willing woman in a place he could explore every inch of her. Kiss. Taste. Take.

He groaned, turning feverish at the thought. His heart pounded, his blood hot.

"Flynn, don't stop. Don't ever stop." She writhed against him, and he licked the words right from her mouth.

He kissed her jaw and neck, utterly dazed but still blazingly aware of every move and sound Jo made. Her breath pelted the air next to his ear in hard little pants. Her fingers tightened on his scalp. The pulse at the base of her throat fluttered under his lips, delicate and fast. She tasted like ambrosia, and he would never get enough.

"Have to stop," he finally managed to rasp out in between firebolts of sensation that tried to incinerate all rational thought. "In someone's front yard…"

She let out a whimper of frustration, gripping him harder despite what he'd said. Flynn wasn't sure how he managed, but he stopped kissing her before someone came out of the house and interrupted them. His chest rose and fell like bellows. Who knew sheer, thumping *want* could wind him as though he'd just run to Olympus and back? It was insanity. Sweaty, shaky, pulse-pounding insanity, his body up in flames.

He moaned with the effort to pull away. Jo let her head drop back, hitting the fence post with a thud that made them both cringe. Flynn tucked his hand between her head and the wood, gazing down at her and marveling at the most beautiful sight he'd ever seen—Jo with flushed cheeks, mussed hair, and kiss-swollen lips. *He'd* done that.

Pride filled him.

Or tenderness.

No, both.

Things that had been jagged and fragile inside him firmed up and slid into place. "I'm your olive."

Jo stared at him. "I've known that forever."

His heart swelled with the promise of the life she offered. A farm. A healing practice. A home. "We have a lot to do. How about we finish this journey so that we can start a new one—for us?"

Her blush-pink lips curved into a smile that rekindled the heat in his groin. "I thought you'd never ask."

CHAPTER 22

They rode all afternoon and evening in the direction of Thassos. Jocasta didn't see the time go by. All she could think about was Flynn, their kisses, their words. Promises. Not yet claiming, but almost as good.

What would happen when they made camp? Would she wake up tomorrow morning no longer a virgin and essentially married? She could finish seducing Flynn tonight. This could be it. Her heart pounded with excitement.

Unfortunately, idiot brigands got in the way.

The bandits struck just before nightfall, and the thieves were sneaky enough to trap them in a difficult place.

"Five horses and likely some gold, judging from those fine clothes and saddles." A yellow-toothed man blocked their path, his eyes greedy, beady, and green. Fisan Magoi green. Who knew what magic he had?

Flynn angled himself and Brown Horse to shield her from the bandit's view. "Walk away, and you might live," he said.

The leader laughed. His band of four men echoed him as two more came out of the shadows, snickering along with them. That made two against seven. Jocasta didn't like those odds, especially when at least one of them had magic.

"Dismount, stand aside, and *you* might live," the leader said. "And we might even leave your wife alone."

Flynn's nostrils flared. Jocasta *heard* it from behind.

Her blood ran cold. Fury—and memories she tried hard to avoid—came surging up like bad well water. Bitter. Sour. Poisonous. There was only one way this would end. There was only one way it *ever* ended with raiders. They took. They raped. They killed.

Or they at least tried to.

She nocked an arrow, drew back, and fired. They never got her before. They wouldn't get her this time.

The Magoi bandit grabbed his thigh. "She shot me!" he hollered.

Jocasta already had another bolt aimed at his heart. "Leave. Now." She narrowed her eyes down the shaft of her arrow.

The Magoi leader motioned with his hand, and the man on his left leaped at Flynn. Two more jumped in the same direction as Flynn drew his ax and started punching, blocking, and swinging with skill and cold purpose beyond any of their reckoning.

With a snarl, the leader snapped her arrow shaft, leaving only a stub sticking out of his leg. He came for her. Jocasta let fly her second arrow. He dodged with a slippery drop and roll and came up running. She nocked another arrow, her hands shaking. He sprinted for her, two men flanking him. All three had long, curving daggers.

A jarring force suddenly hit her from behind. She flew off Panotii's back, landing hard and knocking the air from her lungs. Flynn cried her name. An eighth bandit loomed over her. He smiled in triumph.

Jocasta whacked her forehead into his nose, dislodging him as he tried to pin down her wrists. He reeled back with a howl. She kicked out at another attacker. She hit him—she didn't know where. Panotii clamped his teeth down on the man's shoulder and tossed him away from her.

Jocasta finally managed to inhale again, sucking down a

breath that came back out on a yell when the leader sprang at her. She drew her dagger. He blocked her strike and pressed down until both their blades were at her throat. He trapped her on her back on the ground, and Jocasta didn't dare breathe at all. Her arms shook as she struggled to push him off her.

"Jo!" Flynn's frantic shout spurred her into action. She couldn't see him, but his voice was so desperate it scared her.

A wild sort of strength flooded her, and she heaved with both hands, making enough room to drive her knee into the Magoi's groin. The moment their crossed blades slipped to the side, she cuffed him across the ear.

He shook off both blows and whipped back down on her, landing a ringing hit to her ribs. Pain burst inside her. Gasping, Jocasta doubled in on herself. He pounced. His power flared to life, and he sent a jolt of icy magic into her arm, leaving it numb and limp from fingers to shoulder. Clenching her teeth, she scooted away from him. He grabbed her calf, and her leg went as dead as her arm, the paralyzing cold washing all the way up into her backside.

Jocasta flipped onto her stomach and tried to slither away, using one arm and one leg to propel herself across the ground. Something thumped beside her—a severed head. Flynn swung his ax in her peripheral vision. A man went down in total silence. Another sprang forward, thrusting his knife toward Flynn's abdomen. Flynn spun out of the way and engaged in a fierce exchange of strikes that only took three hits before he stabbed his short sword between the man's ribs. His ax came down at almost the same time and cleaved the thief's head straight down the middle. He pulled both weapons free with a wash of blood and a snarl Jocasta would remember with a dark shiver of satisfaction when this was over.

The scuff of footsteps was her only warning before someone

landed hard on her back and grabbed her wrists, pinning them beside her head. She only felt one of the rough hands holding her, her other arm still completely numb and lifeless. The weight on top of her kept her from moving while someone else started ripping at her belt to try to free her coin purse.

Wouldn't they be surprised to find only a few measly coppers? A frenzied laugh burst from her.

She struggled and kicked, tried to bite, all the while watching Flynn move closer to her. Brigands dropped one by one, fighting him when they should've been fleeing. Blood-boiling rage didn't stop Flynn from being utterly in control of his every movement. Precise. Deadly. Focused on her as much as on the enemy. The easygoing, sometimes standoffish mountain of a man she saw every day was gone. He'd unleashed a no-holds-barred, bone-shattering beast and would finish off these raiders.

"Flynn!" she screamed. "Don't let the Magoi touch you!"

Flynn snapped a neck, his face twisting in fury. He threw the bandit aside, and a thrill went through her. Her monster was coming.

The leader reared off her and leaped at Flynn, his magic-cold hands outstretched and pulsing with darkness. He lost one hand to Flynn's ax along with half a forearm. The blood spurt was glorious.

The Magoi shrieked, clutching the bloody stump to his chest. His breath pounded out of him. He scrambled backward.

"He's a tree farmer, you filth!" Jocasta shouted after him. "He knows how to use an ax!"

A knee suddenly crushed her spine, pinning her so hard to the ground that she involuntarily exhaled all the air left in her body.

Flynn stalked right up to the stumbling Magoi leader and kicked him in the hip. The man doubled over. In the next second, his head left his body. It rolled to Jocasta's feet like an offering, and despite the weight on her back, she smashed her booted heel into the dirt-smeared forehead.

The only bandit left hopped off her when Flynn turned to them. He scuttled back on all fours, begging, "Spare me."

Jocasta flopped over and punched the thief in the face. Which bloody *hurt!* She screamed in fury, tears pricking her eyes, her hand throbbing. Half her limbs still felt lifeless, dead weights attached to her torso.

Flynn advanced like a nightmare. Her dream man. "Is mercy on the table?" His voice could raze mountains. Split oceans. She loved him more than anything.

But Jocasta hesitated. She'd never been the one to utter a death sentence before. Choices didn't seem as black and white once the battle ended.

The decision left her hands before she drew her next breath. A thunderbolt dropped from the sky and smote the last brigand where he crouched in fear before them. The heat and deafening boom knocked Jocasta over again, and she lay there in shock, spots marring her vision, her ears ringing.

Flynn shouted her name, a muffled sound barely penetrating the chaos in her mind as he quickly closed the distance between them. He dropped to his knees beside her, blocking the too-bright sky from her sensitive eyes, which still had the burning outline of a jagged lightning bolt seared across them. She blinked, trying to chase the fiery remains from her vision.

Flynn hovered over her, his hands cupping her face, his thumbs gently stroking her cheekbones. Worry etched lines into his bloodied face. His *beloved* face.

Jocasta reached for him with her good arm, smiling to reassure him. Flynn scooped her up and carried her away from the smoldering crater. As his long strides moved them farther from the body-strewn area and blood-soaked ground, Jocasta looked around. The horses had scattered, but they'd come back. Panotii would make sure of it.

She curled into Flynn's warm, sweaty chest, her lips brushing his collarbone. "My gods," she whispered, trembling from the shock of everything.

"'My gods' is right." He clutched her hard, and she reveled in the pressure of his arms around her. Despite the heat of the battle, cold still built inside her, and she worried about how long the Magoi's power would last. The arm and leg he'd sunk his icy magic into still felt as numb as ever.

"That was a god bolt." Jocasta could barely conceive of it.

Flynn nodded. "Helping us helps Cat—and all of Thalyria. I wouldn't have believed it yesterday, but it looks like the gods haven't forgotten us after all."

No. Zeus was watching from Mount Olympus. She wondered who else was paying attention.

———— ⑥ ————

Thassos turned out to be stunning, a beautiful port city with boats of all shapes and sizes bobbing in the bright-blue harbor, colorful homes with generous terraces and swooping sunshades climbing up the surrounding, sometimes steep hillsides, and views over the sparkling water to take a person's breath away and never give it back again. Pockets of rocky shoreline turned into long sandy beaches. Frothy waves lapped at their edges, the ceaseless thrust and pull of the tide engraving uneven patterns into the sand for miles.

Jocasta simply couldn't stop *looking*. Everything was brighter here—the sun, the sea, the paint on the shutters. She'd never dreamed of anything like Thassos, and her imagination wasn't lacking. She couldn't understand why the entire population of

Thalyria wasn't converging on this place and vying for property, although it might have something to do with the dangerous sea creatures apparently lurking just beyond the inner waters.

People were friendly. "Hello! Welcome to Thassos!"

A greeting they inevitably followed with a warning phrase and a sign to ward off evil. "Stay close to the shore! Beware of the ketea!"

By the umpteenth word of caution from a well-meaning resident, Jocasta found her immunity to their warnings rising along with the tide. So what if there were sharp-toothed sea dragons off the coast just waiting to take bites out of careless sailors? She didn't care—at least not today. The danger was in the deep, and Thassos was beautiful.

"Have you ever seen anything like it?" she asked in wonder. She sat on Flynn's lap atop Brown Horse—a place she would've loved to be under less painful circumstances. Even partial paralysis couldn't keep her from constant awareness of the warm, muscular body cradling hers and the strong arm circling her waist to hold her steady. It only kept her from thoroughly *enjoying* it.

Flynn simply shook his head, either rendered speechless by Thassos or too tired to answer after hauling her and five horses around for the last three days with little rest and a lot of worry.

Despite her own worry over her barely improved condition, Jocasta couldn't help marveling at the scenery. A million sunlit jewels rode each glittering wave rolling toward the shoreline, and it was hard not to wonder if the nereids didn't try to capture the twinkling lights from the water's surface as a game when they weren't busy doing Poseidon's bidding. The fifty daughters of Nereus and Doris surely had the most coveted home of all the deities, because the sea was *magnificent*.

But as the day wore on and they checked tasks off their lengthy to-do list, even Jocasta's pleasure at the exotic sights started to wane in the face of burning pins and needles. The pain in her arm and leg got worse in the evenings, pulsing through her whole body until she wanted to erupt in tears of agony and frustration. By the time Flynn finished renting a private villa by the shore and setting her up in a rocking chair overlooking the water, she was almost ready to use Persephone's heliotrope amulet on *herself* to end her suffering.

She wouldn't, even if she thought about it. The bespelled gemstone was for a life-or-death situation, and this wasn't that. She could even move her previously entirely limp limbs a little more each morning, giving her hope that every day would bring improvement. In the meantime, though, it was awful. Her brave face was starting to twist into a grimace, and Flynn had run out of anecdotes to distract her.

Besides waiting for the numbing magic to finally fade on its own, their other option was to try to locate a Magoi healer. Since she and Flynn were both Hoi Polloi, neither of them believed for a second a Magoi healer would accept her as a patient. Cat and Griffin were fighting this kind of prejudice, but they'd only just begun, and Fisan Magoi were widely known for being the most elitist in Thalyria. Short of revealing her identity as a royal—which Jocasta couldn't prove anyway—there was simply no way a magical healer would help them unless they stumbled upon a truly exceptional person.

Unfortunately, bribery was currently out of the question. Without Bellanca and her jewels, they needed everything Flynn had in his coin purse to secure safe lodgings with a stable and caretaker, restock their supplies, and buy a boat.

As for a Hoi Polloi healer, Jocasta already knew there wasn't an herb, pressure point, or salve that could help her. She'd tried everything she could think of.

Their first morning in Thassos, she rose somewhat refreshed

and hopeful. Sleeping in a comfortable bed next to Flynn had helped. Waking up to the sound of the waves hadn't hurt, either. But a day of rest at the villa while Flynn was out and about just left her bored and antsy. Now, as dinnertime approached, the pain was worsening, and Jocasta was already looking forward to the next morning when it would probably feel marginally better again.

While Flynn clomped and banged around inside, she rocked to the rhythm of the waves lapping at the beach below her. Her good leg propelled the soothing motion, and Jocasta blocked out the stabbing pain in her other leg as best she could. She might've downplayed her discomfort more than once so that Flynn would take care of their overall needs instead of just hers. It was hard to regret her decision when, by the end of their first full day in Thassos, he'd gathered everything they needed for a sea journey, including a boat and someone to show them how to sail it. He'd also left word of their whereabouts for the rest of Team Elpis at the two largest inns along the coast road going north. Her brother, Bellanca, and Prometheus would know exactly where to find them.

Flynn was efficient. She loved it. They'd make a perfectly efficient couple.

Warmth engulfed her at the idea of them really, *finally*, having a future together.

An *incendiary* and efficient couple.

She grinned. *Oh yes.* This was happening. Flynn was beginning to act as though it—*they*—were inevitable, and the idea didn't even seem to terrify him. Or at least not entirely. What could be better?

A working arm and leg?

Jocasta snorted, her own thoughts mocking her as usual. Well, a full set of working limbs would come eventually, and on the bright side, Flynn had gotten so used to helping her and holding her over the last few days that he did it naturally now, the awkwardness burned away by necessity.

In fact, Flynn went above and beyond the necessary at every opportunity. His take-charge attitude over the last several days made her wonder why he'd always stayed so unobtrusively in the background when he was clearly just as capable a leader and decision-maker as Griffin. Had he not realized his own capabilities before taking over as captain of the royal guard? Or had he simply not wanted to step on Griffin's toes? There was no doubt her brother liked to boss people around. And that Cat was just as bossy as Griffin.

Of course, that didn't stop her from loving them both dearly. And Flynn would be the first to jump to their defense if anyone dared voice a disparaging thought about either Cat or Griffin.

Sighing, Jocasta took one last look at the sunset colors and then dragged herself off the terrace overlooking their secluded beach. She would see to her private needs and wash in the small, adjoining bathhouse while Flynn finished cooking their dinner. His meal already smelled delicious and might help her forget the throbbing in her limbs for a few minutes.

The entire time she was out of sight, however, Flynn stood just outside the bathhouse doorway, calling out to her at regular intervals and waiting for her to call back to him. He was apparently more worried about her doing a one-legged, one-armed face flop into the pool and never coming out again than about their dinner situation.

He wasn't wrong. She tottered twice and scared herself but managed to come out of the ordeal bathed and unscathed, if a little winded.

"How are you doing?" Flynn looked her up and down is if checking for injuries when she appeared in fresh clothing and

with squeaky-clean hair again. He'd already bathed before starting the cooking.

Jocasta made a noncommittal sound to answer his question
and drag-hopped herself to a chair at the table. Shortly after,
Flynn set her dinner in front of her—lightly herbed lamb steak,
baby potatoes, and tender-crisp carrots. Her stomach rumbled.

"I've always liked carrots." Emotion stirred up entirely by
Flynn and his thoughtfulness condensed into a lump in her
throat. She swallowed.

"I know. You used to eat them raw, straight from the garden."

"Not exactly. I at least dunked them in a bucket of water
first."

He chuckled. "Don't tell me you weren't crunching dirt."

She bit down on a grin. "Never. Not once."

He lifted skeptical brows as he set a loaf of fresh bread on
the table. It smelled divine. So did Flynn—clean with a hint of
brine. The salt air clung to them both, a little cool and sticky.
Now that Helios had dragged the sun all the way across the sky,
Jocasta shivered when the sea breeze drifted past the diaphanous
fabric framing the open arches to the veranda. Heat didn't attach
to the land here, as it did in Sinta. It flew away with the gulls that
disappeared at sunset.

He cut a piece of bread for her and then one for himself, his
lips curving in a smile. "No dirt? That must've been a beard on
your little-girl chin, then," he murmured.

"We're nothing if not robust in my family," she replied,
scratching her imaginary whiskers.

Flynn's rumble of laughter made her feel as though she
could float away on the sea, light as one of those sunbeams she'd
watched dance over the water. She even forgot about her partial
paralysis for a second. It was lovely.

Still grinning from their exchange, Flynn brought a plate

over for himself and sat across from her. The table was small—a family table. Nothing like that royal monstrosity back in Castle Thalyria. All she had to do was reach over to touch him.

She didn't. Just knowing she could was enough for now. And she was hungry.

Jocasta picked up her fork and stared at her dinner. Unfortunately, she couldn't cut anything.

Without a word, Flynn stood, rounded the table, and cut her meat and vegetables into bite-sized pieces. He sat back down and served them both wine and water.

Jocasta's first delicious, butter-rich mouthful of still slightly firm carrots elicited an involuntary moan of pleasure. Flynn's lamb was very good, too, the seasoning light but flavorful and the meat pink and bursting with juices. The royal cooks couldn't do better.

And all she'd done while he worked was sit on the veranda.

He reached across the table and helped her when she chased a tiny potato across her plate without managing to stab it.

"I'm sorry to be so useless." Being about as helpful as that potato irked her, although there was a certain charm to Flynn knowing exactly what she needed without a word from her.

"You're the farthest thing from useless to ever grace this kingdom."

She blushed, pleased down to her toes by his gruff compliment. Even the numb ones tingled with a little more warmth now.

"How's the lamb?" He eyed her half-full plate. Was he really worried she might not like it when it was the best thing she'd tasted in days?

"Delicious." To prove it, she took another bite and savored it with obvious, almost sensual delight. Flynn ignored his own meal and watched her chew, seeming captivated. He hadn't kissed her since before the bandit attack, and Jocasta was so ready to feel his lips on hers again that she wasn't above some persuasion tactics.

She slowly licked a spot of juice from the corner of her mouth. Flynn's heavy stare turned heated, and he tracked her tongue like a hunter hungry for his next meal.

"Mmm. So good." She took another bite, her low, husky praise hanging between them.

Flynn's hand fisted on the table. His lips parted. When his hooded gaze eventually lifted to hers again, the intensity in his brown eyes made her blood sizzle. "You're doing this on purpose."

"Doing what, Flynn?" Innocence was surprisingly easy to fake. She just had to keep her lips from twitching.

He cleared his throat. "Making me burn from the inside out."

Her heart leaped in triumph. "Oh, that sounds dreadful. I'm sure I have a tonic for that."

He laughed, the deep sound of amusement rewarding her for teasing him. Shaking his head, he asked, "How can you make me smile and *want* at the same time? Is there some magic involved?"

There was definitely magic involved—the magic of them finally communicating. Flirting. Touching—even if Flynn's arms around her were mainly to keep her from falling off a horse. She knew he was joking about magic, or rather, speaking metaphorically, but she decided to tease him again. "I've been sneaking a love potion into your food for the last week. The results are conclusive. I'm pleased."

He grinned again. "I saw your sly tampering, and I've been switching our plates before meals. What do you say to that?"

Her eyes widened in mock surprise. "I *have* been feeling particularly fond of myself."

His low laugh tickled her senses again.

Slowly, Jocasta sipped her wine, once, twice, drawing Flynn's eyes to her lips again. "Then I suppose that means you must be falling for me all on your own," she added boldly.

Flynn hesitated long enough to make her wish she'd kept her mouth shut. Finally, he said, "I fell years ago. It felt like sliding into a deep, dark pit."

Jocasta blinked in true shock this time. Now she *really* wished she'd kept her mouth shut. Her insides turned over in dread.

"And then, not long ago, a wall at the back of the pit crumbled, and I started to tunnel my way out. Certain things didn't seem so...impossible anymore." He leaned forward, his eyes intent on her face. They seemed to be asking for understanding, for patience—from her. "There have been pitfalls and delays. A cave-in here and there. Sometimes, I'm still clearing the path."

She nodded, still nervous but more hopeful now. "Is there a light at the end of this tunnel?"

He nodded back. "And inside, too. I'm not alone. There's a torch leading the way out."

"A torch?"

Flynn looked her up and down as best he could when she was seated across from him. His expression regained some humor, helping her to better breathe again. "It's about this tall"—he indicated her approximate height—"with eyes bluer than the Fisan Ocean and the most kissable lips I've ever seen. In fact, I want to devour them right now."

Heat exploded inside her. "That sounds like quite a torch."

"It is," he answered. "The only torch that could ever have tempted me down this path I seem to be taking."

"*Seem* to be?" As if he had no say in it? Or wasn't sure?

His expression froze. "Did I just snag my toe on a root and trip headfirst into the dirt again?"

Jocasta couldn't help softening. "Maybe." But her smile told him not to worry.

"I thought that sharp question meant something."

"I have a tendency toward quick prickliness, but I also have a selective memory." She tapped her head with her good hand. "I only remember the compliments."

Flynn's shoulders relaxed, and that unsettled look faded. Then his gaze turned to the table. They'd hardly eaten.

"Would you have preferred fish tonight?" He frowned. "Or fowl?"

"Gods, no." She picked up her fork. "I'd take red meat over fish any day, and birds are mostly bones and feathers—although Perses wasn't terrible."

"That's because you didn't have to pluck him."

"True." She grinned. "But I'd probably have gotten impatient and decided to perform surgery, which might not have left us much for dinner."

He grinned back at her. Humor and tingling awareness wrapped around them as they concentrated on the meal again, finally doing justice to Flynn's cooking. Jocasta struggled with a slippery potato, and Flynn helped her skewer the rosemary-and-butter-dotted vegetable. This time, he used *his* fork to feed her.

For the second time that evening, she forgot entirely about the shooting pains in her arm and leg and simply melted like the butter on her vegetables. Feeding someone was so…intimate.

"Thank you," she murmured.

He smiled, which somehow only made the scorching look he gave her more searing.

Jocasta slowly exhaled. Where was that breeze now? She could use some cooling off. She resisted fanning herself.

"Tell me about the boat." She finished off her precut bites of lamb steak. *Those* she could stab. They didn't roll across her plate. "Is it big enough that we can separate Carver and Bellanca as needed?"

Amusement burst across Flynn's face. "Barely. I'm afraid they'll find a way to capsize us."

She grimaced. "*I'm* afraid I'll chuck them both overboard if I can't stand the squabbling."

"I know you wouldn't, but I do like imagining it." Grinning, he made an exaggerated heaving motion.

Their laughter filled the dining room as they raised their glasses in a toast to the absurd idea.

Jocasta still floated like that sunbeam on the water. Sitting across from Flynn this way felt both surreal and entirely natural. She loved how candid he'd become in the last few days, saying what was on his mind instead of withdrawing into himself. And teasing her. She adored his teasing, even if it made her feel like a restless caterpillar in a cocoon on the verge of breaking free and exploding into a butterfly. Being on the edge of so much potential was invigorating. Moments like these—real conversation—felt like the solid stepping-stones to *more* and *better*.

She especially loved that Flynn didn't go stone-faced and silent anymore at the first sign of conflict. It helped her tame her own thorny nature. And when those tendencies did pop through, their awkward appearance didn't automatically end the conversation.

Flynn reached across the table and fed her another potato. "Tomorrow, Calypso, the sea captain who sold me the boat, will start showing us how to sail it. She said we'd need a few days of practice, especially once the others get here."

"I'm pretty sure I'll mostly be sitting around and watching." Jocasta couldn't keep a heaping dose of sour disappointment from her voice. Sailing sounded wonderful. Sitting idly by while Flynn sailed with another woman sounded awful. "Can her

name really be Calypso? As in the nymph who captures sailors
and seduces them?"

Flynn shrugged. "That's what she called herself. That makes
it her name, doesn't it?"

"So if I decide to call myself Aphrodite, does that mean I'm
the goddess of love and beauty?" she asked playfully.

Flynn went so perfectly still she saw his throat move on a
swallow. "Who's Aphrodite? That position is already taken, and
the goddess's name is Jocasta."

His unexpected words felt like a god bolt to her chest, so hot
and exhilarating she could barely breathe around the excitement
of them. If she weren't half-incapacitated, she would leap across
the table and show Flynn exactly how much his compliment
meant to her. Since she couldn't, she did the next best thing.
She told him.

"I claim you."

His face blanked in shock. "You what?"

"I claim you." She wouldn't take it back, nor did she want
to. Maybe doing things first, leading the way, was her role with
them. She was the torch lighting the path out of his tunnel.
She'd just given herself to the man she loved, and all he had to
do was claim her back now.

"I've never been with a woman," Flynn blurted out so fast
Jocasta almost didn't understand him. A sudden flush painted his
face and neck bright scarlet. He sat back in his chair, tugging at
his collar.

She stared, her heart doing somersaults. "Have you been
with a man?"

"No." He frowned. "Have you?"

She laughed. "Of course not. I've been waiting for you. And
it seems you've been waiting for me, too."

Flynn let out a long, slow breath, his color still unnatural.

His cheeks were so red, his auburn travel scruff looked washed out in comparison. "Are you disappointed?" he asked.

Disbelief drove a few more of the stabbing pains from her limbs, and she managed to lean forward without thinking. "Why in the Underworld would I be disappointed?"

The repetitive crash and retreat of the waves below filled her ears while Flynn stayed silent. Bells jangled on boat masts. Insects chittered. A muscle ticked in his jaw before he answered. "I might not...know what to do."

"I'm absolutely certain you know what to do," she said tartly.

"I might not know how to do it *well*," he muttered. "How to please you."

She shrugged. She wasn't worried. They could learn together. "I don't know how to please you, either. Yet." But she loved that they were talking about making love as a given. It *would* happen.

Flynn scrubbed a hand down his face, hiding a pained grimace. "Pleasing me won't be hard."

Jocasta arched a brow. "Will it not be?"

His face went beyond scarlet. "My gods, woman, you're killing me." Then his eyes narrowed. "How do you know these things?"

Jocasta sipped her wine, part fiendishly pleased at how composed she was while Flynn unraveled and part sympathetic to his obvious discomfort. "I'm a virgin. That doesn't mean I live under a turnip and haven't seen a man with an erection."

A hissing sound left him. "Who is this man?"

The deep, dark thread of possession in Flynn's low question surprised—and thrilled—her. She'd never seen him jealous before. His visceral reaction told her he might not have claimed her back yet, but he would. She was sure of it.

"I'm a healer and, apparently, somewhat attractive," she

answered matter-of-factly. "When I'm examining male patients, sometimes things happen. It's really not their faults. I've come to understand that the penis is a part of the body that's not entirely controllable."

Flynn's jealousy turned into a look of total surprise and then into the biggest laugh she'd ever heard from him. He threw his head back. His shoulders shook. He shook the whole table. "Not entirely controllable!" He laughed harder, finally forced to wipe tears from his eyes. Just when he seemed to get control of himself, he started guffawing all over again.

Watching him, joy flooded her. When was the last time sheer, unfettered amusement had surged from Flynn's chest and leaked from his eyes like that? She couldn't remember. She'd claimed him. She'd made him laugh. And he was opening up to her, forgetting the distance he'd worked so hard to put between them. The closer they got, the more they finally understood each other. She'd go through that bandit attack and its painful consequences again ten times over if each time, it brought them to *this* moment.

"You're perfect." Flynn's huge smile brightened the room far better than the candles on the table or the oil lamps in the corners. "I love you."

They both froze, eyes widening and locking across their empty plates and half-full wineglasses. His smile died, but he kept looking at her and didn't take his words back. Instead, he nodded, proving he meant them.

Emotion, adoration, *triumph* nearly brought tears to Jocasta's eyes. Her pulse raced, each heartbeat tight and fast and ecstatic. Voice trembling, she said, "I love you, too, Flynn."

She'd always known that. She loved him because he was dedicated, dependable, hardworking, skilled, and kind. Being as strong as Atlas and as handsome as Hades didn't hurt, either. And *fierce*—especially when it came to protecting her. She also knew just how much she wanted to show him her love the moment she had four working limbs to wrap around his body. But now she knew something else.

Flynn was a blank slate, and she would be his one and only.

CHAPTER 23

As unpleasant as it was to acknowledge, Jocasta prickled with envy around Calypso. The other woman's flawless rosy-brown skin highlighted a strong, straight nose and high cheekbones that Jocasta could only dream about. Calypso's long rows of tight black braids were unlike anything she'd ever seen before and could never pull off without looking ridiculous. The sea captain was *tall*—not that Jocasta had anything against tall people. And she could sail, which appeared to require a great deal of skill, strength, and knowledge.

Humph.

Jocasta shifted uncomfortably on her overturned bucket. She'd quickly and quite sensibly given up on trying to lurch around the boat on one functioning leg. Calypso, of course, glided about on sea legs as steady and sure as the boat slicing seamlessly through the water.

Double humph.

Stewing in silence while at the same time utterly captivated, Jocasta used the hand she could lift to shade her face from the sun and watched as Calypso adjusted the sail to catch more of the light wind, showing Flynn each step of the process and making sure he understood. The fuller sail immediately propelled them along faster, giving her a good idea of why the two sets of oars adjacent to the tall single mast could be pulled in and rendered unnecessary—along with the extra manpower they didn't have today anyway.

Jocasta absorbed the information and instructions along with Flynn, only from a distance and without any hands-on practice. She wanted to learn, and despite the stinging undercurrent of annoyance inside her, she couldn't have turned away if she'd tried. Their serious, somewhat unrelenting tutor drew the eye—both hers and Flynn's—not because she was especially beautiful but because she had *presence*.

With a pang of resentment, Jocasta realized she'd been wasting her energy all these years trying to be friendly and smiling to draw positive attention. Apparently, there was no need for either. You just had to be fascinating.

The hint of Magoi radiance brightening Calypso's golden-brown eyes from within only intensified her natural charisma. Banked power was always more interesting than anything showy or obvious. It made a person wonder.

Leaving Flynn and Jocasta under the large rectangular sail near the bow of the boat, Calypso moved back to stand between the two huge steering oars at the stern of the vessel. She pulled on one, expertly guiding them away from another of the many dangerous ledges dotting the coastline before effortlessly straightening their course northward again. When she started singing an unfamiliar melody in the old language—and could carry a tune impeccably without any music—Jocasta knew she officially hate-mired the woman. She wanted to *be* her. She also wanted to toss her over the railing.

Perched on the side of the vessel, Flynn listened to the song, seeming just as transfixed by the sliding notes and exotic sounds as she was. Jocasta had no idea what the words meant, but they lent a magic-charged energy to the air around them and made her arms tingle with goose bumps. The wooden hull groaned, ropes squeaked, and the big sail ruffled as though joining the final chorus.

"What song was that?" she called to Calypso after the tune came to a rather bellicose crescendo. She shivered suddenly, in spite of the warm sun beating down on them.

"'The Spear and the Aegis.'" Motioning Flynn over, Calypso stepped back and relinquished the two long handles of the steering oars to him, showing him how to hold them steady before glancing over at Jocasta. Tiny seashells danced at the ends of her dark braids and clinked softly in the breeze that swept them up the coastline. "It's about the weapons Athena carries into battle."

"Arms fit for a goddess." Flynn smiled, probably thinking about the statue of Athena Griffin had insisted on dragging all the way up from their village to Castle Sinta after he and his army conquered the realm. The expertly carved and polished marble had been the centerpiece of their home community and depicted the goddess dressed for combat with her crested helmet, long spear, and divine shield. Griffin had refused to leave the sculpture behind, although he had replaced it with a new one that looked exactly like it. He would probably have the original moved to Castle Thalyria now. Athena represented everything he wanted to emulate: power and authority, wisdom in war.

With a lurch of guilt, Jocasta remembered the decoration in the center of Athena's aegis: Medusa's *other* head, the gift from Perseus.

"What do you know about them?" Calypso asked, directing the question to Flynn. "The spear and the aegis?"

His brow dented in thought. "The spear slices deep and never dulls. The Gorgon face in the shield roars when Athena charges into battle." Flynn kept his eyes on the horizon, his mind seeming only half on the question as he adjusted the steering oars, widening the berth they gave yet another rocky outcropping. Legs braced apart, tunic clinging to his strong torso, skin already sun-kissed and weathered, he looked as though he be-longed out on the sea—unlike Jocasta.

Hot, restless, and queasy, she tore her gaze from Flynn's broad shoulders and square jaw, wishing her uneasy stomach would settle. If not, she'd brew herself an antinausea tonic before their next outing. She knew the principal ingredients, although she'd never needed one before her insides had decided to heave and roll along with the waves beneath them.

"And you?" Calypso asked, glancing at her this time.

Jocasta had never thought much about it, although she re-membered almost everything she read or heard, so some knowl-edge about most things eventually ended up tucked away inside her. "From what I know," she said, trying to ignore the uncom-fortable burble in her stomach, "both weapons are unbreakable. The spear is gold, and the shield is made from the golden scales of a fierce drakon Athena slew while protecting her home city in Attica."

"That city is called Athens—after her," Calypso said. "It's bigger than any city you can imagine. Or so I've heard." She shrugged. "But bigger isn't always better."

Being small in stature, Jocasta tended to agree with that. She wondered if this *Athens* was where her brother Piers ended up. All they knew was that Athena took him to Attica after he betrayed Griffin and tried to get Cat permanently exiled from Thalyria. Did that mean he was there, in Athena's home city?

Jocasta would never know, just like she could never laugh with him again or berate him for sometimes failing to see farther than his own nose. Wherever her older brother was, she hoped he was happy—or at least at peace with his banishment. Piers could never earn Griffin's forgiveness now, so some kind of peace for his soul was probably the best she could hope for.

"The drakon scales are supposed to be impenetrable," she

added, remembering one more fact from old stories as she dragged herself from gloomy thoughts about Piers, "except by Athena's own golden spear, which is how she killed the giant serpent to begin with." The statue from their village didn't contain any gold leaf anymore—if it ever had—but the tall spear was fully intact and dangerously sharp, and the curving outline of hundreds of overlapping scales still decorated the round marble shield in a circular pattern that made Jocasta dizzy if she looked too closely.

Flynn's eyes met hers from across the boat, suddenly somber. "And Medusa's stare can still turn enemies to stone. It's lethal, even with her head severed and mounted on the shield."

Jocasta shuddered. They knew that for a fact. At least the only remaining deadly gaze was fastened to Athena's aegis. Bellanca had burned all the other Gorgon heads to a crisp.

"There's no doubt the spear and the aegis are terrifying pieces of weaponry, made to combat gods, mortals, and monsters." Calypso shrugged. "Or that's what the song says."

The other woman skirted Jocasta's seat near the mast and leaned up against the very prow of the boat, letting salt spray darken her turquoise tunic and dampen her shiny black hair. Like a figurehead affixed to the bow, she lifted her face to the sun and sang the melody again. The waves parted below her, her voice collided with the wind, sea mist bounced off her upper body in rainbows, and Jocasta found herself once again transfixed, lulled almost into a trance as she stared at Calypso.

Halfway through the song, she blinked and broke the spell.

Triple humph.

Jocasta knew she was good at several things but carrying a tune wasn't one of them.

The sea captain eventually stopped singing and turned. "She's a worthy boat." Her golden-brown eyes flicked up the mast to check the rigging. "She'll serve you well."

Jocasta certainly hoped so. She glanced over her shoulder at Flynn. He gripped the two great steering oars, his gaze focused on the ledges dotting the jagged coastline as he concentrated on keeping the boat away from them. He seemed confident and perfectly at ease, both at sea and with Calypso. Jocasta, on the other hand, found both a little unpredictable and intimidating.

A shooting pain went up her leg—those were unpredictable, too—and she winced, tucking herself more fully under the shade of the sail. The sun had clearly gone to her head. Calypso had been nothing but helpful. She'd agreed to sailing lessons and was a veritable fount of local knowledge. She'd even sold them the boat for a reasonable price.

Calypso relaxed against the railing, and Jocasta forced a smile at the other woman, wishing she didn't feel the need. "That's quite a song." The warlike chorus still thumped in her chest.

"It's lovely," Flynn added graciously from the stern.

Jocasta held back a snort. The song wasn't lovely, in her opinion. But it was powerful and stirring, which was maybe what Flynn meant. It definitely made you *feel*, made you want to fight. Also, she doubted Medusa's severed head roared out of any desire to help Athena in battle. More likely, she screamed in perpetual fury. Given their history together, who wouldn't?

Sighing, Jocasta tapped her working toes against the wooden floor of the boat. If their theory about an upcoming Olympianomachy was correct, the Gorgon sisters had placed themselves firmly against Zeus and his allies, probably *because* of his daughter Athena.

Calypso walked back toward Flynn and pointed out the coastal city of Oceaneida to them. Fisa greeted the eye as far as it could see on their left, while the Great Arm of Hera did the same on their right, leaving them sailing northward on the relatively calm Inner Sea, a long body of water peppered with rocky shoals and cream-colored islands topped with greenery.

Calypso's silver jewelry flashed, catching Jocasta's eye. The dangling pieces on her bracelets resembled the shiny gray fish darting below their vessel. How did a person manage to be in such perfect concord with their environment? Skin the dusky rose of the clay streaking the cliffs around Thassos. Clothes the colors of the sky and water. Voice as melodious as the waves and eyes as sharp as the ledges. Calypso seeming to have sprung straight from the elements only made Jocasta feel more useless and out of place as she clung to the mast with her good arm and pushed down her roiling stomach.

She wanted to learn how to sail. She did *not* want to sit on an overturned bucket and hope she didn't vomit.

At least Flynn was learning. He seemed to love being out on the water, and Calypso was a good teacher, patient and informative, even if she remained cool and detached in general.

Calypso took control of the twin steering oars again, turning them back toward Thassos in a wide semicircle. Then she showed them how to use a zigzagging pattern to advance against the wind and instructed Flynn to tighten the sail now that the afternoon breeze was picking up. As soon as he did, the boat tilted less, and Jocasta's unstable insides thanked him for it. After he finished checking the knots, he ambled over to her—*his* sea legs working perfectly already.

"This is invigorating." He grinned, rubbing his hands together as though he couldn't wait to get back to work—sailing work. His short hair hugged his scalp, glinting golden-red in the sunlight. The stubble on his jaw flashed the same gilded auburn, but it was his eyes that truly sparkled. Flynn's complexion had always been fairer than hers, and below his tan, Jocasta saw cheeks turned ruddy from sun and wind and obvious happiness. For a farmer, he'd sure taken to sailing like a fish to water.

She swept her hair back from her forehead, using the same hand to shade her eyes. Even with her hair in a tight braid, the wind pulled strands loose and sent them whipping across her face. She'd imagined coming out of their sailing lesson attractively sun-bronzed with delightfully wind-tossed locks shaped into an artful mess. Instead, she had sticky, tangled hair, and her skin was starting to feel crisp. "Humph."

"What's the matter?" Flynn asked.

Jocasta squinted up at him. At least he was big enough to mostly block out the sun. "Why would something be the matter?"

"If something's not the matter, why do you look like you want to crunch boulders between your teeth and spit them out at me?"

She laughed. "It's not your fault. I'm hot, I feel a bit queasy, and I can't *do* anything. We're going to leave for Circe's garden soon, and what if I can't even really walk yet? What if I can't help?"

His brow knotted into a frown. "I thought you said you were better."

"I am." She shrugged. "I'm better every day, which means it's just a matter of time. It's just taking *more* time than I thought it would."

Flynn placed a warm hand on her shoulder and squeezed. "Even if you can't help on the island, look how far we've come already. *You* brought us here."

Jocasta pursed her lips, holding back a sharp retort. Once she knew she wouldn't snap at him, she said, "If you ask me, 'this far' is halfway to nothing."

"That's not how I see it." He squeezed her shoulder again.

"And helping Griffin and Cat isn't the only thing we'll have accomplished on this journey. There's...us. I'm not so scared anymore. I'm..."

The word *ready* hung in the air between them. She could read it in the suddenly soft, almost awestruck expression on his face.

Her heart pounded, and emotion swelled hard and fast, making her eyes prick. "*Us.* I love the sound of that."

"And I love you." Flynn moved his hand to cup her jaw, his thumb smoothing over her cheekbone. The rough-soft sweep of his skin made her shiver, and the look in his eyes took her breath away. The promise. The passion. It was everything she'd dreamed about for years.

Swallowing hard, she asked, "It's not too hard to say that?" Flynn had never been good at talking about his feelings. The more he felt, the more he shut down and shut up. Lately, she'd started to wonder how much Flynn's decision to abandon his farm and join Griffin and his army had been about avoiding the sadness of his empty childhood home and how much had been about escaping *her.*

"What's been hard is *not* saying it all this time, or even letting myself admit it—in here." He put his free hand over his heart, and Jocasta's skipped a beat.

She turned into his hand and kissed his palm. "That's the most romantic thing I've ever heard." Her eyes stung harder, and her throat thickened, making her trembling inhalation shudder all the way down.

Smiling, Flynn lowered his hands. "Maybe I'm not so bad at this after all."

Jocasta breathed in deeply, clearing the tear-hot burn from her throat and eyes. She finally had what she wanted. Now they just had to make it home from this journey alive. "Maybe you never were."

Flynn snorted. He honest to gods snorted hard, and Jocasta burst out laughing before she could stop herself.

"Fine, you were terrible." She giggled. "The absolute worst."

"Honesty *is* the best foundation for a lasting relationship. Probably." Flynn grimaced, looking a little lost.

"Probably," she agreed. "Or so they say."

His eyes narrowed in playful suspicion. "Who's this *they*? And what do they know?"

"Not sure, really." Her lips twitched. "People? Around?"

"Ah, *people*." Flynn scowled. "We're doomed."

Jocasta nodded, basking in the lighthearted humor shining through his words. "Doomed together," she teased. "It could be worse."

He stepped closer, a deep hum of agreement resonating in his throat. Slowly, he leaned down and kissed her. *Voluntarily kissed her! All on his own!* Her pulse drummed as lightning-quick bursts of happiness sparked beneath her skin. Flynn molded his mouth to hers, lingering there, and she felt the soft, warm weight of his lips all the way down to her toes.

She pressed up and kissed him back, breathing him in and marveling at how far they'd come. He was right; this journey was about so much more than a quest and a potion, even vitally important ones. It was about *them*, about stepping into the unknown but also finding each other again.

Too soon—she could kiss him for hours!—Flynn drew back. "Doomed with you is all I want," he murmured in a deep rasp that dripped through her like honey—sweet and slow.

Her heart squeezed tight. Smiling, Jocasta tilted her head back against the thick mast, her lips still alive with the feel and taste of his kiss. "This is taking a dark turn. At least we have each other now."

"Always and forever." Flynn's gaze turned serious as he

looked down at her with an intensity that stole her breath and melted her bones.

Heat billowed inside her that had nothing to do with potential sunstroke. In his own way, Flynn had just claimed her. She felt it, *knew* it. Elation nearly floated her right off her bucket. It was only a matter of time now before the rest of his barriers fell—or he took them down, one by one. On purpose.

"Always and forever," she echoed hoarsely. "I promise."

"We'll do all right, won't we?" His eyes never left hers.

Nodding, she swallowed the lump in her throat. "Yes, Flynn. We'll do all right. I promise that, too."

"I believe you." A wry smile sprang forth. "Because I doubt you'd stand for anything else."

She cocked her head, wondering if she should take offense. "Is that a compliment?" He made her seem rather...exigent sometimes.

"A compliment of the highest order."

"How so?"

He smoothed his hand down her salt-stiff braid as if it were the finest silk. "If something is hurt or broken, you find a way to fix it. That's all I need to know."

Pressure suddenly clamped down on her. *Fear.* They'd just committed to honesty, though, so pretending she had miracles up every sleeve scared her more than the truth. "I can't fix everything, you know. No one can. Some things just...happen. For good or for bad." *Kato, Piers, Flynn's whole family, this curse...*

"I know. I understand." He smiled, softly this time, and stroked her hair again. "I didn't mean to imply otherwise. I just meant"—he paused, searching for the right words—"I feel more confident with you by my side than I did before."

She melted. She melted right there on the spot.

"What's wrong with your wife's leg?" Calypso called from the stern.

Flynn's wife. A victory thrill swept through Jocasta—the parts of her she could feel, anyway.

"We had a run-in with some bandits on the way here," she answered, even though the question had clearly been directed to Flynn. As much as she liked being mistaken for his wife three times in less than a week, she didn't need him to speak for her. She might barely be able to walk, but she could definitely talk. "A Magoi with some kind of numbing power touched my arm and leg. They've been limp and painful ever since."

"It's getting better, though," Flynn added. "Right, Jo?"

Jocasta nodded. Then shrugged. "Slowly."

His eyes narrowing, Flynn slid her a sidelong look.

Fine. She might've somewhat exaggerated her improvement this morning. She wasn't ready to panic just yet, though, and she couldn't help reveling in the fact that Flynn didn't correct anyone about their marital status. Each time, she expected him to startle and deny. He didn't. He looked utterly unperturbed, which delighted her.

"It sounds like you met that thieving rat, Frosty Fingers Fokionas." An impressed brow arched up Calypso's forehead. "Most people don't come out of an encounter with him and his band of crooks and scoundrels still in possession of enough gold to buy a boat—or at all."

"Well, it's Frosty Fingers and his band who didn't come out of this attempted robbery—at all." Jocasta grimaced, hauling her hot-cold leg around with her good arm so that she could face Calypso better. "He got what he deserved. They all did." She'd grown up in constant fear of thieving raiders—ever since that first time she remembered hiding inside the false wall at the back of the kitchen with her mother and sisters, trembling in the dark and praying to the gods that her father and brothers would still be alive when silence fell.

And that the house wouldn't be burning down around them.

"Bloodthirsty. Interesting." Calypso waved Flynn over and relinquished the two big steering-oar handles to him again. She wandered closer to Jocasta. The other woman looked her up and down with more interest than she'd shown all day. "All of southern Fisa will be safer without Fokionas on the loose. Not that I spend much time on land. And we have our own problems out here..." Lifting her gaze, she swept it around the sparkling Inner Sea as if looking for ketea to appear.

Jocasta craned her neck and peered over the ship's railing. Calypso had warned them to stay close to the Fisan shore to avoid sea dragons and to look for the distinctive, clay-streaked cliffs to locate the port of Thassos again, but they needed to go farther afield once they learned how to sail. They needed to get to the *other* side of the Great Arm of Hera, take to the open waters, and sail straight toward monsters, including Circe.

There existed three narrow passageways through the Great Arm of Hera, commonly known as Hera's wrist, elbow, and shoulder. Only the one across from Thassos was navigable. Unfortunately, this southern strait, known as Hera's Shoulder, was guarded on one side by Scylla and on the other by Charybdis, two of the most terrifying monsters in Thalyria.

At Hera's Shoulder, having to choose between two bad options wasn't just a metaphor, it was a reality. To avoid being battered by both, it was imperative to sail closer to one than to the other and, according to Calypso, six-headed Scylla was the lesser of two evils.

"Scylla might take a few men," the sea captain had told them earlier. "Charybdis will take the whole boat."

Jocasta shivered again, just as she had then.

And if they actually made it through the channel, then they entered territory no human was meant to venture into.

Anything beyond the known continent was god touched—the Impenetrable Desert to the south, the Bottomless Cliffs along the Sintan west, the Ice Plains to the north. The latter was marginally more accessible than the first two but still a dangerous and deadly prospect. And then there was the Great Arm of Hera—world's end to the east.

"I know how to get rid of Frosty Fingers's magic," Calypso said, scanning the water in front of them and then to their left. "Head toward that island there," she said to Flynn, pointing to a green-topped mass with white shores not too far ahead.

Flynn followed the line of Calypso's finger and then put extra drag on the left-hand oar, pointing them in the direction she indicated.

Calypso didn't say anything else until they arrived and splashed ashore. Flynn helped Jocasta wade through the deeper water and then scramble up the steep incline leading to the crushed-shell beach. Blinding sun bounced off the white ground, making her eyes water. Flynn strapped back on her sandals, which she'd held above her head, and then she half dragged herself and half let Flynn carry her toward the rocky path leading away from the little cove where they'd dropped anchor.

"We're headed to the back side of the island," Calypso said. "You'll have a good view of the channel through Hera's Shoulder from there."

"Could we not have sailed around to the back?" Jocasta asked, huffing and puffing more than was dignified. She looked around for something to use as a walking stick.

"There's no inlet on that side. It's all rock and ledges with nowhere to stop." Calypso bent and picked up a piece of wood that was just the right size and shape for a walking stick. She handed it to Jocasta.

"Thank you." Taking it, Jocasta let go of Flynn's arm and

used the crutch, wondering where the branch could've come from. There wasn't a tree in sight.

"So why are we crossing the island?" Flynn asked. "What's on the other side?"

"There's a tidal pool out on one of the ledges." Calypso veered right when the path diverged in a Y shape. "The water in it will wash Frosty Fingers's magic right off you." She glanced over her shoulder at Jocasta. "You'll be good as new."

Jocasta grinned. "How fast can we get there?" Highly motivated, she limped forward with new energy.

Calypso laughed for the first time all day. "Pace yourself. It's still a good walk away."

A good walk away turned into endless minutes of agony, mostly uphill, with the sun beating down. Jocasta groaned out loud several times. Sweat stung her eyes, and she would've given just about anything for a drink of water.

"Is it much farther?" she finally asked, shuffling along with the help of the walking stick. Little bursts of misery accompanied every step, and her body shook with fatigue.

"I'll carry you." Flynn picked her up.

The moment the weight was off her leg, Jocasta decided not to protest. She let go of the branch that had started to rub her hand raw and looped her good arm around his neck, groaning in relief. Sun and wind clung to Flynn's skin, mixing with hints of the scents of leather and rope. She inhaled deeply. She could be anywhere in Thalyria and all she had to do was breathe Flynn in to feel at home.

His arms tightened around her. "How does this tidal pool work?" he asked as they crested the rise and began their descent to the other side of the island.

"People come here"—Calypso gestured to the rough paths crisscrossing the hot stone and dry brush on the hillside—"mostly to try to catch a glimpse of Scylla or Charybdis without getting too close, but very few know what happened out on those ledges two millennia ago—or have any idea of the power of the rock pool. The water in the deep basin is called the Tears of Attica. It's a cure to some and a curse to others. It depends."

"The Tears of Attica? Depends on what?" Jocasta perked up along with her curiosity. She loved learning new things and especially about things that could cure people. She bypassed the *curse* part—for now, anyway.

"If someone has been hurt or poisoned by magic, the Tears of Attica will wash the magic away, restoring the person to his or her previous state." Calypso flashed a humorless smile. "But if you're Magoi, the water will strip you of your magic. Forever."

"You mean, the water turns Magoi into Hoi Polloi?" Jocasta asked in shock.

"No wonder people with magic wanted to hush that up," Flynn murmured. "The balance of power could've shifted a long time ago."

"Maybe. Maybe not." Calypso led them toward the part of the eastern shoreline where a long ledge jutted out, a large rock pool sparkling near the end of it. The Great Arm of Hera faced them from across a narrow section of the Inner Sea.

Jocasta squinted but couldn't see any sign of Scylla or Charybdis from where they stood on the wind-ruffled hillside. She also couldn't imagine making Flynn carry her all the way to the tidal pool over the sharp, uneven terrain.

"Why is the water called the Tears of Attica?" she asked, trying to scout out the best path for them. She could limp along once they reached the ledge, using Flynn for balance.

"What do you know about the end of magic in Attica?" Calypso countered Jocasta's question with one of her own—a move that always annoyed Jocasta to the bone.

"Not much," Jocasta answered. "Little by little, the people there stopped worshipping the gods. As they did, their magic weakened, and they took that as a sure sign the Olympians had abandoned them and left their world. They stopped praying even more, which in turn further weakened their magic. Once enough of them stopped believing, magic died altogether. Gone." She shrugged. That was all she knew—except that Piers was there now. Her brother didn't have any magic. Surely, he'd fit in?

Calypso nodded. "Thalyria and the Underworld are the only worlds with magic now."

"What about Atlantis?" Flynn asked. "Did Atlantians stop believing, too?"

Calypso headed toward the ledge with the tidal pool. "I don't think so. Aren't they being punished for bad behavior? Some kind of offense against the gods?"

Jocasta couldn't imagine what the people of Atlantis could've done to merit such a drastic punishment, especially considering what the Olympians generally found acceptable—at least among themselves.

"What does the water in the pool have to do with Attica?" she asked.

"I'm somewhat of a scholar when it comes to Athena." Calypso looked over her shoulder and waited for them to catch up. "I've dug up some rare knowledge here and there, and I found a scroll linking Athena to the rock pool here."

Jocasta could understand the call to dig up rare knowledge. She did the same with plants and herbs. "What did it say?" she asked.

Calypso drifted off the path and led them over even wilder terrain, heading directly toward the pool at the end of the rocky point. "It said that about a thousand true believers remained in Athena's home city, Athens—that's how I found out about that—even after all hope for magic seemed lost. Those Magoi still climbed the hill to the great temple housing her statue and prayed, brought offerings, and kissed her marble feet. As the patron goddess of Attica, Athena decided to reveal herself to them and bring her last faithful followers to Thalyria before their magic died like everyone else's. Knowing her father—who was bitter about losing power in Attica—would never agree to help the final thousand, she created a secret passageway—there." Calypso pointed to the pool holding the Tears of Attica.

A shiver slid beneath Jocasta's skin. "But humans aren't supposed to travel between worlds."

"It depends." Calypso shrugged.

"On what?" she asked, remembering that Piers had done exactly that—with Athena.

"On whether or not the journey is sanctioned."

"What happened to them?" Flynn asked. He walked carefully with her in his arms, taking care not to skid on loose stones or slip on patches of sea moss.

"Zeus," Calypso answered somewhat bitterly. "He didn't care about Athena's thousand Magoi believers—or that they still believed in *her.*"

"They didn't make it through?" Flynn asked.

Jocasta waited for Calypso's answer on tenterhooks. As far as she knew, Zeus controlled passage between worlds and the only hub was on Mount Olympus—the one place universal to them all. The only exception was the Underworld, where Hades ruled and always had the final word.

"According to the scroll, they made it," Calypso said. "But not the way they thought."

"They lost their magic anyway, didn't they?" Compassion flooded Jocasta for those long-dead souls who'd taken a risk.

"The water in the tidal pool stripped them of their power. It still strips away magic, even today."

Calypso confirmed with a nod. "And they cried and cried. They cursed Athena's name and wailed for days."

"The Tears of Attica." Flynn glanced down at Jocasta in his arms. "Bad news for them. Good news for us."

Good news for Flynn and her didn't stop Jocasta from feeling a pang of distress over the fate of all those people, no matter how long ago it was. "Athena tried to do something good for her faithful, and they were all punished for it, even her. How terrible."

Calypso nodded again. "It's a lesson to every single one of us—even to gods. Zeus is *always* watching." She picked a path over the ledge that turned out to be less treacherous than Jocasta thought. Flynn followed directly in her footsteps, and Jocasta stopped feeling guilty about letting him carry her.

"Zeus must've found out about the secret passageway," Flynn said. "What did the scroll say happened next?"

Calypso stopped in front of the clear tidal pool and gazed down at the inviting water. Not even a ripple tickled the surface, despite the relentless ocean breeze buffeting them from beyond the Great Arm of Hera. "It said that even though Zeus let Athena's followers pass through the portal before he closed it forever, he modified the water so that when they emerged into Thalyria, it stripped them of their magic. They held their breath, dove in with Athena's blessing, and came out here—altered."

The empathy inside Jocasta grew tenfold. "They could've just stayed in Attica, with friends and family, their homes and lives. They came here only to keep their magic and ended up losing everything."

Calypso didn't look up, as though seeing the horror of it replayed in the mirror of the water. "They turned from Athena then. She'd betrayed them—in their minds, anyway. They howled on this ledge so loudly they caught the exiled witch's attention."

"Circe?" In shock, Jocasta swung her legs down and stood on one foot beside Flynn, using his arm for balance. "She's out there?"

Calypso cocked her head at Jocasta. "You know that as well as I do."

Did she? She believed so, hoped, but this was…possible confirmation.

She glanced at Flynn, her eyes wide with excitement. Fine— *triumph.* The satisfied look he gave her in return would warm her for a decade.

"What happened then? To the Atticans?" Flynn asked.

"And with Circe?" Was Aeaea that close? Jocasta's thundering pulse made her deadened limbs tingle.

"According to the information I came across, Circe used to be able to ride the ancient sea creatures for leagues around her island. She could even go into the Inner Sea. Only the mainland was off limits. So she came here—powerful and seductive. The desperate cried out their luck, their joy, their salvation." Calypso stared down into the clear blue Tears of Attica. "But the witch didn't come to help them. She lashed out, angry to have been disturbed by their wailing. To silence them, she turned them all into immortal sea monsters, each and every one."

Jocasta gasped. Flynn let out a low curse, and for the first time, Jocasta started to fear meeting the exiled goddess as much as the dangers they'd have to face to reach her.

Calypso finally looked up again, a wry smile on her lips. "But Zeus was still watching and saw Circe's act of malice. With a great storm, he sucked back her boundary to her own island shores as punishment."

"And she's been there ever since," Jocasta murmured, "some-where beyond the Great Arm of Hera."

"And all the ketea that haunt these shores are Athena's faith-ful thousand. Her last Magoi from Attica," Calypso said.

Flynn shook his head. "How did that story even get out? It sounds like only Athena, Circe, and the sea dragons know it."

Calypso shrugged. "Someone else must've been there to write down the tale and bury it in the knowledge temples. It was a long time ago. No one around here even thinks about Circe anymore, and there are so many other stories about the origin of the ketea that the real one must've gotten lost."

"But you found it," Jocasta said, intrigued.

"Because I went looking for it. Which means I know what the Tears of Attica can do." She gave a pointed look at the pool. "In you go now."

Jocasta shivered, as chilled all over now as her bad leg and arm. Into the pool like Athena's refugees, cursed by the witch of Aeaea.

Could the Tears of Attica help Cat? The tidal pool would strip her of her innate magic—possibly Eleni of hers, too—but there was no guarantee it would eliminate the Olympian Evermagic. Olympian magic couldn't counter the elixir, and the pool's power came from Zeus. Cat would just lose more. Lose again. And remain immortal.

Jocasta took off her sandals. She was Hoi Polloi. The Tears of Attica would cure her, not curse her. And Circe was out there. Her *garden* was out there, which meant Cat's antidote was, too.

She braced herself to jump into water where a thousand people had once lost their magic and their humanity because of Zeus's unyielding need to control everything and Circe's malice. She shivered again, then looked at Calypso. "You've helped us immensely today. Thank you."

Calypso simply took a step back and waited.

Sun in her eyes, salt on her lips, and hot-cold needles shooting through her half-numb body, Jocasta glanced at Flynn. He nodded. She nodded back, turned, and leaped feet first into the Tears of Attica, using her good leg to launch herself safely away from the edge.

The water closed over her head. Jocasta opened her eyes and looked up, needing the reassurance of the glittering surface above. Silver-white light pulsed from below. Slowly, feeling tingled back into her arm and leg, hot like the magic-stripping power in the tidal pool. Her descent slowed, and she kicked, arrowing back toward the surface and the big breath of air she needed now. It felt as though she were swimming in bathwater.

Flynn's backlit face wavered in her salt-stung vision. Jocasta shot out of the water with a gasp, elated. She inhaled, wiping her eyes as her scissoring legs kept her afloat. She was in control of her whole body again, and it felt *wonderful*.

Reaching for the edge of the pool, she grinned at her companions. Flynn helped her out, and she launched herself straight into his arms. They gripped each other hard, Jocasta soaking his clothing. Flynn's sigh of relief tickled the water drops on the shell of her ear, making her shiver.

"Cured?" he asked gruffly.

"As you see." She grinned, hugging him even more fiercely.

He dipped his head and kissed her as if it were utterly natural and not something that would've been unimaginable between them just days ago. She kissed him back just as naturally, her heart swelling to Olympian proportions.

"All in a day's work." Turning, Calypso headed for the path that would take them back across the island.

Jocasta tugged on her sandals and followed the other woman over the rocky point on her own two feet, Flynn just behind her. She'd never been happier to be faced with an uphill trek and started singing the tune that had been stuck in her head for hours.

Calypso glanced back at her. Humor flashed in her golden-brown eyes, something Jocasta doubted happened all that often. Jocasta smiled and kept singing. "The Spear and the Aegis" turned out to be rather catchy.

Surrounded by weather-smoothed stone and low brush that rustled in the breeze rolling in over the Great Arm of Hera, she stopped at the summit to catch her breath and take in the view. It was stunning, although she wouldn't trade it for the sloping woodland leading down to the river between her old house and Flynn's olive grove.

"Is everything all right?" Flynn asked when she didn't immediately follow Calypso down the other side of the hill.

"More than all right. I'm happy. Relieved." She looked up at him and touched his cheek. "With you."

Flynn kissed the top of her head, took her hand, and headed toward the cove. As they walked toward the boat together, Jocasta no longer cared how much pain she'd been in, how frustrated these last few days had made her, or how Fokionas's magic had kept her from doing and appreciating so many things, especially with Flynn. Athena's cursed pool had cured her, she and Flynn had finally figured out how to interact like normal human beings again, and on the way back to Thassos, she'd be sailing.

CHAPTER 24

Flynn was thrilled that Jo wasn't in pain anymore and had four fully functioning limbs again since her plunge into the Tears of Attica, but two things kept him on edge all evening despite the positive turn of events. First, he preferred it when she stayed out of his kitchen. The woman could concoct a tonic with extreme care and precision, but she was a menace to delicate seasoning. Second, now that she was well and their relationship had undeniably evolved, she'd have…expectations.

Flynn was so nervous he could barely eat his overspiced dinner. His heart took to racing, and he found himself short of breath every time he looked at the raven-haired temptress across from him. But to the Underworld with it. The moment he'd climbed under that blanket to keep Jo warm, some part of him must've known he was done fighting the inevitable.

Was he still scared? Gods, yes. Did everything that could go wrong, that could *break* him, still punch into his mind like a whip-fast fist and practically knock him out cold? Of course. It probably always would, but now he looked for rational, calming threads to pull forward—Jo's competence, Jo's strength, Jo's solid health and healing skills, his own good health, abilities, and strengths—and waited until the hard, icy knot of fear in his chest unraveled, and he could breathe again.

He hadn't counted on being rendered ridiculous, though. When her eyes met his, he wanted to spout nonsense about blue skies and sapphires but couldn't find the words. When her laughter pealed across the table, he gathered up her joy, mesmerized, staring like a fool. When her voice rasped with that low, husky tumble that sometimes slipped into her words, he could barely remember his own name, his pulse pounding out one-syllable imperatives that pumped straight to his groin. *Jo. Mine. Love. Want. Now.*

He swallowed hard. *Now* was upon them, commanding his senses and funneling his thoughts. His skin vibrated with awareness. His ideas turned in circles with Jo at the center of them all. They'd reached an understanding since splitting from the rest of Team Elpis, and come Hades or high water, they were doing this.

The immediate *this* being sex. It couldn't be that hard to do it right, could it?

The sweat dotting his brow and his churning stomach told him otherwise. Kato had once called making love an art. Flynn was a terrible artist. All the colors bled together somehow.

But he wanted Jo, desperately, and in *all* ways. Lover. Friend. Ally. Wife. The heat and longing left him aching from the inside out, his hands always half reaching for her. The others would be here soon, and then they'd have no privacy and might die on a boat, or in the jaws of a monster, or during any one of the trials, or by Circe's malicious hand if they managed to reach her hidden island intact.

What if he and Jo made love, and then he died and left her? What if he died and left her *pregnant*?

Flynn coughed, choking on a mix of dinner flavors and abject terror.

Jo leaned forward in concern. "Are you all right?"

No. "Fine." He stifled a grimace and took a sip of water. "Great." He cleared his throat.

Her eyes narrowed. Then she glanced out the open arched

windows to the terrace overlooking the sea. "Shall we take a walk on the beach? The stars are brilliant tonight."

Flynn nodded, more than ready to leave the rented villa behind. It was hot and stuffy and there was a *bed* just around the corner.

Not that a bed was necessary to the operation.

"Operation," he muttered, shaking his head.

"What? You need an operation?" Alarm flashed across Jo's face. She stood.

Shock-still, eyes wide, Flynn searched for something that might make her believe she'd misheard. *Infatuation? Stimulation? Lubrication?*

The grimace he'd been holding back popped out. "Eh…"

Her eyes sharpened on him. "Flynn?"

"If I need an operation, you'll be the first to know." His desire-fried brain gave him nothing to work with. Nothing at all. "You wanted to take a walk. Let's go." He sprang to his feet, bumping into the table. The dishes rattled, sauce sloshed over the rim of the platter, and the wooden legs gave an ear-jarring screech against the marble floor.

Heat scalded Flynn's cheekbones. Embarrassment ate him alive. He'd rather have been gobbled down by Cerberus.

Jo went from alarmed to startled to confused, but then she simply tucked her chair back in and moved to join him, gods bless her unflappable soul.

Flynn skipped clearing the table and ushered her toward the door as though wearing Hermes's winged sandals, snagging a big shawl from the entryway in case Jo wasn't experiencing the same inferno he was.

He could do this. A long walk on the beach. Stargazing. Maybe a swim. The sea would cool him down. It might take all night. Perfect.

Coward, his mind whispered to him.

"Flynn, are you unwell?" Jo reached up and dabbed at the sweat on his brow, a little crease marring her forehead. "Sunstroke maybe? It was very hot and bright out on the water today."

Sunstroke? He'd lived the entirety of his thirty-four years getting cooked by the Thalyrian sun and had the tan to prove it, even coming out of the rainy season and despite his redhead's complexion. "Never had sunstroke in my life," he grumbled, taking her hand and holding on to it as they descended the long, steep staircase to sea level. The waves were louder down here, rhythmic and Flynn would've loved to say soothing, but nothing could soothe him right now. Tension gripped him from top to bottom, with an unruly groin area wreaking havoc in the middle.

"We should swim." Jo turned to him, flashing a moonlit grin. "Now that I can move again, we can play in the water!" Kicking off her sandals, she hurried toward the wet sand at the edge of the tideline. A wave lapped up the beach and over her feet. Her gasp of delight drifted back to him. "It's warm! It's wonderful!" She hiked up her skirts until they barely covered her bottom and stepped deeper into the water with a moan that dropped straight through him like a sunken ship loaded with treasure.

"Play in the water?" Flynn's crushed-shell rasp faded beneath the sound of the waves. His eyes locked on Jo's thighs. He wanted to wrap his hands around them. Spread them. He could just make out the shadowy V where her legs came together.

All the blood left his brain, and he stumbled forward.

"Call it what you want." Smiling over her shoulder, she sent an arching spray of seawater at him with her fingertips. "Play. Swim. Dip. Bathe."

"Bathing usually involves washing salt away, not layering it on." Mouth dry, Flynn pulled off his boots anyway.

Her gaze heated as she strode back up the beach on the

upsurge of a wave. She seemed to float right toward him. Aphrodite riding on seafoam. "Something about this place makes me feel strong. Like I can do anything." Never taking her eyes off him, she unhooked her belt and tossed it up the beach behind him. Flynn's breath shortened. When she reached for the hem of her dress, a punch of adrenaline rocked him like the shock of a thunderclap on a quiet morning.

Jo took the final step toward him and pulled her gown over her head in one smooth motion. Blood drummed in Flynn's veins, in his ears, in his cock. A low sound escaped him.

"Anything," she repeated with feeling.

"Jo..." Her name tore from the center of his body.

"Your turn." She tossed the garment away, shoulders back, head high, eyes glittering in the starlight. The little grin that lifted her lips made him want to lick them.

Marveling at the perfection of her, Flynn forgot to breathe until the urgent lack of air in his lungs reminded him. He sucked down a long, shuddering breath. Jocasta stood naked before him, limned in silver-white moonlight. Magnificent. Unbelievable. Brave. Gorgeous.

"I won't look half as good as you do." He couldn't stop staring. He could stare for lifetimes.

Her dark brows winged up her forehead. "I'm not exactly the tall and lithesome ideal our statues would have women aspire to."

"You're better. So much better." She was pocket-sized and curvy, and one side of her jet-black hair always curled more than the other, as though nature understood that making her slightly off-balance could increase her appeal a hundredfold. "I won't look half as good as you do," he echoed firmly.

She laughed, her tip-tilted eyes brightening with pleasure. "I know exactly what you look like, and it's nothing to scoff at."

Flynn's hands moved of their own accord, a little clumsy.

He unbuckled his belt. It fell to the sand. He dropped the shawl he'd been holding next to it. It seemed normal after that to lift his tunic over his head and send it the way of Jo's dress, losing it in the shadows.

His thundering pulse accelerated as her eyes slowly tracked up and down his bare torso. The desire in them lit a thousand fires under his skin that only she could extinguish. Why had he fought this for so long? She was *everything*.

Jo's gaze flicked back to his, searing. "I love every part of you."

Her voice was a feather tipped with velvet, designed to arouse his senses one by one with every word she uttered. "You haven't seen all of me."

"Maybe not, but I've watched you training shirtless count-less times." She placed a hand on his chest. His heart pounded, throwing itself into her palm. "I know you have a scar here." Her fingers slid down to the knife mark a royal soldier's dagger had left over one of his lower ribs during annual "tax collection" in their village. She leaned down and pressed her lips to it.

Flynn's belly tightened. He lifted his hands and cupped her head. "Jo…" His cock swelled, tenting his pants. She'd see it. She'd know.

"And then there's this burn scar here." She easily slipped out of his hold and brushed her hands and lips around his torso to his back. Goose bumps followed the path of her mouth. She stood behind him, barely touching him, his skin heating and shivering beneath her breath. She lightly kissed the lower curve of his left shoulder blade. "I don't know where it came from, but I know you've had it most of your life."

"Home." A slew of images assailed him, most of the memories involving Jo and her family rather than his own. "Backed into my mother's iron cooking pot when I was five—or so I was told. I don't really remember it."

"Ahh." She brushed her lips over the old burn mark again, sending a white-hot shiver down his spine. "That explains it." Her hands skimming his waist, she circled back to his front and stood between his legs. Jo tipped her head back to look at him, and he stared down into her eyes. "The hearth can be dangerous. Hot."

Flynn let out a groan. Her low, throaty *hot* might've been the most erotic thing he'd ever heard. He brushed her hair back from her shoulders, the strands like silk against his knuckles. He ached to touch her moonlit skin, to sweep his hands down to her full breasts and cup them, to grab her hips and tug her hard against him, but letting Jo set the pace seemed like the smart thing to do, and he was determined to be smarter when it came to them.

But there was no way he wasn't going to kiss her. "The thought of your lips has driven me insane for more than six years," he murmured, pressing his mouth softly against hers.

Jo pressed back. "You hid it well."

"Going catatonic whenever you tried to talk to me worked like a charm."

Her huff of laughter warmed his lips. "I recall more arguing."

His mouth moved over hers again. "That was only lately. I couldn't *not* respond to you anymore."

"Because I'm so irresistible?"

"Gods, yes." Flynn gave her hips the lightest nudge toward him he could manage with his big, awkward hands.

Her gasp was his sweet reward. Her naked warmth pushing up against him much harder was a fiery one.

He shuddered. "I want you so much."

"That's good, because I've wanted you for years."

Jo's shy, husky confession set something loose inside Flynn. He deepened their kiss faster than he intended, wildly and with zero finesse. Their teeth clacked together, but before he could wither in shame, Jo wrapped her arms around his neck and hauled herself flush against him, her bare breasts crushed against his naked chest.

A hot shock of relief blazed through him. He kissed her more carefully, angling his head and coaxing little sounds and movements from her that drove him blind with need. Jo ground her pelvis against him. Her tongue flicked against his lips. Sensation gripped his abdomen and shivered to the base of his spine. Flynn licked her back as though slowly savoring a decadent dessert. They opened to each other, and all clumsiness vanished, replaced by slanting mouths, panting breaths, and heated moans.

"Jo. Are you..." *Sure? Ready? Willing?* "We can stop if you want."

Her nails dug into his back. "If you stop, I swear I'll abandon my vows as a healer and kill you right now. I *want* this."

"That's what...I was...hoping...you'd say." Flynn's words tumbled out in relief between kisses he drank down like a man dying of thirst.

Jo's roving touch dropped to his waist. She slipped her fingers under the waistline of his pants. "Really? You were hoping for threats and violence?"

His skin tightened everywhere. His cock twitched. "There you go, twisting my words again."

"It's my special talent," she said with a breathless laugh.

He cut off her teasing with a kiss that left them both gasping for air. Flynn moved his hands to her soft, rounded bottom. He squeezed. Taking Jo from behind would probably be like taking a gigantic hit of euphoria. He'd never touched a drug in his life, but this, *her*, he could get addicted to in no time.

"I like that." Jo reached down and squeezed him back. She held on.

"Gods, woman. Jo..." Her name shuddered out. His heavy pulse echoed the rhythm of the waves, a whoosh in his ears, a crash in his veins. He drew back enough to press a palm against her breast, slowly moving it in circles until the light abrasion made her nipple gather into a tight bead.

Jo arched into his hand. Her silk-and-gravel voice penetrated the lust hazing his brain. "Why don't you take that satisfied smile and concentrate it down"—she slowly dragged his hand to the space between her legs—"here."

Flynn's heart thudded like a crazed monster in his chest. She guided two of his fingers between her soft folds, slowly rubbing them back and forth.

So hot, so smooth, so slippery wet. "I feel unhinged. Like a beast." His breath sawed in and out. His shaft strained against his pants.

"*My* beast." She rocked against his hand.

"I don't want to hurt you." His whole body shook. What if he couldn't control himself? What was too rough? What wasn't rough enough?

"You won't." She angled her hips so that his finger dipped into her core. Flynn slowly pushed upward, sliding in so easily that he did it again. She groaned. "I'm this ready with just kisses and thoughts. I'm panting, desperate. I need you inside me like I need my next breath."

Flynn curled into her, exhaling raggedly against her neck. Heat washed down his back and into his thighs. Desire jumped like wildfire through every part of him. He knew for certain his woman was about to burn him to the ground.

Good. Then he could rise again, a man transformed. He'd finally be what Jo wanted and needed. He knew he could be that man now.

Flynn slid one hand into Jo's hair and angled her head back, taking her mouth with deep kisses while he used his other hand to discover what made her tremble and twitch. She gripped his shoulders. Her little nail pricks told him what she liked best. She moved her hips, adjusting the slant and pressure. Then she *rode* his hand, and Flynn didn't know how his trousers didn't burst into flames.

With a low groan, he ducked his head and kissed her breasts. He nuzzled between them, breathing her in. A summer garden swelled in his lungs, herbs...sweetness...Jo. How did she always smell like everything he liked best? Ravenous, he turned his head and licked her nipple, rolling his tongue over the tight bud. Jo whimpered. She liked it. *He* liked it. Satisfaction thumped in his chest.

"You are..." *My love. My life. My everything.* "Exquisite," he rasped out. He shook his head. "I'm no good at words."

Jo tilted her head back. She touched his jaw. "You're better than you think."

A harsh laugh escaped him. "I can't think at all."

Heat flared in her blue eyes. "Then don't." She threw a leg around his hip, opening herself wider and angling into him.

Flynn's knees almost gave out. She was fantastic—a dream come true.

Arousal pulsed in his groin. He slid his fingers more boldly against her slick, heated skin, in and out of her and around her pleasure point. Jo's shuddering breath and little sounds of excitement heated the air. Her movements changed, turning tight and straining.

"Flynn..." She gasped. Then she went taut all over, holding her breath. Her inner muscles clenched around his hand, and a hot bolt of triumph lit up his chest. "Oh my gods, Flynn!"

The arousal inside him gathered like a storm and rolled south. He turned his head to the side, gulping down air to try to calm the rising explosion. While he was trying not to embarrass himself, Jo went from stiff as a board to utterly limp in his arms. He gazed down at her. "Are you all right?" he asked.

She didn't answer right away, and worry snapped through him. Had he done the wrong thing? Gone too fast?

"More than all right." She wrapped her arms around his waist and leaned against him. "I'm…marveling."

Relief washed over him. He kissed her. Kissed her again. "You're as warm and soft as I imagined."

"You imagined me?" She started moving her hips again like she couldn't wait for what came next. Jo had never been a passive participant in anything, and her enthusiasm now made Flynn feel like Heracles.

"Every time I close my eyes, I see this…and more."

"More?" It was more honeyed proposition than real question, and a volcanic tremble quaked down his spine.

Their lips met and barely parted. Slowly, Flynn swept both hands down her sides. When he reached the flare of her hips, he gripped and rocked her against him.

"Shall I show you?" he rasped.

"Oh yes." Jo reached for the ties of his pants. "Show me."

Flynn's skin twitched under her fingertips. Despite his offer to show her what came next, he didn't know anything more than she did. It was all hearsay and theory at this point. Her earlier climax had probably been sheer luck, but he'd do his best to keep the luck going.

Together, they tugged down his pants. His cock jumped free, big and ruddy. Terrifying, probably. It had to scare her. It almost scared him.

As he stepped out of his pants, Flynn found himself unsure again. Should they lie down? The sand wouldn't do, but they had the shawl. Had he brought it with them for this very reason without realizing? Or had that been sheer luck again?

He glanced at the big piece of fabric, then back at Jo.

Her eyes locked with his. "Flynn." She looked very serious.

He took a deep breath. It was okay. They could take their time. He braced himself for this to be it for now. "Jo?"

She wrapped her hand around his painfully hard shaft and gave it a gentle stroke. "This *will* fit."

A strangled laugh somehow made it up his throat. "Aren't I supposed to be the one reassuring you?"

Shrugging, she turned with a smile and gathered the shawl from the ground. She gave it a shake to get rid of the sand and then let it billow down into a blanket for them.

"There." She started to drop down, but Flynn reached out and touched her elbow. She stopped and looked at him.

"Jo." He swallowed hard. This was it. But it was so much more. "*Latreia mou.*" *My adored one.* It was true.

Her eyes widened. She stepped forward and cupped his jaw, kissing him lightly and with a lingering sweetness he'd never forget. It made his throat thicken and burn.

"Don't be worried. I don't expect perfection." She grinned. "I expect hours of practice until we're both very good at this, and then I expect to bask in our success for the rest of my life."

He laughed sharply, his face twisting into a smile. His gut was still tight—equal parts nerves and excitement—but the raw fear left him, ripped away by Jo.

"You understand what this means? Doing this?" he asked.

"It means you claim me, Flynn." She lay down on the blanket and beckoned for him. "It's all right. I don't need the words."

He scowled, incredulous she'd ask for anything less than the entire cosmos—which she deserved. Jo wasn't one to let anything slide, and she shouldn't start now, especially with him.

"Don't do that." He joined her on the shawl. "Don't ask me for less when I'm finally ready for more."

Challenge sparked in her moon-dark eyes. "Then say it. Say whatever you feel. Say it all."

Flynn stretched out beside her and swept a hand down her body, savoring all the soft dips and gentle curves. "You're beautiful. Magnificent, inside and out. You inspire me. I can never wait to see what you'll do next."

Her sudden smile told him she liked his words, and not even the darkness could hide the flush of pleasure stealing across her cheeks. So many emotions knocked around in Flynn's chest that he could scarcely breathe. He'd helped accomplish a lot of things in his life, but *this*, making Jo happy, he'd done that all by himself, and he knew he'd crave this feeling of achievement for the rest of his days.

"Even if it's to argue with you?" she teased.

"Even then." Maybe *especially* then, when her eyes flashed, her color rose, and her sharp tongue talked circles around him. "And right now..." He dipped his head and kissed her, softly at first and then with growing intensity. Jo's response was to wiggle closer and touch him *everywhere*. She feathered her warm, questing fingers over his chest, his waist, his hip, his shaft, his balls.

Flynn sucked down a long, heavy breath, his control knife-edge thin. "Jo... My Jo." She commanded his every thought, filled his soul. He found the swell of her hip, the crease of her thigh, caressing and exploring while she moved restlessly against him, driving him to the brink of sanity and control. They tangled and kissed. Kissed endlessly, fiercely, deeply. They had years of lost kisses to make up for, and Flynn wanted them all. He stroked his fingers through her slick heat, seeking whatever made her tremble and moan. Jo arched into him. Her breath shattered against his mouth. Flynn shook as he rolled on top of her. He braced his weight on his forearms, all the feelings he'd fought off for a decade blazing through him in an inferno that burned up everything in its path.

Her knees came up to cradle him. "I'm ready," she whispered, her gaze locking with his.

He groaned. His heart hammered against his ribs. "I'm not. Not yet."

Flynn swallowed, trying to get his chaotic pulse under control. Talking about his feelings had always been about as appealing as the idea of marching into battle weaponless and blind. Now was no exception, and his whole body reacted, trying to lock up tight and keep deep inside the words that would leave him vulnerable—now, tomorrow, *forever*.

Breathing slowly in and out, he pushed past his gut-reaction barriers. For Jocasta. For himself. He had to begin somewhere, and this...this was their fresh start.

He gathered her head in his hands, looked into her eyes, and opened his soul to the woman he loved. "I could *never* not say this to you before we take this step. I only wish I had grander words—words worthy of you, of how much you mean to me..." Gazing down at her, he brushed a wisp of hair off her cheek as he fought through a jumble of words to find the ones that fit. Silvery moonlight outlined her face in a soft pearlescent glow, as though even the night sky recognized the treasure in Jo. *His* treasure. And by gods, he would cherish her.

"I claim you, Jocasta. You will be the sun I orbit for the rest of my days. I will be your home, wherever we are and wherever we go. I will protect you. I will love you. I will always be yours." Voice low, unsteady, he rasped, "I vow this with every part of my body and soul."

Tears welled in her eyes. She blinked them away. "I already claimed you. It wasn't half as poetic." She blinked again, her mouth flattening into an adorable little frown. "And by the way, you *don't* lack for pretty words."

"Do it again," he said gruffly, still holding her head in his hands. "Claim me."

Her brow furrowed. "This isn't something we get do-overs in."

"We can do whatever we want. Now, claim me."

She searched his eyes. Whatever she saw in them must've convinced her he was dead serious and waiting. "All right. A second chance is a gift." Even huskier than usual, her voice hitched, and she cleared her throat.

Holding his breath, he nodded. It was all he could do—besides silently vow not to botch his second chance at a life with Jo.

A slow, trembling exhalation crossed her lips. She swallowed. "I claim you, Flynn. You're my home, my hero, my only one. I'll do everything in my power to make our life happy, complete, *safe*. We already share a past. I can't wait to share a future. I've loved you always. I'll love you forever—in this life, and in the next. You'll never be rid of me," she added with a shaky laugh.

He squeezed his eyes shut against the burn of tears. "Thank the gods for that."

Jo wrapped her arms around his neck and kissed him hard. He kissed her back. They could seal the vow this way or with what came next, but it didn't matter. Every word was seared into his brain, burned into his blood. Their promises already beat in his chest in the place of his heart, and everything finally felt *right* inside him after all these years of nothing truly lining up.

To the melody of the cicadas on the hillside and the rhythm of the waves rolling in, they kissed and moved against each other until they were restless and panting again. Hot with need, Flynn forgot about the nerves riding him earlier and found new places on Jo's body to touch and lick and explore. It was like winning a prize every time she arched into him and moaned.

"Flynn." Tossing her head back, she gripped his hair. "It's... I... Oh!" Her gasp of pleasure tore through the night air.

Satisfaction flared inside him. He'd never heard Jo at a loss for words before. Her chest thrust up against his. She moved her hips, and he shuddered with arousal, barely keeping climax at bay.

"Are you ready?" He held himself above her, poised at her entrance. His arms trembled. "I'm not sure how long I'll last."

A sultry smile curved her lips. "Then we'll do it again."

He groaned. "Yes. Again." They'd get this right. If not tonight, then the next time or the time after that. Flynn wasn't in this for once or twice; he was in this for life.

Jo reached down between them. With her help, he entered her as slowly and gently as he could. She tensed, and he bit down on a curse. Sweat beaded his brow. She was warm, soft, so godsdamned tight. He kept going, but the pressure inside him coiled so hard and fast he gasped.

Fully inside her, Flynn shuddered in pleasure and let out the longest exhalation of his life. *Oh. Good. Gods.* Jo softened beneath him, sighing a sound somewhere between relief and pleasure. Her hands swept down his sides. He held himself completely still. Sensation sparked along his spine and gathered in his shaft. He gritted his teeth against the aching, throbbing pulse mounting inside him and fought off the release his body so desperately wanted. There was not getting this quite right, and then there was humiliating himself. *That* was not happening tonight.

Finally, the crisis averted, he breathed again. Flynn lowered his head and took Jo's mouth in the deepest kiss of his life, one meant to mark them both. They barely parted. He whispered her name, a ragged promise of devotion, ripped straight from his heart.

Tentatively, Jo moved her hips. "It's good now," she whispered against his lips. When he didn't move, she touched his jaw, snagging his eyes with hers. "Really, I'm fine."

Flynn nodded. Swallowing hard, he started to thrust. The first pull through her tight heat made his mind blank out. Jo didn't truly soften until he gave a few more gentle pushes, and then... *Oh gods.* She started to move, meeting him thrust for thrust.

They were gentle and careful with each other at first. Every sensation was already too much. A bonfire blazed inside him, burning hotter and higher with every kiss and touch. He shuddered. "Pure magic," he breathed out.

"Yes." Jo tilted her hips, taking him deeper. Flynn hissed in a breath. Her knees lifted, and he reached down and gripped her backside, keeping her writhing little body still while he worked himself inside her. Every deep thrust sent a hot surge of lust through him. Jo tossed back her head, breathing as if something wild lived in her chest. The sensations were incredible, but Jo was *intoxicating.* He'd never get enough. He moved faster and with more force, her moans of pleasure telling him to stop holding back.

Jo made a needy sound and brought her hands to her breasts. Plump, round, firm... How many nights had he touched himself to thoughts of those amazing breasts?

She squeezed herself hard, and Flynn nearly exploded inside her right then.

Gasping, he stopped moving, somehow keeping himself from spilling his seed too fast. It was an Olympian miracle he held back. His chest heaving, he said, "You're my every erotic dream, and I will not last."

Her brows lifted. Then she smiled as though she'd just walked into a bright, pristine healing room, fully stocked. "That's nonsense. I'm already impressed."

Laughter rose up, unbidden. The flash of humor took the edge off. "It's not nonsense that I dreamed about you. About this..." He touched her full, pink mouth. "And this..." He trailed his hand down to her perfect breast, rolling her nipple between his fingertips. "And this..." He swept his hand over her clearly defined waist to grip the generous flare of her hip. He groaned. He loved her handful hips. Planned on holding on to them a lot.

"Mmm." Jo rubbed up against his chest. "And of course, this." She pointed to her head.

"Your mind's the best part."

"Maybe, but you can't give it a squeeze, a lick, or a bite."

He chuckled. "Gods, woman. The things you say." Flynn shook his head, smiling. "Don't ever stop."

"Oh, believe me, if I could curb my tongue, we'd know by now."

He grinned, but his blood ran so hot that humor evaporated, and need took over again. Jo wanted licks and bites? Good. He wanted to fulfill her every wish.

He dipped his head and took the fleshy part between her neck and shoulder between his teeth. Growling softly, he bit down, gently trapping her beneath him and increasing the pressure as he slid his hand back up her body. He tangled his hand in her hair and gripped.

Jo let out a breath that shuddered toward the night sky. She clenched her inner muscles around his shaft, and the sensation nearly slayed him. He flicked his tongue, tasting her skin—sweet, fresh, a little salty from the sea air. Delicious. He couldn't resist keeping her there a little longer, captive and quivering.

Reluctantly, Flynn released her and kissed the curve of her neck. He trailed his lips over her jaw to reach her mouth again. Jo kissed him back with a panting ferocity that hinted at desperation. He knew what she needed now. He just hoped they could figure it out.

He rolled onto his back, taking her with him. Her hands crashed down on his chest, and she let out a startled sound. Then, smiling, she cocked her head.

"What do you think?" he asked. Jo might not expect perfection, but he would still do his best.

"I think we have a hundred different things to try, and this is just the start." She shifted to get her bearings, her knees hugging his sides. She lifted a little and slid back down on his cock.

Flynn squeezed his eyes shut, fighting for the upper hand against the need to ejaculate. After several thundering heartbeats, he looked at her again. A goddess in the moonlight. On top of him. Jo. His wife. They'd claimed each other. That was all either of them needed to start a life.

"I love you." It seemed so easy to say now, those words he'd refused to acknowledge but had let turn him inside out for so long. He clasped her hip with one hand and lifted the other to her breast, brushing his thumb back and forth across her nipple.

She shivered. "Oh, Flynn."

Jo's velvet-and-honey voice sank deep inside him. Heat tripped down his spine. "I've heard a woman can find her pleasure more easily when she's on top. In control. Shall we find out?"

Her starlit eyes flared. "I'm nothing if not willing to try." Tossing her hair back, she started to move. Her hips rocked in a sensual motion, slowly at first and then faster. All awareness narrowed to Jo and the combustible joining of their bodies.

Want this. Always.

Flynn gulped down air, watching her every move—every twist, every arch, every swallow. Her breast filled his hand. He squeezed like Jo had earlier, and she rewarded him with a throaty moan, her head dropping back in pleasure. She moved with increasing confidence, clearly aiming for her target now. She looked so focused and free—a heady combination as he throbbed inside her. Flynn chased every sensation along with her, burning them into his body and mind. He struggled to last, but it was like climbing uphill on quicksand.

He sank his fingers into her magnificent backside and pulled her tight against him, helping her to grind down harder with every flick of her hips. "You're so beautiful, it hurts."

"*You're* beautiful. And strong." Somehow, he knew she wasn't talking about anything physical. He trembled beneath her. She moved faster. He clenched his jaw, the pleasure-pain reaching a critical level. How long could he hold back?

Their eyes locked. She bit her lip. "Oh gods, Flynn," she murmured. "This is good."

His balls tightened. His spine tingled. *Son of a Cyclops!* This was it.

He pushed up into her, grinding her down hard as he did. He held her there, pinned.

Jo's breathing turned almost panicky, quickening as her muscles tensed. Then she stilled, her eyes widening and her mouth opening on a silent gasp. Her inner muscles clamped around him, and Flynn let go in a thundering rush. Orgasm pounded through him. A groan tore up his throat. His head swam, the pleasure intense.

Jo sank down against his chest. Her forehead rested in the crook of his neck, her warm breath sliding over him. The rightness of *them* and everything this night meant settled into his bones, and he lifted his arms around her.

"You're infinitely precious to me," he said. It seemed the only thing that mattered right now.

"I love you." She relaxed against him, warm and loose. "And I loved *that*."

He chuckled. "Me too." His pulse beat hard from exertion and release, but there wasn't any anxiety in the fast, heavy beat. There was no room inside him for his usual fears. Jo was there instead.

"My heart is full. It's..." Words were inadequate, and he'd never been any good with them. He hugged her tighter instead.

The Fates would still play their parts in his future—*their* future—but he'd no longer avoid the game board just to thwart them. Not when a life with Jo was the prize to win.

He felt her smile against his neck. "If that wasn't perfection, I can't wait to see what comes next."

Flynn grinned, in complete agreement. Happiness rose inside him like the sun cresting the horizon at dawn and flooding him with light. "Thank you for not giving up on me—on us."

Jo snuggled into him, a soft weight on his chest. He drew a corner of the shawl across her back. A sea breeze lifted strands of her hair around his face, and her honey-and-lavender scent teased his senses like a summer garden come to life. She smelled of southern Sinta. Of wild herbs perfuming the sun-scorched hillsides around silvery-green olive groves. Of pockets of lush, shaded bliss near the cool, clear river where they'd caught fish.

Home. Their home. They could go back.

Jo sighed happily, her body still cradling his. He'd never be the same—thank Olympus. It was exhausting shutting everything off and everyone out. He finally felt free, free to live.

Jo eventually lifted her head and, in his ear, a secret just for him, quietly said, "It was you and me, Flynn. Nothing could ever have made me give up."

CHAPTER 25

Team Elpis arrived a handful of days later and only moments after Jocasta tumbled out of bed. It was well past noon—a fact certainly noted by everyone. As was the fact that Flynn was still half-naked, and she had a bedsheet tucked around her like a dress. There was no mistaking that they were both a flushed, wild-haired, thoroughly satisfied mess.

Carver glared at them, but not even her brother's narrowed-eyed, pinched-mouth stare could dampen Jocasta's mood. She'd been incandescently happy ever since Flynn had claimed her, and Carver could take a long walk off Thassos's short pier if he wasn't on board.

She grinned at Carver, despite his glower. She was thrilled to see him and Bellanca and Prometheus alive and well. Bellanca and Prometheus grinned back. Then Jocasta smiled at Flynn. Life was wonderful and filled to the brim.

The others began shedding cloaks and weapons, but Carver just looked back and forth between her and Flynn, a muscle ticking in his jaw. "I see you've been busy."

Jocasta lifted her chin. "Indeed. We've accomplished several things." And they had. It turned out improvements *could* be made upon what had seemed like perfection on the starlit beach. She and Flynn were fast learners and thoroughly invested in studying each other from head to toe. She knew things about his body—and her own—that she couldn't even have imagined a week ago. The places a tongue could lick…that fingers could explore…

Heat flooded her. She wanted more.

Carver's mouth flattened. He took one last look at her and then swung his scowl on Flynn. "You'd better have claimed her first."

"Or what?" Jocasta drew her brother's attention back to her. His overbearing nonsense *would not* ruin her good mood.

Carver's nostrils flared like a bull's. His eye twitched.

"I did," Flynn answered evenly, stepping forward to take the brunt of Carver's volcanic stare.

Carver swallowed whatever rubbish he was about to say and visibly relaxed, although his eyes stayed granite hard. "Then I guess felicitations are in order."

Neither Flynn nor Jocasta responded. She eventually nodded, but Carver's congratulations felt too forced to count as a blessing.

Griffin's pre-curse happiness had turned their brother into a grumpy drunk. Would hers turn him bitter? Damn Konstantina for choosing a rich Magoi over her brother. Carver had claimed his childhood love, she had no doubt. He'd always believed their pretty, dark-haired neighbor from three houses down and two fields away was it—for life. Too bad life had been about wealth and security for Konstantina, and she'd left Carver behind for the city and a man with marble statues and peacocks in his garden. And then she died.

"What do you mean by 'several things'?" Bellanca sat at the table, grabbed a handful of grapes, and started popping them one by one into her mouth. She propped her feet on the opposite chair, looking road-weary and ready for a bath. "Our boat?" Grape. "This house?" Grape. "Where're we at?"

Everyone stared at her. Prometheus took the seat next to her but didn't reach for the fruit.

"What?" Chewing loudly, she scraped back a hank of tangled red hair that clearly hadn't seen a brush on this side of the Arcadian Wilds. "Oh wait…" She swallowed. "Are there two conversations going on here? Because I'm no good at that."

Laughter snorted out of Carver before he could stop himself. Humor melted the chips of gray ice in his eyes, reminding Jocasta of the fun, teasing brother he'd been a year ago. His joviality had been a well-practiced facade, one they'd all come to see as real over time, but it was a relief to know the real Carver could still smile.

He pulled out the chair across from Bellanca's, making her feet thud to the ground. "You'd think you were raised in a barn instead of a castle." He stole the bowl of grapes from her.

"Other people controlled everything I did for years. I'm expressing myself. Deal with it." Bellanca chomped more grapes from the stash in her hand.

"Then express yourself with your mouth closed." Carver eyed the grapes. Then Bellanca.

"You know, for a—and it *pains* me to admit this—smart man…" She tossed back a few more grapes, chewed, then cleared her throat. "I'm pretty sure that's the most idiotic thing I've ever heard."

Carver must've agreed because he shut up about it. He also probably knew that Bellanca would've liked a barn better than Castle Tarva. She was terrible at normal human interaction for a reason: lack of experience. But that also made her unique and… refreshing. A lot like Cat.

Carver—who honestly wasn't doing much better than Bellanca at normal human interaction these days—rooted around in the grapes. Finally, he raised a bunch as though in toast, turning to Jocasta and Flynn again. "Well, claiming is good enough for me. Here's to the happy couple!"

Jocasta heaved a sigh, mostly for show. She was delighted Carver had left all sarcasm aside this time. He meant it. He was happy for them, and how her family reacted to her choices and ideas had always been important to her. Maybe too important.

She laced her arm through Flynn's, smiling at the sibling she was nearest to in age and had always been close to. "Thank you for your approval, you overbearing lout."

Carver smiled genuinely but without remorse, clearly embracing his inner watchdog. She rolled her eyes at him, adding a good-natured shake of her head.

"Claiming is barbaric." Bellanca dragged the fruit bowl back to her with a loud scrape. "Gods, I'm famished." She looked around, evidently hoping a several-course meal would magically appear. When it didn't, she settled for the grapes. "Really, why do you Sintans do that?"

"What? Claiming?" Carver reached for the grapes, and she hugged the bowl to her chest, giving him a warning look. He drew his hand away. "What's barbaric about it?" he asked.

"You can't just tell someone their yours and expect it to be true." She frowned at him. "Expect them to *believe* it."

Carver's jaw went slack. He stared at her. "That's not what it is at all."

Frowning, Bellanca unhanded the fruit bowl and nudged it toward him. "Then what is it?"

"It's complicated." Carver shook his head, seeming to search for words. "Claiming has nothing to do with *ownership*. It's about…devoting yourself to someone. And hopefully receiving their devotion back." Pain flashed in his eyes. He glanced at his lap.

"Huh." Bellanca still looked confused. "Like a pledge?"

Nodding, Carver looked back up, his expression wiped carefully blank.

"Then why not just get married?" she asked. When Carver

didn't respond, she turned to Prometheus as though he had answers.

The Titan's eyes widened in a how-should-I-know-I've-been-locked-up-and-tortured-for-eons kind of way. "It sounds the same to me," he said.

"But is it?" She looked at Carver again. "What about children? Are they bastards?"

Carver choked on a grape.

"Hosting a wedding can be expensive and delay couples from starting the next phase of their lives," Jocasta explained while her brother spluttered and coughed. "This type of vow developed in places where funds were lacking. If both parties publicly recognize a mutual claiming, they can ask to sign the temple registry where they live, and that's that. To make a union legally binding, the local holy man usually expects a minimal donation, though. I've seen ours paid in fish."

"Ahh." Bellanca nodded, finally seeming to grasp the idea of a mutual claiming being synonymous with marriage. "But you don't lack funds."

No. They hadn't back in the village, and they certainly didn't now. Jocasta shrugged. She liked a comfortable life as much as anyone, but her comforts satisfied her more if she worked for them. Being handed coins by her brother—the king—sometimes felt like a slap to all the years she'd spent learning the healing arts.

"We can always host a wedding later. Griffin wanted both—the temple, the traditional vows, the blessing…" Flynn turned to her, seeming worried he'd somehow shortchanged her. "Would you?"

An internal rebellion cropped up inside Jocasta, waving flaming pitchforks at the idea. "I think our vows were perfect just the way they were. I don't need anything more than to sign the temple registry wherever we decide to live." She only wanted to finish this quest and start their new life—their *together* life. "Do you?"

Flynn shook his head, his brown eyes warm with love and something more now, something new.

Intimacy.

Her belly swooped. Would she ever get used to this? The memory of his taste, his mouth, his touch, his tongue? Imprinted on her skin, cleaved to her soul, a part of her—inside and out.

Ease. Trust.

They knew each other like they never had before. They'd peeled back layer after layer since leaving Castle Thalyria, and she wouldn't go back to their awkward, wary dance for all the riches in the worlds.

"What do you mean, wherever you decide to live?" Carver narrowed his eyes at her.

"Exactly what I said." She smiled up at Flynn, remembering the soft rumbling of his voice in the dark as they'd talked about their future together, about how they might go back to where it all began.

Flynn bent down and kissed her in front of everyone.

"Ugh." Bellanca made a face. "Congratulations and all, but *please* don't make us watch you moon over each other and kiss." She sat up straighter and let out a gusting breath. "Now, about our journey, the royal baby, and saving Cat from a fate worse than death… What have you two accomplished in Thassos so far besides, you know, the *obvious*?" Her gaze flicked to Flynn's naked chest and stuck.

Carver threw a grape at her.

She threw one back twice as hard. It bounced off his eyebrow, hit the table, and rolled into Prometheus's lap. The Titan ate it without a second thought.

"Do we have a boat? What about provisions?" Prometheus asked. "And what happens to the horses while we're gone?"

"We have a boat and food and water ready to go," Flynn answered. "I've arranged for all the horses to lodge at a local farm and be returned to Castle Thalyria in two months' time if we haven't returned by then."

"Eight horses now," Prometheus noted. "The three of us have two each."

"Will you want to keep them or sell?" Jocasta asked.

"Keep," they all said at once. Then they looked at each other and laughed, making Jocasta wonder about their adventures between Kos and Thassos. She knew what she and Flynn had been up to. But what about them?

She didn't have time to ask. Carver's stomach gave a mammoth rumble—loud enough to make him blush. He turned toward the breezy terrace overlooking the sea, pretending his body hadn't just roared for food, but Jocasta was thrilled he had an appetite. A few months ago, he'd seemed to think he could subsist on wine alone.

"I'll be right back." Flynn strode down the hallway and disappeared into their bedroom, moving as though a decade of tension had drained from his body. She'd done that. Or *they* had.

She grinned, following him and wishing she could be as relaxed as Flynn about Carver catching them half-dressed and just crawling out of bed. In all honesty, she would rather have been caught by her parents. They were more lenient with her than her brothers had ever been.

But then, what did it matter now? Claiming was marriage in her family's eyes. To make their union binding in the eyes of the authorities, all they had to do was sign their names in a temple registry and give a holy man some fish.

Flynn only needed to throw on a tunic and left again to get

lunch on the table. Jocasta took her time choosing clothes she felt comfortable and confident in and then spent several more minutes taming her hair into a loose fishtail braid that started high and draped over one shoulder—a style she'd picked up from the women in Thassos.

Satisfied with her appearance, she returned to the main living area. Flynn was already feeding everyone, which was no surprise. It was his way of saying, *Family, gather round. Let me care for you*, and his quiet efforts were even more poignant now that she understood them for what they were.

Stepping in to help him, Jocasta picked up plates piled high with flaky, cheese-filled phyllo triangles, tightly wrapped dark-green dolmades, and fat herb-and-garlic-marinated olives. She placed them on the table next to the lamb stew and glazed... something Flynn had already brought out for the visibly famished trio. They fell upon the food like rabid animals.

"Is that a Perses?" she asked, crossing paths with Flynn in the kitchen doorway. She glanced back at the feast item in question. It was bird-shaped and about the right size and plumpness to match their mysterious feathered dinner from Fisan bandit territory.

"I think so." Flynn eyed the already half-eaten bird on the table. "They're all over the marketplace here. The agora's bursting with them. And fish. I figured you'd rather eat a Perses."

She nodded, smiling. He knew her well. You couldn't go three days in Thalyria without someone serving you fish, but she'd never really enjoyed it—and some kinds less than others. The saltwater varieties here in Thassos were better than the river fish she was used to, which always tasted like mud to her. Besides, she was perfectly happy to stick a knife into something they'd named after a mean, rotten god like Perses.

Brushing past her, Flynn headed back to the table while Jocasta smiled all by herself and a little inanely. She and Flynn had a joke—one no one else knew about. The idea of a lifetime of shared secrets made her giddy.

Flynn cut a portion of Perses for her before it disappeared entirely, nodding to her place across from his and setting the plate there. He'd been out and back to the agora a few times for fresh food while she'd slept between bouts of bone-melting lovemaking, every muscle deliciously used, fatigued, and aching. Jocasta had mostly only left the villa or their private beach for sailing lessons with Calypso, but Flynn had found time to shop, cook, and, as the time drew nearer, prepare a feast to welcome the rest of Team Elpis to Thassos.

"Everything looks wonderful," she complimented, taking her seat and picking up her silverware.

Flynn's eyes warmed as their gazes met across the table. He barely ate, seeming content to watch everyone else enjoying the meal.

Bellanca reached for the cheese platter, practically salivating despite having just devoured half a Perses and fought with Carver over the last leg. Carver won this time. Prometheus stayed out of it and ate lamb stew instead.

"Not much sustenance on the road?" Jocasta lifted a brow at the sheer amount of food Bellanca heaped onto her plate. She'd be digesting that for a week.

Bellanca's mouth was too full to answer, so Carver stepped in. "The inns were mostly closed or else serving the bare minimum and shooing people out. Between the Great Roars, the Gorgon attack, the Arcadian Wilds dying off overnight, and then that colossal earthquake, everyone's been hunkering down and closing up shop."

"Fear spreads fast," Bellanca said after swallowing. "Especially along the Continental Road. People seem less worried here. All they talk about are the ketea. 'Beware! Beware!'" she mocked.

"Come face-to-face with a sea dragon, and maybe you won't be so flip." Carver reached for her plate.

"Maybe I'll throw *you* at it." She slapped his hand. "Don't touch my cheese."

"It was a challenge just to buy new horses," Prometheus said. "Then we half starved until we reached Exo Ipeiro. The coast road was somewhat better. People along the shore seem to have escaped the worst of it so far."

"The worst of it?" Flynn frowned. "There's more?"

"Great Roars are popping up all over Thalyria now." Prometheus sat back and spread his hands. "The Continental Road was buzzing with stories about panic in this place or that. People are asking where the queen is, why she's not putting a stop to it, what will happen next..." The Titan winced. "And if not Cat, then Griffin. But he's just as absent, and no one's providing any answers. Our time to fix this is running out fast."

Jocasta set down her fork, no longer hungry. "I'm almost certain the Great Roar is Pan. Someone must be startling him awake on purpose to create disturbances wherever he decides to take a nap. He's probably moving all around the kingdom looking for a pocket of peace but then getting violently jolted out of sleep and letting out his terrible shout."

Prometheus pushed back his plate with a growl. "Of course. I should've thought of that myself." His eyes darkened, and his hand curled into a fist. The whole thing stank of the Olympianomachy they'd talked about, and he'd already lived through one War of Gods.

"You were isolated for so long," Jocasta pointed out. "It's normal to forget things."

The Titan's nostrils flared. He didn't look convinced.

"We—Flynn and I—thought maybe the Gorgons were the ones startling Pan since they came on the heels of a Great Roar, but…" She shrugged, trying to keep Medusa's hissing whisper from invading her head.

Traitor to abused women. Betrayer of women wronged.

She glanced down, biting her lip.

"But they're gone now," Flynn finished for her. "So someone else must be waking Pan up."

"Why is Pan even here? Where was he before?" Carver asked.

"He could've been here in Thalyria, in Attica, in Atlantis, on Mount Olympus…" Prometheus scratched his jaw. "He wasn't in Tartarus and couldn't have been in the Underworld. Only Hades, Persephone, and Hermes can travel to and from there."

"So Pan might've been here all along, just no one was startling him awake?" Carver's brows rose in question. "Who's waking him up now, then?"

"Who knows?" Jocasta wasn't even sure it mattered. If a god was startling Pan into panic-inducing shouts, what could they do about it? "But whoever's behind the upcoming Olympianomachy—if that's really what's happening here—is gathering momentum as we speak."

Flynn refilled everyone's cups with the clear, fresh water he'd drawn from the private well in the villa's courtyard that morning. *Family. Gather round. Let me care for you.* Tenderness welled in Jocasta's chest.

"Jo has a theory," Flynn said, glancing at her before turning to the group again. "Whoever's trying to take Mount Olympus from Zeus is weeding out those loyal to him by seeing who takes pity on Thalyria and on Cat—Zeus's favored world and his direct descendant. Those who don't give a damn are likely fair game. They can be swayed, bribed, convinced…"

"That's brilliant," Bellanca said. "Horrible, but brilliant. Someone slipped Cat the Elixir of Eternal Life, and now they're using her misery and the unrest in Thalyria as a measure of loyalty to Zeus."

Carver breathed out a low curse. "Cat's just a pawn again. We all are."

Jocasta nodded. "Anyone who stands with Cat can be discarded. Someone very powerful is using her to try to divide the pantheon and steal Mount Olympus."

CHAPTER 26

Flynn gripped the steering oars and stared out at the rolling sea. They were on their own now, on their way, but a few days of sailing lessons with Calypso had given the whole team their sea legs and confidence that showed in the way they moved around the boat and handled the wind and ropes.

He glanced at Jo, once again finding his eyes drawn to her and his blood singing beneath his skin. Gods, he loved her. And wanted her. She'd made him crave sinking into her soft body like he'd never craved anything in his life. She'd made him want to *talk*, and if that wasn't an accomplishment, he didn't know what was. He'd opened up more in the last week in the privacy of their bedroom at the villa than he'd ever opened up in his life.

Positioned at the prow, she had her bow and arrow at the ready and had already stared down a few of the ketea that slithered through the water and sometimes bumped the boat. Maybe they hoped someone would fall overboard and provide an easy meal. The sea dragons had kept their distance when Calypso was aboard, lulling them all into a false sense of security. *Now* Flynn understood why everyone in Thassos went on and on about the ketea. The bastards were aggressive. And everywhere.

Jo let fly a warning shot at a particularly insistent green-and-yellow monster. She narrowed her eyes, shaking her head in a way any sentient creature should heed with caution. Team Elpis had no interest in killing any ketea, especially knowing they'd once been a group of unfortunate humans. But they would defend themselves and their boat, no matter how much humanity might remain under fins and scales.

With a last petulant flick of its shiny tail, the sea creature dove and didn't come back. Flynn had no doubt another would take its place.

Jo looked at him and grinned, her wide smile lighting a fire inside him from across the boat. He nodded his approval, the small dip of his head not reflecting the leap of pride in his chest. He'd tell her how incredible she was later. When they *talked*.

She cocked a brow, seeming to know exactly what he was thinking, then swung back around to scout for more ketea. Flynn's lips twitched. They'd spent years misunderstanding each other, and now they could communicate with nothing but body language. *Perfect*.

He kept watching her, even though her attention was elsewhere—or maybe because of it. He still snuck furtive glances, sometimes forgetting he could look his fill, and no one would think twice about it, especially not Jo. He loved what she'd started doing with her hair. That high braid that draped over one shoulder and led the eye straight to her breasts. She'd tanned, too, turning her eyes so sapphire-bright against her sun-bronzed skin that they almost glowed. And her body... Heat stirred, and Flynn let out a low groan, snatched away by the wind. He had big hands, and every part of her was just enough to fill his palms.

Gripping the oars harder, he exhaled a steadying breath. They'd have no privacy for the foreseeable future, so he'd better curb his thoughts.

Turning his gaze to the sea again, he kept a shoal he knew to avoid on their left while not getting too close to the ketea stirring up the deeper waters on their right. Carver and Prometheus each manned a big oar on either side of the boat, speeding them along with the help of a stiff breeze coming out of the west. At the bow, Jo caught his attention again, moving to one side to make room for Bellanca, who'd wandered up from the stern. The two of them kept watch for creatures and ledges. Both could smash the boat.

For a while, all was quiet except for the cries of the gulls. Bellanca played with a ball of fire in her hand, making a show of it for the constantly circling ketea. Jo just watched for danger, primed to react, her eyes scanning the water. She seemed more in her element than the Magoi. Maybe because fire didn't mix with water. Or maybe because Jo had spent more time on the boat. Once she'd gotten rid of Frosty Fingers's magic, she'd thrown herself into sailing lessons with the kind of determination he'd come to expect from her. But then, Jo excelled at everything she put her mind to. She had ever since he'd known her—her whole lifetime.

Flynn pursed his lips, watching her from afar again. Jo didn't just need to be good at the things she did; she needed to be perfect. It was a trait that sometimes worried him. She put too much pressure on herself.

The boat rocked violently, nearly throwing him to his knees. Flynn craned his neck to see what hit them, but Bellanca was already hurling fireballs at a sea serpent that thrashed at the surface before diving to escape the flames. Jo trained an arrow toward the depths but didn't shoot. After the sudden jolt, there was nothing.

"This is fun," Carver said, never breaking his rowing rhythm. "I love being hunted for dinner."

"It's breakfast time, you idiot." Bellanca brushed her hands together, putting out the lingering sparks.

"Tell me when I have permission to throw her overboard," Carver said to no one in particular.

Prometheus cracked a smile.

"Well, she's right, you know," Jo said. "It's barely midmorning."

Bellanca gave Jo a thank-you smirk that made a vein pop in Carver's forehead.

"Are women always so literal?" Again, Carver's question didn't seem to go to anyone in particular. Flynn knew better than to get involved. He wanted to live for at least the next twenty minutes.

His thoughts turned somber and tension gripped him as they neared the eastern side of the Inner Sea. An unmistakable prickle of danger loomed like a lightning-charged storm cloud above their heads. He could see through the narrow southernmost opening in the Great Arm of Hera now to the bright, sparkling ocean beyond—which meant they were mere minutes from being caught between Scylla and Charybdis.

His jaw tight and his mouth a hard line, Flynn kept their course steady, but it took all his force of will not to turn the boat around and deposit Jo back on the shore where she'd be safe from this.

Her choices had already been ripped out from under her time and again. Home. Lifestyle. Profession. He wouldn't do that to her. He couldn't.

The wind picked up even more as they neared the opening, pushing them along as though Poseidon himself were blowing them toward the open ocean.

Maybe he was. He'd always been there for Cat, and they were just an extension of her now.

Thalyria needed a win to get back on track to the *Elpis* it knew only months ago at Cat's crowning. The kingdom needed the baby it had been promised in prophecy to unify people who were used to being separate and to quell the stirrings of ambitious nobles who eyed the throne as they circled the worried new royals like vultures. Zeus needed to shore up his reign or face rebellion on Mount Olympus, and Flynn and Jo needed to make it home safely, because there was no way in the Underworld he was losing her.

Flynn angled them slightly northeast as he narrowed his eyes. And there they were. Scylla on one side, Charybdis on the other. The ketea to eat all ketea—the stuff of nightmares.

"Danger ahead." He nodded toward the creatures, his body automatically tensing to fight. Heart pumping. Hands searching for a weapon. Senses on edge.

Jo looked back at him, and their eyes locked from across the boat. She seemed to swallow down a gulp of sudden fear, but maybe that was just his worried imagination filling in the gaps.

There was no longer any need for Carver and Prometheus to row, so they took up vigilant stances on either side of the boat and gave the evil eye to the remaining ketea prowling the waters around the narrow gap. The sea dragons had thinned out as the boat neared the real monsters, but who knew how many of Athena's unfortunate followers haunted the other side of the peninsula.

"Hades, Hera, and Hestia," Flynn murmured as they drew closer. Scylla examined their approach from the right-hand side of Hera's Shoulder, all her heads turned and watching. Six long serpentine appendages grew out of a huge female upper body. Her humanlike head made seven sets of eyes, so calling her six-headed Scylla wasn't quite accurate. Shiny green scales covered the sea creature's enormous, muscular torso like armor but her skin pinkened into flesh near her navel. She appeared to turn into a barnacle-covered blob below the water. The sea crashed and churned against the cliffside behind her. She perched on a partially submerged ledge, staring.

Hating the looks of this even more than he thought he would,

Flynn turned to the left-hand side of the strait. Of Charybdis, he could only see a giant, sharp-toothed mouth, slowly opening and closing. It sucked in seawater and spat it out again, creating a gigantic whirlpool that seemed to lead straight into an endless, dark gullet. The rest of the sea monster remained hidden beneath the vortex.

"So Charybdis is out," Carver said dryly.

Prometheus shot him a look. "'Evade Charybdis's swirling fall.'"

"That's what the scroll said." Jo looked back and forth between Scylla and Charybdis. "Certainly makes sense now—and confirms that Scylla is the only choice."

Everyone swung their gazes back to the colossal sea creature. One of Scylla's serpent heads shot forward and hissed.

Carver swore under his breath. "Anyone else wishing Cat were here right now?"

Bellanca nodded. "She could just fry them both with lightning bolts, and that would be that."

"Cat's magic is still unpredictable," Flynn reminded. "Especially when she's not well."

"Not to mention that it's *insane* to throw a heavily pregnant woman at monsters, even if it's Cat." Jo flashed Carver a stern look. "Let's stuff *you* full of a baby and see how ready you are to hop up and fight."

Prometheus grunted his agreement. "Not sure these creatures have any magic for her to steal, either. I think they're just muscles, tentacles, and teeth."

Big muscles, a lot of tentacles, and very sharp teeth. Flynn kept his thoughts to himself. They didn't help him, and he couldn't imagine they would help anyone else.

"We'll throw Pro at them instead." Bellanca winked at the Titan to show she wasn't serious. "His parts grow back."

Flynn tensed. Leave it to the utterly tactless Magoi ex-princess to *tease a god* about having been mutilated for millennia on end.

Prometheus barked a laugh. "Try it, and you're coming with me—straight into the belly of the beast. You're sure to give it heartburn," the Titan teased back.

Bellanca grinned. Then her expression lit up, the unmistakable spark of an idea flashing across her face. "Maybe that's exactly what we should do. I go in and burn Scylla up from the inside out."

"That. Is. Not. Happening," Carver ground out.

Bellanca frowned. "Why not? It could work."

"It could work. Or you could get ripped to shreds, digested, and come out as ketos dung. Is that what you want?"

She wrinkled her nose. "Well, no. I can't imagine anyone would want that."

He glared at her. She glared back.

"What makes you think Scylla would swallow you whole instead of chewing you up?" Prometheus asked. "That's probably a long shot."

"Fine." Bellanca tossed up her sparking hands. "What do you all suggest?"

"We sail closer to Scylla to avoid Charybdis's whirlpool." Flynn adjusted their course, angling them toward the many-headed sea creature and away from the huge, water-gulping vortex. "If she attacks, we fight back."

"What Flynn said." Jo nodded to him. He nodded back.

The west wind carried them into the channel, high cliffs on either side and monsters dead ahead. Of course, Scylla attacked. As soon as the boat came within striking distance, a head shot out and thumped the mast. The boat rocked. She nearly tore the sail. Another head lunged for them, trying to shred the canvas.

Bellanca released a scorching wave of magic to drive the creature back, and Scylla screeched, her female eyes burning with fury, her serpentine eyes as cold as ice.

Prometheus grew, splitting his tunic down the back. His trousers shredded at the thighs. His belt popped off, and he caught the leather strap, swinging the heavy buckle at a snake head diving for Carver. Metal thumped against the scaly face, and a fang broke off with a crack. Carver ducked as Scylla's appendage veered away, trailing blood.

The swordsman popped up again, blades in both hands. "Thanks, Pro."

Prometheus sighed. "Pro." He shook his head.

Scylla attacked again. All six snake heads lunged at once, three underwater and three above, trying to overturn the boat. Everyone widened their stances and held on to whatever they could as the creature shoved the vessel across the channel. The sturdy boat stayed upright and intact, but the rising roar of Charybdis's whirlpool filled Flynn's soul with dread.

"Flynn!" Jo shouted. "Other way! Other way!" She shot an arrow into a serpent eye. The creature recoiled with a hiss. She hit its other eye, blinding one whole head.

Gritting his teeth, Flynn leaned heavily against one oar, putting all his weight into steering them back toward Scylla and away from the whirlpool.

Fire flew from Bellanca's hands, driving a looming head away. She launched volley after volley, trying to keep her flaming magic away from the wooden boat. Burns blistered the creature's reptilian skin. Pockmarks smoldered the length of its neck. The serpent recoiled from Bellanca's onslaught, sinking underwater to escape the flames.

Scylla cried out in pain and anger, her shout echoing off the cliffs. She pulled the appendage Jo had blinded to her chest, cradling it in her giant arms. Hate flashed in her eyes—and maybe surprise. For a split second, she looked uncertain.

Flynn used her moment of doubt to straighten out the boat and race forward. The wind caught the sail, propelling them directly alongside Scylla. They were halfway through Hera's Shoulder, at the narrowest point and right between the two creatures. With his team in danger—*Jo* in danger—it was torture not to pick up his ax and fight, but he kept his grip on the steering oars and concentrated on getting them through the channel intact.

Scylla's burning gaze left the two women at the prow of the boat and snapped to the men in the middle. Carver and Prometheus stabbed at the three heads below them, their swords slicing in and out of the water. Flynn couldn't see what damage they caused, but the sea on that side of the boat darkened, and the female at the heart of the monster let out a bloodcurdling shriek as she yanked her serpentine parts out of their reach so fast the boat got caught in their current and tilted.

Everyone gripped the railings for balance. Water sloshed into the vessel. The eddy swung them toward Scylla, and the wind suddenly came across them, buffeting the boat. The sail snapped and ruffled. Flynn hauled on one oar, trying to right their course again. Salt spray stung his eyes, and he squinted against sun and water, his muscles straining. Waves slapped the hull, rocking them, and their hardy little boat suddenly felt like a speck of dust in a heaving maelstrom.

"To the left!" Carver shouted.

Flynn grimaced. He knew that.

"Not too far left!" Bellanca countered. "There's Charybdis!"

Flynn growled, pulling on the oar with all his strength. He *knew* that.

Before he could point the boat forward, Scylla used her huge bulk to send a wave crashing over the bow. Bellanca ducked just in time, but Jo lost her grip as water smashed over the railing. The surge washed her across the deck. Worry knifed through him. Jo flipped onto her belly, reaching for something to grab on to. She missed a rope by a fingertip and slid toward the mast, her outstretched hands squeaking on the wood.

"Jo!" Flynn nearly let go of the oars and raced toward her. He caught himself just in time. His hard counterpressure against the swirling current was the only thing keeping them out of Scylla's clutches. He doubled his efforts, bringing them around just as Jo hit the mast with a thud. He winced, cursing. She didn't move for the longest seconds of his life, and Flynn shouted her name like a madman.

Jo finally lifted her head. Their gazes locked. "I'm okay." She turned to Carver and said the same thing. Her brother was halfway to her. Carver nodded and swung back to Scylla, sword up, jaw tight, eyes fuming.

Jo stood, a little unsteady and rubbing her hip. She looked around for her bow, righting the quiver on her back and checking for arrows. She still had some. Some were missing. Flynn swallowed the taste of fear in his mouth and concentrated on getting them out of this death trap.

They caught the wind and moved forward through the channel again. Scylla narrowed her eyes. Charybdis's vortex swirled on their other side, closer than before, a roar in their ears, a nightmare for a lifetime.

Everything was quiet for a moment. Too quiet. The kind of quiet when behemoths lie in wait, stalking their prey and sharpening their claws.

Bellanca popped up from behind the railing, swiping sodden hair out of her eyes and coughing up seawater. "You couldn't have gotten us a bigger boat? Scylla's tossing us around like a plaything!"

"There are five of us," Flynn shot back, his focus on Jo. She limped toward the bow. "How were we supposed to man a bigger boat?"

Prometheus eyed the too-quiet creature. "She's retreated for the moment. Maybe I can reason with her."

"What? God to god?" Carver snorted.

"She's no god." Prometheus looked Scylla up and down, his lip curling. "She might be tough, but if I gut her, her insides won't grow back like mine will." The Titan sneered at the creature, and for the first time, Flynn saw the powerful, disdainful, utterly detached ancient being Prometheus could be if he decided to embrace his magic and ancestry and give being a mighty, manipulative deity a go. The thought made him shudder. He'd gotten used to thinking of Prometheus as one of them, but he wasn't, was he? He predated their entire world.

"Gut her," Bellanca said.

Carver agreed.

"How?" Flynn asked. Gutting Scylla sounded good right now. Better than trying to reason with her.

"Maybe we don't have to kill?" Jo still sounded winded from her crash into the mast. She must've had the breath knocked out of her.

Flynn's focus darted back and forth between Jo and the creature. Jo bent and picked up her bow. He just hoped she was ready to use it and wouldn't let her guilt over Medusa's death stay her hand with the furious sea creature tracking their every move.

Scylla scuttled along the cliffside, keeping pace with them. They'd almost left the huge whirlpool behind, but there was no way Scylla wouldn't attack again before they reached the open ocean.

People didn't go beyond the Great Arm of Hera, and if they

tried, they never came back. Calypso had confirmed it. She'd also taken their gold and handed over her boat.

Flynn eyed the monster as the strait narrowed and put them well within Scylla's reach again. He couldn't say the sea captain hadn't warned them. "She's too big and far to cut with a sword." And he was *not* sailing closer.

"Her scales will probably protect her anyway," Jo added from the bow.

"Her underbelly looks soft enough to me. And there's always that female torso in the middle." Prometheus made a wrenching motion, looking ready to punch through Scylla's chest and rip out her heart barehanded.

Flynn nodded, more than willing to let the Titan lead the attack. They'd wanted Prometheus to move past the trauma of Tartarus, embrace his true self, and take charge of his abilities again. Fighting the Gorgons hadn't fully done the trick, but it looked like coming face-to-face with Scylla might lead to a breakthrough.

The sea monster struck fast. Scylla's five in-use snake appendages shot out in a blur, catching them all off guard even though they'd been waiting and ready. Flynn ducked on instinct, shouting a warning as an inhuman shriek split the air, covering a chorus of hisses.

Movement erupted everywhere—scaly green, fang white. The boat rocked violently, and Flynn braced himself, keeping the steering oars in line. One snake head knocked over Carver, sending him sprawling. His sword slid across the deck and clattered against the opposite railing. Another tried to clamp its jaws around Prometheus and got a Titan-powered punch in the nose instead. It recoiled, its eyes flashing red-hot with the promise of retribution. Two serpentine appendages went for Jo at the same time, foiling their own attempts at lethal bites but hitting her square in the chest. Their combined force sent her flying over-board. She screamed in the air, and Flynn's world went black.

"Jo!" Silence. His heart thudded in dread. "Jo!" Flynn leaped forward, grabbed Carver, and hauled him to his feet. "Take the oars!" he shouted.

He shoved Carver toward the stern without looking back and ran to the bow. He scanned the waves, searching wildly for Jo.

She was nowhere in sight.

CHAPTER 27

Jocasta held her breath, her lungs already aching. She didn't have much breath to hold. Two giant snakes had just bashed it out of her. They'd knocked over Carver, too.

Anger burned inside her. To the Underworld with trying to show Scylla mercy. She wanted that ketos dead.

Her pulse thumped in her ears. Currents dragged at her. She kicked hard, aiming for the surface. The dark hull of the boat already seemed frighteningly distant. So did the sky. Where was Scylla? And where was Charybdis?

She broke free of the water and sucked down air. Her first breath barely satisfied. She tried to wheeze in another and got a mouthful of salty liquid instead as a wave crashed over her with a slap.

Currents pulled at her again, yanking her down. No air in her lungs. Light dimming. For a terrifying second, Jocasta didn't know which way was up. A serpentine body sliced through the water next to her. Panic shrieked in her head. She found sunlight and swam wildly. She barely got a hand above the churning surface when another wave slammed into her, pushing her under again.

Jocasta sank, fear wrapping icy fingers around her salt-seared throat. Darkness crowded in on her vision. Daylight faded. She stopped thrashing, tired. Too tired. No breath.

Eyes open, heart breaking, she watched the shadow of their

boat get smaller. Then a sudden flash of light seared the water above her. Golden, *powerful*, the light reached down to her from the vessel, and she found the strength to reach back to it, kicking with all the force she had left in her.

Progress was slow. Her lungs screamed for air. Jocasta shed her empty quiver. She wasn't done fighting. For herself. For her family. For Flynn. She finally hit the surface and opened her mouth for a huge breath of air.

Yes!

She sank again.

No!

She kicked, her legs weak and leaden.

Air! Need air!

Desperate, she reached for the sun-dappled world above, fingers outstretched. A big hand reached down and grabbed hers. The strong grip pulled her to the surface.

Flynn hoisted her onto his chest, keeping her face above water. "Breathe!" he shouted, banding one arm around her. With his other hand, he slashed out with a knife, driving back one of Scylla's serpents. He kicked hard, jostling them both as he awkwardly fought off the creature, held her, and treaded water.

Jocasta coughed and gagged, sucking in air, her lungs on fire. "Flynn!" she choked out, her throat stinging with seawater.

"Gods damn it, woman! You terrified me!"

Tears leaked from her eyes. She couldn't answer.

She finally dragged in a decent breath, filling her lungs enough to satisfy. *Sweet Olympus!* She gulped down air by the mouthful. "Oh my gods." More tears leaked from her eyes. Salt prick, sun glare, terror, relief—*everything*. She clutched Flynn's arm. He still felt warm. She was *freezing*.

Bellanca's fire magic arced over them, bright and blazing. Flames hit the scaly body arrowing straight for them. The beast swerved and sloshed water over Jocasta. She blinked, trying to clear her vision. Warning shouts erupted. More fire. A wave crashed over her head, and she held her breath, her pulse pounding in her waterlogged ears. She and Flynn bobbed back to the surface, and she sucked in a breath, her eyes opening to chaos. Flames, waves, Scylla on a rampage.

Flynn held her tight, his arm a welcome anchor. He breathed hard, trying to haul her through the turbulent channel, stay above water, and fight off the long, vicious serpents attached to the sea monster. Jocasta kicked weakly, wanting to help. She ended up tangling their legs together. She stopped kicking and filled her lungs, becoming as buoyant as possible.

Flynn sped up. "That's better."

She nodded, trying to rest for now so that she could swim if she had to.

"Almost...there," he puffed.

She tipped her head back and found the boat. They were *not* almost there. A current must've dragged them halfway to Charybdis!

"Watch out!" she cried, a fang flashing in her peripheral vision.

Flynn sliced out behind them and missed. He cursed in frustration. His grip around her torso turned almost painful. Jocasta looked frantically from side to side. The creature might've changed course, but it was still close—right around them. She could feel its bone-deep malice icing the water.

"Where is it?" She craned her neck, dread mounting inside her as Flynn fought the anarchic currents of the channel. Swells hit the cliffsides on either side and bounced out again, meeting in the middle. A breeze whipped down the center. Charybdis pulled, eternally hungry. Serpents lashed out at them from Scylla's gargantuan body.

Flynn kicked with powerful legs, propelling them toward the others. Jocasta waited and watched, her heart pounding. She could hear the crackle of Bellanca's magic. The hiss of serpents. Prometheus shouted something about dropping the sail, turning, and rowing. She hardly dared look. Last she'd seen, the boat was moving steadily away from them.

The snake appendage she'd lost sight of surged out of a wave, jaws open, striking at them. Jocasta screamed a warning just as a dagger flew past them and pierced its skull. Scylla's serpent crashed back down, sending a gush of seawater over them. The life faded from its eyes as it sank below the surface.

Shaking, Jocasta exhaled sharply. It was more of a sob, and she clamped her mouth shut. Flynn kept moving.

Scylla shrieked, a pained, grieving, dreadful sound that battered the cliffsides. Jocasta whipped her head around, new tension gripping her. She recognized a final war cry when she heard one.

The female at the core of the creature heaved her giant lump of a body up out of the water and then smashed it back down, generating a huge wave that rolled out from her. The sudden surge crossed the channel sideways. It hit the boat first, making it list precariously. Barrels that weren't strapped down tumbled overboard, and Team Elpis scrambled to hold on to something. Jocasta's eyes widened. For a horrible second, she feared the whole boat would tip over. Then the sturdy little vessel lurched back into place with a creak and a shudder. The wave pushed onward, scooping up Flynn and her and taking them on a stomach-flipping ride up a mountain of water and then back down again. Flynn's arm stiffened around her. Jocasta held on, terrified.

The swell reached the opposite side of the strait and struck the cliffside with enough force to spray them halfway across the channel. Before she could catch her breath, more serpents split the bucking surf with their scaly backs. Most rocked the boat, trying to capsize it. Others headed their way, chilling her to the marrow.

"Flynn! They're everywhere!" How many snake limbs did Scylla have? "This is more than six!" And they'd put two out of commission.

"There must've been more underwater. Here." He shoved his knife into her hand and swam harder.

Despite Flynn's strength, their progress seemed nonexistent. The water was too rough, and she was a burden.

"I can swim now." She rolled off Flynn's chest, and they aimed for the boat together. At least it was no longer moving away from them. Those aboard had dropped the sail, and the vessel bobbed in the channel, a sitting target.

Flames roared to the sea, driving serpents away from them. Jocasta didn't dare think about what might lurk beneath, where Bellanca's magic couldn't reach. She kept her feet close to the surface and the knife in her hand, even though holding the blade made already difficult swimming even harder. If she dropped it, she thought she might scream. She slashed at shadows, hitting nothing. A dagger plunged into the water in front of her. The sunlit glint of metal disappeared, and a cloud of blood billowed up for her to swim through. She held her breath until she reached the other side of it.

"You all right?" Flynn called, turning and treading water.

No. "Yes!" Fear and sheer determination kept her going. "Don't stop! I'm right behind you."

She glanced up and saw her brother tracking their progress from the railing, another dagger at the ready. Bellanca stood there, too, arms out and flaming to the elbows. She hurled fire at anything that dared make a sudden move toward either of them in the water. Carver disappeared, then popped back into sight with Jocasta's backup bow and arrows. He sheathed the knife and started shooting at snake limbs he saw move near them beneath the surface. Between the two of them, fire above and arrows below, they kept a path open to the boat, which still seemed impossibly far away to Jocasta.

"Hang on! We're coming!" Prometheus shouted. He sprinted across the deck, took up a side oar, and started swinging the bow around. The current they'd been swimming against—Charybdis's steady pull, she realized with a shock of terror—was already moving the boat back toward them. Now that the sail was down, they'd meet up quickly, but the trick would be getting them going in the right direction again before Charybdis pulled them under.

Or Scylla smashed them. The sea monster seemed to be driving them straight toward the vortex.

Good gods. Were they working together?

That thought doubled the nightmare of swimming in Hera's Shoulder.

Flynn pulled ahead again, motivating her to move faster. The constant drag of Charybdis proved an even greater incentive, as did all the snake appendages lying in wait for either Carver or Bellanca to falter. Jocasta plowed through the water. Just one of those serpents could swallow her whole. The horrifying thought kept her going.

The prow of the boat lined up with them the next time she had to stop and catch her breath. She stared at it, shock echoing through her. "Flynn!"

His strong body stopped slicing through the turbulent waters. He turned back to her, yelling, "Keep moving!"

"No, Flynn!" She pointed to the bow, her heart pounding. "It's the spear and the aegis. Look." The golden glow she'd seen from below must've come from them—from Athena's legendary weapons. *Appearing.*

Treading water, Flynn turned, his gaze following the line

of her finger. "They're on our boat." His voice ringing numb, awestruck, he repeated, "The spear and the aegis."

"Athena gifted them to us. She was here!" The gigantic golden spear ran the entire length of the prow, its bottom disappearing below the water and its tip lining up with the front angle. The huge shield hung from it, the dizzying spiral of impenetrable golden drakon scales glinting in the sunlight. In the center of the famed, ancient aegis, Medusa's first severed head slumbered—the one taken millennia ago by Perseus.

Jocasta swallowed, her salt-raw throat suddenly thick with emotion. Athena, the Olympian her family had always revered above all others, had put her weapons aboard. For them.

"Let's go!" she called, swimming with renewed energy. The spear was too big for her to wield, too big for Flynn even. "Prometheus can slay Scylla with it!"

"Calypso?" he asked as they swam.

"*Is* Athena." Jocasta could hardly believe it. *Athena* taught them to sail! Her mesmerizing presence, her sternness, her knowledge, her easy strength and flawless physique... And all that in a muted form, without ever flaunting her power. No wonder the ketea in the Inner Sea had avoided them. They had history. "That song, the first day out on the water. She did this then." Wonder filled her along with relief as the boat finally came alongside them. "I'm sure of it."

"She knew we'd have to fight Scylla to get to the open ocean." Flynn reached for the rope ladder Carver threw over the railing. He held it steady for her. "She wants us to succeed!"

Jocasta grabbed a rung, her heart hammering from exertion and excitement. Athena definitely wanted them to succeed. She was one of Zeus's key supporters.

"Come on! Climb! Climb!" Carver shouted. He held out a hand to her while Bellanca stayed vigilant, watching the water.

Jocasta started up the ladder, saying over her shoulder, "They appeared when we needed them." They appeared when *she'd* needed that golden light to continue fighting for her survival.

Gratitude filled her. Breath and life had started to feel impossible until that golden glow reached out to her and made them seem attainable again. *Thank you.* For once, she was certain her silent prayer reached Athena. *Thank you*, she thought again, this time for the Tears of Attica.

Jocasta understood the value of the knowledge temples and the buried treasures in them, so she hadn't truly questioned "Calypso" uncovering a story so ancient and unknown. Right now, she'd bet her life only Team Elpis knew the fate of Athena's Attican thousand—or about that magic-stripping pool.

Carver grabbed her under the arms the second she was within reach and pulled her over the railing. She tumbled to the deck, breathing hard and shaking with fatigue, her muscles weak and trembling. But there wasn't time to rest. A god bolt from Zeus. A hands-on intervention from Athena. Cat still had allies on Mount Olympus who were watching, who wanted them to triumph. And Jocasta knew just what to do next.

Flynn vaulted over the railing, looking battle-ready but tired. Prometheus steered while Bellanca single-handedly kept Scylla's serpents from capsizing them, her face bone-white now and her movements sluggish and labored. Jocasta had never seen the Magoi's fire magic dwindle before, but Bellanca was clearly reaching her limit. A few snake limbs snuck through the gaps in her declining barrage, pounding into the hull and rocking them. At a side oar now, Prometheus dug into the water and managed to point them toward the exit of Hera's Shoulder and open ocean. Flynn leaped for the mast. He hoisted the sail while Jocasta ran for Prometheus.

"Pro! I know what to do! Come with me!" She grabbed his

tattered tunic, hauling him toward the bow as the boat caught the wind and sped forward. Flynn sprinted for the steering oars at the stern. Carver started shooting arrows again, covering the places Bellanca couldn't.

"What?" Prometheus followed Jocasta without question. They vaulted over scattered items and dodged writhing snake limbs, keeping their heads low.

They slid to a stop at the front of the ship. "Spear," she panted, pointing down. "Aegis."

Prometheus glanced over the prow. Then his startled gaze whipped back to her.

Too exhausted to speak in full sentences, Jocasta mimed the stabbing part. "You. Scylla."

The Titan immediately got to work pulling the god-sized weapons onto the boat. Everything was solid gold and must've weighed as much as a Cyclops. Even Prometheus's muscles bulged as he slowly, hand over hand, hauled the spear out of the golden loops attaching it to the hull.

Scylla scuttled alongside them, keeping pace with the boat and thumping her big body to create turbulence. She hissed and spat, some serpent appendages floating dead in the water and others attacking the boat. The vessel suddenly veered toward Scylla and the cliffside ledges. Jocasta's pulse leaped in fright, and she glanced over her shoulder. Flynn was frantically loosening the sail, trying to gather more wind, which meant no one was manning the steering oars.

She sprinted for the stern, skidding into place and grabbing the big wooden handles. With a groan, she pulled hard on one oar, angling them back toward the middle of Hera's Shoulder. Too far and there was Charybdis. The vortex haunted the other side. Too close and Scylla's endless snake limbs might finally overwhelm Bellanca. The Magoi had saved them so far, but she was tiring fast. Jocasta aimed for the narrow area where they could still avoid certain death, fear keeping her every nerve on edge.

The boat straightened out, moving away from the snakes. Only the longest could reach them now. Scylla followed from the rocky edge of the channel, her shriek of rage making Jocasta's hair stand on end. The steering oars chafed her hands, the wood cold and wet. They'd caught the breeze, but they still weren't moving quickly enough. The strongest current pulled them toward the whirlpool. Charybdis seemed to have gotten bigger and hungrier since they entered the channel, sucking them in with swirling strength.

Flynn and Carver used the side oars to try to counter Charybdis's relentless pull. Prometheus gripped the spear but was having trouble freeing the aegis. He cursed in the old language, trying to detach the shield from the bow.

Seeing her chance to crush a weakening Bellanca, Scylla ripped a huge rock off the cliffside and hurled it at the boat.

"Get down!" Jocasta shouted just before the boulder hit the railing near the Magoi, shattering a whole section with a sickening crack.

Bellanca dove sideways at the last second. She staggered to her feet, slow to react. She tried to retaliate with fire, but her magic fizzled. Her fingers sparked once and then went dark. "Oh my gods," she murmured, staring at her hands in shock.

The giant sea creature reached for another massive rock. Jocasta watched in terror as Scylla threw it at the boat.

"Bel!" Carver leaped for the Magoi from across the deck.

Prometheus swung around just in time, the huge aegis shielding all three of them at once. The boulder bounced off the golden drakon scales, Prometheus's strong, crouched body absorbing the shock. Carver pulled a staggering Bellanca away from the broken railing just as Prometheus let out a huge shout and took a flying leap off the boat. The force of his jump made the vessel dip hard and sent them sloshing sideways across the channel. Jocasta and Flynn gripped their oars for balance. Carver and Bellanca fell to the deck.

Prometheus landed on the ledge in front of Scylla. The sea monster recoiled in horror, all her snake appendages turning as one and racing back to defend their body.

"Pro!" Jocasta yelled a warning. He turned in time to slice his razor-sharp spear tip across the throats of three snakes, half severing their heads from their bodies. Scylla howled, venom frothing at her mouth. More snakes lunged at Prometheus.

Another roar suddenly filled Jocasta's ears—Charybdis! Prometheus's powerful leap had pushed them toward the vortex. The boat crept sideways, caught in the hungry current. "Flynn!" she screamed, throwing all her weight against one of the steering oars. On her left, sharp teeth rose like rocks, ready to shred them. "Carver! Row!" Her feet squeaked across the deck as the oar pushed back at her. Her pulse spiked. Her breath quickened. "Flynn!" she cried again.

As Jocasta tried to steer them away from Charybdis, Flynn and Carver took up the long wooden oars on either side of the boat again and rowed with all their might, digging deep and slowly inching them out of the whirlpool's clutches. Bellanca sat up, so ashen and drained of fire that even her hair looked dull orange. She crawled toward the railing, watching Prometheus battle Scylla.

Jocasta gripped the steering oars, keeping the boat pointed forward. The water in Hera's Shoulder turned red with the blood of serpents. Fang marks and puncture wounds covered Prometheus, and she had no idea what Scylla's venom might do to him. Maybe nothing. He kept fighting as if he didn't even feel his wounds. The moment he cleared a path to her fleshy underbelly, he drove the spear deep into the monster.

Scylla gasped. Pain and rage flared in her eyes, but she kept fighting, savage and unyielding. It would take more than that to kill her. Prometheus yanked the spear out, thumped it against the shield, and cried, "Wake!" He lifted the aegis in front of Scylla.

Medusa's slumbering head awoke with a terrifying bellow. The Gorgon caught Scylla in her poison gaze and turned her to stone, ending the ancient creature in an instant.

Jocasta breathed again, not having realized she'd stopped. Prometheus hit the shield with the spear, commanding Medusa's deadly head back to sleep. Weapons in hand, he turned and crossed to the boat on the long body of a stone snake, leaping only a small distance back to them. The boat still creaked and shuddered under his weight—and that of Athena's treasures. Without a word, he sat near the mast, staying god-sized and picking at his snakebites.

At the stern, Jocasta aimed them straight ahead, using the big oars to prop up her aching body and letting the wind and rowers carry them out of Hera's Shoulder. They hit the open ocean within minutes, although she was certain it would take her years to stop hearing Charybdis's hungry rumble and Scylla's angry hissing.

As an endless blue horizon opened before them, Jocasta used slow, measured breathing to try to calm her rattled nerves and raw emotions. One trial down. Four to go. She couldn't stop shaking.

As soon as they cleared the first of the ledges on the far side of Hera's Shoulder, Bellanca gave up on trying to pretend she had an iota of strength left and simply dropped where she stood. She curled up and fell asleep on the hard deck, her head near Carver's foot.

Jocasta's chest gave a painful lurch. Since the moment she met Bellanca, she'd thought of the redhead as an endless source of fire and energy. She'd somehow thought Bellanca could yell, fight, annoy, and insult forever, an endless geyser of Magoi power and abrasive commentary. Seeing she was wrong hurt her heart more than she could've imagined.

Carver kept glancing at Bellanca's motionless form as he pulled rhythmically on his oar, looking both weirdly incensed and utterly lost. He called her name. She didn't respond. He couldn't stop rowing—the waters were still turbulent and pushing them back toward the rocky outcroppings guarding the peninsula—but he managed to tug off his tunic one-handed and stuff it under Bellanca's head. She settled into it, and Carver pulled hard on his oar again, one eye on her and one on the ocean.

Jocasta found the energy to smile. They were a team when it counted. That was all that mattered.

When only a few bigger, easy to avoid islands dotted the horizon, Prometheus got up and adjusted the sail. The *Athena*— because that was clearly the right name for their boat, Jocasta decided—caught more wind and sped forward, skipping over the waves as though she had wings.

Flynn and Carver stopped rowing. Carver sat between Bellanca and the big hole in the railing, and Flynn came back to her, taking the steering oars when she offered him the twin handles with a nod of encouragement. She kissed him lightly on the shoulder as she shook out her aching fingers. Prometheus stood at the bow, spear and aegis in hand. Jocasta couldn't help thinking how powerful and majestic he looked, with his big, toned body, heavy brow, flat cheekbones, and straight nose. His injuries didn't seem to be bothering him, and for the first time since she'd known him, Prometheus looked comfortable in his own skin and ready to go.

Good. Because this was it. They were on their way to Aeaea. They were in god-touched territory now—just them, a thousand ancient and angry ketea, and who knew what else. She tipped her face to the sun. Despite her being soaking wet, near collapse, and in unknown waters, Jocasta's spirit soared along with the boat. She had high hopes for this quest.

And that was when she heard the most beautiful, mesmerizing song saturating the air around them.

CHAPTER 28

*"Do you hear that?" Jo asked him. "Siren song. We're not sup-*posed to listen." She tilted her head toward the melody.

Flynn nodded. The enthralling music swirled down to them on a gentle breeze, filling him with awe and a sweet sense of serenity he'd never found in his life, even in those soft moments between asleep and awake. The piercingly beautiful song felt like sunshine on bare skin, fine wine going to his head, and orgasm all at once. It was the most alluring sound to ever grace his poor mortal eardrums. He needed more. More now. More always. *Please, oh gods, don't let it stop.*

"It's incandescent." Jo slipped from his side and wandered to the railing. She looked around, eyes bright, cheeks flushed, and lips parted. "Glorious."

Flynn lifted his gaze, searching for the source of the spell-binding music. The sirens were surely as beautiful as their melody. Whoever warned people away from the creatures were idiots. Wrong. Jealous. Afraid to share the mesmerizing music. It was birdsong, with a sweet trill and warble, but female, too, with notes so clear and pure his soul longed to bask in them for eternity.

His heart thumped in triumph. *There!* High above a rugged island in the distance, large birds with the heads of lovely maidens circled, calling to them with golden voices. They replaced all other need and thought. They were all Flynn wanted.

He turned toward the beautiful creatures and their captivating song, turning the boat along with him. The vessel slowed, not capturing as much wind in the big square sail anymore, and he moaned in frustration. No matter. They still moved toward the island. Toward the magnificent notes chiming on the sea air, beckoning them closer.

Carver stood, his face aglow with wonder. Gazing up at the creatures, he stepped straight off the boat through the hole in the railing.

Prometheus reached out and caught him by the tunic. The Titan hauled Carver back aboard, and Flynn grunted in protest. As soon as he got the boat closer to the ledges, he was going, too. He would savor the sirens' song and listen. Just listen—forever. Three sirens circled overhead. Surely, they never stopped singing. That would be tragic. The thought filled him with misery, and he contemplated jumping overboard and swimming.

"Where do you think you're going?" Prometheus asked, holding Carver at arm's length and glowering.

Carver's feet dangled above the deck. He gave Prometheus an owlish blink. "I'm going to hear the singing."

"What? That horrible screeching?" Prometheus knocked Carver's hands away when the other man started batting at him. Carver fumbled for his sword, and Prometheus knocked that away, too, sending it toward the barrels lining the far side of the deck.

Flynn frowned. Carver was the best swordsman in Thalyria, but his reflexes didn't seem too good. Then again, he felt a bit lethargic himself. It must be the fatigue of battling Scylla. Jo seemed to be moving at half speed as well. Carver's long limbs tangled as if they weren't coordinated by the same brain, and Flynn's own feet felt like lead. Swimming probably wasn't a good idea. He'd bring the boat right up to the island instead.

"You want to turn now?" Prometheus snapped back to him

at the stern. "Or do you not see that ledge? Or that one? Or those huge cliffs up ahead?"

Flynn ignored him. The singing grew stronger, louder, more beautiful the closer they got. His whole body vibrated. He started singing, too. He didn't care what he said.

"Bloody sirens this close to the mainland," Prometheus growled. "I thought we'd have time to prepare."

Prepare for what? Flynn didn't care. He kept singing as loudly as he could, at the top of his lungs. "Ahhhhhhhhhh!" he screamed to the wind. The bird ladies sang back, welcoming him in.

"Stop squawking!" Prometheus yelled.

Who's squawking? Carver, Jo, him… They all sang, and they sounded *fantastic*, just like the beautiful creatures up ahead. Who'd have thought he could sing like this? Whoever told him to be wary of magical creatures was a liar. Too bad Bellanca was asleep. She was missing the concert. She'd be sad. Her perpetual fear of being left out came across in her constant need to comment on *everything*.

Hmm. Maybe her being fast asleep wasn't so bad.

Jo climbed up and stood on the railing, swaying along with the boat. "I'm coming!" she called to the creatures, a wide smile pulling at her mouth, and her arms flared out. Flynn watched her, thinking of doing the same.

No. He'd keep sailing. Get a bit closer. Right up to the ledge.

Jo tipped toward the water, beautiful birdsong rolling off her tongue.

Dropping Carver, Prometheus took a flying leap toward the stern. He caught Jo by the ankle, and she grunted when her upper body thumped against the hull of the boat. Flynn wondered vaguely if she'd hurt herself. He hoped not. Prometheus pulled her back aboard and stomped over to Carver, Jo still upside down in one hand.

"Don't you know sirens are deadly? Those voices are treacherous. A lie!" He pushed both brother and sister up against the mast and strung a rope around them, arms and all. "They call sailors to their doom!"

Poor Jo and Carver. Now, like Bellanca, they'd miss out, too.

Flynn let go of the steering oars. They were close now. In the background of the beautiful singing, he could hear waves colliding against the rugged cliffs. The sound of the powerful, crashing surf just made the music more dramatic. He needed to get a better look.

He moved toward the sail. Prometheus looked at him warily, but Flynn wasn't aiming to untie the hostages. He wanted to climb the mast.

He found footholds amid the ropes and started climbing, his voice still joining the marvelous chorus. Prometheus grabbed at his foot and missed. Flynn smirked. He was a fast climber.

The boat tossed, the surf rougher and rougher the closer they got to the island's jagged coast. If he reached the top of the mast, maybe he could jump off and touch the sirens. They circled just overhead, their crystalline birdsong filling his ears, their melody the new rhythm of his heart.

Below him, Prometheus swore—he wasn't singing at all for some reason—and rushed to the stern. The Titan heaved on one steering oar and brought the boat parallel to the island. A long finger of ledge scraped the hull, and Flynn got ready to jump. Maybe he could make it to the rocks. They were far below, but he didn't care. He wanted to join the singers and listen without Prometheus getting in the way. The boat started to stick on the ledge, but the Titan shifted his colossal weight, and the stone released them. They were on their way again.

Damn it! Flynn growled the next part of his song. He would have to swim after all. There were plenty of rocks between them and the island to help him along. Waves smashed into them. It would be so much easier if they just smashed into them, too.

He reached the top of the mast and looked out over the water, scouting for the best place to jump. Prometheus used a barrel to block the steering oars, keeping them on a trajectory away from the island. Flynn scowled. He needed to move fast, or the Titan would sail him away from the sirens.

Poor Jo. He glanced down. He'd have to leave her behind with that killjoy, Prometheus.

Speaking of Pro, the Titan clomped over. "Down. Now."

"I'm not a dog," Flynn called back. He sang it, of course. Singing was all that mattered.

"Then stop barking like one and get down here. Can't you tell they're enchanting you?"

"Bah!" He wasn't barking. He'd never sung so well in his life. He could make a career of it!

Prometheus lifted Athena's golden spear and poked him.

"Ow!" Flynn swatted at the weapon.

Prometheus poked him again. "Down."

Flynn shrugged. Fine. He primed to dive into the water.

"Oh no, you don't!" Prometheus jumped into his path and poked him again. He drew blood this time. "And there's more where that came from," the Titan threatened.

"Who put you in charge?" Flynn sang. "You're ruining everything."

"I'm in charge because you're all *under a spell*," Prometheus shouted.

Bellanca sat up, rubbing her eyes. "*What* is that awful screaming? Can't a person get a moment's peace on this stupid boat?" She blinked at the sky. "Oh. Sirens."

Flynn shook his head in disappointment. *Awful screaming?* "You too, Bellanca?"

"It's bloody *dreadful*! Now get down here, you big ox, or I'll burn your toes off one by one."

Flynn snorted. "You're out of magic."

Bellanca's hands flamed to life. "No, I'm not. I re-re-re-reeee...sted!" Bellanca sang.

Flynn grimaced. She sounded terrible. Nothing like Jo, Carver, and him. Clearly, they'd missed their calling as bards.

"Their song doesn't effect Magoi or gods." Prometheus poked him again when Flynn moved to jump. "This lot, though... Catastrophic."

"The singing is. That's for sure." Bellanca gave Carver a little kick. "Shut up."

Carver tilted his head back and looked at her. "You're just jealous because you can't sing."

"Yes, that's it." She rolled her eyes. "You know me so well."

"Oh, I know everything about you." Carver smirked, singing loudly, "Ultra-competitive. Argumentative. Never tentative. Usually very, very negative." He bopped to his song, his shoulders moving. "A flaming-red lesson in expletives. Lacking in sane relatives."

"Are you done yet?" Bellanca's lips twitched.

Carver kept singing. "Dimples when you grin. Fire through thick and thin. Incessant need to win. Cute freckles on your skin."

Bellanca's eyes widened. "Okay, that's enough." She dug out a spare handkerchief and none too gently stuffed it in Carver's mouth. He mumble-sang around it.

Jo took up Carver's song. There was a lot of *la-la-la-ing* and a lot less rhyming. It wasn't really about Bellanca.

"Oh my gods." Bellanca grabbed another cloth and gagged Jo. "She's squawking like a gull."

"I prefer the gulls," Prometheus said darkly.

Flynn tried to jump again and got a spear in the backside for it. It was a damn good thing he didn't plan on riding anytime soon. That spear was no joke, and his arse hurt. He rubbed the injury, scowling.

"They're following us with their awful screeching." Bellanca shaded her eyes, glaring daggers at the beautiful sirens.

"Yes! Follow!" Flynn cried to the marvelous and talented creatures. "Ahhhhhhhhhh!" he sang. They sang back to him. What a chorus!

"That's it." Prometheus picked up Jo's bow and arrows. He nocked an arrow and took aim at the singers.

"No!" Flynn started down the mast. He had to protect the feathered females!

Prometheus let fly, and Flynn's heart jolted. His song faltered. The siren closest to them tilted in the air, and the arrow flew past her. Flynn sighed in relief. Prometheus cursed and readied another arrow.

Flynn jumped the last bit and landed heavily on the deck. He got his balance and heaved himself toward Prometheus.

"Pro!" Bellanca warned.

The Titan turned, sidestepping Flynn with ease. Prometheus dropped the bow and arrow and slammed his giant fist down on Flynn's head.

Flynn staggered. The singing grew distant. Color faded, then light, then everything. His legs folded, and darkness overtook him.

———————— (6) ————————

"What happened?" Flynn moaned. His head ached as though a herd of centaurs had played kick-the-melon with it. He glanced around. Jo and Carver sat together, looking utterly dejected. His eyes met Jo's. She remembered. *He* remembered. He just didn't like it.

"You all went insane," Bellanca said tartly. "It would've been hilarious if you hadn't almost shipwrecked us. Good job with the 'Heed not the deadly sirens' call.' I mean, really. It was right there in the scroll."

"We can't all be Magoi or primordial deities, can we?" Carver snapped.

"What a shame," she snapped back. "Maybe then we wouldn't all *die* out here."

Gods, her voice was strident. Flynn winced. He'd be nursing a headache for hours. "Did Prometheus really need to punch me in the head?" he asked, gingerly touching the top of his skull.

Bellanca crossed her arms and leaned against the railing. "Yes."

"Hmm." What did he expect? Bellanca was nothing if not blunt. "Then I guess we should thank you. And Prometheus."

"Don't thank me. I just woke up to the worst concert ever. Pro did all the work. He saved us. And the ship."

Everyone looked at Prometheus. He shrugged. "It's a fair trade. I have bribery material for the rest of your days."

Flynn huffed a laugh. *My lovely, feathered females, ahhhhhhh-hhh!* was going to come back to haunt him, wasn't it?

Jo got up and inspected his head. Her hand lingered in his hair, and he reached up and squeezed her fingers. "There's a lump. I'd suggest not sleeping too heavily right away, but the next part of our plan involves falling into a very, very deep sleep."

"Right. Fun. The tricking death part." Carver scratched his jaw. Dried sea salt flaked from his stubble. "I get to steer the boat in random directions looking for a mystical island no one's ever been to while you all get to take a nice long nap under the influence of Nyx's Shallow Grave." He pressed his lips together. "Got it."

"It won't be so bad." Bellanca turned and gazed out at the

water. "At least you'll get some peace and quiet from aggressive, confrontational, cynical *me*. Isn't that what you want?"

Carver stared at her back. Eventually, he said, "Exactly."

Flynn almost reminded Bellanca about dimples and freckles and fire through thick and thin but then decided to stay out of it. He wished they could just forget the whole thing.

Jo glanced skyward, frowning. "Wait. What happened to the sirens? I was tied to the mast and didn't see."

Prometheus looked uncomfortable. Bellanca straightened off the railing. "We survived their singing," she said, "so as we sailed away, they hurled themselves into the sea and drowned."

Flynn stared in shock, some part of him still longing for the sirens' beauty and music even though he *knew* they'd been trying to kill them. "Their song was so wonderful."

"It really wasn't." Bellanca grimaced. "Magic made you think that, but one squawked like a gull, one barked like a seal, and the other just bellowed."

"It was horrendous," Prometheus confirmed.

"And so were *you* all." Bellanca shuddered.

"Yes, well, I think our perception was a little off-balance," Jo murmured, her cheeks heating.

"Off-balance!" Bellanca snorted. Loudly.

"How 'bout you give it a rest, Freckles?" Carver said.

"Why should I?" Making a face at him, she sang, "I'm argumentative and very, very negative."

Jo was the first to laugh. Her laughter traveled to him, and Flynn went from chuckle to full-out belly laugh so fast he figured siren-induced trauma had something to do with it. Prometheus joined in, then finally Carver.

Bellanca flashed a grin, and it was true. She did have dimples. "Just wait until I write a song about you," she threatened Carver.

His gaze burned into her. "I can hardly wait."

She abruptly stopped laughing.

"So…" Jo rubbed her hands together as though trying to wipe away the sudden tension on the boat. "Here we are in god-touched territory, on the open ocean, with no idea where to go. Any thoughts?"

"Our only clue is that people think Aeaea is about two days out from Thassos." Prometheus manned the steering oars, keeping them on a course due east, the sun at their backs now.

Jo nodded. "Hearsay, though. No one really knows anything."

"We could pray," Flynn said, surprising himself. "Ask the gods for guidance."

"We have a god." Bellanca pointed to Prometheus. "He's currently guiding."

"Pro doesn't count," Carver said. "He's lived in Thalyria for a matter of months and had never been here before."

"What about that can-see-what's-up-ahead magic you used back on the mainland?" Jo asked the Titan. "The map in your mind."

Prometheus shook his head. "It's not working out on the water. I don't see anything more than you do."

Jo looked crestfallen.

Flynn leaned over the railing and caught some sea spray in his hand. Drops glistened on his palm. The idea of praying to Poseidon wouldn't leave him. They were on the water. Poseidon was Cat's godfather and many-times-removed uncle. While there was constant infighting on Mount Olympus, Poseidon always stood with Zeus during the main conflicts. He'd do the same now. Flynn was sure of it.

He held up his hand, letting the sun and breeze dry his wet fingers. "Poseidon!" he called to the waves. "Please guide us. Which way to Aeaea and Circe's garden?"

Nothing happened. Everyone stared at him, and he felt like

the biggest fool, on or off the continent. Jo must think him an idiot. Heat scalded his cheeks. He'd stopped praying years ago and never put much store in it to begin with. Gods didn't listen to him. To farmers. To soldiers. To Olympians, men like him were only playthings. Despite everyone's fervent devotion back in the village, Athena had never been there for his family. She'd shown up for Cat. Cat was who counted.

So maybe praying right now wasn't such a stupid idea. They were out here for Cat. For Eleni. To preserve the royal lineage and keep Thalyria united. Flynn called Poseidon's name again.

He'd almost given up on the idea when a huge golden trident rose in front of them, cascading seawater and glinting in the sunlight. Flynn gaped. Everyone gaped. It worked!

"What in the Underworld..." Carver's eyes narrowed on the little old man riding the trident, seated between two great prongs, his scrawny legs swinging. "I know him. From the stampede outside Kos."

"We brought him to safety," Jo said. "Wait! He wouldn't blindfold himself and was patting Panotii. I was sure Panotii was scraped raw and bleeding, but when I looked again, there was barely a scratch on him. The old man—*Poseidon*—must've healed him while we were fighting the Gorgons!"

Flynn tore his eyes from the astonishing sight to look at Jo. "God of the sea but also of horses." He didn't even try to disbelieve. The proof was in the trident.

"Maybe he could've helped out with the Gorgons," Bellanca said acerbically.

"He did," Jo murmured. "He told me they couldn't look at each other, either." And she'd turned Stheno to stone with Euryale's severed head.

"So that's Poseidon?" Prometheus looked the old man up and down. "Smaller than I remember."

The little old man smirked at that. Shedding half his years in an instant, he jumped off the trident and grew, grew, grew until only his gigantic upper half emerged from the water, long curling hair and a wave-washed beard floating around his huge, muscled torso. Calypso popped onto his shoulder, sitting cross-legged. She smiled at them before standing and morphing into the tall, majestic Athena they knew from statues.

Flynn sucked in a breath. Long, straight nose. Spiraling dark hair. A stern expression that spoke of wisdom. She wore a chiton and her crested helmet. Her spear and aegis were missing. Even without them, she radiated power and authority. Flynn had sailed with Calypso for a week and found her fierce and intriguing, but he was in utter awe of Athena.

Poseidon lifted his trident. At the same time, both he and Athena pointed northeast. Prometheus adjusted the oars, bringing the boat into line with their directions. The wind shifted to push from directly behind them, the sail grew taut, and the boat sped forward. Aeaea dead ahead. Flynn was sure of it. Before he could call or wave his gratitude, the Olympians vanished.

"I didn't just imagine that, did I?" he said to no one in particular.

"You mean Athena and Poseidon?" Jo asked. "*Not*-Calypso and the big golden trident? I saw them, too. We all did." She looked around for confirmation.

Everyone nodded, as dumbstruck as Flynn. Besides, what were the chances of a collective hallucination? Not much, he figured.

"Calypso is Athena?" Bellanca looked at him accusingly. "Why does it seem like you knew that?"

"Because I did. *We* did." Flynn glanced at Jo. "We heard her singing about the spear and the aegis the first day on the boat, before you got there. As Calypso, she must've placed them on the bow with an enchantment, and they revealed themselves to us when we needed them."

"Their connection to Athena was too obvious to miss," Jo said. "As soon as we saw them on the boat, we knew Calypso must be Athena."

"'Too obvious to miss,'" Bellanca parroted in a sour voice, rolling her eyes as she flounced to the stern with Prometheus. Crossing her arms, she huffed, "Magoi here. I'm supposed to know these things. Or really, you should, Pro." She glared at the Titan, arching her brows. "Falling down on the god job, are you?"

"Careful, Red, or you might go for a swim," Prometheus growled. There wasn't a person on the boat who thought he was serious.

"Northeast it is." Carver joined Bellanca and Prometheus at the stern. He leaned against the back railing and crossed his legs at the ankles.

Still god-sized, Prometheus continued to steer. Bellanca scowled as usual, her fiery hair flying on the wind. Carver picked at the dried salt in his budding beard, squinting against the diamonds flashing off the waves ahead. The sun gilded them all from behind—a golden frame for a colorful mosaic. They made quite the tableau. Deadly. Powerful. Messed up and endearing. Flynn got the insane urge to hug them all.

They were a trio now, he realized. The earthquake in the Arcadian Wilds had separated their group in more ways than one. They were still a unit—Team Elpis—but with two poles. The separation had given him time to accept his feelings for Jo and finally act on them. He couldn't be more grateful—or sure that Poseidon was watching their every move. After all, he was also the god of earthquakes.

Jo had been certain that deep crevasse was supposed to swallow them whole. Flynn wasn't so sure anymore. Maybe the uncrossable divide had done exactly what it was supposed to— remake them into what they were now.

Carver straightened, a frown tugging at his mouth. "You don't have to fall into that deathlike sleep right away, do you?" He glanced first at his sister and then at Bellanca. For someone who'd done his best lately to drive away everyone who cared about him, Carver sure looked like he didn't want to be alone. "We can at least... I don't know... Sit and have a meal?"

"Definitely. There's plenty of time." Jo wandered toward the stern, shading her eyes from the sun. "I was thinking of administering the potion a little later than this time tomorrow. If Aeaea is about two days off Thassos, we need to still be under the influence of the sleeping draught when we get near it, or the island won't think we're a ghost ship and reveal itself."

"And let's hope I'm *dead enough*," Carver said a little dully, "or I might sail us right past it, and the gods only know where we'll end up then."

Flynn had a feeling Carver's brief trip to the Underworld had left enough of a mark on him to count. Even if Carver had been pulled back to the land of the living before it was too late, he'd be able to see Aeaea and sail them safely in. He'd drop anchor off Circe's prison, they'd find their way to the marble statue of her in the center of her garden, and they'd get what they came for—a plant grown with magic that wasn't Olympian in nature. A plant that could be converted into an antidote for Cat.

Flynn gave Carver a reassuring nod from across the boat. "You'll find it." He sounded confident. He *felt* confident. He'd never doubted Jo's ambitious plan, and now, he'd never been more certain of it.

Jo returned to his side and slipped her hand into his, small, warm, and perfect. He loved her so much, his heart ached with it.

"We'll reach Aeaea." She squeezed his fingers, but her gaze lifted to her brother. "And everyone except for Carver—sorry, big brother—will be very well rested for whatever comes next."

CHAPTER 29

Jocasta doled out the vials of Nyx's Shallow Grave, her palms sweaty and her heart racing. It wasn't that she doubted herself—she'd checked the doses, double-checked them, and her mother had been watching and helping during the entire brewing process—but no one was mistake-free in life, and she really didn't want any mistakes in this case. When an error could be fatal, it was best to read the labels twice.

When everyone taking the potion had their designated vial in hand and a comfortable place to curl up on the deck, Jocasta took a moment to visit with Carver before they sank into the sleep of the dead. Standing at the stern, he looked relaxed at the steering oars. He might be comfortable guiding the boat northeast as Poseidon and Athena had instructed, but she had a feeling her brother was far less at ease with the idea of a good twelve hours alone with his thoughts.

No wonder he argued incessantly with Bellanca. Carver didn't like the quiet. If his mind wasn't occupied, it likely turned too often to Konstantina and her poor choices in life.

Her back to them, Bellanca got ready to settle down for her long sleep, plumping her bag into a pillow and pulling out a cloak. Carver hadn't been easy lately, but Bellanca had skin as thick and tough as it got. You could probably slice her up and throw vinegar on her, and she'd still laugh in your face and burn you to a crisp.

"How's my big brother doing?" Jocasta asked, dragging a barrel closer to Carver and taking a seat. She'd leave it there for him. At some point over the long hours ahead, surely, he'd also prefer to sit.

"Which one?" Carver's mouth twisted into a semblance of a smile. "One's tearing his hair out while the woman he loves suffers and his new kingdom wobbles on shaky legs. Another is off in Attica somewhere—hopefully alive. And me..." He shrugged. "As you see."

"What I see is a man who just avoided my question."

Carver's gaze flashed to hers, his smile turning more genuine. "And here I always thought it was Kaia who was a pain in the neck."

"Kaia is...determined," Jocasta agreed with a laugh.

Carver snorted. "*You're* determined. I never thought you'd crack Flynn's shell. I'm impressed."

"Well, it took years. I first kissed him when I was eighteen, you know."

"You *what*?" Carver rounded on her, no smile this time. "Flynn was a man, and you were—"

"Well into womanhood," Jocasta cut in. "You know very well I haven't changed size or shape since I was fifteen."

"Size and shape don't make for maturity," he said, still scowling.

"Oh, please." She rolled her eyes at him. "You're not one to lecture me about maturity. Stop harassing Bellanca with every other sentence out of your mouth, and then we'll talk about being a grown-up."

Carver gaped at her. "She harasses *me*."

"I'm not saying that's false." Jocasta conceded his rather fair point with a sigh. "Just that it goes both ways."

"So?" He looked genuinely confused.

"So maybe you're both...misdirecting your energy." Was she being too subtle? Probably.

"Nah." Carver grinned suddenly. "She keeps me sharp. Sharpness is important for a swordsman."

Jocasta nodded, pressing her lips together. Definitely too subtle. "And you keep her constantly on the verge of flaring up—important for a Magoi with fire magic."

"You see?" He chuckled. "Symbiosis." Carver's gaze strayed to Bellanca as she said something to Prometheus, her long braid glinting fiery red in the late afternoon sun. "You think she's comfortable on the deck?" He looked pensive. "She's a princess...used to castle life. Fine beds, soft pillows, and all that."

No one was comfortable on the deck. It was hot and hard, and they hid behind barrels to perform bodily functions that shouldn't be anybody else's business. Afternoon jaunts on the *Athena* were great. The five of them stuck onboard for the foreseeable future was not.

"She *was* a princess. We deposed her, remember?" Sintan, Tarvan, and Fisan royals didn't exist anymore. There was only the Royal House of Thalyria now, with Cat at its head and Griffin as her king. And baby Eleni—the unborn heir to it all.

Carver watched the Magoi across the boat. "Maybe that's why she's always so prickly."

"She's prickly by nature. And she wouldn't trade her new life for her old one. I'm sure of it."

"You're right." He lifted his eyes to the horizon, a smile pulling at his lips. "She's too smart for that."

Jocasta sighed. If Carver would just *listen* to himself, he'd see that Bellanca didn't aggravate him half as much as he thought.

"So you're all right?" she asked. "You. Carver," she added, just in case he wanted to deflect her question again.

He leaned toward her, touching heads. "I'm all right. Actually, I'm a lot better than I have been in a while."

Trying not to smile too obviously, Jocasta stood, slid both

arms around him, and squeezed. Carver kept his hands on the oars, but he dropped a kiss on the top of her head, and her smile widened. If only she could pass the sudden joy flooding her straight into her brother. The healer's curse was to not always have the right panacea or the means to administer it. A hug would have to do. "I'm sorry none of us realized how hard things were for you, between when Konstantina left and... lately."

Carver shrugged as she let him go. "It's not your fault I'm an excellent actor."

Her smile turned wry. "You are." She looked up at him, catching a flicker of warm gray eyes as he briefly glanced down. "But don't act anymore, okay? You don't need to. I want my real brother, even if he's a testy grump sometimes."

"Don't worry." Humor laced his words. "This testy grump will still bite heads off regularly, especially Bel's."

Jocasta barely held back a smile and kept her eyes on the wide blue ocean. "You do that," she said, knowing *Bel* would bite back hard.

Carver tipped his head toward Flynn. "Speaking of good acting, I had no idea there was a thing between you and Flynn until he went berserk at the Agon Games. You offered to join the team, and the man who never argues about anything went insane."

"It was impressive," she agreed.

"*You* were impressive." He leveled one of those heavy looks on her that the men in her family were so good at. Instead of the usual demand for caution, this one conveyed respect and pride. "You refused to back down. You convinced Cat and Griffin. You insisted on helping. And you *survived*."

Carver's unexpected praise pushed up such a strong surge of emotion that tears pricked her eyes. "But you died protecting me. What if Persephone hadn't been there to pull you back? And when you saw Konstantina in the Underworld, it stirred up so much. It made you miserable. I'm so sorry."

"Don't be." His short laugh was more of a scoff, and his self-deprecating smile arrowed straight to her heart. "I needed stirring up. Konstantina was on the far side of the Styx. Even if I'd crossed the river and never come back, we might not have been together. She didn't choose me in life. I don't know what made me think she'd choose me in death."

Jocasta forced herself to nod, sniffling. If Carver's angry, drunken spiral after the Agon Games had actually resulted in some kind of catharsis, then so much the better. Hopefully, it was bringing him relief.

"And you were right," he added. "What you said below the arena before the games? I didn't really know you until that night. Now, I see who you are."

She swallowed. "And who's that?"

"The woman who stepped in to save the day, despite the danger to herself. The woman who called everyone together and proposed a solution to a problem that could tear a kingdom and a family apart. The woman who made a plan when not even the gods had one."

Her sharp inhalation shuddered in her throat. She wiped a tear from her eye. "Let's just hope my plan works."

"I'm done hoping." Carver's flat tone made her look up at him, hurt. "I *believe* instead."

Her frown turned into a smile. She stretched up on her toes and kissed Carver's scruffy cheek. "Fair winds, Brother."

"Sleep well," he answered. "I hope you'll see Aeaea when you wake."

Me too, Jocasta thought as she wandered back to where Flynn had set up bedrolls and blankets. He'd managed to carve out a nook for them on the far side of Bellanca and Prometheus. Between the thick mast, the side oars, their weapons, drinking water, food, and other supplies, there wasn't much room on the *Athena* for the sleepers to spread out. Just the spear and the aegis took up more room than the four of them combined.

"Mmm. Cozy," she said, eyeing the Titan and the Magoi right next to them. They eyed her back.

"Pro takes too much room." Bellanca gave Prometheus's ankle a shove with her foot.

"That swim is still on the table," he growled, shoving back.

"Keep your god-sized feet to yourself. No kicking." She kicked him, of course.

Prometheus grabbed her foot in an invisible rush of movement and then slowly, very deliberately placed it as far away from him as possible. Letting go, he ground out, "You are. Downright. Impossible."

"Well, I'm better than Tartarus," she snapped, wiggling into a more comfortable position.

His eyes narrowed. "Debatable," the Titan said.

Bellanca's jaw dropped, wounded feelings making her gasp out loud.

Prometheus winced but didn't look ready to apologize. Jocasta couldn't blame him. With her wholly unfiltered interactions, Bellanca often started things but didn't like how they finished.

"A deathlike sleep could be just what the healer ordered," Jocasta said a bit too brightly. "How about a little break from one another?"

"I'll drink to that." Scowling at Prometheus, Bellanca raised her vial of Nyx's Shallow Grave. "Cheers." She downed the potion. After wrinkling her freckled nose and smacking her lips a few times, she turned her scowl on Jocasta. "You messed up. It's not doing anything. I feel nothing." A second later, she slumped to the side and would've slammed her head on the deck if Prometheus hadn't caught her.

"One down," Flynn said as Prometheus gently put Bellanca's head on her makeshift pillow and pulled her cloak around her. Bellanca would never know it, but that looked to Jocasta like the Titan's way of saying he was sorry for hurting the Magoi's feelings.

Prometheus took the precaution of lying down before he drank his dose. He settled into his temporary bed and within seconds was snoring loudly enough to rattle the boat.

Flynn grimaced. "Thank the gods I don't have to listen to that for the next twelve hours."

Jocasta giggled. "He'll stop in a minute. Once the potion truly kicks in, he'll barely breathe, let alone snore like the Erymanthian Boar."

Flynn eyed the sleeping Titan. "More like thunderbolts from Olympus."

Laughing, Jocasta scooted back from the racket and snuggled in to Flynn. "It really is tragically loud, although I don't remember hearing it on the road."

Flynn looped his arm around her waist and tucked her closer. "True. It must be the potion."

It likely was, because soon, Prometheus settled into such a deep, quiet sleep it frightened her a little after the deafening honking.

Jocasta resisted the impulse to lean over and check for a pulse. This result was *good*, not bad, she reminded herself. Deep sleep was the whole purpose of a sleeping draught.

"I guess it's our turn." She rubbed her vial between her fingers. It was warm to the touch—maybe because she'd been holding on to it for several minutes.

"If Carver wasn't awake and just steps away, I'd lobby for holding off and enjoying a moment of privacy."

The Flynn effect exploded inside her, only now, it was a welcome feeling. Desire stirred, tightening her belly. "Shall we throw him overboard?" she suggested.

Flynn chuckled. "Ruthless. I'm actually considering it." His hand brushed the side of her breast. Warmth shimmered through her. "We could always haul him back onboard in a little while."

Jocasta stroked her free hand up Flynn's muscled thigh, remembering the feel of his body wrapped around hers, pressing her down, moving inside her. A riot of sensation burst between her legs and spread to her middle. "What about the ketea?"

Flynn nuzzled her neck. "Have you seen any lately?" He planted a light kiss below her ear. Then another.

She shivered. "One. Not an hour ago."

"Hmm. He'll survive." He captured her mouth and kissed her, long and deep. She arched into him, need unfurling inside her. They moved together, their bodies inching closer until they tangled into one and clothing became an insufferable barrier.

Breathless when they broke apart, Jocasta asked, "Are we actually considering this?"

Flynn's low laughter sounded almost pained this time. "I wish."

"I have a wish, too," she said, suddenly serious. She took his face in her hands and kissed his mouth. It was a light, lingering press, tender but full of promise and fire.

Flynn's gaze flicked up, meeting hers. "What, *latreia mou?*"

My adored one. Would that ever not send a thrill through her? Give rise to a shiver of pleasure through her senses, a flutter in her heart, and a hot little thump in her core? "I want to get what we need, and I want to make it home. With you."

Flynn nodded. She didn't need to explain that by *home*, she meant their Sintan village. With the healing practice she'd begun building. With his olive groves.

When this journey was over, there wouldn't be any war to fight. Or if there was, it wouldn't be theirs.

There would be a whitewashed farmhouse, furniture that needed dusting, and flowerpots to fill.

"That sounds like the right ending to this quest." Flynn kissed her back, his brown eyes hopeful and warm. "And the perfect beginning to so much more."

CHAPTER 30

Flynn squinted against the glaring sunlight, opening his heavy eyelids only a slit. The boat rocked beneath him. Waves lapped against the hull, a gentle *slap-slosh* that didn't sound like open ocean. They didn't seem to be moving, and he was sure he was the anchor, his body leaden enough to stop the boat.

Groaning, he blinked and rubbed his eyes. Jo was a warm weight against his side, her body still heavy and slack with slumber. It took a moment for his brain to unfog and even longer for his arms and legs to respond to his cues to move again. Nyx's Shallow Grave was one doozy of a potion. He *did* feel as though he'd been dead. Sleep was one thing. This was a void, empty and dark.

So worse than death. At least with death, there came an afterlife.

A tight pang hit his chest as he thought about Kato. They hadn't found Kato's body, but his brother-in-arms had never been without an obol to pay his passage across the River Styx. Kato was living his second life in the Underworld, and if there was any justice, the golden path to Elysium had unfurled before him as he crossed the river. Kato deserved more than just an afterlife. He'd earned a glorious one.

Sliding away from Jo, Flynn corralled his strength and sat up. Carver perched on a barrel near the mast, eating an orange. His shadow shaded Bellanca's fair, freckled face from the blazing-hot sun. She slept on, blissfully unaware that Carver tossed orange peels onto her head. Next to her, Prometheus was just waking up. Like Flynn, he went from sluggishly blinking to finally sitting up. He rubbed his hands over his face, scrubbing hard.

"Did we make it?" the Titan rasped, twelve hours of gravel in his throat.

"Look for yourself." Carver tipped his head to the right.

Flynn craned his neck and peered over the edge of the boat. "Hades, Hera, and Hestia," he breathed out. He'd never seen anything like it. "Aeaea?"

"I sure hope so." Carver spit an orange seed over the railing. "I kept sailing in the direction the trident pointed, and nothing else ever showed up."

Jo moaned and flopped an arm over her eyes. "Whazz happening?"

Flynn lifted her arm off her face and kissed her. "You're amazing. That's what's happening."

She squeezed her eyes shut. "Aeaea?"

"Yes."

Her eyes flew open, and she launched herself toward the railing, stumbling as if she'd had one too many cups of wine. "Oh my gods, we did it!" She shaded her eyes with a trembling hand, her face scrunched against the glare. "Great Zeus." She stared at the high marble wall blocking access to the island as far as they could see in both directions. One wide-open door faced them. "That's the maze, isn't it?" She turned back around, her eyes as big and round as Athena's aegis.

Flynn, Carver, and Prometheus stood and took in the imposing sight along with her. The immense structure rose from the wide, sandy beach, that one towering door gaping like a giant mouth ready to eat them. Through the doorway, Flynn could already see several possible paths branching out. The maze was impossibly huge, with walls five times as high as any man. Not even Prometheus would be able to jump high enough to see the lay of the land over the sides. There wasn't a hint of green—just white marble and sand—and the heat the thing threw off made Flynn think he could cook a lamb steak against the stone in less than three minutes.

Circe's palace loomed in the distance. The huge hilltop citadel must rival anything on Mount Olympus, with its marble columns, wide arches, and lush, tiered gardens cascading down the slope until finally disappearing from view behind the maze.

Nervous awe sat like a lump in Flynn's throat. He swallowed. Circe's island. *Circe's garden.* The magic here was palpable, even to him. The power and mystery blanketing everything was what he'd always imagined feeling if he stood in the shadow of Mount Olympus. Jo was right. The hidden island was the reason the whole of Fisa had always been awash with magic more than anywhere else. Olympus in the north. Aeaea in the south.

"You did it, Jo," he murmured to the woman beside him. "You got us here."

"We're all going to die," she murmured back.

Flynn laid his hand over hers on the railing and squeezed. "Now's not the time to doubt."

She nodded but agreeing with him didn't wipe the terror from her face. "Carver…" She glanced at her brother. "You brought us right to the gate."

He popped a wedge of orange into his mouth. "Looks like my temporary death finally came in handy."

"That's not funny," Jo said.

Carver had the decency to look sheepish. He gave a good-natured shrug. "It wasn't that hard in the end. That castle was all lit up like a beacon throughout the night. I saw it from hours away. The ocean was calm, the winds good…"

"Did you have to sail around the island?" Prometheus asked.

Carver shook his head. "From farther out, you can see there's nothing but cliffs on either side of the maze. This gate was pointing right at us as we sailed in."

"The only door to Circe's prison." Flynn would've dropped anchor here, too, with no other choice and the entrance to the maze staring them in the face. "Has anyone figured out who Asterion might be?" *Navigate the maze where Asterion rules all.* They all knew that scroll by heart now—or at least the part detailing the five trials by sea and land. They'd done sea. Now came land. And the witch of Aeaea.

Gooseflesh rose on Flynn's arms.

"I guess we'll find out." Jo stared through the open doorway as though it were the entrance to Tartarus. She shivered despite the heat.

Bellanca sat up with a groan. "You killed me, you stupid Hoi Polloi healer," she moaned. "I honest to gods feel dead."

"It'll get better," Jo said, clearly not taking offense. "Welcome back."

"Welcome to Aeaea," Carver added, looking almost proud.

Frowning, Bellanca picked an orange peel out of her hair. Seeing the rest of the orange in Carver's hand, she threw the peel at him. He dodged. She plucked another piece off her shoulder and threw that one, too. Carver dodged again. He grinned, obviously enjoying himself. Standing, Bellanca fumed, steam practically coming out of her ears.

No, that was *actual* smoke. Fire erupted down her braid.

"That's more of an incendiary incident than usual!" Jo warned, pointing to the redhead's hair.

Bellanca batted at her head, trying to snuff out the flames. "The magic's too strong here. I can barely control it!" Her voice rose in fear. Sparks sizzled to the hot planks of the deck, smoldering there. "The boat!" she cried.

Carver stomped on an ember, grabbed her arm, and pulled her overboard with him through the hole in the railing. The splash nearly showered the *Athena*'s deck. Bellanca came up flailing and spluttering. Carver—somewhat more prepared for the sudden plunge—calmly treaded water.

"Was that really necessary?" Bellanca ground out, wiping now-sodden hair from her face.

"I think so." He grinned.

She hmphed. As Bellanca and Carver swam toward the shore, the Magoi got her first good look at what they faced. "I hate this already!" she called over her shoulder, probably aiming the words at Jo. Steam rose from her wet head.

The rest of them quickly gathered weapons and supplies and then floated them in watertight baskets as they swam for the beach. Just tall enough in his god form for his feet to touch the bottom, Prometheus carried the spear, the aegis, and a satchel holding Jo's essential healing supplies above his head.

"I think we should eat and drink and shake off the effects of the potion before we enter the maze," Flynn said. They needed to gather their strength.

Jo slogged up the beach beside him. "I second that," she panted. "Then, we go into the maze and see what happens next."

Bellanca scowled, already half-dry and sizzling again. "It's massive. We'll never find the way through. *Or* back."

"Lucky for us, I have Ariadne's thread." With a dazzling smile, Jo pulled a silvery ball of twine from her pocket.

Flynn's jaw dropped. "Did Cat give you that?" He hadn't even thought about the magic thread, a gift to Cat to help navigate another labyrinth on a different quest.

A smile tugged at his mouth as he wryly shook his head. Cat had a habit of squirreling away magic to suddenly pull out in an emergency and of keeping lifesaving talents to herself until she actually needed them to save someone's life. She always said not to flaunt your abilities, since you never knew when they could give you the edge. He'd thought her lessons in discretion were funny at first, since Cat was probably the least inconspicuous person he'd ever met. But in the end, her well of magic and mettle ran so deep there was always another layer to dig up. She *did* show only the periphery of her strength, as impressive as that already was. Jo was the same, Flynn realized, not advertising all the strategies in her head, all the courage in her heart, or all the aces up her sleeve, but pulling them out one by one, as needed in a pinch.

He couldn't have been prouder of her. His chest swelled with admiration for the woman, the healer, the *warrior* by his side.

Jo held out the magic twine, letting everyone take a good look. "Cat kept it from when she and Kato navigated the caverns on the Ice Plains. Since a labyrinth was listed as part of our trials, she gave me the thread."

The ball in Jo's hand was the size of a small goose egg, but Flynn knew that meant nothing. Ariadne's thread would go on forever—for as long as they needed until they could retrace their steps out of the maze.

"It will not end. It will not tangle," Carver murmured, remembering the same words Flynn had heard what seemed like a lifetime ago. A different journey. A different team. Kato still with them.

His eyes met Carver's. Then Jo's. The pause was brief. The grief profound. Loss like that never got easier, it just got…more distant. Until the day they met again in the Underworld.

Before letting themselves sit down to a much-needed meal in the shade of the huge doorway, Jo and he tied the end of the string to the big metal ring anchored to the beach—a mooring for boats that never reached here. Or *almost* never. Jo kept the rest of the twine in her pocket. It would seamlessly unravel as they navigated the labyrinth.

———— 6 ————

"Another dead end," Jo growled, whipping Ariadne's thread back around the useless bend.

Prometheus slashed his palm and left a bloody streak at eye level on the marble wall. In their countless turnings, they'd already come across several dried blood marks, which meant they were both spinning in circles and exploring new paths.

Jo had quickly stopped asking if Prometheus needed a numbing salve or bandages every time he marked another dead end. His hand healed practically before he finished marking the wall. Either the Titan was getting stronger as he used his magic more—and assumed his full size again—or being on Aeaea amped up his godliness to a new level. Even Flynn, knowing he was as Hoi Polloi as they came, could feel the buzzing prick of magic on the hot dry air. Jo felt it, too, her heat-reddened face pinching from the constant sting. Carver kept muttering about how Aeaea felt like one big bug bite to him.

And Bellanca… She constantly struggled for the upper hand over magic that wanted to break free and burn.

"Stop complaining." The redhead shoved Carver away from her. "I can barely control my fire as it is, and you keep making me want to roast you alive."

He angled back toward her, unperturbed by either her fiery ire or by the *actual* fire curling around her head. "Maybe you'll cook my bug bites."

"You don't *have* bug bites. That's magic. It stings."

Carver studied her from under lowered brows. "You mean you have to live like this all the time?"

"Well, this is worse. Far worse. It must be if even *you* can feel it." She wiped sweat off her upper lip. "But yes, otherwise. There's always at least a faint prickling, unless there aren't any other Magoi—or gods"—she tossed a glare at Prometheus—"around."

Carver pursed his lips. "No wonder you're always so grumpy."

"*I'm* grumpy?" Bellanca squeaked.

"Is that why you spend time with me?" he asked. "Because I don't make you sting?"

Her mouth opened. Closed. "I just singed your eyebrow. That one." She jabbed a finger at his face.

Carver touched his eyebrow, putting out the spark. He shrugged. "It'll grow back."

Bellanca decisively faced forward and walked a little faster, gaining the lead for herself.

Several minutes later, she stopped up ahead, holding out a warning hand. "Did you hear that?" she asked softly, her head and shoulders starting to flicker and flame again.

Flynn hadn't heard anything, but he trusted that Bellanca had. He nodded to her to follow her instinct.

Her eyes narrowing, she moved toward a route they had yet to take, raising both arms in that direction. Sparks danced between her fingers. There was nothing unusual about that— her hands were weapons, her magic ready in an instant—but in the maze, her fire crackled an eyeball-searing blue-white.

Flynn approached the entrance to the path, keeping Jo at his side. The sun bounced off the white walls and beat down on the fine sand beneath their feet. Flynn was convinced Circe's island had already half roasted and half blinded him. He'd never been so blazing hot in his life.

He squinted down the long, high-walled corridor Bellanca watched with predatory stillness, little flames licking up and down her arms. The others all stopped and waited with him, listening. Everyone but Carver shook their heads. The dark-haired swordsman took a few silent steps toward Bellanca, cocking his ear down the path.

"Scuffing," Carver finally said, staying just out of her flaming reach.

Flynn finally heard something, too, distant but worrisome. Or maybe good news?

Bellanca listened again. "Scraping?"

Carver nodded. He and Bellanca moved forward as one.

"Careful," Flynn warned as they cautiously advanced. "We don't know what it is."

"Asterion?" Jo quietly guessed. She inched closer to him, Ariadne's unending thread a shiny gray line trailing from her pocket. She unsheathed a dagger, gripping it hard. "Maybe we should take the path away from the noise, not toward it?" she whispered.

"We've been in here for hours," Prometheus said with the confidence of an immortal who knew for a fact that relentless torture wouldn't end him, even when he wished it would. "I say we check it out."

"You're also practically unkillable," Jo said with a hint of exasperation. "The rest of us aren't."

With a few quick steps, the Titan took the lead from Carver and Bellanca. "Then I'll go first. Unless something chops off my head, I'll recover."

Out of the corner of his eye, Flynn saw Jo press a nervous hand to the satchel she carried with her healing supplies. He was glad she'd brought it. Depending on what they faced, they could go from whole and hale to dying in the blink of an eye. They'd all seen it happen.

Flynn slowed so that he could take up the rear position and watch everyone's backs. With Prometheus in the lead, they continued, cautious and quiet. No one spoke another word. They heard the scuffing scrape again at an unmarked crossroad and headed in its direction. They didn't hit another dead end, and the twists and turns got tighter and closer together, as though they finally converged on the center of the maze.

"I think we're nearing the heart of the labyrinth," Flynn said.

"Maybe." Jo bit her lip and glanced down at the thin magic rope marking their path back out for them. "I'm hopelessly turned around."

He was, too. Worry tightened his chest. Flynn kept his battle-ax ready and Jo close. Sweat stung his eyes. The fiery ball overhead told him nothing. It seemed to have been dead noon for hours. Could time move differently on Aeaea? Or just in the maze?

His nostrils flared in frustration, the island's scorching air burning the insides of his nose. Endless labyrinth. More questions. No answers.

Jo took long, deep breaths. Prometheus forged silently ahead. For once, Bellanca and Carver kept quiet.

Holding up his hand to halt them, Prometheus stopped at another intersection and listened. After a moment, he turned left. They rounded another corner, and the high, confining walls of the maze suddenly opened into a big central courtyard with a fountain in the middle. A huge marble statue of Poseidon jutted out of the spraying water, his golden trident pointing toward an exit on the opposite side of the courtyard. Flynn knew without a doubt that was the way out of the labyrinth toward Circe's garden.

Jo's feet dragged to a stop. "We made it." Her eyes zeroed in on the fountain. "I'm so thirsty." They'd already finished the water they'd carried in with them—a fact that had been weighing on Flynn's mind as their time in the oven-like maze continued.

He'd been minutes from suggesting they turn around, follow the thread back to the boat, and try again later.

"Made it where, exactly?" Bellanca asked. "Navigate the maze. Fine. Then what?"

Prometheus took a few steps forward, bone-dry stone dust swirling around his feet. It wasn't sand here. It looked more like incredibly fine, crushed marble. Bits of minerals sparkled in the sunlight.

A loud, slow, sarcastic clapping sounded from behind the fountain. Flynn froze, instinctively reaching out an arm to shield Jocasta. She stopped, lifting her dagger. A dry swallow clicked in her throat, and Flynn's lip curled in aggression. *Nothing* would get close enough to harm her.

In front, Prometheus remained a barrier for them all. Carver drew his sword, and Bellanca burned already.

"Reveal yourself!" Prometheus boomed like thunder.

"With pleasure," answered a low, grating voice.

Flynn's eyes widened. No human followed those confident words around the corner of the fountain. What emerged from the shadows had the body of a man and the head of a bull. It was the Minotaur.

A burst of adrenaline sent Flynn's heart kicking against his ribs. Hadn't the Minotaur been killed centuries ago? In Attica?

He was no historian, but he knew his basic stories. Enough magical creatures roamed the worlds to bring the biggest legends even to the ears of simple olive farmers in southern villages. The monster in the maze was no exception.

"Asterion?" Jo broke the silence, the name the scroll had given them for this king of the labyrinth rasping like rust in her mouth.

The creature's golden eyes fixed on her, raising Flynn's hackles. "Not many know my true name. The name my mother gave me."

A chill slid through Flynn at the labored, grinding rumble.

The Minotaur formed human words in the mouth of a bull. It shouldn't have worked and almost didn't. It made the monster even more monstrous. Two sharp, curving horns put the creature a head taller than even Prometheus. Its barrel chest, strapping arms, and powerful thighs spoke of strength that went beyond even the Titan's.

"How's Pasiphaë?" Prometheus asked. He stepped forward, keeping everyone else behind him.

"My mother thinks Theseus killed me," the Minotaur said. "She doesn't know her magic protected me from true death and that I appeared again, whole and woundless, on her sister's prison island—and once more trapped in Daedalus's same accursed maze."

So this was the famed Cretan labyrinth—or an exact replica of it. Flynn processed the information he understood as quickly as he could. Circe was the Minotaur's aunt. Circe and the creature's mother, Pasiphaë, were both skilled witches and the immortal daughters of the sun god, Helios. Prometheus was their cousin. Which made the monster...Pro's second cousin? Flynn had no idea.

"I see you've been consorting with that traitor Ariadne." Asterion's golden eyes narrowed with hatred on the thread trailing from Jo's pocket. "My sister never liked me."

"Are you surprised?" Bellanca snorted. "You're a flesh-eating monster."

An enraged bellow resonated around the courtyard. Eyes blazing, the Minotaur scraped a huge foot against the ground, sending marble dust flying.

"Good gods, Bel. Keep quiet," Carver muttered.

"No!" Jo threw her hands out to stay the creature. "Don't charge! Maybe we can help you. The maze *is* escapable. We'll find the way out—together."

Asterion's brutal laugh whipped out like a lash striking a stinging blow to Jo's offer. "I know the way out, puny human. I *can't* leave. They trapped me here. The Starry One must stay at the center of his constellation or the Great Bull will come crashing from the sky and cause cataclysms across the worlds."

Flynn blinked. *What now?*

Jo gasped. "That's why you ended up in a place no one is ever supposed to reach? Healed? Your mother's magic tied you to the balance of the cosmos, so the gods—Poseidon," she guessed, glancing at the statue of the Minotaur's Olympian grandfather, "were forced to keep you alive and safe somewhere." She lowered her hands. "But not happy, I imagine."

"Who cares about happy?" the creature spat out. "I'm hungry." He lowered his head and charged.

First in line, Prometheus barely had time to flip the giant aegis off his back and deflect the Minotaur's attack. Asterion staggered sideways, landing on one knee in front of Carver. The force of the Minotaur's blow knocked Prometheus flat on his back at Bellanca's feet. Asterion lashed out at Carver with a heavy arm. Carver sprang out of the way. Bellanca set the arm on fire. The beast howled, jumping back from the trio while Prometheus leaped to his feet and aimed the spear at the Minotaur.

"Don't kill him!" Flynn shouted before the Titan could either skewer the monster or wake the Gorgon head on the shield.

Prometheus pulled up short, growling, "Why in the name of Hades not?"

"Cataclysms!" Flynn hissed, stepping forward to stand with the others. Jo hung back. Smart woman.

Prometheus leveled a battle-hot gaze on the bull creature. Eyes narrowed. Shield up. Spear in hand. "He'll just be reborn."

"It sounds like he was *healed*, not remade." Flynn edged back toward Jo as Asterion ignored Prometheus's clear challenge and turned his tawny gaze on the woman with only a dagger in her hand and healing supplies for armor.

Jo backpedaled, brandishing the knife. "I'll throw this," she warned, "and I don't miss."

The Minotaur grated a low, monstrous laugh, hitching his distended chin at Jo in a ghastly show of humor. "You're for later." He winked. The godsdamned monster winked. At Flynn's *wife*. "There's plenty of food here already, and you, my delectable black-haired human, have hips made for a bull." He mimed a crass rutting motion.

Jo's absolute silence was the most terrifying thing Flynn had ever heard. Lava boiled in his veins. "Touch her and die."

Asterion didn't even look at him as he ambled toward Jo. "This coming from the one who just shouted, 'Don't kill him!'" The creature's scraping laugh grated on Flynn's last nerve.

Gripping his ax, Flynn backed up until he stood in front of Jo, the Minotaur matching him step for step. Jo was finally his. For life. In death. She was a fire in his heart, a beacon in his soul, and nothing ended today. Anything coming at her would have to go through him, but he knew she was far from defenseless. Any god, man, or monster underestimated Jo at their own peril. He'd learned that twice.

Flynn let a deep growl build in his chest. "I've killed plenty of monsters in my life, human and magical creature alike. Cataclysms might be worth the risk." He hardly knew what he was saying. He just knew he had to keep the Minotaur looking at him while Prometheus, Carver, and Bellanca crept up on the beast's back. Pro looked like he was gauging where to stick Athena's spear without killing Asterion. Bellanca had murder in her eyes, and Flynn almost wanted her to act on it. Carver's face was such a mask of fury that Flynn could only imagine the violent thoughts going on behind it. Threaten his family, and Carver turned as cold and calculating as the gods were hot and impulsive.

"You're awfully confident." Words coming from an animal's mouth added a repulsiveness to the already nightmarish situation. There was no mobility of lips, no elasticity of expression. Speech emerging from a dark, half-open maw was just as unnatural as the rest of this.

"That's because I know something you don't." Flynn kept his eyes from straying to the trio sneaking up on Asterion. "We. Don't. Lose."

The Minotaur's eyes gleamed, the twin disks like golden suns. "My mother lusted after a bull. I lust after flesh and blood." He shrugged as though cannibalism were to be expected. "And I know something you don't."

"What's that?" Flynn ground out even though he had no desire to humor the beast.

A chilling laugh fell like a mudslide from the Minotaur's throat. "I. Always. Eat. My. Fill."

Prometheus raised the spear behind Asterion. Despite the Titan's utter silence, Asterion whipped around, lowering his head and lunging as he turned. He gored Prometheus through the chest, both horns sinking so deep they came out the other side.

"Pro!" Bellanca shouted. She sent a wall of fire crashing into the Minotaur. Carver followed her barrage with a hard downward strike that sliced open Asterion's shoulder.

Asterion tossed Prometheus off his horns. The Titan flew through the air and slammed headfirst into the huge statue of Poseidon. The spear and aegis clattered to the ground. Blood poured from Prometheus's head and chest, staining the marble base of the fountain.

Twisting with preternatural speed and strength, the Minotaur lashed back around, aiming a sharp horn at Carver's middle. The swordsman darted out of the way. Bellanca attacked, and Asterion dodged, tucking and rolling under her flames. He came up midway between the two poles of Team Elpis.

Flynn didn't waste a second. He threw his ax, burying it deep in the Minotaur's back. Asterion didn't even seem to feel it. He spun and lunged for Flynn. Flynn evaded, but the Minotaur followed up with a lightning-fast kick that clipped Flynn's elbow. His bone ringing, his fingers almost numb, Flynn reached for the sword on his back. He pulled a dagger from his belt at the same time and struck low with the smaller blade, plunging it into the Minotaur's thigh while the creature deflected the sword with his horns.

Roaring, Asterion landed a blow to the side of Flynn's head that nearly knocked him senseless. Flynn staggered. For a moment, all was silence. Then a whoosh of heat spurred him into action, and he ducked under Bellanca's flames, lashing out with his dagger.

The Minotaur reared back. He twisted, catching Carver's sword with his horns just before the blade skewered him. He sent the sword flying end over end into the fountain. Weaponless, Carver dove to the side, and Bellanca diverted the monster with a blast of blue-hot fire that left him smoking from hips to shoulders.

Asterion turned his sunburst eyes on Bellanca. "You die first," he snarled.

Darting in from the side, Flynn threw a handful of marble dust into the creature's face, momentarily blinding him. Carver saw the opening, heaved Prometheus's spear off the ground, and drove it straight into the Minotaur's stomach.

After that, they attacked from all sides. Flames. Blades. Kicks and punches. Flynn got in a blow that would've felled a mortal. Then a second one. Asterion kept fighting. There were three of them, and they were *losing*. Heat, fatigue, and thirst made Flynn sloppy for a split second. That was all it took for the Minotaur to grab Flynn's head in his huge hands and mash his thumbs into Flynn's eyes. Flynn wrenched away with a roar, his eyes aching and watering.

Carver grabbed the spear and yanked it out of Asterion's middle. Spinning, he swung the heavy weapon like a club, landing a ringing hit to the Minotaur's head. Asterion made a sound so terrible it would rattle in Flynn's mind for a decade. Then with a lunge no one saw coming, Asterion grabbed Carver, lifted him in the air, and threw him down so hard that Carver just lay there on his back, sprawled out and gasping. Bellanca raced in, and Asterion backhanded her in the face without even looking. She spun like a top and dropped, blood spraying.

Standing in the middle of the courtyard, braced for action, chest heaving, unaffected by his injuries, the Minotaur suddenly seemed invincible. His golden eyes blazed with hatred and hunger, and Flynn started to fear that Asterion would eat, gore, and slake every depraved appetite inside himself until his was the only heartbeat in the center of the maze again.

His vision still blurry, Flynn stumbled toward Carver. Jo shouted her brother's name. Her knife landed in the Minotaur's already damaged torso. Asterion ignored her and aimed his vicious charge at Carver. Flynn cried a warning. Carver was slow to move. Bellanca scrambled forward. She heaved herself between Carver and the Minotaur, and Asterion's big horn cleaved her middle as easily as a hot knife through butter.

Flynn gasped. Jo screamed behind him. Asterion ripped his horn free, sending Bellanca's innards flying across the courtyard. Carver went dead still under Bellanca, her blood soaking him.

Then he howled the most anguished sound Flynn had ever heard and gripped her hard against him.

Suddenly, Jo was there, launching herself onto Asterion's back and hanging on with her legs while she shoved a vial into his gaping maw. She slammed his snout shut with both hands and a crack of glass and held on, forcing Asterion to swallow what was in his mouth, shattered container and all. She leaped off the creature, fast on her feet and leading the Minotaur away from Bellanca and Carver.

Asterion lunged, trying to catch her. He staggered. One leg buckled. Then the other. He crashed down on all fours like the animal he was, panting.

His head tilted up, his fury boring into Jo. "What...did... you...?" His already grinding and guttural speech grew garbled and slower. He blinked, his exploding-star eyes dimming. His lids drooped. He fell to his side. "Witch," he accused, unmoving.

"Healer," Jo corrected. "I could cut off all your limbs right now, and you wouldn't even feel it."

The Minotaur didn't answer. For the first time, fear glittered in his golden eyes. He stared at Jo until his lids closed, and his huge body relaxed in forced slumber.

"Bel?" Carver's voice hitched on her name. "No. *Why?*" Carver dragged the tortured question straight from his soul. It nearly brought tears to Flynn's eyes.

Her breathing sharp and irregular, Bellanca still managed to laugh as Carver maneuvered her gently to the ground and leaned over her. "And let you die instead?" Blood bubbled up with her words. "I'd be so godsdamned bored without you. Now *you* can be bored. Serves you right."

"Jocasta!" Carver's scream racked his lean body. He looked wildly around for his sister. His eyes landed on her, the whites huge, the pupils dilated in terror. "Jocasta! Help! Pro!" He

turned to the Titan. Prometheus moaned and clawed his way
closer. He got halfway there and collapsed. Carver's frantic gaze
swung back to Jo. "What can we do? Can you do something?"
His face twisting, he begged, "Please. Please help."

"I'm here." Jo dropped to her knees beside them. With
trembling hands, she unclasped Bellanca's ripped and bloodied
leather armor, which had done nothing to stop the Minotaur's
horn from gouging straight through it—and her. Jo pulled it
aside, and Carver gasped at the sight of the huge, ragged hole.
He turned away, retching.

Jo didn't say a word. Her hands steadied. She gently peeled
Bellanca's bloodstained tunic away from the wound. "Cut this,"
she said to Flynn.

He sliced the garment from top to bottom, and Jo spread the
two sides, leaving Bellanca without anything in the way of the
injury. The sight of it was enough to turn Flynn's stomach, and
he'd seen all manner of atrocities. The damage was irreparable.
There was no cure for this.

Carver must've believed the same because he held Bellanca's
hand, convulsively squeezing. "You can't heal that. Only a
Magoi healer can."

"Have hope." Jo dragged an egg-shaped pendant out from
under her tunic. "Elpis abandons no one."

Flynn's pulse leaped at the sight of Persephone's heliotrope,
cradled in its delicate wire cage of golden leaves and spring
flowers. Did the others even know about it? They'd been across
the courtyard when Cat gave Jo the amulet. As the Queen of the
Underworld, Persephone, like her husband, Hades, had a hand
in life and death. She'd ripped Carver from the Underworld.
Now her magic would rip Bellanca from the jaws of death.

Jo pulled the chain over her head. "This was a gift from
Persephone to Cat. It has the power to heal one mortal wound."

Bellanca's eyes closed, her skin already the color of ash. Her breathing seemed to stop, and Carver stared at her in utter, panicked shock.

"Do it! Do something!" he urged Jo in a rough, raw rasp.

Jo held the stone over Bellanca's wound. Magic instantly ignited, a flash of green, searing and bright. It took a moment for Bellanca's body to begin knitting back together. Once it started, it was miraculous to watch.

"It's working," Carver whispered, still gripping Bellanca's hand. Flynn watched in awe. He'd never seen healing magic work so fast.

Jo's nostrils flared. Her hand started to tremble, then smoke.

Flynn's eyes sharpened. "Jo?" She pressed her lips together, her muffled sound of pain echoing in his ears like a thunderclap. "It's too hot. Jo!" The little leaves and branches glowed white-hot between her fingers. Most of the pendant nestled in her palm, scorching her.

"Leave it," she grated.

He clenched his jaw, fighting the impulse to knock the stone away from her. She would never forgive him. His heart pounded in fear, ached for her pain, but he didn't move. Jo made her own choices.

Pain-pale, she shook. Flynn's insides cramped as he watched her and waited. Her mouth popped open. She breathed hard and fast. The stone branded her, and she took it. She took it until Bellanca healed, the stone went dark, and the magic disappeared.

Jo slumped against him, her chest heaving. She made a sound—a tiny whimper. It was her only concession to pain and fear. Within seconds, she worked on calming and controlling her breathing.

Flynn gathered her more fully in his arms, murmuring

praise. "You did it. You're strong. You're brave." He brushed his lips across her forehead. "You brought down the Minotaur. You and Theseus. Both heroes. We talk about him a world away and centuries later. What do you think they'll say about you?" He smiled, wondering how he managed but doing it all the same. "And she did it all while looking fabulous?"

A short, hard laugh burst from her. It might've been a sob. Voice hoarse, she said, "I'm a parched, sweat-soaked mess."

Flynn's own mouth felt as dry as week-old bread. "And she did it all while severely dehydrated?"

Jo laugh-sobbed again. "Don't make me smile. It's unfair when my hand hurts like this."

Flynn gently took the now-cool stone from her. "I'm so proud of you," he said.

She looked at him and then at her red, puckered hand. Her skin would forever bear the mark of Persephone—new vines, spring flowers. Life renewed. "I'll need a salve," she said as if talking from far away. "This magic was for Cat. Cat would've healed almost instantly."

But Jo would carry this reminder in the palm of her hand for the rest of her days. As she should.

"This is a moment to remember," Flynn said solemnly. "This is the moment you saved *everyone*."

Tears sprang to her eyes. Her voice wobbled. "I love you."

"I love you, too. More than anything." Flynn wrapped his arms around her. He'd look in her bag for a soothing salve in a moment. Right now, he just needed to hold her.

Near them, Bellanca slowly came back to herself. She took a few deep breaths and then gingerly touched her stomach. After a moment, she looked at Jo with grudging admiration. "I thought I was done for." Then she winced in Carver's direction. "Can we just pretend this never happened?"

On his knees, still gripping her hand, Carver glared at her. "Are you kidding me?"

"Fine. Whatever." Bellanca tugged her hand from his and stood, clasping her leather armor back into place. Stone dust covered her. So did blood. "Don't get yourself almost killed next time."

"Me?" The look on Carver's face would've been hilarious if Flynn had been capable of laughing right then.

Jo stood. "We should go before that anesthesia wears off and Asterion wakes up. Prometheus? Can you walk?" she moved toward the Titan, checking on him.

Prometheus struggled to his feet. "Get me out of this maze." Staggering, he looked around for the spear and aegis, somehow picking them up. "Poseidon's trident is telling us *that* way." He limped toward what had to be the exit.

"Bellanca?" Jo asked.

The Magoi nodded. "Good as new." She pressed on her stomach. "I'm not even sore or tired, like with regular healing magic. I'm energized." Carver moved to help Bellanca walk, and she brushed him off. "I said I'm fine."

"Forgive me for wanting to help you after you *saved my life!*" he snapped, holding up his hands in mock surrender. "You were all but dead just minutes ago. You terrified me!"

Bellanca's cheeks flamed bright red. She turned and followed Prometheus. Carver fished his sword out of the fountain and stomped after them, muttering a curse.

"I guess everything's back to normal," Jo said, doctoring her own hand while Flynn picked up their weapons, including the ones still sticking out of Asterion. He replenished their water at the fountain.

"How long will that last?" he asked, glancing at the Minotaur. "Long enough for us to finish on the island and retrace our steps through the maze?"

"Half a day?" she guessed. "I'm not sure. He's not human."

No, he wasn't. Asterion was part Titan descendant from a line of powerful immortal sorceresses and part sacred bull of Poseidon. What a mix. Apparently, not one to whip up again—in any place or lifetime.

"Jocasta Thalyria—healer and hero." Flynn glanced at her. Did she like it?

She smiled, despite what had to be throbbing pain in her now-wrapped hand. Burns always pulsed as though they had a heartbeat of their own. "You give me too much credit. I barely did anything while you all fought like mad."

"But you jumped in when it counted." He took her uninjured hand. "And you did it with intelligence."

She snorted. "So my brain is my biggest muscle?"

"If only we could all claim the same," Flynn said, utterly serious.

When she leaned her head against his shoulder and laughed, Flynn knew that for once in his life, he'd said the right thing.

"To the lotus eaters," Jo said, starting down the trident-indicated path.

"To the lotus eaters," he echoed, following the rest of Team Elpis out of the blood-soaked courtyard. "And Circe's final test."

CHAPTER 31

Jocasta stared, incredulous. "Those are the lotus eaters? They're just people." People in all shapes and sizes and shades of skin color. Mostly men, some with the remnants of faded and tattered soldier's gear still clinging to their bodies. Otherwise, clothing seemed optional in the blissfully shady hollow behind the maze. "How did they end up here?"

"Magoi rulers, especially Fisan ones like Andromeda, have sent out ships to try to find Circe's island." Bellanca swept her hand toward the dozens of people lounging under the trees. "Clearly, some of them made it."

"Unless they knew about the whole ghost-ship problem, they must've just crashed into it." Jocasta frowned. What were the chances?

"That might explain why there were no boats bobbing around out there." Carver shrugged. "Crash against the cliffs. Swim to the beach. See a big door. Go through it. Once you're close enough, Aeaea isn't invisible to the living anymore. You all saw it when you woke up from the sleeping potion, which was the plan all along."

"I guess some ships might've just gotten lucky," Flynn said. "Sailed the right way, and there it was."

"And I'd bet some sailors also went in, never came out, and their boats left without them," Jocasta said. Whatever the case, those ships hadn't made it back to the mainland that they knew of. Maybe Scylla and Charybdis had something to do with that.

"What about Asterion?" Flynn looked skeptical—and rightfully so, in Jocasta's opinion. "*We* barely made it past him, and we're not exactly inexperienced in battle."

"Survival is about numbers a lot of the time," Carver said, sheathing his sword. The lotus eaters didn't seem aggressive. They didn't even seem to *notice* them. "We're only five people, and we stopped to defend each other. A large crew, probably made up mostly of mercenaries who barely know one another, aren't going to put someone else's survival above their own. Asterion can only kill and eat so many at once. Others will be able to run past him."

"True," Flynn conceded with a nod. "And the maze was easy after the fountain. No more dead ends."

Jocasta gazed out over the heaps of people, all heaped up under the lotus trees. Survival to the fast, slippery, and heartless. Lovely. Although this didn't seem like much of a life in the end.

"I'd say they either weren't ready to risk the maze back out again, or they didn't have a ship to go back to," Bellanca remarked, glancing over her shoulder at Prometheus. The Titan had recovered enough to move a big stone onto Ariadne's thread, locking the ball of twine down to pick up again later when they were ready to return to their boat. "And they obviously got hungry enough to eat the lotus fruit."

The hugest belch Jocasta had ever heard reached her ears. She turned toward the source, wrinkling her nose. A sandy-haired man who might once have been handsome plucked a pinkish-orange fruit off one of the trees. It resembled an apricot, only about twice the size. Every person here moved with a sort of dazed-eyed lethargy—presumably from eating their weight in narcotics every day.

"Looks like no one warned them about the indifferent thrall," Prometheus said, joining them at the entrance to the pre-garden. On the far side, a narrow bridge spanned a large moat. Beyond that, Circe's domain rose in tiered gardens toward the marble citadel on the hilltop.

"So should we cross over to the land of the not-wasting-away-in-apathy?" Bellanca asked.

Jocasta chewed her bottom lip. "Can it really be that simple?"

"The scroll just says to not fall into the thrall," Bellanca said. "No fruit. No thrall."

"I suppose..." Jocasta still worried. She couldn't imagine every single one of these people choosing to forget their homes and lives and families—everything that mattered to them—rather than try to get off the island somehow.

Could they take the lotus eaters back with them? They had plenty of food and water on the boat—and could even survive the two-day journey back to the mainland without any supplies at all—but not even a fraction of these people would fit on the *Athena*. It was too small.

If Asterion woke up before they reentered the maze, though, they'd increase their chances of making it past him with more people around.

Guilt twisted inside Jocasta. She'd gone from wondering how to save the lotus eaters to contemplating using them as people fodder for the Minotaur. What kind of a healer was she?

"Onward?" Flynn asked rather than directed.

"It seems like the only choice," Jocasta answered.

They moved toward the bridge. As they advanced across the glen, the lotus eaters took more notice. They started trying to give them fruit.

"No, thank you," Jocasta said, politely at first and then with more force as the eaters insisted. "No. Ugh. No!" She turned her face away and got a lotus fruit in the ear. It split, and juice dribbled down her neck. She grimaced. Better than in her mouth.

The rest of Team Elpis wasn't faring much better. They sped up. Jocasta kept her arms out as a barrier, increasingly nervous as the horde converged, shoving fruit at them. The more they said no, the more aggressive the lotus eaters became. Several tried to force-feed them. Others blocked the bridge. Dozens of mostly naked bodies piled up, barring the path to Circe's garden. They weren't fast, but they were *insistent*. Jocasta slipped around one just to run smack into another. They squashed fruit all over her face and head, trying to get it in her mouth.

"Flynn!" she called, unable to shake a particularly zealous male. It was the one who'd burped earlier. He wasn't apathetic now. He was all over her. "Flynn!"

Flynn yanked the man away, but others just replaced him, crowding in and separating her from Flynn again. There were so many of them—everywhere. Panic started to claw at her chest. She couldn't escape them. Blank-eyed faces. Pressing hands. Lotus fruit. She had no air!

Carver and Bellanca made it to the moat, the Magoi's little bursts of fire driving the mob away from them.

"Come on!" Carver waved frantically from the bridge. Half the glen still separated them.

"At what point do we start fighting back?" Prometheus asked. He picked up a rotund lotus eater and threw him at three others, knocking them all to the ground.

Jocasta ran into the opening he'd created, but more lotus eaters swarmed in to block her path. The throng swayed and moaned, flashing rotten teeth and milky eyes. They didn't speak. They groaned and shoved and piled on top of each other, trying to force-feed them fruit and keep them off the bridge.

Bellanca shot off little fireballs to scare the lotus eaters away. The throng stopped caring about her magic, choosing burns over unblocking the only path away from them. They started throwing fruit. Eating. Throwing. Spitting it out. The ground grew slick and wet. Jocasta slipped and almost went down under a tangle of limbs. The lotus eaters converged. Those on the outside passed fruit to the ones on the inside, creating an endless supply. Jocasta kept her mouth shut tight, but she had lotus juice all over her. Could they be contaminated through contact? She wiped wildly at her face, trying to get the juice off with her sleeves.

"Pro!" Flynn's frantic voice reached her. He was far. Too far to help her. Lotus eaters dragged at her, holding on, holding her back. Jocasta stumbled and fell. Bodies piled on top of her, shoving squashed fruit in her face with manic hands.

Suddenly, Prometheus was there. He picked her up and plowed straight through the horde, batting lotus eaters away with his Titan-sized fists. Flynn fought his way over to them and did the same, shielding Jocasta as she clung to Prometheus's chest, half-blind with mashed fruit and spitting lotus juice from her lips.

"Wasn't planning on hurting them, but I've had enough," Prometheus grumbled.

Jocasta scrubbed her sleeve across her mouth. She shook. Being attacked by a mob was about as horrible as she could've imagined. How many of the lotus eaters had eaten willingly, and how many had been forced? The enchantment might not be their fault, but they spread it like a disease to anyone they caught.

They only made it to the bridge thanks to Prometheus being an immovable rock, even with dozens of barely sentient people trying to drag him back. The Titan set Jocasta down on the wide wooden planks. She gripped Flynn's arm, still trembling, her heart beating fast. The five of them backed away from the groaning, reaching horde.

The lotus eaters stopped at the bridge. Either they couldn't cross it or wouldn't for some reason. They swayed at the brink, making guttural sounds, hands searching for them, eyes huge and barely seeing, long-nailed fingers dripping pulp and juice.

Jocasta shuddered from head to foot. "Would you believe that somehow terrified me as much as everything else?"

Flynn wrapped an arm around her, tucking her close as Team Elpis traversed the bridge and headed into Circe's garden. "There's not much scarier than a mindless swarm. They don't fear pain, they won't stop coming, and you never know what they'll do next."

Jocasta swallowed the last of the unsteadiness in her voice. "Thanks for the help, Pro. I needed it."

"Pro." Rolling his eyes, the Titan shook his head. Jocasta didn't miss the hint of a smile, though, as he turned his focus ahead.

Nothing else got in their way as they climbed the manicured pathway up the hill of Circe's garden. Insects droned. Plants Jocasta had never seen before crawled up terraces and tumbled down trellises. Nerves buzzed inside her as loud as the cicadas, her pulse thudding like the waves below. This was it. They'd made it. One test to go.

Would Circe come out to greet them? Would she come out to kill them? To curse them? To make this whole journey worthless in the end?

Jocasta pulled her shoulders back. She didn't like her thoughts, so she did her best to stop them and concentrated on breathing evenly and putting one foot in front of the other until they reached the top, each exhalation a rejection of fear, each footfall a denial of doubt.

A central fountain finally came into view, the white castle behind it. In the middle of the fountain stood a marble statue of an imposing, shrewd-faced goddess. Jocasta stopped and took in the sight, both immensely relieved and wholly intimidated. That statue was exactly what she'd been aiming for since the day she'd called a meeting and set this whole expedition into motion. They'd made it this far. And now, according to their information, the witch of Aeaea was obligated to give them one last trial.

And a reward when they passed it.

Her pulse a tempest in her veins, Jocasta reached over and squeezed Flynn's hand. Team Elpis gazed at the fountain together, at the marble statue of Circe in the center of her garden. The garden was still and eerily quiet at the top of the hill. No movement came from the sparkling white citadel. No breeze stirred the air. The only sound apart from the creak of their leather armor was the splash of water cascading from the wide-open mouths of the stone sea dragons carrying the statue of Circe, her feet riding their scaly backs, her hands holding their reins.

"Here we are." Jocasta's insides flipped over with a mix of triumph and fear. Somehow, she knew she had to touch the statue. That was how to reach Circe. She let go of Flynn's hand and reached forward, brushing her fingers against Circe's marble gown.

She didn't know what would happen, but she didn't expect the statue to come to life. Jocasta leaped back, her heart pounding. Marble turned to flesh and flat eyes to bright, green irises. Stiff, stone hair softened into long flowing curls the color of a Sintan sunset. Circe stepped onto the rounded edge of the fountain and then joined Team Elpis on the ground, standing as tall as Prometheus. The now-living ketea dove into the fountain and disappeared.

Hardly daring to breathe, Jocasta stared at the sorceress, awed and frightened. Circe was striking in the way of deities. Stern. Powerful. Unforgiving.

The ancient goddess whisked cool eyes over them. "I've been watching you." What curved her lips might've been a smile. It might also have been their one and only warning to run from a predator who'd show no mercy. "In millennia, two groups of travelers have reached me in the heart of my garden. Odysseus didn't stay long enough. You've perhaps overstayed your welcome." She glanced at Prometheus, looking him up and down without a flicker of warmth. "How do you fare, cousin?"

"Better than you, I think. My interminable imprisonment in Tartarus finally ended."

Envy flared in her eyes. "Did Zeus free you?"

Prometheus shook his head. "A human queen with a heart of iron freed me from his clutches."

"Perhaps this queen should come here and free me, too," Circe mused. "Or did she send you for that?"

Prometheus once again shook his head. "This queen is caught now in a game of gods. They work to crush an uncrushable spirit."

"For what purpose?" the goddess asked.

"To advance their sly games of power."

"You're here for her, then." Circe's interest appeared to wane, though she asked, "Why come all this way? Why make such a difficult journey?"

"To help her. And to help her help everyone else." Prometheus's love for Cat, his eternal gratitude, shone through in his expression and every word. Cat inspired him, as she did so many others. Jocasta's hair stood on end. She felt it, too. The surge of passion. The need to be a part of something that went so far beyond herself, she saw no beginning and no end. "To keep Elpis alive."

"Hope?" Circe scoffed. "There's little of that here. The beauty of Aeaea is nothing in the face of endless boredom. Loneliness. Exile."

Could she not even consort with Asterion or the lotus eaters? Was she trapped right here, alone in her castle and garden?

"I don't know if we can help you," Prometheus said. "I'd like to. But we came here because you can help us. We have a boon to ask."

"Of course." Circe's lip curled as she surveyed them one by one. "No man or god is ever selfless."

Jocasta had to wonder what stock Circe put in being selfless. She hadn't heard it was in the witch's nature, and yet here she was, almost demanding it of others.

"That might be true. But I think you're obligated," Prometheus pointed out coolly.

Circe turned as stone-faced as when she'd been a statue. She pivoted on Jocasta. "You brought everyone here. You touched my statue. What do you want?"

Jocasta tensed. Fear churned inside her, hollowing her out. Flynn inched closer. Was she terrified? Yes. But she hadn't faced monsters, killed living beings, and come all this way to shrivel like a grape in the sun. She lifted her chin. "Our queen was given the Olympian Elixir of Eternal Life against her will. It put her in active stasis. She's pregnant, which means it also stopped the baby's development. Right now, neither can ever change again—never age, never grow. We need both mother and child to regain their normal, healthy, *mortal* existence and age according to the laws of nature. Day by day. Year by year. Until a natural end."

Circe shrugged, utterly indifferent. "I fail to see how this is my problem."

"It's not your problem," Jocasta said, "it's your *solution*. Your garden is the source of any plant you choose to create. Your magic is Titan. Olympian magic can't counteract the elixir, which Olympians consider an untouchable gift, but *Titan* magic can provide an antidote. You can grow a plant to reverse the effects of the elixir and brew it into a potion to help our queen. With it, we can set her—and her unborn child—back on track, as though the elixir had never crossed her lips."

Circe dipped her fingers into the fountain, swirling them back and forth. "With my great power and talent, this is possible." Her eyes hardened. "But you must earn my help."

The final test. Anxiety knotted Jocasta's stomach, but she nodded. "We're ready," she said.

"Not *we*," Circe shot back. "*You*. This was your idea. I've known it from the start."

Jocasta nodded again, a hard swallow scraping down her throat. Flynn shifted nervously beside her. He didn't protest. "*I'm* ready." She hoped.

Circe gazed at her with eyes so green they reminded Jocasta of Cat's, magic-bright and unyielding. She began to think there was no loss of Elpis here, despite the prison of Aeaea. A glimmer of hope always lived on, tenacious, resolute, *stubborn*. There was a reason why Elpis, the original spark from which all hope sprang, remained even in Pandora's box, the most dismal and terrible place in all the worlds. Circe hadn't given up. This wasn't a female resigned to the fate others had imposed on her. This was a powerful sorceress biding her time—and with eternity to plot revenge.

A cold sweat tickled the small of Jocasta's back. She doubted the gods had seen the last of Circe.

Circe eventually—*pointedly*—gazed down into the now-statue-free fountain as if inviting Jocasta to do the same. Uneasy, Jocasta stepped closer, looking more carefully. "It's a well." Deep.

Shadowed. Did something shimmer at the bottom? Where were the ketea now?

"Where you're going, escape is possible. For *you*, anyway." Bitterness laced Circe's words. "To ensure you don't run away through the well, I'll take some collateral."

Dread knifed through Jocasta. Something horrible was about to happen. She felt it from her bones out, as though Circe's gathering magic spoke to her on the deepest, most visceral level. The attack came, whip-fast and devastating. Flynn, Carver, and Bellanca turned into pigs. With a swipe of the witch's hand, they went from human to animal!

Jocasta's heart exploded in her chest like a shattered dream. She lunged for what used to be Flynn, touching tough, pink flesh before he slipped from her hands and ran. The other two followed him, barrel bodies swaying and hooves marking the grass. She watched in horror as the three of them began rooting around and snuffling. They were pigs. *Pigs!*

Her pulse pounded so hard she shook. Acid stung the back of her mouth. She swallowed. This wasn't entirely unexpected. And she could fix this. Pass the final test. That was the only solution. To *everything*.

Jocasta swung on Circe, cold anger and burning determination filling her to the brim. They hadn't come this far to turn into bacon for the witch's table. "I'll be back for them. Do *not* harm them." Jaw tight, eyes spitting fire, she drew her spine straight and turned to Prometheus. "Guard them well."

The Titan nodded. Jocasta stepped closer to the fountain. She peered into its depths, watching the faint shimmer of magic reach up to her from below.

"In you go." Circe tipped her head toward the fountain. "Jump in and we'll see what you're made of."

CHAPTER 32

Not giving herself time to second-guess, Jocasta vaulted over the edge of the fountain and into the well. The cold shocked her. The current shocked her more. A strong downward pull dragged her toward the bottom. The need for air started to claw at her chest, and panic set in as the surface got farther and farther out of reach. The more she struggled, the faster she sank, the sky fading to a pinprick of light.

Her body begged her to open her mouth and breathe. Jocasta fought the natural reflex. Her chest ached. Her vision darkened. She yelled Circe's name, burning up the last of her air on a furious scream.

Just as her lungs spasmed, she dropped out of the water and onto a hard stone floor, jarring every bone in her body. Gulping down air, she gingerly rolled to her knees, aching, shaking, and miraculously dry. She trembled on the floor, waiting for her pounding heart to settle and her vision to adjust to the dimness at the bottom of the well. Torches burned on the walls next to five arching doorways leading down long, dark corridors. The hallways speared off like the points of a star, the circular room she'd landed in at the center of them all.

Jocasta used the ancient-looking wooden table next to her to haul herself up. She looked around again, breathing more normally now. Water sloshed above her head, a strange and un-dulating ceiling. The corridors faded into darkness. She had no idea how long they were or where they led. Three rough clay cups sat in a line on the table. Each contained a dark liquid. In front of them, four ominous words jumped out at her, scrolled in thick black ink across a parchment. *Drink one entire cup.*

Jocasta swallowed hard. Here was the test. Two cups were obviously poisoned. One was safe. They all looked the same, like the red wine you'd find on any table.

But looks could be deceiving. And how did they smell? This had to be more than just a game of chance. The gods could be counted on for that much, at least.

Without touching the cups, she dipped her nose to the first, then the second, then the third. The only liquid that smelled a little different to her was the first. All she detected in the other two cups—at least at first sniff—was wine.

Still shaky from their encounter with Circe and the terrifying descent through the well, Jocasta didn't feel quite ready to concentrate on something so delicate and crucial to all their futures. She took a moment to explore her surroundings instead. She hadn't noticed the faint markings on the stone walls at first, but upon closer inspection, she saw that each corridor was labeled with a word. She moved toward the one closest to her.

"Atlantis." As Jocasta stopped directly in front of the tunnel, the view down the long corridor changed. She gasped, going perfectly still. It wasn't dark anymore. A large island zoomed toward her, growing until she felt as though she could step right onto the bright, wide beach with turquoise waves lapping at the sand. A huge castle dominated the coastal city beyond the shore, a serpentine of colorful houses climbing up to it. "Beautiful." And not unlike Thalyria, especially around Thassos.

She shuffled to the next tunnel, reading *Attica* on the wall. She sucked in a breath. Was this a passageway? To Piers? Could he come back this way? Back to Thalyria? Back to them?

Her heart racing, she peered down the hallway only to scramble back at a sudden wailing noise. Something red and blue flashed by, screaming a high-pitched *woo-woo* that pierced her eardrums. She cringed, the brightly lit nighttime scene so unfamiliar she had no words for what she saw. Great metal objects sped by faster than horses. Buildings rose so high they scraped the stars. It was crowded, sounds and people everywhere. Jocasta didn't see a single weapon, but everyone wore unfriendly expressions, and they ignored each other, passing by without a word.

Tears stung her eyes. What a horrible world. She shuddered to know her brother was there.

Jocasta practically leaped to the next tunnel. "Tartarus." Shadowy. Gray. Dismal, as though this might be the one place where Elpis couldn't exist. Shivering, she hurried away without a backward glance.

"Thalyria." At the next corridor, her pulse sped up. That was Oceaneida on the other side. She recognized the port city from their sailing lessons. Had Athena been showing them Oceaneida on purpose? So Jocasta would recognize it and know it wasn't far from Thassos? If they all jumped into the well, this passageway could take them back to the known continent without them having to face the lotus eaters, Asterion, the ketea, or Charybdis. Circe had said escape was possible, just not for her—the prisoner of the island.

Jocasta's jaw slid open. How utterly Olympian as a punishment. Zeus added that extra touch of cruelty by putting access to *everywhere* right at Circe's feet but preventing her from going anywhere.

She stared down the tunnel to Thalyria. They weren't bound by the same curse. Her pulse accelerated. This was a huge opportunity. Abandoning the *Athena* would be worth it.

Losing Ariadne's thread would be worth it. They'd bypass all the dangers they faced on the way back.

Shaking now with something other than fear, Jocasta took a few steps and looked down the last tunnel. The name next to it didn't surprise her. *Underworld.* She gazed into its depths. It was dark, murky. Not what she'd imagined. She bit her lip. Wasn't the afterlife supposed to mirror this life? Not something to race toward, but not something to dread, either?

The hope she'd felt just moments ago soured. Tears stung her eyes, her heart heavy, this time for Kato. She'd imagined better for him. Better for all their future lives.

A fiery light in the distance caught her eye. A moving torch. Perhaps it was only nighttime there.

Jocasta leaned in for a closer look. Then, as though thinking of the man they'd lost conjured him, Kato dashed across the tunnel at a sprint.

Her heart exploded in her chest. "Kato!" she screamed.

The light whipped around and came back. The brother from her childhood, the man from just months ago, moved cautiously toward her, each step bringing him closer to the mouth of the tunnel as she shook, her breath shuddering, her mind reeling, and her eyes stinging with a teary mix of grief and love.

"Jocasta?" His blue eyes widened. He looked her up and down as if checking for injuries. "Are you all right? What are you doing here?" His expression turned abruptly stark, and he reached for her, only to draw his hand back before it crossed the mouth of the tunnel. "Are you dead?"

"No." She shook her head. Sniffling, she inhaled deeply through her nose, trying to calm the rising tide of tears threatening to break all dams. "I'm in some kind of hub. A star-shaped hub on a hidden island. I can see all the gods' worlds. Everything they've linked together. I'm here trying to help Cat."

"Is she okay?" Kato frowned, stepping forward again only to stop as if blocked by an invisible barrier. "The baby?"

Jocasta couldn't let him worry. She lied. It just sprang out. "She will be. I know what to do."

He nodded, believing her. He also seemed in a hurry, glancing over his shoulder at another torch that moved their way. "You always were the smartest of us all."

"I miss you," she blurted out.

His eyes softened. "It's different here. You remember everything, *everyone*, but you also just...live." He looked behind him again, rubbing his neck where the tattoo of Titos—one of Poseidon's creatures—watched her with black eyes and a forked tongue that unfurled with every breath. Titos had protected Kato in life. She hoped he protected him in death.

Jocasta nodded, breathing unsteadily and not sure she fully understood. Were memories muted in the Underworld, to make the wait for your loved ones bearable until they joined you, one by one, as Atropos cut their threads?

She held back her tears—glad to know that grief might only be a plague of the living—but the urge to hug this man who was as much a brother to her as her own blood kin overwhelmed her, and she stepped forward, her arms outstretched.

She got halfway through a prickling barrier of magic and almost touched Kato when the second torch flashed beside her, carried by an athletic blonde woman who shot from the gloom and shoved her back. Jocasta staggered, nearly falling on her backside in the room beneath the well. Regaining her balance, she peered at the newcomer, who stood beside Kato now.

"Don't," the stranger said. "It's a one-way trip. You can come through. But you can't go back."

Jocasta nodded. She swallowed, but the sob she'd been holding in burst out. She put a trembling hand to her mouth.

She backed up, backed away from Kato. "We miss you. So much." For a while, it had seemed like life just couldn't go on without him. But then it did. It always did. And good things and bad things happened all the time, just as they always had.

"We'll find each other again," Kato said gently, backing away as he did. The blonde matched him step for step, keeping a wary eye on something behind them in the shadows of the Underworld. "That's how it works."

Jocasta's mouth quivered. She nodded again, incapable of speech. The snake tattoo on Kato's neck suddenly slithered to the other side, perking up in the direction of a noise that rang out like heavy footsteps. The sound drew Kato's attention. The blonde woman cocked an ear down the corridor as she pulled a knife from her belt. Fire sprang to life in her free hand, swooping around her wrist on golden wings.

"We have to go," the stranger quietly insisted. "Perses won't let up until he takes the crown of death from Hades himself."

Kato acknowledged her with a swift jerk of his chin, and she sped off down the corridor again. Turning back to Jocasta, he said, "All's not well in the Underworld. Perses made a deal with Zeus to get out of Tartarus and ended up in the Underworld not long after I did. He's restless and hungry for power, and Hades is distracted by something else."

"War is brewing on Mount Olympus," Jocasta said. "It must be that."

"Do you know who's behind it?" His impossibly blue gaze sharpened on her. "Someone's backing Perses here. He's been too lucky by half."

Jocasta shook her head. "We're trying to figure it out."

"Kato!" the woman with fire magic called. "He's headed for the temple!"

"I have to go." His feet scuffed backward, more than three

decades of memories in his eyes and growing brighter by the second. Maybe this was why the dead couldn't mix with the living. Jocasta saw cracks forming and emotions seeping out of them that hadn't been there when he'd first seen her from the Underworld. "Tell them all..." His voice turned rough. "Tell them..."

"I will," she said with a wobbly smile. "Go clobber Perses for us. He's an ass."

Kato flashed a brilliant grin. It didn't hide the tears now glittering in his eyes. Regardless, he turned and sprinted after the blonde. There was no coming back to them. This was his life now. This, and maybe that woman. Jocasta watched him disappear. Kato was the first of them to cross the Styx, but he wasn't alone. He had someone to watch his back. Someone to count on, and someone who counted on him. That lightened her heart.

It took Jocasta a long time to stop fighting tears and peering down the tunnel in the hopes of seeing Kato again. Her view into the Underworld remained empty and dim. Kato didn't come back, and she finally forced herself to focus on the living again—on her task. She was the lucky one. She'd seen Kato. The others would only hear the story.

She dragged in a long, calming breath and pulled her shoulders back. She turned to the three cups again, staring at them. Circe was a potion master, skilled herbalist, and witch. She'd been brewing concoctions for thousands of years. Everything about these mixtures would be subtle and designed to trick.

"Be systematic," Jocasta murmured, approaching the table. "Use your skills." Her mother had repeated those very words to her on countless occasions. Right now, Nerissa wasn't here to remind her, so Jocasta reminded herself.

One by one, she sniffed the liquids again. She swirled them in the cups, seeing if the odor shifted, or the color, or if any residue stuck to the clay sides to hint at ingredients. The contents of two of the cups would undoubtably kill her and leave Flynn, Carver, and Bellanca as pigs forever and Prometheus trapped on Aeaea with his bitter cousin. She pursed her lips.

Pulling off her tunic, Jocasta unwound the white linen cloth that bound her breasts and sliced off three narrow strips before tying it back in place and throwing her dark-blue tunic over her head again. Since she'd come out of the well dry, only her own sweat might contaminate her experiment, but it was a risk she'd have to take. She took a spoon from her medicine bag—the one with markings she used to administer precise doses according to weight.

Using the spoon to avoid touching anything or pouring out too much, Jocasta gathered a sample from the first cup and dribbled it onto one of the white strips. The stain remained wine-red and soaked straight in without any graininess or residue. She put her nose as close as she dared. Wine was definitely the main ingredient, but a sweet smell clung to the more acidic odor of fermented grape juice, one she began to recognize as she repeatedly breathed it in and sorted through her knowledge. Nepenthe. When mixed with wine, it quieted all sorrows to the point of them being entirely forgotten.

She straightened away from the drug, sensing how strong it was in the cup now that she'd pulled the cloying scent out of the more prominent perfume of red wine. So not deadly, but as good as lethal. If she drank that whole cup, she'd forget her problems and die down here, leaving Team Elpis to their fate, Cat immortal, and Griffin crushed.

Wiping the spoon on a dry corner of the linen, Jocasta took a sample from the second cup. She repeated her process, watching how the stain spread and studying its color and odor as it dried.

Nothing popped out at her, which was worrisome. Surely, Circe wouldn't simply put a cup of wine down here?

How many poisons were colorless, odorless, and tasteless? Not that she'd tried tasting anything yet. And not all toxins came from plants. Minerals crushed into fine powders could be just as deadly. And then there was venom.

Her eyes narrowed in thought. Venom could harm or kill because a bite dumped a toxin directly under the skin and into the bloodstream. Poisons worked by ingestion or inhalation, being absorbed into the body that way. Conceivably, sending a venom through her digestive system could destroy it, whereas the same venom might kill her if it went directly into her veins.

Not sure what to think of the contents of the second cup, Jocasta moved on to the third and took a sample. Like the second, it simply looked and smelled like wine. Sniffing and observing as it dried told her nothing.

Frustrated and starting to feel the press of time, she opened her medicine bag and sorted through the contents, hoping for inspiration. The silence grated on her, the only sounds her own breathing and the clink of her supplies, so she talked to herself as she set items on the table.

"Lance. Catheter. Ampoule." Nothing she needed. "Antifungal. Antiparasitic. Antiseptic." The last was her personal concoction, and she'd seen infection rates fall by half since she'd perfected the mixture. "Antidiarrheal. Expectorants." Neither helpful. "Antivomitives. An emetic." She pulled up short. She had a container in her hand that would make her vomit up all the contents of her stomach. What if she drank a cup, any cup, and then threw it all up again?

She hesitated at the idea. Circe would know. Jocasta needed to get Cat's antidote before she did something the goddess might consider cheating.

Still, she slipped the vomitive into her pocket. If she didn't choose the right cup, she'd need it.

A few parchments crinkled at the bottom of her satchel. A study in herbs with illustrations. A note from her mother from the day Jocasta left for the Agon Games—not that anyone had expected her to end up in the arena. A treatise on venomics.

"Ah." She pulled out the scroll. At the new healing center outside Ios, near where her family had first taken up ruling residence in Castle Sinta, a group of Hoi Polloi and Magoi healers had begun collaborating on a project to study the potential beneficial properties of snake venom. They'd discovered that about half of snake venoms could help reduce bleeding. Those venoms encouraged blood coagulation and could help turn potentially fatal wounds into more manageable ones. Of course, other venoms thinned the blood. It was a work in progress.

An idea sparked. Jocasta took a clean lance from her supply of cutting instruments and made a small incision on her inner left arm. She did the same to her right arm. As thin lines of blood dribbled down her skin toward her elbows, she spooned out a tiny sample from cup two and poured it over the left-arm incision. She had no desire to mix either venom or poison with her bloodstream, even in this minor way, but she needed to take a risk to test a theory. She spooned a minute portion of the liquid from the third cup onto the cut on her right arm. Then she waited.

Soon, it became clear that the bleeding on her left arm was slowing more quickly. She took that as a sign that the middle cup *might* contain snake venom. It was a guessing game, but weren't guesses all she had at this point?

She washed off her arms with her antiseptic solution. She'd found out what she wanted to know—or at least, she thought so.

After putting everything she'd taken out back into her satchel and slipping the strap over her head and across her body, Jocasta stood there and stared down at cup three—her nemesis. Either it was perfectly harmless—just wine—or it was the most dangerous cup of all. It could easily contain arsenikon, the most subtle of all poisons. Symptoms from a small dose could resemble food poisoning. A large dose could drop a person dead in a few hours, although it might take longer. Horrible stomach cramping, diarrhea, and vomiting usually started quickly, and by then it was probably too late for any treatment. The poison would already have caused lasting if not irreparable damage, and the person would die in agony.

She grimaced. Three cups. Drink one. *Entirely.*

Unfortunately, Jocasta wasn't convinced there was a single cup that was harmless. This was *Circe.* Prometheus had described his cousin as bitter, predatory, and always having a trick up her sleeve. And Jocasta had no doubt the witch was trying to trick her.

"Nepenthe. Unknown venom—maybe. Possibly arsenikon." She swallowed. "Or nothing."

No. She shook her head. She wasn't naïve enough to believe the third cup was just a cup of wine. That would be too easy.

But what if that was the trick? What if Circe was trying to make her doubt the obvious and choose another cup, when cup three was exactly what she needed?

Jocasta growled in frustration, wishing Flynn were here to talk her through the possibilities.

"I could use some help here," she said loudly. "Anyone want to give me a sign? Rattle the right cup?" She looked down each tunnel. "Hello? Olympus?" There was only silence.

The gods could do boats and directions and heal horses and send down thunderbolts, but *no one* could be bothered to show up now with a little advice and encouragement?

"Damn it." She obviously couldn't count on the gods, so she'd count on herself. She'd trust her instincts.

Jocasta reached for the middle cup. If she was right and it contained venom, it might make her sick, but she doubted it would kill her, especially if she emptied her stomach as soon as possible.

She brought the cup to her lips and tossed back the contents. She was used to sipping wine, not gulping it, and downing it like water turned her stomach. Fear heightened her disgust. She was in no way certain she hadn't just killed herself.

Jocasta forced the last drop down and hurled the empty cup against the wall next to the tunnel to Tartarus. "Circe!" she screamed toward the watery ceiling. "I'm ready!"

CHAPTER 33

A great force sucked Jocasta back up through the deep, churning waters of the well. She landed next to the fountain, perfectly dry again. She staggered, sucking down air after holding her breath almost to the point of breaking. Two more seconds, and she'd have been coughing up water now. Prometheus reached out a hand to steady her, and Jocasta glanced up at him, grateful to see a friend. Tears sprang to her eyes. Seeing him brought home how very alone she'd been.

She blinked back her tears, straightening. Her pulse galloped like a herd of centaurs. She shook from head to toe again. Three pigs still milled around the large grassy area surrounding the magical well in the center of Circe's garden. Her chest hurt at the sight of them. Flynn-pig didn't even look at her. He snuffled the ground, bumping into Carver.

Circe stood by the fountain, exactly where she'd been earlier. Her eyes shimmered with temper. "Interesting choice."

Jocasta lifted her chin. "Was it the right one? Did I pass your test?"

"Your logic was sound." The goddess didn't elaborate, but Jocasta took that to mean that cup three had, indeed, been deadly.

A shudder went through her. "Care to tell me what I drank?"

"No."

Of course not. So much more fun to keep Jocasta scared

and guessing. She curled her hands into fists, trying to contain the nervous energy that made her want to strike out at Circe. "I drank an entire cup, and I didn't run away through one of the tunnels. Can you please turn my companions back into themselves now?" Jocasta might've added a *please*, but there was nothing courteous about her tone. She wanted Team Elpis human again. *Now*.

Stone-faced, Circe reversed her spell with a flick of her hand. Flynn, Carver, and Bellanca slowly straightened onto two legs, gradually returning to normal again, the snouts and tails the last things to go. They looked confused at first. As realization dawned, horror replaced their confusion—and definitely some embarrassment.

Flynn got over it first. He rushed to her side and took her in his arms. "Are you all right?"

"I think so." She squeezed him back. "Are you?"

"Fine," he answered. "Although you might check for a tail later."

His joke rattled a laugh from her. Stepping out of the warmth of Flynn's arms, Jocasta turned to Circe. "I drank the middle cup. I'm alive and lucid, so I must've passed your test. Will you reward us with what we came for? Will you make the antidote for the Elixir of Eternal Life?"

"I don't have a choice." As the witch spoke, a bitter pill seeming to break between her teeth, a plant grew in the palm of her hand, blue petals unfurling. Each delicate petal shimmered with golden veins that reminded Jocasta of the ichor in the blood of gods, that rare fluid that made them so powerful and immortal. "My brethren set up my prison with *rules*. Males seek to control powerful females. The reward for strength and cleverness is banishment and exile."

Her hard green eyes on Jocasta, Circe closed her hand and

crushed the flower she'd brought to life. When she opened her hand again, an ampoule of dark-blue liquid with golden rivulets had replaced the bloom. "At least I got to choose your final test. And I find that you, too, are a powerful female." Jocasta stared at the goddess in shock. "With this, your queen will move forward again with her mortal life, since that is her wish." She handed the potion to Jocasta.

Very carefully, Jocasta slipped the potion into the padded pocket of her satchel. She had Cat's cure, Eleni's future. They'd done it. Her spine tingled. Her fingers shook. Either excitement, relief, and adrenaline were whipping up a nauseating storm inside her, or the middle cup was starting to make her sick.

She made sure her bag was firmly closed and the antidote secure. Her eyes met Carver's, then Bellanca's. They seemed to have recovered from their time as pigs—hopefully enough to hold their breaths for a good long while.

"Will you allow us to take the tunnels?" Jocasta asked, glancing into the well.

Circe nodded. "I think you've earned that, too. Think of it as a gift. And perhaps, one day, you'll discover a way to cure me of *my* curse."

Jocasta *would* think about it, although she wasn't sure that Circe on the loose in Thalyria would be any better than Perses running amok in the Underworld.

"Oceaneida is only steps away at the bottom of the well," she explained to Team Elpis. "Just hold your breath and let yourself be dragged down to the room under the water. It's scary, but don't fight it. There are magical passageways. We can be back on the mainland in minutes."

Flynn peered into the well's cavernous depths, preparing to jump in with her. "It's a long way," Jocasta murmured.

"Deep breath, then." He looked more than ready. She nodded.

Before jumping, Jocasta looked one last time at Circe, nodding her thanks to the witch of Aeaea. She might be one of the most powerful and scheming beings alive, but she'd done exactly as promised.

Or exactly as dictated by the rules laid out for her by her jailers—rules Jocasta had found and exploited.

She leaped into the well, leading the way for the others, zero remorse in her heart. She didn't know to what extent Circe deserved this interminable prison sentence, but they'd *earned* their reward. They'd fought hard for it. Now, it was time to go home. They'd make things right in Thalyria, and Olympus could burn on its own.

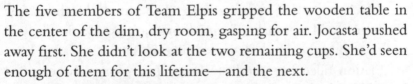

The five members of Team Elpis gripped the wooden table in the center of the dim, dry room, gasping for air. Jocasta pushed away first. She didn't look at the two remaining cups. She'd seen enough of them for this lifetime—and the next.

"I hated that." Carver straightened away from the table and shook himself out.

Still coughing, Bellanca reached out and touched his hair. "You're not even wet."

Carver tensed from head to toe. "Neither are you."

She shrugged.

Prometheus picked up the spear and the aegis. He'd sunk fastest, probably due to their enormous weight.

Flynn studied the table, the scroll, the shattered remnants of pottery on the floor. Then he looked at her. His eyes softened, the sympathy in them wrapping around her like a warm blanket on a cold day. Until then, Jocasta hadn't realized just how chilled she'd been. In fact, she *had* chills.

She placed a hand over her churning stomach, wanting to vomit up the contents right then. Something still told her to wait until they'd left Aeaea and truly finished this test.

Rubbing her goose-bumped arms, she moved toward the passageway to Thalyria. Flynn followed.

"You're right. It's Oceaneida." He gazed down the tunnel. "We'll lose Ariadne's thread and the *Athena*, but we can be in Thassos in a day and on our way to Castle Thalyria the day after that."

"Worth it," Prometheus rumbled.

Bellanca peered over their shoulders. "I agree to agree to this plan with zero argument."

"That's a first," Carver muttered.

"I agree with *good* plans." She grinned. "When you have one, I'll concur."

Carver snorted.

"Are we ready?" Jocasta asked. "This should be the easiest trip home we'll ever make." *Home* didn't look like Castle Thalyria to her anymore, though. It looked like Flynn.

Elation filled her—and dizziness. The sooner she emptied her stomach, the better. She gripped Flynn's hand.

"Wait!" a strong female voice commanded from the next doorway over. Persephone herself stepped out of the shadows of the Underworld and into the circular room with them.

Jocasta blinked, wondering if hallucinations might be setting in, but she clearly wasn't the only one staring in shock at the goddess who hadn't shown up again since telling Cat she'd been cursed with the elixir.

Jocasta's heart started to pound, pumping queasiness through her. Why was Persephone here? Was something wrong with Cat? *More* wrong? Was there a problem at home?

The room grew brighter as Persephone entered it, illuminating the cold, dark stones at the bottom of the well with her intense presence. Palpable power pulsed from her. Her magic was the only crown the Queen of the Underworld wore—and the only one she needed.

Jocasta asked the only question tearing up her throat. "Where have you been? Cat needed you."

Persephone focused on her, and a cold sweat broke out on Jocasta's skin. It wasn't entirely nerves. There'd definitely been something in that cup that wasn't good for her.

"Cat was safe for now. In fact, safer than many." The goddess's nostrils flared, aggravation and maybe even worry darkening her expression. "Pressing matters are cropping up all over the place." Her blue eyes darted to the entrance of the tunnel almost directly across from Thalyria and then darted back to them, landing on Bellanca. "Fire mage, you need to take the road to Atlantis."

"Me? I…" Bellanca stared at the goddess. "Why?"

"Zeus punished Atlantis by taking away its magic. The rulers there grew arrogant and believed they could rival Olympus, even though they were human. Powerful Magoi, but human." She stepped forward and slipped a chain around Bellanca's neck. A circular bronze medallion the size of a fist dangled from it. It sat right on Bellanca's chest. "Their pride was their downfall. No one defies Zeus without consequence."

As Bellanca looked down at the medallion, Jocasta had to wonder if Persephone was talking about now, too, and whoever was gearing up for a Power Bid on Mount Olympus.

"We need powerful people ready to defend our interests." Persephone backed toward the hallway to the Underworld. "We need Magoi across the worlds."

"Am I supposed to lead a Magoi army? In Atlantis?" For once, Bellanca looked at a complete loss. She clutched the medallion. "How, if they don't have magic anymore?"

"Give them back their magic." Persephone looked point-edly at the medallion. There seemed to be an empty spot in the middle, as though an oblong jewel belonged there but had fallen out. Engravings decorated the edges of the big bronze disk. A thunderbolt. A trident. A helmet? "Find the key. Rekindle magic in Atlantis before the enemy can do it first."

"What enemy? Rekindle how?" Bellanca asked. "I don't understand."

"There's no one alive with more powerful fire magic than yours." Bright and starkly powerful against the nighttime back-ground of her tunnel, Persephone said, "Use it to fan the flames."

Eyes huge, Bellanca shook her head. Persephone doled out information like puzzle pieces, and Jocasta was just as confused as the Magoi.

"The passageways only work for you in one direction. There is no hub in Atlantis." Without another word, the goddess turned and walked back into her world—or the world she spent part of her time in.

Jocasta stared after her. Only three beings could move freely between the land of the living and the land of the dead. Hades. Persephone. And Hermes, the messenger of the gods.

No, four beings. There was also Cerberus.

Persephone faded from sight just as Kato had.

"Did she just tell me to go to Atlantis but say I can't come back?" Bellanca's voice had never seemed quieter or more uncertain.

Jocasta couldn't believe it, either. Bellanca—gone forever? This couldn't be.

She glanced at Carver. Her brother stood stock-still, his hands fisted at his sides. His eyes never left the redhead.

Pale and visibly shaking, Bellanca backed away from the hallway to Thalyria, bumping into Prometheus. She stopped, still gripping the medallion, the Titan at her back, two worlds before her.

"I guess…" Her eyes flicked to the passageway to Atlantis. "I guess Persephone thinks I agreed to that."

"Have you?" Carver asked in a tight voice.

Bellanca didn't answer at first. She swallowed hard. "What choice do I have? *Persephone* just told me to go lead a world."

"To war," Carver snapped.

Her chin notched up. "To defend our pantheon. To defend the gods that have helped us."

"When it was convenient for them," Carver reminded her sharply.

"Get over it, Carver." Eyes suddenly flashing, Bellanca stepped toward him. "That's just the way they are. And life's just the way it is."

"You don't have to answer a call if you don't want to." His gaze drilled into hers. "You. Don't. Have. To."

She shook her head, seeming steadier and more certain of her choice. "I do. All of this… It's connected. The elixir. The Great Roars. Trying to stir up unrest—first in Thalyria, next in Atlantis. Looming Olympianomachy." She stepped in front of the hallway to Atlantis, and the white, sandy beach zoomed in to greet her. Her eyes widened. "Persephone said to bring magic back to Atlantis. She said to light a fire before the enemy does. I can do that."

Carver flinched. Stiffly, Bellanca turned to the rest of them. "Tell Lystra…" Her face twisted. She fought back tears. "Tell my sister…"

"Lystra will have people to care for her. And to care *about* her," Flynn said. "It's already true, but every single one of us will make sure of it."

Bellanca's composure nearly cracked. She dragged in a

shuddering breath and wiped a hand over her eyes. Voice trembling, she said, "She'll be alone."

Jocasta's heart ached for Bellanca. And it ached to lose a friend to another world, just as she'd lost a brother. "Flynn and I will take her with us if she wants. She can live without the shadow of the past hanging over her. She can start fresh." They'd already told Team Elpis about their plan to return to their village in the province of Sinta. They could provide a home for Bellanca's sister if Lystra chose to leave Castle Thalyria behind.

Bellanca nodded. She sniffled and wiped her eyes again. "Well then. I guess this is goodbye." She backed toward the gateway that would take her to Atlantis, to a new life. She wasn't the hugging type and didn't try. "Bye, Pro." She swallowed hard. "Carver." Her voice cracked on his name.

"You didn't think you'd be going alone, did you?" Carver asked. Their eyes met. His pinned her, halting her midstep.

Jocasta's heart splintered in grief. Not another brother. *No!*

A sharp laugh shattered from Bellanca. Incredulous, she shook her head. "Your family. You can't."

"My family loves me no matter what. They've proven that several times." He joined Bellanca near the entrance to Atlantis.

Devastation ripped through her, but Jocasta forced herself to hold still and not try to pull him back. Carver had every right to choose his own path, just as she'd chosen hers.

"You'll never see them again," Bellanca warned. "*Ever.*"

Carver nodded. "I know."

"Don't you get it? You can't!" Bellanca practically shouted.

"I can," Carver replied calmly. "I am."

"Carver..." Jocasta's voice quaked, and she cleared her throat. Her chest burned like all the fires of broken hearts left strewn across the worlds. "You're the best brother I could ever have had. I love you."

Carver suddenly leaped for her. Clasping her tightly, he whispered, "Say my goodbyes. You'll find the right words."

Jocasta nodded, holding back the sob of a lifetime. She'd let it out when he was gone.

Carver hugged Flynn, too. He shook Prometheus's hand, clapping the Titan on the shoulder. "My brothers," he said in a voice that nearly broke.

Flynn's eyes glistened. Jocasta reached for him, and side by side, they held each other's hands.

"Carver, you can't—" Bellanca began anew.

"Stop arguing!" Carver growled. "*For once*, just let me have the last word."

Her chin wobbled. "You'll regret it."

"Then that's my problem, not yours." Carver lifted a hand, tersely indicating the gateway to Atlantis. "After you, firebringer."

Bellanca's mouth flattened. "Fine." She looked at each of them one last time and then whirled and stomped through the archway. Within seconds, she turned into a distant figure in another land. She walked up the beach without looking back, her red hair glinting in the sun. Maybe she didn't want to know if Carver actually followed. Jocasta knew he would.

Carver looked right at her, smiled that teasing smile he'd perfected years ago, winked, and backed through the archway.

Jocasta gasped. It was over. Done. Carver grew small so fast. Just a splash of darkness, he turned and followed Bellanca up the sand.

Jocasta's heart shattered. She whimpered, cold and shaking, her legs weak, and sorrow doubling her over.

"Let it out," Flynn said softly, pulling her into his arms.

Jocasta turned into his chest with an anguished howl. She cried. She cried in great, heaving sobs until Flynn picked her up and held her close as he carried her home to the continent.

CHAPTER 34

Flynn sat in a chair in Cat and Griffin's big bedchamber in Castle Thalyria, not quite sure what to do with the baby in his arms. Not drop her. Maybe bounce her? Pat her hair?

He tried the bouncing idea, and little Eleni let out a sudden burp. Nearly transparent milk dribbled from one corner of her mouth onto his arm. Her face wrinkled into a grimace.

Flynn stopped bouncing her, holding perfectly still. That was probably better, at least until she digested. Although who knew when that would be. The voracious little monster seemed to nurse around the clock. She'd quickly and with surprising authority established a routine that had an entire family revolving around her. Cat cuddled and fed her, Griffin walked her all over the castle, talking her to sleep and showing her off to whoever he crossed paths with, and then adoring aunts and grandparents took their turns holding the tiny sleeping princess until she woke up again and wailed for food. He wasn't sure when anyone slept, especially Cat and Griffin.

Flynn had been by Jo's side the entire time as she welcomed her niece into her heart and doted on the adorable princess, but this was Flynn's first time holding the baby. Thank the gods, he was sitting. His knees felt weak. His heart pounded. He loved this little girl, and he didn't even know her. But that was how family worked, he supposed.

He stared down at the half-naked little bundle in the crook

of his arm while Jo fluffed Cat's pillows and listed different herbs that could help ease Cat's discomfort after childbirth without negatively affecting her milk. Standing behind him, Griffin leaned over Flynn's shoulder, gazing down at his sleeping daughter as though he'd never seen anything so wonderful or so terrifying in his life.

Flynn could only concur. Princess Eleni was a beautiful little person, with tufty black hair, bright-green eyes, rosy-tan skin, and lungs that could howl as loudly as Cerberus—Cerberus, who watched from the corner of the room, four eyes open, one head sleeping. The big, ugly, deadly hound hadn't left the baby's side. Where she went, he went. Cat and Griffin had gotten used to the canine guardian in their bedroom. Eleni was also the smallest, most delicate thing Flynn had ever held in his arms. What if he dropped her? Squashed her? Made her cry? No wonder Griffin looked terrified half the time.

Flynn shifted uneasily. A baby was so helpless. Dependent. Fragile. So many things could go wrong. His chest constricted with familiar anxiety, but he breathed deeply, evenly—something he'd learned from Jo—and pushed those thoughts aside, keeping in mind who Eleni's parents were. There was a good chance the little princess wasn't as breakable as she looked. They already knew she was immune to Cerberus's poison slobber. Gods, the heart attacks they'd all had when the hound first licked her. Flynn could barely think about it without breaking out in a cold sweat.

He untensed muscle by muscle. If there was one thing he was sure of, it was that this baby was in good hands—and paws.

Jo left Cat's bedside and gazed down at Flynn with Eleni in his arms. She smiled softly, and his heart melted from the inside out. He loved Jo more than anything. He was a lucky man.

Flynn handed her the baby, settling them both on his lap.

"This could be us one day," she murmured. "Would you like that?"

"The sooner the better," he said, meaning every word. He kissed her temple. He'd always wanted a family—with Jo—but paralyzing fear of loss had held him back. No longer. He'd take each day as it came, recognizing it for the gift it was.

They'd arrived in Oceaneida what felt like only a blink and a breath ago. Jo had pulled herself together in the shadow of the sandstone walls of the southern port city and downed a mixture that made her vomit. The moment they were free of Aeaea and Circe's magic, she'd made sure that whatever was in that cup she drank came back out again as fast as possible. He'd held her while she shook and cried, heaving for long minutes. *He'd* shaken and cried, terrified of poison. But Jo was Jo, indomitable, and when she'd looked him in the eyes and said it would take more than the witch of Aeaea to kill her, he'd believed her.

They'd collected the horses in Thassos and been on their way home at a breakneck pace the day after they set foot on the continent. Flynn doubted anyone had ever made it halfway across Thalyria faster than they did. He still ached from the journey.

As expected, their homecoming was bittersweet and tumultuous, with only three returning when five had set out on the expedition. Cat took the antidote, hope, shock, and heartache all ringing through the castle. Baby Eleni didn't take long to make her appearance. They hardly even had time to discuss what they'd learned from Kato and Persephone.

Jo's description of her encounter with Kato left everyone as stunned and bewildered as they were heartsick and worried over Carver and Bellanca. Two would never come back from Atlantis. One was in the Underworld.

Kato's missing body had always somehow given Flynn hope

that his friend wasn't truly gone, that maybe Kato could come home. He let that hope go, along with some of his grief. Kato was living his life again. For now, it just wasn't with them.

Flynn glanced at Griffin, who could barely take his eyes off his wife or his child. Griffin no longer had a brother in Thalyria, but maybe Flynn could be enough of a brother to him to help him through the pain. Losing Carver didn't feel like losing Piers to exile. Piers had been dragged away after a betrayal based on things he didn't fully understand. Carver had made his own choice, and he wasn't alone. That eased Flynn's mind, and he hoped it eased Griffin's.

As for Bellanca, everyone was just now realizing how much the Magoi ex-princess meant to them. Like the fire she wielded, Bellanca was a spark that lit every room she entered and a hot-burning forge that welded everyone together. They'd sorely miss her, as would Lystra. Bellanca's little sister had cautiously agreed to move away with Jo and him, but for now, she still hid in her room. Flynn hoped a fresh start would free her.

Jo shifted in his arms, cooing softly to baby Eleni, and Flynn's heart swelled with so much love that a sweetly painful ache filled his chest to bursting.

He'd brought up the question of a wedding in private, but Jo had just shaken her head, saying a big celebration was the last thing on her mind after everything that had happened. So together, along with Kaia and Prometheus as their witnesses, they'd gone that morning and signed the registry at the Temple of Athena in Tarva City, handing over a sizable donation not only there but also at the temples dedicated to Zeus and Poseidon. And that was that. They were married in the eyes of their family, according to their customs, and with traceable signatures for any authority that cared to question.

For the occasion—quiet as it was—Jo wore a striking blue

gown that matched her eyes and the bronze bracelet with the polished blue stones Flynn had given her on her eighteenth birthday. She hadn't thrown it in the river after all. Seeing it, seeing that she'd kept it, nearly brought him to his knees. Part of him wished he hadn't wasted so much time, but part of him knew he wouldn't be the man he was now, ready for his own family, without those six years to truly understand that family wasn't only who you were born to, but who you chose, and those you fought for.

And now, he was married to the most stunning, courageous, and intelligent woman he could ever imagine. She still wore the bangle, and every time Flynn saw it on her wrist—saw *her*—he couldn't wait to start their life together, the life they'd begun planning the moment the word *home* went from meaning this castle to a whitewashed farmhouse with blue shutters.

"Oh, she's waking up," Jo whispered, stroking a gentle finger down Eleni's cheek. She touched the baby's little chin dimple.

"I guess that's my cue. *Again.*" Cat settled into her nest of pillows and held out her arms. Her beleaguered sigh didn't match the excitement glowing in her expression. Everyone here knew she was eager to hold her baby and care for her in all the ways that had been missing in Cat's own infancy and childhood.

Jo stood and relinquished Eleni to her mother, her blue eyes lingering on the princess's little scrunched-up face as the baby hovered between waking and sleeping. Flynn watched them and smiled. With any luck, Jo and he would be juggling babies for years to come, and cousins would grow up like siblings, forming friendships that lasted from this lifetime into the one beyond.

Even in southern Sinta, they wouldn't be so far from each other—not with the vast network of road improvements Griffin was working on, the best and fastest horses in Thalyria, and grandparents who'd undoubtedly insist on regular visits.

Eleni let out a little noise, and Cerberus sat up, surveying the room. Having three heads must be convenient for a watchdog.

Cat smiled adoringly at her child. "You're going to have big magic, aren't you, little monster? And a nanny with poison drool." Her eyes flicked to Cerberus, who answered with a snarl.

Eleni settled down to sleep again, apparently not hungry yet after all.

"Do you think she'll have fire magic?" Cat asked, gazing down at Eleni. "Bellanca would've liked that. She probably would've said it was obvious." Cat chuckled. Cat had been the first to truly trust Bellanca. And she'd been right. Bellanca had never let them down. "Or like my sister, Eleni. We named you after her," she told the infant. "She could make birds out of what looked like sunbeams. They matched her hair. Golden and pretty—but when they attacked, her burning little sparrows could scorch holes in a man's hide *through* his armor." Cat glanced up, grinning. "Several idiots learned that the hard way."

Jo cocked her head, a little frown creasing her forehead. "Did you say birds made out of fire?"

Cat nodded. "They'd dance around her hands and up her arms. I never saw fire keep its shape and move that fast. Or stay that sunbeam color—almost transparent."

Jo took a step back toward Cat. "I saw golden fire swooping like birds around the wrist of the woman Kato was with in the Underworld."

Hades, Hera, and Hestia. Flynn's pulse started to pound. In life, Cat had found the closest thing to a true brother in Kato. In death, could Kato have found Cat's sister?

"She had blonde hair, green eyes, and fire magic," Jo continued. "Now that I think about it, she might've resembled you, Cat. Something about the way she moved..."

Cat's breath shuddered. Her eyes filled with tears. "Kato and Eleni? Together in the Underworld?"

Jo winced, uncertain. "I don't know. I think it might be. He didn't call her by name, but they'd united against Perses. They looked like they'd known each other for a while, like they had each other's backs."

A watery smile spread across Cat's face. It was pure joy—flooding out of her. She reached over and squeezed Jo's hand. Flynn knew displays of affection weren't easy for Cat. To initiate one showed how far she'd come since the day he met her.

"You could *not* have given me a better gift," Cat said in a tear-thick voice. "Except for the antidote to that stupid elixir. That was pretty good, too," she said with a shaky laugh.

They all laughed. And it felt good. Because loss never really left you. New beginnings also meant endings. Hope was what you found on the other side of suffering. And life was good, but it would never be the same.

HERA

Hera gazed over the marble wall of her private terrace, ignoring the two lesser beings at her back and the human she considered so useless she was sure a goblet of wine would serve her better at this point. Where was Dionysus when you needed him?

Thalyria spread out before her. This world her *husband* adored. She hissed in anger and closed her eyes against it.

Humans in Attica had perfected the art of divorce. Why couldn't they install a similar tradition on Mount Olympus? She saw no reason to be bound for eternity to a brutish, cheating male who expected—no, *demanded*—her blind loyalty and devotion.

She swung around, so angry at the latest turn of events that she saw fire behind closed eyelids.

Her burning gaze opened on Pan. "You did your part. I cannot fault you."

The goatish god of flocks, shepherds, and the wilds bowed his horned head to her. "Thank you, my queen. Though I'm sorry we lost Medusa and her sisters."

Hera's nostrils flared. "The Gorgons overstepped their mandate. I did not authorize more than threats against the new queen of Thalyria and her people."

"Yes, my queen. They got what they deserved."

Hera growled in frustration. She hadn't said that, either. Did no one understand the subtleties of manipulation? She was the goddess of marriage and responsible for the welfare of women and children. She no more wanted to harm Catalia Thalyria and her child than to sanction the atrocious treatment of Medusa and her sisters. That didn't mean she wouldn't *use* them. And she had. She now knew exactly who had watched out for the human queen and her people. Who had helped them. And who hadn't.

She turned to Hermes. "Go. Continue what you've started. Take Pan with you and round up the others."

Her faithful messenger nodded. They exited the high marble patio, leaving her alone with the human. He trembled.

"My queen…" His mouth opened and closed like a baby bird's. Was he waiting for her to feed him?

"I am not your queen. Your queen is Catalia Thalyria. And you betrayed her."

"I did your bidding." His frantic eyes darted to the side, then back to her.

No, little bird. There's no escaping.

"Worse, you betrayed a sister." Hera's eyes narrowed. "Who *spared* you."

The human's mouth finally snapped closed. Fear was a color. Hera had always seen it, and he oozed that gray sludge of terror from his nostrils. "Priam, isn't it?"

He nodded, swallowing.

She circled him. He turned with her, wary. "I always believed it was a curse of queens to be unhappy. But that seems untrue. Misery comes from others still being able to control and punish you. So what does the unhappy queen need to do?" Priam shook his head, his eyes a mix of fright and awe. "She needs to rule her kingdom. Above *all* others. *Alone.*" Hera stopped and gripped his chin. "You fed your own sister an elixir you knew would ruin her life—*for eternity*—and yet today, she celebrates. Today, she holds her baby. Today, her kingdom rejoices. *Her* kingdom—*hers."*

"I couldn't control what happened after. I didn't know there was an antidote. I did your bidding. Please! Spare me." Priam's jaw moved under her hand, small and so easily crushed. Hera allowed him to speak. She'd always enjoyed a little begging.

She gazed into his bright-green eyes, wondering how many lifetimes it would take to dull them. "You did. And you played your part in my plan. I got exactly the information I needed."

Hope brightened the gray muck swirling between them. "So...I can go home now?"

She nodded. "I know exactly where to put you."

In a blink, they stood in the circular room at the bottom of the mountain. Deep in the stone-cold heart of Mount Olympus, a star-shaped hub granted them passage between worlds. Two were one-way trips, even for deities: the Underworld and Tartarus.

Hera threw Priam through the barrier to the land of everlasting punishment. He had no need of the Elixir of Eternal Life to know eternal torment. Tartarus took care of immortality all on its own, and the petrified gray sludge leaking from the human would fit in perfectly there, adding to the gloom.

"No!" Priam clawed at the transparent doorway, a dark cloud of terror folding in on him. "Please! No!"

"No one made you betray your sister. I asked. You agreed. You're a human of the Kingdom of Thalyria who worships the gods of Olympus. It's within my purview to punish wicked deeds knowingly perpetrated against family." Hera flicked her fingers and sent the screaming human straight into the now-empty cliffside chains that had bound Prometheus for millennia. The location was available, and the eagle was hungry.

EPILOGUE

Jocasta quickly came to the very logical conclusion that there was nothing better than surprising her husband down by the river as he rinsed off the dust and sweat of a hard day's work before coming back home for a proper bath and dinner. She had plenty of dust and sweat to wash off, too, and what better way to do it than with Flynn stalking her into deeper water, catching her with a wicked grin, and thrusting inside her as they drowned each other in kisses that boiled the cool river every time they went in.

Privacy was guaranteed. Their property bordered the section of the river they frequented on both sides—Jocasta's family home on one side and Flynn's farm on the other. *Their* farm. The bridge they'd all used as children stood strong, still carrying them daily between their two houses.

Jocasta's healing center was up and running in her childhood home, her mother's huge medicinal herb garden cleaned up after the family's long absence and more thriving than ever, especially with the additions Jocasta had made. Several beehives, more of all the most essential herbs in order to meet increasing demand for her various tonics, sideritis to make Fisan shepherd's tea—a recipe she'd learned from Lukos, who'd taken over from Flynn as captain of the guard—and apricot trees.

Alexander had sent two dozen seedlings as a wedding present to her and Flynn, and the trees were thriving under the hot Sintan sun. Feeding patients a wholesome and nourishing fruit was already a good thing, and Jocasta looked forward to developing her own press to extract the useful oil from the apricot stones. She already had olive tree leaves and olive oil in abundance from her next-door neighbor—herself.

Lystra lived in Jocasta's old house and was learning the healing arts from her. The youngest born into a powerful Magoi family, Lystra had been ridiculed, berated, threatened, and beaten for her lack of magic. She was as Hoi Polloi as Flynn and Jocasta. Bellanca had protected Lystra as best she could, but the poor girl still grew up thinking she was worthless. Jocasta's own theory, which she kept to herself, was that Lystra had somehow been switched at birth, and that a young Tarvan woman of the ex-royal line was out there somewhere, as powerful a Magoi as Bellanca and her now-dead brother and sisters had been.

All her life, Lystra hid because coming out meant abuse. It had taken weeks, but she'd finally realized she wasn't different here. In southern Sinta, she was just like everyone else. She still barely left the house, but that hardly mattered when the whole village and the people of the surrounding towns came to her. Jocasta's healing center was quickly becoming a focal point of the region, and she couldn't have been prouder of the useful services and products she provided her community—or of the young woman helping her there. Lystra's quick mind and innate willingness to help had been hidden under a heavy cloud of fear, even once she'd been with the new royal family. Maybe she'd needed to escape the castle she grew up in to truly break free. Once the dread had dispersed, her ideas had begun running rampant and in every direction. She could hardly stop talking some days.

Griffin and Cat had insisted on sending servants with them, two couples and their children who'd expressed an interest in rural living. They'd been meant for Jocasta's new household, but she and Flynn had set them up in the healing center with Lystra. Flynn and Jocasta liked their privacy and fending for themselves. Besides, no one cooked a better lamb steak than Flynn.

Griffin, Cat, and baby Eleni would be visiting soon, along with Anatole and Nerissa. They were on a tour of southwestern Thalyria to oversee the progress being made in building and staffing new schools and healing centers dedicated to Hoi Polloi communities, including Jocasta's. Egeria sometimes rode down from Sinta City with her partner, Lenore, and Jocasta was grateful to see her older sister whenever she could spare a moment. Egeria remained the royal family's arm in western Thalyria while Ares continued to keep an eye on the more petulant and Magoi-heavy east, along with Cat's younger brother, Laertes. Cat's other remaining brother, Priam, had mysteriously disappeared. The only ones who hadn't made plans to visit yet were Kaia and Prometheus. Kaia spent her days trying to fuse the Hoi Polloi and Magoi contingents of the main army into one cohesive unit—and Prometheus was there to glare down anyone who didn't like it.

They never found out who slipped Cat the elixir, but there hadn't been a single Great Roar since their return from Aeaea, Thalyrians were back at the forefront of their new ruling family's minds—and starting to see the changes they'd been promised— and the shadow of Olympianomachy seemed less dark and looming to Jocasta under the endless bright-blue sky of *home*.

As she neared the edge of the woods, she glimpsed Flynn's auburn hair catching the last rays of the slanting sun as he peeled off his clothing. He tossed everything onto the bank, his muscled body glowing golden as he stepped into the water.

Jocasta bit her lip, anticipation tightening her breasts and tingling in her lower abdomen. Heat sank through her, pooling between her thighs. She could already feel Flynn's touch—the hard plane of his chest against her nipples, his big hands gripping her backside, the slow, delicious slide of him inside her body, his unsteady breath pounding against her mouth.

She exhaled sharply.

Shucking off her clothing, Jocasta joined Flynn in the river. He turned at the sound of her approach. Desire blazed through the space between them. He stayed where he was, the river lapping at his navel. She slipped through the water, the light current caressing her thighs. She shivered even as her blood caught fire. There was nothing like Flynn's eyes on her. Just his searing gaze made need pulse inside her.

His voice a deep rasp, he said, "You look like a woman on a mission."

"I'm always a woman on a mission." Right now, it was to replace the cool touch of the river with something hot. "My mission is you. Inside me. As soon as possible."

Flynn's eyes flared. His lips parted. "Gods, woman, just looking at you makes me hard as a rock."

Jocasta's eyes flicked down. Unfortunately, the part of him in question was hidden beneath the surface. Her eyes flicked back up. "That can only help the quest."

Groaning softly, Flynn reached down and fisted himself underwater. The way he stroked, his jaw tense, his muscles rippling, sent heat whipping through her. She couldn't wait to replace his hand with her body.

Stopping in front of him, she slid her hands over his shoulders. Their eyes locked. She jumped, and he caught her. She wrapped her legs around his waist. His shaft prodded her entrance. She sank down on him with a moan, not caring that she wasn't quite ready. The tighter-than-usual friction felt so good that she shuddered with pleasure.

Slowly, Flynn started moving. His strong arms held her steady, and he filled her deeper with every thrust until her body adjusted and took him fully.

"Jo... I..." Shaking his head, Flynn kissed her instead of trying to form words he still thought he wasn't good at. He kissed her as only he knew how, with passion that touched her soul and everything he needed to say written on his lips.

Her body coiled tight. Jocasta rocked faster, her arms wrapped around Flynn's neck and their mouths fused in a long, deep kiss. She rubbed against him, and Flynn pulled her in with firm little tugs. Sensation grew, brighter, hotter, sparking strong. She panted and strained, but Flynn stayed gentle with her— gentler than he needed to be. He was still adjusting to the slight swell of her belly between them and to the idea of the baby they'd made.

Bow-tight pressure reached its pinnacle inside her, and Jocasta climaxed, her mouth opening on a gasp. Pleasure pulsed through her. Her core still throbbed around him when Flynn followed her over the edge, his satisfied groan the sound she'd come to crave most.

Neither of them moved. Still joined, they held each other close. The river lapped at their waists. The sun's last rays warmed her back, Flynn warmed her front, and happiness warmed her heart. This was the life she'd fought for, and she loved it.

Jocasta's heartbeat gradually calmed. Languid heat slid like sun-warmed honey through her limbs, and a slow, sated smile curved her lips. "You're my olive," she murmured.

Flynn's soft, lingering kiss was sweet and scorching all at once. "You're my everything."

THE KEY PLAYERS

JOCASTA
QUOTE | "Because you're all so excited about this possible wild-goose chase?"

FLYNN
QUOTE | "You haunt my dreams, daytime and night."

BELLANCA
QUOTE | "Thank you for slapping yourself. You saved me the trouble."

CARVER
QUOTE | "If you want to chase me again for an hour, be my guest."

PROMETHEUS
QUOTE | "She might be tough, but if I gut her, her insides won't grow back like mine will."

CAT
QUOTE | "Do that again and Cerberus gets to lick you."

GRIFFIN
QUOTE | "Never underestimate the value of moral support."

GUIDE TO THALYRIA AND THE GODS

ADELPHE MOU
Greek for *my brother*.

ADONIS
An incredibly handsome young man in Greek mythology; the mortal lover of Aphrodite.

AEAEA
The fabled island where Circe lives in exile.

AEGIS
A shield carried by Athena and Zeus; made of serpent scales and containing the head of Medusa.

AGAPI MOU
Greek for *my love*; a term of endearment.

AGORA
Greek for *gathering place*; a central, outdoor, public area used for markets, socializing, politics, and debate.

APHRODITE
Olympian goddess of love, beauty, passion, and fertility.

APOLLO
Olympian god of the sun and light, music and poetry, healing, plagues, prophecy, archery, and more; the son of Zeus and Leto; twin brother to Artemis; his symbols include the lyre, a laurel wreath crown, and a bow and arrows.

ARES
Olympian god of war with a predilection for violent, destructive battles; son of Zeus and Hera; his symbols include a four-horse chariot, helmet, shield, spear, and sword.

ARIADNE'S THREAD
A magical string that allows a person to retrace his or her steps to find the way back out of a labyrinth.

ARTEMIS
Olympian goddess of the hunt, the moon, the wilderness, and chastity; a virgin deity; daughter of Zeus and Leto; twin sister to Apollo; her symbols include a quiver of arrows, the bow, deer, and the moon.

ASKLEPIOS
God of healing, rejuvenation, and the medicinal arts; son of Apollo.

ASKLEPIOS'S ROD
The serpent-entwined staff wielded by Asklepios, the god of healing, rejuvenation, and the medicinal arts.

ATALANTA
A fast and skilled huntress from Greek mythology; abandoned at birth and raised by bears; she lived in the wilderness and devoted herself to Artemis.

ATHENA
Olympian goddess of wisdom and strategic warfare; a virgin deity; daughter of Zeus; her symbols include the owl, the olive tree, the spear, and the aegis (or shield).

ATLANTIS
Another world created by the gods; from Plato's writing: a seafaring, island civilization that fell out of favor with the gods and sank into the ocean.

ATLAS
The Titan war leader during the War of Gods; after the Titans were defeated, he was condemned to eternally hold up the heavens.

ATTICA
One of the largest and most ancient worlds created by the gods; still the favored world of Athena; a place without magic because the people there stopped worshipping the Olympian gods.

CENTAUR
A creature with the body of a horse and the head, torso, and arms of a man.

CERBERUS
The hound of Hades; a huge three-headed dog usually found guarding the entrance to the Underworld to prevent the dead from leaving.

CHAOS
The whirling mass without form from which the cosmos took shape and all life emerged.

CHAOS WIZARD
An all-knowing conduit for information and prophesies from the Olympians, especially Zeus.

CHARON
The cloaked ferryman charged with collecting an obol and rowing the recently deceased across the River Styx so that they can begin their afterlife in the Underworld.

CHARYBDIS
The immense underwater sea monster creating a huge whirlpool on one side of the strait known as Hera's Shoulder.

CHIMERA'S FIRE
A deadly magical fire named after the fire-breathing chimera, a hybrid creature mixing lion, goat, and snake.

CHIRON
A centaur who traveled the worlds, bringing stories from Attica; the son of the Titan Cronus and known for being wise, intelligent, civilized, and a good teacher.

CIRCE
The sorceress daughter of the Titan sun god Helios; a skilled herbalist and potion master, also known for her wicked temper and manipulative ways; the gods, led by Zeus, banished her to eternal exile on the hidden island of Aeaea.

CIRCE'S GARDEN
The fabled garden on the island of Aeaea where Circe resides in exile; the source of all plant life in the gods' worlds—past, present, and future.

COSMOS
The universe, in particular the universe seen as an all-encompassing and orderly system.

CRONUS
Titan ruler of the first generation of gods after the primordials; he was the youngest son of Gaia and Uranus, consort and brother to Rhea, and the father of Hestia, Demeter, Hera, Hades, Poseidon, Zeus, and the centaur Chiron.

CYCLOPS (CYCLOPES, PL.)
Giant with a single eye in the center of its forehead; the Cyclopes were the children of the primordial deities, Gaia and Uranus.

DEATH MARK
A long, thin scar left by Magoi healers when their only option is to make an incision into the skin of the upper arm and pour healing magic directly into a person's blood; only used in urgent, near-death situations.

DEMETER
Olympian goddess of agriculture and grain, fertility, and the seasons; daughter of Cronus and Rhea; sister of Hestia, Hera, Hades, Poseidon, and Zeus; mother of Persephone.

DIONYSUS
Olympian god of fertility and wine; son of Zeus and the mortal Semele.

DODEKATHEON
The twelve principal gods of the Olympian pantheon: Zeus, Hera, Poseidon, Demeter, Athena, Apollo, Artemis, Ares, Aphrodite, Hephaestus, Hermes, and either Hestia or Dionysus; while a major deity and brother to the first generation of Olympians, Hades is not included because his domain is the Underworld.

DRAGON'S BREATH
The deadly magical fire produced in the mouth of dragons.

DRAKON
Snakes of all types and sizes.

DRYAD
A tree nymph; a nature spirit in Greek mythology specifically linked to oak trees.

ECHIDNA
The part woman, part serpent she-dragon previously controlled by the now-deposed Sintan Alpha.

ELIXIR OF ETERNAL LIFE (THE)
Also known as Olympian Evermagic, this well-guarded potion may be bestowed on demigod offspring who powerful Olympians believe have earned the right to become immortal; an irreversible gift, untouchable by Olympian magic once ingested.

ELPIS
The personification and spirit of hope in Greek mythology; the ancient spark from which all hope springs.

Elysian Fields (the)
The area of the Underworld reserved for the afterlife of the great heroes and warriors favored by the gods.

Fates (The)
Three goddesses whose role is to make sure that all living beings, human and god alike, live out their destiny, represented as a thread; Clotho spins the thread of life; Lachesis measures it, deciding length of life and purpose; Atropos cuts it; usually considered to be above the gods in their control over destiny; also called the Moirai.

Fisa
The eastern province of Thalyria.

Frostfire
A location on the Ice Plains where a hermit who makes powerful potions resides.

Furies (the)
Three ancient goddesses of vengeance in Greek mythology; they punished those who swore false oaths, committed acts of evil, or perpetrated crimes against the natural order; also called the Erinyes.

Gaia
The first primordial deity to emerge from Chaos; the origin of all life and the mother of the Titans, the Cyclopes, and other giants, all of whom she conceived with Uranus.

Gia Panta
Greek for *forever*.

GLIKIA MOU
Greek for *my sweet* or *sweetheart*; a term of endearment.

GOD BOLT
The lightning strike, sometimes called the thunderbolt, sent down by Zeus to warn, punish, or kill.

GOD TOUCHED
All the areas surrounding Thalyria that are outside the known continent and barely, or not at all, accessible to humans.

GOLDEN FLEECE
The golden wool from the winged ram, Chrysomallos, in Greek mythology; a great prize, quested after, and a symbol of power and authority.

GORGONS (THE)
Three sisters in Greek mythology: Stheno, Euryale, and Medusa; daughters of primordial sea gods, these winged creatures had hair made of living snakes, and their powerful gazes could turn anyone who looked into their eyes to stone.

GREAT ARM OF HERA (THE)
The huge peninsula guarding the eastern coast of Fisa from the greater, god-touched ocean; has three openings, but only the southernmost channel, known as Hera's Shoulder, is navigable.

HADES
God of the Underworld and ruler of the dead, husband of Persephone; son of Cronus and Rhea; brother of Hestia, Demeter, Hera, Poseidon, and Zeus; his symbols include the scepter, the keys to his kingdom, the cornucopia, and Cerberus.

HARPY
A hideous winged creature with the body of a bird and the head of a woman, known for stealing food and abducting people.

HELLIPSES GRASS
A prolific type of long, sturdy grass in Thalyria; used by the southern tribes in thatching, weaving, and the making of various decorative and household objects.

HEPHAESTUS
Olympian god of fire, forges, and blacksmiths; son of Zeus and Hera (or Hera alone); married to Aphrodite; he was a creator, sculptor, and crafter of famous weapons and pieces of armor; his symbols include the hammer, the anvil, and tongs.

HERA
Queen of the gods and wife of Zeus; Olympian goddess of marriage; daughter of Cronus and Rhea; sister of Hestia, Demeter, Hades, Poseidon, and Zeus.

HERACLES
The son of Zeus and a mortal woman; greatest Greek hero; best known for performing twelve nearly impossible tasks (labors) and becoming immortal.

HERMES
The winged messenger of the gods; the son of Zeus and the only Olympian other than Hades and Persephone to be able to cross the boundary between the living and the dead.

HESTIA
Olympian goddess of the hearth; daughter of Cronus and Rhea; sister of Demeter, Hera, Hades, Poseidon, and Zeus.

HOI POLLOI
Commoners, people without magic; Greek for *the many*.

HYDRA (THE)
A many-headed, serpentine water monster.

ICE PLAINS (THE)
The dangerous and largely inaccessible region in northern Thalyria where magical creatures roam and live and where the gods reside; Mount Olympus is located in the northeast corner of the Ice Plains.

ICHOR
The golden fluid that runs like blood through the veins of the gods and other powerful immortals in Greek mythology.

IPOTANE
A fierce and volatile magical creature with the body of a large, powerful horse and the head, arms, and torso of a human.

KARDIA MOU
Greek for *my heart* or *my sweetheart*; a term of endearment.

KARDOULA MOU
Greek for *my sweetheart*; a term of endearment.

KNOWN CONTINENT
The part of Thalyria accessible to and inhabited by humans rather than gods and magical creatures.

KOBALOI

Gnome-like magical creatures fond of playing tricks.

LATREIA MOU

Greek for *my adored one*; a term of endearment.

LOTUS EATERS

Anyone who eats the fruit of the lotus tree and falls into a drug-induced state of apathy, losing all interest in returning home or finding their loved ones again.

LYRE

An ancient stringed instrument, similar in appearance to a small, U-shaped harp.

MAGOI

People with magic and consequently belonging to the privileged class.

MATAKIA MOU

Greek for *my little eyes*; a term of endearment.

MEDUSA'S DUST

A deadly magical concoction that will turn anyone who touches it into stone.

MINOTAUR (THE)

A creature with the head and tail of a bull and the body of a man; also called Asterion; King Minos had the Minotaur confined to a labyrinth built by the famous architect, Daedalus; human sacrifices were sent into the maze to appease the creature's hunger until Theseus, with the help of Ariadne, was (supposedly) able to slay the Minotaur and escape the maze.

MORO MOU
Greek for *my baby*; a term of endearment.

MOUNT OLYMPUS
The home of the Olympians and the source of magic in Thalyria; a gateway for deities and magical creatures connecting the different worlds created by the gods.

NEREIDS
Sea water nymphs, companions to Poseidon, and often helpful to sailors in need; they are the fifty daughters of Nereus and Doris.

NIKE
The goddess of victory, also known as the winged goddess; of Titan descent.

NYMPH
A minor female nature deity in Greek mythology associated with a specific location (trees, freshwater, seawater, mountains).

NYX'S SHALLOW GRAVE
A powerful sleeping potion that induces such a long, deep slumber that a person can be mistaken for dead.

OBOL
The coin used to pay Charon, the ferryman who rows the dead across the River Styx in the Underworld.

OIKOGENEIA
Greek for *family*.

OLYMPIANOMACHY
War among the Olympians, potentially to establish a new rule.

OLYMPIANS
The third generation of gods; they overthrew their Titan ancestors and made their home on Mount Olympus.

ORACLE
A magical creature representing an Olympian deity with the power to gauge a person's worth and bestow magic on worthwhile aspirants; an oracle will kill anyone who fails its test, usually by swallowing the person whole.

ORIGIN (THE)
The half-Olympian, half-Titan son of Zeus and the first king of Thalyria; Zeus created Thalyria to offer his son a world over which to rule.

PAN
The god of flocks, shepherds, nature, and the wilds; often associated with sex and fertility.

PANDORA'S BOX
A jar containing sickness, suffering, violence, and generally all the evils known to man as well as the unshakable, undying essence of hope (Elpis).

PANIKOS
The word used to describe the sudden fear that sends animals and people fleeing in terror.

PANOTII
A mythical people with ears as big as their entire bodies; the name of Cat's big-eared horse.

PERSEPHONE
Olympian goddess of the springtime, wife of Hades, and queen of the Underworld; daughter of Zeus and Demeter; unlike Hades, Persephone only spends part of her time in the Underworld; her symbols include the pomegranate, seeds of grain, and flowers.

PERSES
The Titan god of destruction.

PERSEUS
The son of Zeus and the mortal Danaë, one of the greatest Greek heroes, and the founder of Mycenae; he beheaded Medusa and gave his prize to Athena, who mounted the still-deadly Gorgon head on her shield.

PHOENIX
A bird in Greek mythology that cyclically rises from the ashes of its predecessor to live again.

PHOIBOS
A powerful Fisan Magoi who helped expand his realm in the past by destroying the opposition with his rare, fast, extremely hot-burning magical fire.

PHOIBOS'S FIRE
A rare, fast, extremely hot-burning magical fire; named after Phoibos, a powerful Fisan Magoi who helped expand his realm in the past.

PLAIN OF ASPHODEL

The dreary, shadowy, hopeless area of the Underworld where the dead arrive before moving on to their afterlife *if* they have an obol to pay for passage across the River Styx *and* are not being held back for the punishment of evil deeds.

POSEIDON

Olympian god of the sea, earthquakes, and horses; son of Cronus and Rhea; brother of Hestia, Demeter, Hera, Hades, and Zeus; "godfather" to Cat; his symbols include the trident and the horse.

POWER BID

Approximately every forty years, current, aging rulers find themselves challenged by their own children, who vie for power both within their families and their realms; it's not unknown for Power Bids to extend to attempted takeovers of neighboring realms.

PROMETHEUS

A god of Titan descent who sided with Zeus in the War of Gods; he fell out of favor with Zeus after stealing fire from the gods and gifting it to humans; Zeus punished Prometheus for his defiance by chaining him to a rock and sending an eagle to tear out and eat his liver every day in a cycle of endless torment; freed by Catalia Thalyria.

PSIHI MOU

Greek for *my soul.*

RHEA

Titan goddess; daughter of Gaia and Uranus; sister and consort of Cronus; mother of Hestia, Demeter, Hera, Hades, Poseidon, and Zeus.

RIVER STYX

The body of water the recently deceased must cross in order to begin their afterlife in the Underworld; the payment of one obol to Charon is required for passage across the river.

S'AGAPO

Greek for *I love you*.

SATYR

A lustful and often inebriated male nature spirit with the ears and tail of a horse; companion of the gods Dionysus and Pan.

SCYLLA

The deadly many-headed female sea monster guarding one side of the strait known as Hera's Shoulder.

SINTA

The western province of Thalyria.

SIREN

In Greek mythology, the sirens were part woman and part bird; used their beautiful singing voices to lure sailors to their deaths on rocky shores.

SISYPHUS

A cunning and deceitful king in Greek mythology whom Zeus eventually punished for his arrogance by sending him to Tartarus to roll a boulder up a hill, only to have it roll back down again, forcing Sisyphus to perpetually start over.

STYMPHALIAN BIRD
A type of man-eating bird in Greek mythology with a sharp bronze beak and pointy metallic feathers it can hurl at its prey.

SYBARIS
The vicious, fire-breathing she-dragon previously under the control of the now-dead Alpha Fisa.

TARTARUS
A realm of eternal imprisonment, and often torment, for gods and mortals who displease or defy the ruling Olympian gods; the bleak prison holding most of the Titans after their defeat in the War of Gods.

TARVA
The central province of Thalyria, between Sinta and Fisa.

TEARS OF ATTICA (THE)
A magic-stripping tidal pool on an island in the Inner Sea off the coast of Fisa.

THALYRIA
The finite world created by Zeus for his son, known as the Origin; a once-splintered kingdom now reunited into one.

THANATOS
The personification of death in Greek mythology; the name Cat gives her sword.

THEA MOU
Greek for *my goddess*.

TITANOMACHY
The ten-year series of battles that resulted in the Olympians, led by Zeus, overthrowing their Titan ancestors and establishing their new pantheon on Mount Olympus; also called the War of Gods.

TITANS
The twelve children of the primordial deities Gaia and Uranus; the generation of gods directly preceding the Olympians.

TITOS
Poseidon's magical drakon, or snake, that previously lived inside the Chaos Wizard but transferred its residence, and protection, to the warrior Kato.

UNDERWORLD (THE)
The land of the dead, ruled over by Hades and Persephone.

URANUS
The son of Gaia and the second primordial deity to emerge from Chaos; he formed the primordial couple along with Gaia; father of the Titans, the Cyclopes, and many others.

VRYKOLAKAS
A vicious, soulless, undead creature that can take a humanoid form or that of a huge, misshapen wolf.

WAR OF GODS
The ten-year series of battles that resulted in the Olympians, led by Zeus, overthrowing their Titan ancestors and establishing their new pantheon on Mount Olympus; the War of Gods is also called the Titanomachy.

ZEUS

King of the gods and ruler of Mount Olympus; Olympian god of the sky and thunder; son of Cronus and Rhea; brother of Hestia, Demeter, Hera, Hades, and Poseidon; husband of Hera; father of Athena, Apollo, Artemis, Ares, and Persephone, among others; his symbols include the thunderbolt, the oak, and the eagle.

ACKNOWLEDGMENTS

A heartfelt thank-you to the incredible team at Sourcebooks, who took this story from the manuscript I didn't know what to do with to the beautiful books and series we see today. Also, thank you to my agent, Jill Marsal. I'm so lucky to have you in my corner. To my family and friends, I'm forever grateful for your encouragement and understanding. And finally, my sincere gratitude to you, my readers. Your enthusiasm and support are why I get to sit down to a job I love every day. I can't wait to dream up more stories for you.

ABOUT THE AUTHOR

Amanda Bouchet is a *USA Today* bestselling author of fantasy romance and space opera romance. She was a Goodreads Choice Awards top 10 finalist for Best Debut in 2016 with her first novel, *A Promise of Fire*.

For more about Amanda's books with equal parts adventure and kissing, connect with her online:

amandabouchet.com
@AuthorABouchet
@amandabouchetauthor
facebook.com/AmandaBouchetAuthor

A PROMISE OF FIRE

Kingdoms will rise and fall for her.

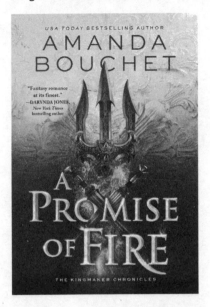

Cat Fisa isn't who she pretends to be. She's perfectly content disguised as a sooth-sayer in a traveling circus, avoiding the destiny the Gods—and her dangerous family—have saddled her with. As far as she's concerned, the magic humming within her blood can live and die with her. She won't be anyone's pawn. But then she locks eyes with an ambitious warlord from the magic-deprived south and her illusion of safety is shattered forever.

Griffin knows Cat is the Kingmaker—the woman able to divine truth through lies—and he wants her to be a powerful weapon for his newly conquered realm. Kidnapping her off the street is simple enough, but keeping her by his side is infuriatingly tough. Cat fights him at every turn, showing a ferocity of spirit that burns hot...and leaves him desperate for more. But can he ever hope to prove to his once-captive that he wants her there by his side as his equal, his companion—and maybe someday, his queen?

"Fantasy romance at its finest!"

—Darynda Jones, *New York Times* bestselling author, for *A Promise of Fire*

For more info about Sourcebooks's books and authors, visit:

sourcebooks.com

BREATH OF FIRE

And she will be their queen.

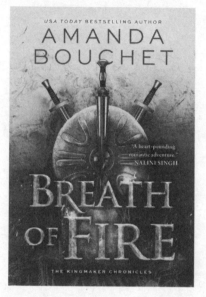

Cat Fisa's warlord captor-turned-lover may have crowned her with the symbols of the three realms, but war is far from over. She believes in what Griffin is trying to accomplish. She believes that peace will finally come when the realms are united. And she believes that with her by his side, Griffin has the strength to change the world. But with her dangerous past resurfacing and the neighboring royals out for blood, Cat and Griffin must strike soon if they want to unify the land without full-scale war.

They'll do anything to avoid innocent bloodshed, including crossing the treacherous Ice Plains or entering the deadly Agon Games to win access to the royal court...and the very family they plan to usurp. When their desperate battle for survival is over, Cat and Griffin will either be standing side-by-side in the heart of their future kingdom—or not at all.

"Fantasy romance at its finest!"

—Darynda Jones, *New York Times*
bestselling author, for *A Promise of Fire*

For more info about Sourcebooks's books and authors, visit:

sourcebooks.com

HEART ON FIRE

With the power of the gods at her fingertips.

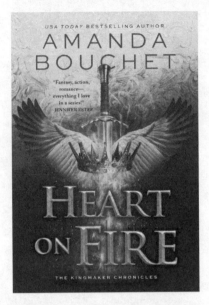

Cat Fisa's destiny has finally caught up with her. But fully accepting her fate means taking a final, terrifying step—reuniting all three realms and embracing her place as queen with warlord-turned-king Griffin at her side. Yet forging their kingdom can only mean going to war with Fisa and its violent Alpha—Cat's own mother, Andromeda. Although Cat used to be Andromeda's sole weakness, that's no longer true. And while Andromeda seems to know every trick and spell, Cat's own magic refuses to work like it should. When tragedy strikes, Cat unleashes the power she's been afraid of all her life, but her misuse of the Gods' gifts comes with a terrible price.

Ripped away from Griffin and the home she's come to love, Cat's only option is to fully accept the power she's always denied so that she can return to the people she loves, confront her murderous mother, and finish restoring her kingdom—no matter the ultimate cost.

"Fantasy romance at its finest!"

—Darynda Jones, *New York Times* bestselling author, for *A Promise of Fire*

For more info about Sourcebooks's books and authors, visit:
sourcebooks.com